MARK BILLINGHAM

The Murder Book

Little, Brown

LITTLE, BROWN

First published in Great Britain in 2022 by Little, Brown

7 9 10 8 6

Copyright © Mark Billingham Ltd 2022

The moral right of the author has been asserted.

A CIP catalogue record for this book is available from the British Library.

Hardback ISBN 978-1-4087-1245-0
Trade Paperback ISBN 978-1-4087-1246-7

Typeset in Plantin by M Rules
Printed and bound in Great Britain by Clays Ltd, Elcograf S.p.A.

Papers used by Little, Brown are from well-managed forests
and other responsible sources.

Little, Brown
An imprint of
Little, Brown Book Group
Carmelite House
50 Victoria Embankment
London
EC4Y 0DZ

An Hachette UK Company
www.hachette.co.uk

www.littlebrown.co.uk

Mark Billingham has twice won the Theakston's Old Peculier Award for Crime Novel of the Year, and has also won a Sherlock Award for the Best Detective created by a British writer. Each of the novels featuring Detective Inspector Tom Thorne has been a *Sunday Times* bestseller. *Sleepyhead* and *Scaredy Cat* were made into a hit TV series on Sky 1 starring David Morrissey as Thorne, and a series based on the novels *In the Dark* and *Time of Death* was broadcast on BBC1. Mark lives in north London with his wife and two children.

Also by Mark Billingham

The DI Tom Thorne series
Sleepyhead
Scaredy Cat
Lazybones
The Burning Girl
Lifeless
Buried
Death Message
Bloodline
From the Dead
Good as Dead
The Dying Hours
The Bones Beneath
Time of Death
Love Like Blood
The Killing Habit
Their Little Secret
Cry Baby

Other fiction
In The Dark
Rush of Blood
Cut Off
Die of Shame
Rabbit Hole

For Thalia Proctor. Incomparable,
irreplaceable . . .

He watches the gate and wonders. Fifteen minutes now since the old woman went inside with the rest of them. Enough time, surely. He's smoking, which is not something he does very often, and he's trying to stay calm.

He's thinking about pain.

About the great many things that can cause it or take it away, about thresholds and about those people who think they know what pain is, but who should count themselves lucky that they really don't have the first idea. He thinks about living with pain, or the memory of it, which he knows better than most can be equally bad. For obvious reasons though, bearing in mind where he is and what he hopes is happening on the other side of that gate, he's thinking about those who live to inflict it.

About a man who has done exactly that for far too long.

He turns and moves away when the first of the visitors begin to emerge, their precious time with loved ones cut tragically short by the dramatic events inside. He lets a few of them drift past him. One woman already jabbering into her phone – 'You are not going to *believe* this' – and two more muttering and shaking their heads. Now, walking towards his car through the ragged shadow of the prison behind him, he hears snippets of conversation and he doesn't bother trying to keep the smile from his face. Just a word or two here and there, but it's more than enough to tell him the job is done. Not *done* done ... he can't be sure of that, but he knows it will all be over soon enough.

The old woman had passed on his token of admiration.

An offering that had been eagerly accepted.

All that fiddly business with the needle and the food dye had been worth it ...

He doesn't know exactly how long it will take, because it typically depends on body weight and metabolism, but he knows it won't have been pleasant. He's seen a few jerky videos and read descriptions online. He keys the fob to unlock his car, remembering those words that had jumped out at him from various articles – *gasping, seizure, coma* – and decides that he should probably do something about his search history.

No rush though. A few drinks to celebrate first.

He tosses what's left of the cigarette away.

The only disappointment is that he couldn't be there to see it, but he has no problem imagining. He's been doing little else. The flare of panic in the man's eyes before they glassed over and the spasms kicked in. Anger even, at the horrified old woman who would almost certainly have been screaming by then, but mostly at himself for being such an idiot; for being too greedy and too trusting.

As he turns the wheel and pulls out of the car park, he's hoping that it wasn't over too quickly. That there was just enough time for the man to know exactly who his final visitor was. That death, having tapped the bastard on the shoulder, had put its feet up for a few minutes at least and made itself at home.

More than anything, he hopes it wasn't painless.

PART ONE

A HAPPY ENDING

ONE

Detective Inspector Tom Thorne stood and looked around the bedroom of what was – the corpse aside – a perfectly unremarkable house in Gospel Oak. There was a low rattle in his throat as he sighed and the plastic of his bodysuit crackled when he turned his head. The man's clothing lay tangled at the foot of the bed – trousers, shirt, socks and underwear – but everything else in the room pointed to occupants who, until very recently at least, had been tidy and organised. A selection of motoring magazines was perfectly aligned on one bedside table. Several paperbacks, a make-up bag and a couple of pill bottles sat neatly on the other. The doors of the wardrobes had, he presumed, been opened by those conducting the initial sweep of the scene and revealed shirts arranged by colour, sweaters folded carefully and shoes that had been polished and lined up perfectly in pairs. One look at the contents of the adjoining wardrobe was enough to confirm that the woman had been equally fastidious and, while half a dozen coppers, photographers and CSIs went quietly about their business in all parts of the house, Thorne could not help but imagine an altogether less grim routine as husband and wife moved easily around one another in what had once been a warm and welcoming room. A place of safety. The pair of them gently bickering as they hung up clothing or deposited it in the painted wicker laundry basket, before getting ready for bed.

An ordered life that, for one of them, had ended in carnage and chaos.

A CSI dressed in a similar plastic bodysuit to Thorne's sidled up next to him. Left a beat or two. 'I *so* hope the poor sod's name was Douglas.'

'Come again?'

The CSI nodded towards the bed next to which the on-call pathologist was making notes, and Thorne stared again at its lifeless occupant. The duvet was sky blue, a faded pattern of fluffy clouds now spattered scarlet. Higher up, it looked as though someone had emptied a bottle of red across the man's chest, but it had not been wine that had leaked from the gash in his throat, or pooled on his pillow; a small puddle of blood on either side of his head.

'Get it?' the CSI asked.

'I'm not with you,' Thorne said.

The CSI raised his arms and pointed gloved fingers to the sides of his head, just in case Thorne needed it explaining. 'Then he'd be Lugless Douglas.' He stared at Thorne, waiting for the laugh, the wry smile at least and, when neither was forthcoming, he wandered away, shaking his head as though sadly disappointed that his joke had gone unappreciated.

Fallen on deaf ears.

Thorne turned as DI Nicola Tanner walked in from the landing, a second CSI close behind her. Tanner caught Thorne's eye and shook her head. 'No sign of them.'

The CSI mock-shuddered. 'Looks like our killer took the ears with him.'

'Oh, fuck,' Thorne said.

'One of those,' Tanner said.

'There is good news, though.' The CSI – a woman who looked disturbingly like Theresa May but was a lot less scary – held up a handful of plastic evidence bags. 'No shortage of trace.' She selected one of the bags and dangled it, like treasure. 'Found this nice little clump of hair just sitting there, trapped in dried sweat on the victim's chest.' She grinned. 'And we've got bulbs.'

Thorne leaned forward to get a closer look at the strands of what appeared to be blonde hair. He understood why the woman was so cheerful. He knew that an intact bulb or root on a single hair meant DNA. 'Pulled it out during a struggle, you reckon?'

'Or during something else,' Tanner said.

Thorne looked at her, then looked again at the dead man.

The CSI took a step away. 'I'm guessing we'll want this fast-tracked?'

'You guess right,' Thorne said.

Thorne and Tanner watched her walk away and, a few moments later, as soon as the look on Thorne's face suggested that he wanted a rather more private conversation, Tanner moved towards the door, knowing that he would follow. The two of them stopped on the landing. They lowered their hoods, then pressed themselves in unison against the wall to allow two more technicians struggling with a battery of equipment into the bedroom.

'It could be gangland related,' Thorne said.

'Could it?'

'Why not? We've both seen this sort of thing before.' He raised his hand and mimed the cutting. 'Worse.'

'You serious?'

'Someone needs to send a message, whatever.'

'Gangland?' Tanner nodded back towards the bedroom. 'He looks like the sort of bloke who irons creases into his pyjamas.'

'Maybe he got involved in something he shouldn't.'

'Oh, I think he definitely did that.'

'I'm just saying we shouldn't rule anything out.'

'And *I'm* just saying we shouldn't piss about avoiding the obvious.'

The CSI who fancied himself as a comedian stepped out on to the landing carrying a plastic toolbox. Thorne said, 'Nice way to round off the weekend,' but got only a perfunctory nod in return. Thorne thought it was about what he deserved. He had heard worse jokes. He had heard sicker jokes, plenty of them. The banter and the off-colour cracks were important, they were *necessary*, and he guessed there was likely to be a good deal of such whistling in the dark in the days and weeks ahead.

Thorne turned to Tanner. Said, 'Yeah, all right . . .'

He wasn't sure who he'd been trying to fool, because he knew Nicola Tanner well enough.

One of those.

He'd known what she meant straight away, because he'd been thinking the same thing himself. Every murder changed you, or it should, but there were those that bit a little deeper than others, left scars that were more vivid and scabs that could be picked at for longer. Some who committed murder, most of them, were ordinary and killed for ordinary reasons: they were angry, they were jealous, they were greedy, they snapped.

Some others were not.

Sweating and swaddled in a square, pale pink bedroom that stank of rotting meat, Thorne had known straight away that the individual he was now tasked with catching had not taken a life for any reason he would ever understand. Or would ever want to. That CSI had been trying to diffuse a little of the horror they were all confronted with, no more than that, but it had been impossible for Thorne to react the way he was expected to when something like a scream had already begun to build inside him.

When he'd been staring that horror full in the face and knowing that there was worse to come.

'Where's . . . ?'

Tanner stepped across to the banister and nodded down. 'She's in the kitchen. They're going to take her to a friend's place for the night, get Family Liaison organised, then we can interview her tomorrow.'

Thorne was already on his way down the stairs. 'Let's see if she's up for a quick chat before she goes.'

Andrea Sumner was sitting at a long kitchen table, with a uniformed PC on either side of her. Both coppers stood when Thorne and Tanner entered. They stepped away from the table and offered to make tea, but Andrea Sumner shook her head. Taking the chair alongside Tanner, Thorne guessed that by now she'd probably been given enough to put her off the stuff for life. Not for the first time, he wondered why reaching for the PG Tips was so many people's first instinct in times of crisis. It certainly wasn't his.

'Something stronger?' he asked.

The woman shook her head again, as though she'd barely taken the question in.

'We're very sorry for your loss,' Tanner said.

Andrea Sumner smiled and nodded, like she presumed it was something they habitually trotted out on such occasions. It was, of course, and they were words which always made Thorne bridle slightly, because nothing, and certainly not a man's life, had been *lost*. It had been taken. Even so, nobody had come up with a better alternative, besides which he knew that Tanner had meant it. He'd heard it in her voice. Her own partner, Susan, had been stabbed to death on the doorstep of the house they shared only a few years earlier. She still grieved, and even if sometimes she struggled to express it, she was the only person in the house at that moment who came close to understanding how Richard Sumner's wife felt.

Richard Sumner's widow.

Thorne guessed she was in her mid-fifties. Thanks to the creeping ravages of rigor and lividity, he could not be sure if she was older or younger than the man in the bed upstairs. She was tall and slim. She wore a cream blouse beneath a brown V-neck sweater. She was pale-skinned, with red-rimmed eyes magnified by wire-rimmed glasses, and she was very still.

What she wasn't was blonde.

'I gather you'd been away for the weekend,' Tanner said.

Another nod.

'Liverpool, is that right?'

The woman had been staring at the space between them, out through the open doorway, but now her eyes slid slowly across to meet Tanner's. 'A teaching conference,' she said. Her voice was flat, a hint of a northern accent perhaps. 'It was just the two nights. A few of us go up there every November.'

'And you got back late morning, today?'

'I told them.' She nodded towards the hallway in which the two uniforms were now lurking. 'I told them all this.'

Which was how Thorne and Tanner knew as much as they did, but both were well aware that stories often changed, if only subtly, when people had lived with a situation such as this for a few hours. However hard it was to live with at all. Thorne leaned towards her. 'We're really sorry to be asking you these questions now, Andrea, and I promise you that we wouldn't if it wasn't important . . . but is there any way you could be a bit more specific about the time?'

She shook her head. She lifted her hands off the table then let them drop again. 'Just after twelve, maybe. Quarter past . . . something like that. I was listening to some comedy thing in the car. Radio 4.'

'That's great,' Tanner said. 'We can check that. Thank you.'

'So, is that about the time you were always due to come back?' Thorne asked.

'Sorry?'

'You weren't expected back any earlier?'

She looked at him and said nothing for a few seconds, as though trying to work out what his question might mean.

'No. I was always meant to be coming home this morning. I've got work tomorrow ...' She stopped, realising what she'd said, that she would not be going back to work for a long time, if at all.

'Right. So when did you speak to Richard last?'

'Last night.' Andrea's mouth fell open and it seemed as if closing it again was causing her great discomfort. 'He called me at the hotel about seven o'clock,' she said finally. 'We didn't talk for very long. He told me he was going to get an early night.'

Tanner said, 'Thank you,' again before glancing at Thorne. They knew that when it came to time of death, the on-call pathologist would only provide a rough estimate. Now, at least, they had parameters. 'That's really helpful.'

Thorne looked past Andrea Sumner and out through the glazed back doors. Not quite four o'clock and it was already getting dark, but Thorne could make out the fence at the far end of the small garden, a narrow gate to one side of it. He was too far away to see if the bolts at top and bottom were open or not. He would check later. 'The back gate leads out to an alleyway or something, does it?'

Andrea nodded, then turned suddenly to stare at the gate herself, as though Thorne might have spotted something; as if there might still be some visible trace of whoever it was the policeman clearly suspected of using it. 'It runs behind all the houses. Why? What are you thinking?'

'I'm not thinking anything,' Thorne said. 'Not yet.'

Now, Tanner leaned towards the woman and stretched out a hand until it was almost touching hers. 'Andrea ... you told our colleagues that everything seemed perfectly normal when you got back.'

'That's right.'

'Like you left it, you said.'

'Yes, everything was just fine.' She nodded again and began to fiddle with the gold bracelet around her wrist. 'That's what I thought, anyway. The way it's supposed to be ... you know?'

'OK.'

'It wasn't until I went upstairs ...'

Tanner heard the woman's voice crack and watched her head drop, so she raised a hand to let the officers in the corridor know that she and Thorne were about done. Thorne pushed his chair back and grimaced at the scraping noise while Tanner was saying something about ongoing support and counselling services. He let her get on with it because she was so much better at that stuff than he was.

'Absolutely,' he said, when Tanner had finished. 'Please don't hesitate.'

Thorne wasn't surprised that Andrea Sumner had once again chosen not to mention the opened wine bottle and those two dirty glasses that the first officers on the scene had discovered in the sitting room. She *might* not have noticed them, but Thorne was fairly certain that she had. A bottle and two glasses that had been carefully bagged up and boxed by CSIs and which Thorne was damn sure had not been there when Andrea had left the house two days earlier.

It would be hard enough coming to terms with the fact that her husband had been killed. *How* he had been killed. She would not want to spend too much time wondering what had happened to that early night.

The road had been sealed off at both ends and crime scene tape strung across it on either side of the Sumner house.

There were half a dozen emergency vehicles parked in the middle of the road or up on the pavements and a good many onlookers were being kept politely at a distance. As he waited for coffee at the Met Police branded drinks wagon, Thorne saw one woman, who had found herself a nice little gap between cars and coppers, reach out to touch the tape and nod, satisfied.

When he and Tanner stepped away, coffees in hand, Thorne noticed a woman waving at him from the garden of the house opposite. He walked across and asked if he could help.

The woman peered at the lanyard around Thorne's neck. 'Is everything OK with Richard and Andrea?'

She would find out soon enough anyway. Police could instruct the street's occupants to stay inside temporarily, but could hardly insist that curtains were drawn or windows blacked out. They would see the body bag being removed from the house.

'Not really,' Thorne said.

'Oh God,' the woman said. 'That's awful.'

'So you know them, then?'

'Well, yes, they're neighbours. I mean . . . not *well*. Just a few words in the street every so often, popping over there for a drink at Christmas, that kind of thing.' Then, 'Oh, God,' again.

'Did you see Richard yesterday evening?'

'Not to talk to, no.'

'Any comings and goings?'

The woman took a few seconds, as though she was thinking about it, though Thorne guessed that she simply didn't want to appear over-eager. 'I saw his car pulling off

14

the drive . . . I don't know, about seven, half seven? Then I heard him come back later on, maybe a couple of hours after that. Well, I *actually* heard his garage door opening. He's got one of those remote things for it and the door's really bloody noisy.'

'Right.'

'I couldn't tell you the last time he used it, because him and Andrea usually just park in the drive, but when I heard the noise and looked out last night, I saw him driving into the garage. Maybe he wanted to work on the car or something.'

Thorne already had a fair idea of why Richard Sumner had parked the car out of sight, but said, 'Yes, maybe.' The car was still in the garage, of course, and Thorne had already seen that there was a door at the rear of it that opened directly into the Sumners' garden. He thanked the woman for her help and walked back across the road to join Tanner. He told her what the neighbour had seen, what he thought the implications of it were.

'Where would we be without curtain twitchers?' Tanner said.

'Yeah.' They would be starting a full house-to-house as soon as possible, but it was useful to have information like this good and early.

They stood in silence for half a minute or so, sipping their coffees.

'So, a woman, you reckon?'

Thorne looked at her. There might have been a time when, despite knowing full well that women could be every bit as homicidal as men, a degree of violence such as the one they were now confronted with might at least have given the average detective . . . pause for thought. Thorne

15

remembered the last case of multiple murder he and Tanner had worked on together; the woman at the centre of it.

He said, 'Looks that way.'

'Doesn't *have* to be a woman, of course,' Tanner said. 'Maybe Mr Sumner had a different kind of secret life.'

'Maybe.'

'We might find out when we talk to the wife again.'

Thorne poured what was left of his coffee into the gutter, thinking about what was likely to be an extremely awkward conversation. 'That's going to be fun.'

'I don't think it's going to be a barrel of laughs for her either.'

Thorne turned at a wave from the Sumners' front door. A signal that they were ready to bring out the victim's body. 'Fair point,' he said.

TWO

He called Melita on the drive home to Kentish Town.

'I'm going back to the flat,' he said.

'Really? OK ...' The plan made that morning had been for him to spend the night at her place in Crouch End. She sounded disappointed.

'We caught a nasty one and it's going to be pretty full on for the next few days,' Thorne said. 'Blanket clearance on overtime, all the usual. It's obviously an early start tomorrow, so it makes sense—'

'It's not a problem, Tom.'

'Thought I should try and get an early night.' At least *he* meant it, although, with so much to think about, the angry static in his head that was refusing to quieten, Thorne was already doubtful that he'd actually get the sleep he needed.

'Do you want to talk about it?'

'Can I call you when I get home?'

'Course.'

'I should probably fill you in anyway, because I wouldn't be surprised if Russell asks you to come in on it. If things don't pan out.'

'Oh,' Melita said. 'One of those.'

The timer had been set for the heating to come on for a couple of hours early evening, but the flat already felt chilly by the time Thorne got back, so he turned it on again. He stuck a ready meal in the microwave. He opened the post he'd missed that morning, then binned it. He took a can of lager from the fridge, carried his 'Luxury Chinese chicken chow mein' through into the living room and scrolled idly back and forth through the sports channels as he ate. Deciding against golf and tennis and ignoring Formula One – even though it might have helped him sleep – he stopped to stare at what was allegedly a sporting offering from the US, featuring men with beards throwing hand axes at a wooden target.

He said, 'Christ,' but watched it anyway.

'Have you eaten something?' Melita asked, when he called her.

Thorne told her that he had. He sat back, cradling his lager, and explained how grateful he was that the supermarket had specified in its labelling that his chicken chow mein was 'Chinese'. Up until then, he had stupidly thought it was a staple of French cuisine.

Melita laughed. 'It's a shame you couldn't come over,' she said. 'I made a curry.'

'Will it keep? I mean, having said that, it might be a couple of days.'

'Don't worry, I'm perfectly capable of eating the whole thing myself.'

Thorne was well aware how much his girlfriend enjoyed her food, how much of it she could put away. Not that anyone would know it from looking at her, which was definitely something he enjoyed.

'She's so far out of your league it's ridiculous,' Phil Hendricks had told him numerous times. 'If this was the first round of the FA cup, she'd be Arsenal, obviously, and you'd be . . .'

'Yeah, I know, Wigan Athletic or whoever. You're hilarious.'

'I was thinking more like one of them teams halfway up the Evo-Stik League, mate. Grantham Town, maybe, or Witton Albion.'

For the first time in many hours, Thorne managed something like a smile thinking about it. The journeymen of Witton Albion had been holding their own against a younger, fitter Arsenal for a little over a year now, due in large part, Thorne reckoned, to the decision early on against moving in together, but rather to maintain their own places. To alternate home and away fixtures. Each had given the other a front door key, but neither had felt the need to make use of it, as yet.

Thorne's 'home turf' was the ground-floor flat he'd bought more than twenty years ago. He'd lived there on and off ever since, the *off* being a period when he'd rented it out while in a long-term relationship with a fellow officer called Helen Weeks. When that had gone the same way as the long-term relationship preceding it and the marriage that had run its course before that, Thorne had found himself back in Kentish Town, mightily relieved that he'd never sold the place.

He felt very happy – yes, and lucky – to be spending quality time with Dr Melita Perera, but was equally happy to have a space that was all his; where he was as comfortable as he was ever likely to get and where, when he needed it, he could find some time alone.

Even if he wasn't always the best company.

He told Melita about the crime scene in Gospel Oak.

'I see what you mean,' she said. 'There's no chance it was a torture–robbery thing?'

'Wife says there's nothing missing.'

'Maybe they just wanted information . . . financial details. Maybe their bank account's been emptied.'

Thorne was not sure if anyone had checked and he would make sure it was done, but he doubted Richard Sumner had been butchered for his PIN number. He told Melita about the wine and the dirty glasses. 'Certainly seems like whoever was in that house with the victim had been invited.'

'Welcomed, for sure.'

'Woman, it looks like.'

'Well, actually that's very much *not* what it looks like,' Melita said. 'I'm not saying you're wrong, of course, but the degree of violence you're describing would certainly make a female perpetrator unusual.'

'Yeah, but you and I both know—'

'I'm not saying you're wrong, Tom. It's . . . rare, that's all.'

Thorne glanced across at the now muted TV. In a thrilling development, they had moved the axe-chuckers' targets several feet further back. He wondered if there was a version where the competitors were given blindfolds, or better yet threw the axes at each other. 'So, what do you think about the ears?'

'Trophies?'

'I was afraid you were going to say that.'

'Come on, it's what you were thinking.'

The static in his head turned itself up a notch; that thought and a dozen others, equally unwelcome, hissing and popping. He downed what was left of his lager and let out a long breath. 'Anyway, how was *your* day?'

She laughed. 'Not to make you feel bad, but it was perfectly lovely. Just private patients today, so I didn't even have to leave the flat.'

'Jammy sod,' Thorne said.

When she wasn't providing her services as a forensic psychiatrist to various police forces, or consulting at prisons and secure hospitals, Melita divided her time between private and NHS patients. The days spent seeing patients at home were what subsidised the rest of her work, and if Thorne had some concerns about her treating potentially dangerous clients at her flat, he'd learned to keep them to himself. He'd raised the subject once a few months before and it had not gone down well.

'It's my job.' Melita had said it as though she was talking to a six-year-old. 'Clients with certain ... predilections, or a history of violence, just happen to be part of it.'

'I know that.' Thorne had immediately wished he'd kept his mouth shut, but he was already committed. 'And that's all well and good at a hospital where there's security, but when they're just walking into your flat—'

'You think I should pick and choose a bit more?'

'Well, vet them a bit, maybe.'

'I do vet them, Tom, because I'm not an idiot and obviously I need to know exactly what I'll be working with. If

21

that happens to be someone you'd class as dangerous I will take that information on board and my approach to that client, personal *and* professional, will be adjusted as and when it needs to be. Fair enough?' She'd stared at him for a few seconds after that, to be sure she'd made her point, then her expression had softened, just a little. 'Besides which, look me in the eye and tell me that the dangerous people *you* go after, the *really* dangerous ones, aren't always the most interesting.'

Thorne had not been able to tell her any such thing.

Now, Melita said, 'I don't think *jammy*'s the right word. Not after the hour I had to spend listening to a clinically depressed klismaphile.'

'A what?'

'Someone who is sexually aroused at the thought of giving or receiving enemas. This particular gentleman is a giver.'

'Oh, I definitely think he's picked the best option,' Thorne said.

Melita laughed, but Thorne knew she had encountered plenty of clients whose predilections were anything but amusing. She might not share Thorne's taste in music – one of the reasons Phil Hendricks was so taken with her – and she was a damn sight tidier than he was, but they had rather more important stuff in common. When it came to the very worst things one human being could do to another, each had seen or heard about their fair share of horrors. Outside of those cases they'd worked on together, their deeper feelings about such things – the pictures inside their heads or the voices of those who had put them there – were not something they chose to discuss very often.

Another very sensible decision.

He could count on the fingers of one hand the number of times Melita had lost her temper for no obvious reason or even been in a shitty mood that wasn't down to him for very long, so Thorne couldn't help but wonder sometimes how much she held inside.

How loud *her* static was.

'I should let you go,' she said. 'So you can get to bed.'

'Fair enough, but you know I'll be thinking about you.' Thorne lowered his voice. 'About what I'm going to do, I mean, the next time I come over.'

'Same,' she said.

He left it a few seconds. 'You do know I'm talking about that curry in your fridge, right?'

THREE

Predictably, Andrea Sumner did not look like someone who'd had anything approaching a restful night. Her face was as pale and creased as old paper and the shadows that had spread like ink underneath her eyes were bruise-black.

'Did you get any sleep at all?' Tanner asked.

It took her a second or two, as though she was responding via a video link from a distant country and they were fighting the delay. 'My sister gave me some herbal sleeping tablets.'

'That's good.'

The woman sat up a little straighter and tried to smile. It seemed suddenly to be an expression that was entirely unknown to her and she quickly abandoned the struggle. 'Didn't make a blind bit of difference.'

'I'm sorry,' Thorne said, though he was not surprised. A memory, unbidden and – as was so often the case in situations such as these – wholly inappropriate, barged into his head. He remembered when he'd been having trouble sleeping a couple of years before and Phil Hendricks, no stranger to insomnia himself, had suggested that he lie there and count up the number of people he'd slept with. In order, if possible. Hendricks had said it was way more fun than counting sheep and swore it had always done the trick for him. Thorne had given it a bash, but thirty seconds later, when he'd reached the end of the list, he had still been wide awake, as well as being vaguely depressed.

Tanner leaned to pour out the water. 'Thank you so much for coming in, especially so early. I know this is a terrible time, but it's important that we get all the information we can, as fast as we can.'

Andrea nodded. 'OK.'

It was a little after nine o'clock on Monday morning and they were seated in one of the informal interview suites at Colindale station. A dark brown sofa and matching armchairs were arranged around a low table. There were biscuits on a plate, a water jug and glasses. A box of tissues had been placed within easy reach. Unlike the formal interview facilities in a different part of the station, the chairs had cushions and the only unpleasant smell was down to cheap air-freshener. There was no panic-strip and the furniture wasn't bolted to the floor. The interview *was* being video-recorded on the off chance that something said might later need to be produced in court, but when Thorne informed Andrea of the fact she just stared up at the camera for a few seconds and nodded, before turning back to him.

'Do you know what happened?' she asked.

Now it was Thorne's turn to take a few moments. She'd spoken matter-of-factly, as if they were here to discuss a tragic accident and he might set her mind at rest by saying,

I'm afraid your husband had a heart attack at the wheel, or *It looks like the brakes failed*. What had happened to Richard Sumner was horribly obvious, but that wasn't what she was asking. 'It's early days, I'm afraid.'

'To Richard . . . what happened to Richard?'

'I promise we'll keep you informed every step of the way,' Tanner said.

Andrea grunted and began looking around the room, blinking slowly as she turned her head. She stared for several seconds at one wall after the other, at the chairs and then the table, as though searching for something, anything, that might give her the answers these two detectives were unable, or unwilling, to provide.

'Andrea? Mrs Sumner . . . ?'

The woman turned back to Tanner and sighed, ready for whatever was coming.

'We wondered if you might be able to tell us if Richard had said anything about expecting visitors over the weekend.' Tanner was making it sound nice and casual. 'On Saturday evening, specifically.'

She shook her head. It was the answer Thorne and Tanner had been expecting, of course, but it didn't make the line of questioning they were about to take any easier.

'I told you. I spoke to him on Saturday and he said he was going to get an early night.'

'Of course,' Thorne said.

'That's what he told me.'

'Yes, and he might have meant to.' It was about as much sugar as he could coat the pill with. 'But I'm sorry to say it looks like that isn't the way things turned out.'

Andrea Sumner sniffed, then reached across to snatch

a tissue from the box, aware that she would soon have need of it.

'There was evidence to suggest that Richard had a visitor on Saturday night.' It sounded stupid when Thorne said it. Obviously the dead man had been visited, he would not be dead otherwise, but that was not what he meant and he could see that Andrea knew it.

'What evidence?'

'A half-empty wine bottle and two dirty glasses,' Tanner said.

'They were found in your sitting room,' Thorne said.

'I didn't see them.'

Thorne nodded and sat back. Answering a question which neither he nor Tanner had actually asked was enough to confirm his suspicions. Andrea Sumner was clearly lying to them, but he knew it made no material difference to the investigation and that the denial was clearly important to her. She still had so much to process and deal with. While the pain was, as yet, still too raw to allow even grief to get a decent foothold, she could not bear to consider for a moment that the man for whom she *would* eventually grieve was not quite the man she had believed him to be.

She would have to deal with the unpalatable truth eventually, of course, and it was not the first time Thorne had seen the nearest and dearest of murder victims struggle and flail when a loved one's darker secrets were revealed. Right now, Andrea Sumner's suspicions about her dead husband's fidelity seemed shocking enough, but Thorne had encountered worse. He recalled one memorable case when the innocent victim of a pub brawl – a mild-mannered and happily married father of two – had turned out to have not

27

one, or two, but *three* entirely unknown families scattered across the country. A trio of other wives and just shy of a dozen other children, undreamed of by his widow.

His *widows*.

'I went straight upstairs, you see?' Andrea was already putting the tissue to good use and leaning down for more.

'Right,' Thorne said.

'I didn't think anything was wrong. The house seemed normal.'

'Sadly, we know that it wasn't. Which is why we have to ask these questions.' Tanner leaned forward and waited until Andrea was looking at her. 'Have you any idea who Richard's visitor might have been? Maybe he mentioned someone to you before you went to Liverpool?'

'I'm sorry,' Andrea said. 'I really don't know. I mean, one of his mates might have popped round to watch football or rugby or whatever. Someone from work or something. But that doesn't explain what happened, does it?'

'No,' Tanner said. 'It doesn't.'

It had been no more than a shot in the dark, of course. The kind of 'visitor' they already suspected the killer was, the kind Richard Sumner had been expecting, was not the kind he would have been likely to mention to his wife.

Have fun in Liverpool, love. Oh, by the way, I thought I might phone out for an escort one of the nights. That a problem?

Five minutes in that house had been enough to tell Thorne they were not dealing with a marriage of that sort. He wasn't sure there *were* marriages of that sort, but even if there were, he didn't suppose they lasted very long.

See you on Sunday . . . you enjoy yourself. Don't worry about me, my long-term girlfriend/boyfriend/sex slave is popping over

28

on Saturday night to keep me company. I've been meaning to tell you . . .

'When can I go back to the house?' Andrea asked.

'Not just yet, I'm afraid,' Thorne said.

'Only, if I'm going to be staying with my sister for a while, I'll need a few things.'

'If you give a list to one of the Family Liaison Officers they can pick everything up for you.'

Andrea nodded, resigned, and said, 'Fine,' though it was obviously anything but.

'Actually, there's one or two things *we* need from the house and we were wondering if you could maybe help us with that.' Thorne smiled, like it was no big deal. 'Richard's phone and computer? I mean, we're presuming he *had* a phone and computer because, well, everyone does, but we couldn't find them.'

'I've got them.' She began to pick at the damp clump of tissue clutched in her fist, plucking off pieces and letting them drop. 'They were on the kitchen table, so I put them in my bag while I was waiting for the police to arrive. It was just a reflex, really. I wanted to look after them, for him.'

'Right.' Thorne could see that, walking back into her house the morning before, Andrea Sumner had known straight away. Not what was waiting for her upstairs, but what had been going on before that. She had known the minute she'd seen that wine bottle and those glasses. Her actions afterwards hadn't helped the investigation, but they had delayed it by a few hours at most and she hadn't done anything illegal. Taking the phone and computer had been an attempt to preserve a little dignity, no more than that, knowing full well what might be on them; the kind of information that Thorne and Tanner were clearly after.

'We'll need you to hand them over to us,' Tanner said.

'Why, though?' It was a mumbled plea, but a plea nonetheless. 'I mean, I know you do that, I've seen it on the news and on the crime shows, but those are the kinds of things you take from suspects, aren't they?'

'Usually,' Thorne said.

'Richard was a victim.'

'It's daft, isn't it? I mean, people keep their whole lives on their phones these days.' Thorne looked to Tanner who grunted her agreement. 'On laptops and whatever. I know I do and I'm sure you're the same.' Andrea shook her head, but Thorne pressed on. 'Being able to access the information on there will tell us a lot more about Richard and, hopefully, help us shed some light on why this terrible thing happened to him.'

'If you want to know about Richard, you just have to ask me.'

'Well thank you,' Tanner said, 'and we will, but—'

'I knew him better than anyone. I knew everything about him.'

'Of course you did,' Thorne said.

Tanner leaned forward and spoke slowly. 'We'll also need a DNA sample, if you wouldn't mind.' They could have easily helped themselves to a hairbrush or whatever – there would be something suitable in the evidence bags – but a simple swab while the woman was in the building would be rather more straightforward. They certainly didn't need a sample of her dead husband's DNA. 'It's purely for elimination purposes, obviously.' Tanner waited. 'I hope that's OK, Andrea. It would really help us.'

It was hard to be sure if Andrea had taken in a word

Tanner had said. She was still looking at Thorne, eyes as wide as she could force them, the pieces of damp tissue scattered in her lap and at her feet.

'I *knew* him.'

Twenty minutes later, Thorne and Tanner stood outside the entrance to the station and watched one of the FLOs lead Andrea Sumner back towards the car they had delivered her in. The heavy frost that had settled overnight didn't look like it was going anywhere. An hour and a half before, Thorne had stood outside his flat, hunched-up and swearing, spraying de-icer on the car windows, and it already looked as though that might be the most enjoyable thing he'd do all day.

Andrea Sumner glanced back at them as the car door was opened for her and she bent to climb inside. Tanner raised a hand to wave, looked at Thorne. 'After Susan was killed, it felt like *I* was the one who was dead,' she said. 'Dead in all the ways that count, anyway. Walking around like a zombie and waking up every morning as if I'd forgotten what I was there for. Back then, I thought that was probably the worst anyone could ever feel.' She nodded towards the car that was now pulling out on to the main road. 'So how does someone get past *that*?'

Thorne wasn't altogether sure it was even possible, but he guessed that catching whoever was responsible for Richard Sumner's murder might be a start.

Of course, *that* was only a possibility, too.

'No idea,' he said.

Shivering, they turned gratefully to head back inside and Tanner looked at her phone. 'You'd better get a shift on.'

Thorne checked his watch, his breath pluming in the cold as he swore underneath it. He moved quickly ahead towards the Gents before hurrying to collect his jacket and bag from the office, keen not to miss the start of the post-mortem.

He needed cheering up.

FOUR

One post-mortem was more than enough for most people and Thorne had been present at a good many more than that. Hundreds, probably. Though he had become . . . accustomed to the unique sights and smells and the terrible whine of the bone-saw, he still put the Vicks and the earplugs to good use every time, and, unlike the heavily tattooed man sitting opposite him, he was certainly unable to face a full English breakfast immediately afterwards.

Full English Option Three, to be precise, with two eggs, double sausage and extra bubble and squeak.

The man was an animal.

Phil Hendricks was not quite as delicate with a knife and fork as he was with dissecting scissors and rib-shears, so just watching his friend tucking in was making Thorne feel gippier than he had while watching him work on Richard Sumner's body twenty minutes earlier. He groaned to make his feelings clear.

The pathologist lifted a fork dripping with baked beans and jabbed it towards the single piece of toast on Thorne's plate.

'Pussy,' he said.

'Pig,' Thorne said.

Hendricks shook his head, disgusted, and the rows of rings, crosses and dangling skulls in each ear moved in unison. 'Could be worse, I suppose. If you'd ordered muesli, I might not have been responsible for my actions.' He turned and raised a thumb to the balding colossus behind the counter, who grinned and gave a thumbs-up in return. The café was a five-minute walk from Hornsey mortuary and Hendricks was a regular customer. He raised his voice so that the owner would hear. 'Mind you, if they served fucking muesli, I wouldn't come here.'

The PM itself had been relatively straightforward. 'No giant moths shoved down the victim's throat,' Hendricks had said early on. 'That's always a plus, right?' As usual, his deadpan Mancunian commentary levelled out the horror with banality, though predictably he'd been unable to resist a gag or two when he'd first seen the body. 'Bloody hell, talk about ear today, gone tomorrow.' Seeing the look on Thorne's face, he'd shrugged and said, 'Chill out, mate, it's not like he can hear us, is it?'

'Doesn't work,' Thorne had said. 'He's dead, so he wouldn't hear us anyway.'

'Bloody hell, everyone's a critic.'

Richard Sumner had died sometime between nine and midnight on Saturday evening, Hendricks had said. The cause of death had been a single stab wound to the neck. 'Slit his throat, with a very thin blade . . . a scalpel, Stanley knife, something like that. He'd have bled out pretty quickly. Same weapon was used to remove the ears and, trust me, I'd love to tell you they got lopped off post-mortem, but the amount of blood on the pillow would suggest otherwise.'

'Jesus.'

'He was probably too busy worrying about all that claret gouting out of his neck to care a great deal.'

Thorne realised that, by the end, Richard Sumner would not have been able to hear himself screaming. He wasn't sure if that was a blessing or not. 'What about drugs?'

'Yeah, I reckon so. Rohypnol, ketamine ... some kind of benzo. I'll know when I get the toxicology results back, but I think it's a fair bet. Especially if you think the killer might be female.' He'd looked down at the body laid open on the slab. 'He was a fairly big lad.'

Something in the wine, Thorne guessed. They'd be getting those results back soon enough.

'Oh, and there's a decent amount of half-digested spaghetti in the stomach,' Hendricks had said. 'Unless he had a seriously nasty case of worms. So, looks like him and his killer plumped for Italian. Talking of which, you up for a late breakfast ... ?'

Now, the café owner sloped across to remove the dirty plates and cutlery, came back almost immediately with fresh mugs of tea.

'Anyway, how's Melita?'

'She's good.' Thorne nodded and smiled. He was hoping he could get over to see her later on.

'Right, or as good as anyone can be with low standards and serious eyesight problems. I'm amazed those glasses she wears aren't a damn sight thicker.'

Thorne clutched at his sides theatrically.

'Mind you, at least she *can* wear glasses.' Hendricks nodded out towards the mortuary. 'Unlike that poor sod back there.'

'That doesn't make sense either,' Thorne said. 'He's dead, so why would he be wearing glasses?'

'You do know how jokes work, right? I mean Englishmen, Irishmen and Scotsmen don't *tend* to walk into bars together.'

Having dealt swiftly with Thorne's love-life, Hendricks talked for a few minutes about his own partner, Liam. '*My* Irishman.' He seemed as settled in that department as he had been in a long time and, barring the unlikely prospect of Arsenal winning silverware any time soon, Thorne could not imagine him any happier. A good deal of the tattooing and many of the piercings were there as notches on Hendricks's bedpost, but he hadn't paid a visit to the tattoo parlour in a good while. Thorne could only hope it stayed that way. It wasn't like there was too much unmarked flesh left.

He winced, remembering one such area of his friend's skin that had been forcibly removed some years before. *Excised*, before being popped into an envelope and hand-delivered to Thorne himself.

He tried not to think too often about the man responsible for it.

'So, Nicola working with you on this one, is she?'

Thorne looked across the table. Hendricks's face showed nothing.

It was a simple enough question, but still there was a second or two's hesitation before Thorne was able to answer; a second or two when their eyes met and the acknowledgement was made.

'Yeah, course.'

'Good job,' Hendricks said, the momentary awkwardness dismissed.

Though Nicola Tanner, who could be somewhat squeamish, baulked occasionally at one or two of Phil Hendricks's ... excesses, the three of them had always been close. But now they were bound together by their actions two years previously. By what had been done to a man named Graham French, bludgeoned to death *after* he had been caught and restrained. By the story one of the three had concocted to protect another, and by the professional jiggery-pokery of the third, done to keep his friends from losing their jobs, or worse. The secret they shared was rarely mentioned or even referred to, but it hung around, heaviest when the three of them were together; stinking of blood and wet hair in moments such as this.

'Because I reckon you'll need all the help you can get.' Hendricks slurped his tea and swallowed. 'Judging by the state of our auditorily challenged friend in the morgue. She—'

Thorne's phone buzzed on the table and he glanced down at the screen. 'Talk of the devil ...' He read the text message.

DNA results back from hair at Sumner house. XX

'Give me a sec.' Thorne called Tanner's number. 'You're not usually *that* affectionate,' he said, when she answered. 'Two kisses?'

'They're not kisses, you arse. They're chromosomes.'

'I don't—'

'Two X chromosomes, which means our killer is definitely a woman.'

Thorne glanced across the table to see Hendricks, who had clearly overheard, snigger before sticking his tongue behind his bottom lip and rolling his eyes.

'Yeah, obviously.' Thorne pressed the phone to his ear and turned away. 'I knew that's what you meant.'

FIVE

Back at Becke House, once she and Thorne had conferred about the PM, Tanner led the first major team briefing. As she spoke, leaning against a desk and gesturing when necessary at the whiteboard behind her, the twenty or so men and women gathered in the incident room studied relevant pages in the case folders that had been put together and handed out by DS Samir Karim. More than a few shook their heads at the crime scene photographs, or sucked in a breath. Karim would also be working as the team's Exhibits Officer, while others would be responsible for overseeing outside enquiries, co-ordinating interviews and managing intelligence. Tanner herself had selected two members of civilian support staff – only marginally less anal-retentive than she was – and tasked them with indexing every statement, message received and suspect profile on to the HOLMES computer system.

There was plenty to do.

Tanner and several others had spent the morning studying

footage from local CCTV and automatic number-plate recognition cameras. It was a laborious process and there was still a long way to go. House to house enquiries had been completed in the road where the Sumners lived, but they had already taken the decision to widen the operation to neighbouring streets. A standard search had been conducted for any record there might be of Richard Anthony Sumner in national police systems. They were carefully examining the couple's financial records, looking at clubs or associations of which they were members, and had begun tracking down and talking to as many of the victim's friends and work colleagues as possible.

At this stage of the game, the net was cast wide, but not overly deep.

'We're just getting started,' Tanner said. 'There's going to be a lot more to get stuck into when we get full forensic results back, and we'll be up to our eyeballs by the time the techies have finished with the victim's phone and computer. *Hopefully*, we will. So, everyone needs to get their nut down, and anyone who doesn't wants to stop and ask themselves if it's really worth pissing me off. No stupid mistakes, nothing half-arsed and no cutting corners, fair enough? That said, we need to do this on the hurry-up . . . '

She let that sink in.

She made eye contact with a few of them to make sure it *had* sunk in.

Obviously, Tanner told them, their job, the job of any homicide unit, was to catch every perpetrator as quickly as possible and, more often than not, speed was the most effective weapon they had. The first twenty-four hours, hot irons, all that. Still, there were newbies on the team, so although she did so rather less dramatically – less forcefully, at any rate – than Tom Thorne might have done, she wound things up by telling them exactly why, with a case such as this, time was not on their side.

Ten minutes later, Thorne and Tanner closed the door of the DCI's office behind them. Russell Brigstocke, the nominal SIO on the case, had been watching the briefing from the back of the room and nodded at Tanner as she and Thorne sat down, to let her know she'd done a good job.

'Sir.' Tanner did not need to be told.

'So, where the hell are we, then?' Behind his desk, Brigstocke began leafing through the case file; a 'murder book' that was, as yet, a rather slim volume, but one which they all knew would fatten rapidly. What had once been a luxuriant quiff was a little shambolic these days and the chain attached to his specs gave him the look of a somewhat dotty headmaster, albeit one who could still dish out a good kicking if he needed to. Tanner was relatively new to the team, but Thorne and Brigstocke had worked together for a long time. In Thorne's admittedly chequered experience, most officers of DCI rank and above were more politician than plod, but Brigstocke was a welcome exception. They'd fallen out, of course, spectacularly on more than one occasion, but Thorne was confident that, when it mattered, he and his boss had one another's back.

Fairly confident, anyway.

'Looks like they had an arrangement and Sumner went somewhere to meet her,' Thorne said. 'Dinner.'

'Spaghetti,' Brigstocke said, looking at the notes. 'Worth talking to Italian places nearby?'

'It might have been local, I suppose, but my money's on somewhere a bit further out. Wouldn't want to risk being seen.'

'Don't shit where you eat.' Brigstocke nodded, like it made sense.

'One way of putting it.'

'We picked his car up going past Gospel Oak station just after seven-thirty,' Tanner said. 'Then again ten minutes after that, heading north towards Highgate. We've got him coming back past the station at nine forty-five. There's obviously a passenger in the car, but it's not a clear image.'

'Sod's law,' Brigstocke said.

'He opens his garage with the remote and drives straight inside,' Thorne said. 'Because he doesn't want his nosy neighbour, or anyone else who knows that his wife's away, clocking that he's brought a woman home with him. The pair of them go out through the back of the garage and into the house through the kitchen door.'

'Then she drugs him,' Brigstocke said.

'Well, obviously we're waiting for forensics to confirm it, but I reckon she slips something into the plonk. Maybe they sit snogging on the sofa for half an hour or whatever, until she's pretty sure the drug's kicked in, then she takes him upstairs and does what she's really there for.'

'What we can't find,' Tanner said, 'is any sign of a woman leaving that area on foot in the time frame we've got. Nothing on any of the cameras that picked Sumner's car up.'

Thorne turned to look at her. 'I don't think she did leave on foot. I think she left the house through the back gate, slipped along that alleyway and walked to whichever street she'd left her own car in.'

'Covered in blood?'

'It's dark and she's wearing a coat.' He waited. 'Why not?' Tanner still seemed unconvinced, so he looked at Brigstocke.

'All right, I'll go with it.'

'She knows where he lives, susses out the area, where the cameras are, all of it. She drives over there beforehand, parks up on a road nearby, then heads off to get ready to meet Sumner later on.'

'You saying she'd planned it well in advance?'

'Come on, do any of us think this was a spur-of-the-moment thing?'

The short silence that followed, the shifting in the seats, made it obvious that none of them did. 'So, how did he meet her?' Brigstocke asked.

'We're still waiting on the nerds,' Thorne said.

'If you're talking about the Digital Forensics Unit, those *nerds* are probably responsible for seventy-five, eighty per cent of all our decent results.'

Thorne nodded, impressed. 'Still nerds, though.'

Tanner smiled and so, eventually, did Brigstocke.

'They've promised a preliminary report by the end of the day.'

'We'll know then,' Thorne said. 'It'll all be on the phone or the laptop, or both.'

This was the information they were really waiting for, counting on. The forensic scientists dealing with physical evidence had worked quickly and already provided enough to secure a conviction, but it was largely academic until such time as an arrest was made. There had been no short-age of DNA and print evidence found at the crime scene, though nothing that had yet been matched with anything

43

on the database. They had also identified a partial footwear print lifted from the bathroom floor as belonging to a size six Dr Marten, which was certainly not a shoe owned by Andrea Sumner.

Thorne was already picturing those shoes, tapping nervously against the floor of an interview room.

Until such time . . .

'So, one of those dating apps, you think?' Brigstocke looked at them. 'An online escort agency?'

'Got to be favourite,' Thorne said.

Tanner nodded her agreement. 'He wanted sex, basically. All tarted up with dinner and a bottle of Merlot, but that's the long and short of it. So I doubt very much this woman is someone our victim met at the bus stop, or in the queue at the post office.'

Brigstocke hummed and nodded. He took off his glasses and rubbed his eyes. 'What about the killer taking the ears?'

'Yeah.' Thorne let out a long breath.

'Might need to put your Dr Perera on standby, Tom. If and when we make an arrest.'

'She's not *my* Dr Perera.'

'No?'

Thorne could see that Tanner was trying to suppress a grin. 'You know what I mean. Not when it's a job.'

The DCI set the file down on his desk and rolled his chair away. Thorne turned to stare out of the office window for a few seconds, across the lush green sports field and the pulsing M1 towards the grim sprawl of the industrial park beyond. Then he let his head drop back and spoke to the dirty-white ceiling tiles. The words themselves were rather more . . . dramatic than those Tanner had used when talking to the team twenty minutes earlier, but he said them as casually as if he were asking for another sugar in his tea.

'If we don't catch her, she's going to do it again.'

SIX

The headless corpse of a mouse had been waiting for Tanner in her kitchen when she got home and for once it had been a fairly easy case to crack. She was not best disposed towards the cat for a while, but by the time Mrs Slocombe sprang on to her lap an hour or so later, all had been forgiven, even though the guilty party was a notorious recidivist. Tanner allowed the cat to settle as she finished what was left in her glass. The red wine and the warmth of the cat were a pleasantly soporific combination, and soon she was struggling to stay awake, while the rhythmic purring and the snare-roll of rain on the roof drowned out the chinless moron on TV who was begging Alan Sugar not to fire him.

I'd fire him, Tanner thought, as she let her eyes close. *In a heartbeat, the useless pillock.*

Drifting, she thought about the kick-arse speech she'd made to the team earlier in the day, her best *Henry V* routine. Better than Lord sodding Sugar, anyway. The need

46

for commitment and for urgency which Tom Thorne had stated rather more bluntly in Brigstocke's office afterwards. She remembered the veiled threats of disciplinary action she'd bandied around; the ton of bricks she would bring down on any idiot who didn't pull their weight or do things the right way.

Anyone who did not follow the correct procedure.

As was so often the case, it was Susan's voice she heard, saying, *Who the hell do you think you're kidding?* and Tanner sat up fast when she felt claws in her chest. The cat jumped away and the rain had stopped and all she could think about was the warm spatter on her face and the weight of a poker in her hand.

She stood up, cold suddenly, and followed the cat into the kitchen. She stood for half a minute, wondering what she'd gone in there for, then decided that a herbal tea would help her sleep. Camomile, maybe, or one of those fruity ones Tom Thorne enjoyed taking the piss out of. Leaning against the worktop, she remembered their conversation outside the Sumner house, when they had talked about the level of violence, about whether a woman could really be responsible. As the kettle began to grumble behind her, Tanner remembered the blood soaked into those clouds on the duvet and a victim who had been unable to defend himself, and thought:

Am I any better than . . . ?

Don't be daft. Nic . . . don't be so stupid.

Susan's voice again. Not in any sort of spooky way and not because Tanner was losing it, but just because she constantly found herself imagining what her dead partner would say in any given situation. Hammering at a brick wall of *no comment* in an interview room, or if the car wouldn't start, or when they'd run out of those biscuits they'd both loved in the supermarket.

The kettle turned itself off.

'Yeah, you're right,' Tanner said.

Susan was bang on, same as she usually was. Tanner was in no way similar to the woman they were now trying to catch, not even close. What was done was done – one moment of madness when rage had got the better of her – and the best way to make up for it was by working to put things right for anyone facing the same hell *she'd* once been in. For the likes of Andrea Sumner.

Justice now was the best thing Tanner could offer, or at any rate it would have to do. Justice was ... atonement. Wasn't it?

Atonement? Listen to you.

Tanner smiled. Susan would never have said anything as poncey as that.

She turned round to make the tea, shushing the cat who had begun to pester her again, nosing around her shins and yowling insistently. As if a bowl of Felix Double Delicious and a mouse's head had not been quite enough.

Thorne and Melita lay reading in bed, each having eaten far too much of Melita's seafood curry to even consider anything more physically demanding. Melita was reading a novel about old people solving a murder, while Thorne flicked through the latest edition of *Country Music*, which the permanently miserable newsagent round the corner from his flat ordered in for him.

Seriously? You like all that twangy stuff?

I do, yeah.

Blokes in big hats?

He was excited to see that there was a new album by Sturgill Simpson out soon and decided that he'd get it. That he'd go to a shop and buy it. He knew he could download it on to his phone, stream it or whatever, but he couldn't be arsed to learn how all that carry-on worked. He still bought CDs, listened to them in the car or played them on what he refused to think of as anything but his 'stereo system'. He still played his records now and again, and would buy a lot more if vinyl hadn't become so bloody expensive. A few months earlier he'd wanted to replace his copy of *Johnny Cash At San Quentin*, which was scratched to buggery. They'd been asking forty-odd quid for it, so Thorne had learned to live with the scratches.

'How was Phil today?'

Thorne turned. 'He was fine.'

She looked at him, a question in her expression he couldn't work out and didn't want to think about for too long.

'Yeah, you know, his usual self. Gobby, and not quite as funny as he thinks he is. He sends his best.'

Melita smiled and turned a page. 'Send mine to him.'

Thorne was keen to change the subject. 'How was your . . . what did you say it was . . . kistophile, today?'

She shook her head. 'It's klismaphile, and I didn't see him today. He's a private patient.'

'Right.' Thorne went back to his magazine, trying to come up with something. 'Public enema number one.'

Melita grunted, like she wanted to get back to her book.

'Oh yeah . . . Brigstocke talked about bringing you in on the case.'

She lowered the paperback and turned to him. 'Right. Well, I'll have to check my diary, see if I'm available.' She reached over and punched him on the arm. 'I'm kidding.'

'If and when the time comes, you know.'

'Obviously.'

'I mean, I wouldn't want to do you out of a payday, but I'm hoping it won't come to that.'

'No, fingers crossed it doesn't. Seriously though, it's good that *he* brought it up.' She narrowed her eyes. 'You hadn't said anything . . . ?'

'No, I swear.'

'OK, then.' Melita leaned across to put her book on the bedside table and switched her light out. 'I wouldn't want anyone thinking it was nepotism. Or that I was working in return for sexual favours from a certain detective inspector.'

Thorne rubbed his stomach. 'Not tonight, you weren't.'

'Well, let's see how we feel in the morning,' Melita said.

Thorne turned his own light off and lay in the dark for a few minutes, the ghost of the bulb dancing behind his eyelids. He'd meant what he'd said; he hoped this case would never reach the stage where Melita's services were called for. It wasn't so much that he didn't believe he could catch the killer. He wasn't short on confidence, misplaced or not. It was more about the kind of case that called for his girlfriend's expertise and how he was likely to feel about it afterwards, whatever the result. The marks a case like that would inevitably leave. *Had* left.

'Night,' Melita said.

In the end, of course, he knew there wasn't a fat lot he could do about that, that all he *could* do was his job, so he tried to tell himself there was very little point in worrying about it.

Thorne rolled on to his side and tugged at the duvet.

He'd learned to live with the scratches.

SEVEN

In the bedroom of a small flat on the other side of the river, Rebecca Driver was wide awake at her computer and making up stories.

She had been doing it ever since she could remember, trying to write things that were funny at first, that might make the other kids at school laugh, if she was lucky and got called up to the front of the class. They did laugh, too, most of the time, and it was the best feeling in the world. Then, a bit later on, when things had turned to shit at home, she didn't much feel like being funny any more.

It was just monsters after that, and nobody liked those stories very much.

Age: 26.
Location: Essex, but happy to travel.

She stared at the screen and racked her brains. She had already come up with a name for this new character and

51

now she was trying to describe her, to think of the things she liked. The films and music she always went back to, favourite food, all the usual. This was the part she enjoyed the most, the bit she put most effort into. Not that any of it was much effort. The story was what really sold it though, she reckoned; the details that would catch the eye, the message it gave. The pictures could come from anywhere, of course, and they were always the thing she left until last, anyway. It was never any problem explaining that discrepancy away.

Smoker: No. Horrible habit.
Traits in a partner that would be unacceptable:

She typed *Erectile dysfunction*, giggled then deleted it.

She still enjoyed making up stories, did it in her head all the time, but it could never come close to the pleasure she got from reading them. She'd spent a lot of time alone in her room after things had turned ugly, with the door locked and always, *always* a book to lose herself in. Headphones pumping out metal, so she could tune out the noise downstairs. She could still feel it, though; vibrating in the walls when things were starting to get smashed downstairs and her mother was screaming at him about something that didn't actually matter, because deep down she knew.

Losing herself wasn't just a treat back then, it was a necessity.

It was the scary stuff she'd needed, right from the off, not that any of it actually scared her. Nothing scared her. Those kinds of books were the best escape route, that was all, so she devoured them. Thrillers with gore-spattered corpses on the cover, dark fantasy, horror of course . . . until eventually she had discovered true crime.

She smiled and started to type again.

That was when all this had really started, obviously.

Looking for: Fun. Passion. Use your imagination!

She swallowed a mouthful of the coffee which had gone cold and glanced at the clock on the screen. She'd give it another couple of hours, try to release as many characters into the world as she could come up with before she got too tired. Work in the morning, on top of all this.

To this day, she always carried a book in her bag, still grabbed every chance she could find to rummage around in one strange world or another. She wasn't that messed-up teenager any more, but some things would never change, even if these days the headphones were only there to dissuade one of the other till-monkeys from disturbing her at lunchtime.

What you reading for?

What kind of a moronic question was that?

Once upon a time it had been because she was desperate to get lost. On a dark and stormy night, in a land of fire and demons, whatever. Looking back now though, she knew damn well that it had been every bit as much about trying to find herself.

Rebecca still loved a good story, but she was very happy she didn't have to do that any more. She'd found out exactly who she was.

EIGHT

It was a dry afternoon and traffic was unusually light on the North Circular as Tanner drove towards Muswell Hill, but that was not why she and Thorne were feeling rather more positive than they had been twenty-four hours earlier. Or at any time since catching the case. The information found on Richard Sumner's phone and laptop might well have eluded his wife, should she have been inclined to look for it, but the Digital Forensics Unit had found everything they needed easily enough.

The nerds had come good.

'So, he just swipes her?' Thorne made the gesture as he asked the question.

'Right, simple as that,' Tanner said. 'Then "Jasmine" or whatever her real name is swipes him back. We can't confirm what the actual sequence was until we've talked to the people at the app, but that's how I'm guessing it went. That Sumner made the first move.'

'Well, he was obviously keen.'

'Though there's still a chance she was the one to swipe first.'

'Either way,' Thorne said. 'He must have thought all his birthdays had come at once.'

'Whichever way it went, why choose Sumner?' Tanner was an extremely careful driver – certainly better than Thorne – and rarely took her eyes off the road, but now she glanced across at him. 'I mean he wasn't loaded and he wasn't what I'd call great-looking.'

'You're hardly the best judge,' Thorne said.

Tanner took her hand off the wheel just long enough to give Thorne the finger.

'Besides which, this "Jasmine" wasn't actually after anything like that, was she? We don't know *what* kind of bloke she was looking for.' He thought about those severed ears. 'What weird boxes she needed ticking.'

'Still.' Tanner shook her head. 'I'm betting she had dozens of desperate blokes swiping, so why him?'

Thorne turned to stare out of the window at a kid in the back of the car on their inside who was pulling faces at him. 'I'm tempted to say that's the sixty-four thousand dollar question, but you know how tight our budget is. I *will* say that if you come up with the answer, I'm willing to splash out on a pint and a pasty in the Oak.'

Richard Sumner had registered with an online dating app called *Sugar-Dad-E* a month or so before. It appeared to be aimed squarely at married men and at women who were looking to be 'taken care of'. Sumner had not chosen the premium option (£9.99 per month for unlimited swipes) which was probably because he had not wanted to hand over any payment details, but the basic service had done the trick.

For the woman he'd found himself matched with, certainly.

Once mobile phone numbers had been exchanged, there had been no further activity within the app itself, but the DFU had been able to retrieve the sizeable series of deleted text messages the victim had sent and received, between his wife leaving for Liverpool on Friday afternoon and Sumner setting off for an assignation in Muswell Hill the following evening.

So, Jasmine, you fancy meeting up?

ok

How about Saturday?

i think so

Dinner?

sounds good.

You like Italian? I know a nice place in Muswell Hill . . .

Nine times out of ten, that would have been job done: number, mobile provider, name, address and inside leg measurement. Thorne and Tanner might now be on their way to make an arrest had the woman they were looking for not been understandably keen to avoid such an outcome and taken precautions. The number from which 'Jasmine' had been texting was attached to a pay as you go burner phone and the line had been inactive since the night of the murder.

56

Ten minutes later, Tanner turned on to Muswell Hill Broadway, and once they'd spotted Arturo's, she began looking for somewhere to park. 'Well, whatever the reason she chose him, the poor bastard did the chasing after that.'

'You think?'

'You read those messages,' she said. 'He suggested a time, he picked the restaurant.' She parked on double yellows and reached into the map pocket for the police business sign. 'He was making all the running.'

'She let him think that's what he was doing,' Thorne said. 'She was always going to be the one doing the "taking care of".'

Calling ahead had given the owner plenty of time to line up the relevant footage from the restaurant's security camera. Luca Gemelli, who had already let it be known that Arturo was actually his late father, sat down in a small office behind the kitchen and showed Thorne and Tanner how to scan through the footage on his computer. Attentive and helpful to the point where Thorne started wondering if the man was dealing coke in his calzones, Gemelli said that he and his staff would be more than happy to answer any questions the police might have when they had finished. Then, as soon as one of the waiters had brought in a pot of coffee and a plate of biscotti, which he urged Thorne and Tanner to 'enjoy', he left them to it.

Tanner put on reading glasses and went to work, while Thorne sat down behind her and poured the coffee. He proffered the plate. 'Want a biscotti?'

'It's biscotto.' Tanner did not take her eyes from the screen, but reached for one. 'Biscotti is plural.'

Thorne told her she was a smartarse and would have been happy to elaborate had he not taken a mouthful of coffee and forgotten what he was going to say. 'Bloody hell, that's nice.' As someone who thought that beans were something you had on toast, Thorne was not what anyone could call a coffee snob, but he was used to the liquefied slurry on tap at Becke House so knew nice when he tasted it. 'Nic, you really need to try—'

Tanner held up a hand. 'There they are . . . '

It had only taken a minute or two. Thorne stood up and peered over Tanner's shoulder. She had frozen the frame on a black and white image of the soon-to-be-murdered Richard Sumner, raising a glass and smiling at his dinner companion.

'Poor sod,' Thorne said.

Tanner let the silent footage resume, then sped it up. Sumner did a lot more smiling as he ate. He listened and nodded, laughing once or twice at whatever his new friend was saying and topping up her glass when it was necessary. Unfortunately, the woman who would mutilate and kill him some time in the following few hours was sitting with her back to the camera and resolutely stayed that way until their meal was finished. There was one fleeting moment of hope when she rose from the table and turned, presumably to visit the Ladies. Tanner and Thorne leaned close to the screen, but on her short walk away from and, a few minutes later, back to the table, 'Jasmine' kept her head down and her face hidden.

'She knows where the camera is,' Tanner said.

Thorne sat down again. He poured more coffee and helped himself to the last biscuit on the plate. 'When did Sumner send the text where he mentioned the restaurant?'

Tanner thought about it. 'Friday afternoon.' She grunted. 'While his wife was still on the train to Liverpool.'

Thorne stepped out to fetch Gemelli and told him that they'd need to look through the security footage from Friday early evening all the way through to the Saturday afternoon. The owner said that would not be a problem and, once he'd replenished the plate of biscuits, he lined up the footage then sat down with them to watch as Thorne and Tanner went through it.

It took a little longer this time, but after half an hour or so, towards the end of the Saturday lunchtime service, Thorne told Tanner to stop and pointed to a woman in the back of shot, standing alone near the entrance to the restaurant. 'What's going on there?'

Gemelli stood to peer at the screen. 'That's the takeaway counter. Looks like she's picking up a pizza.'

Unlike the woman in the footage they had already seen, the figure at the counter was wearing her hair down, a good deal of it conveniently masking her face. As if that wasn't enough, she was wearing a baseball cap and sunglasses, though Thorne could not recall more than half an hour of sunshine at any time the previous week. The woman kept her head lowered this time too, but as her pizza was handed over and she pushed payment across the counter, she turned her head quickly to take in the restaurant's interior. For a few seconds before she turned to leave, when she'd spotted what she was looking for, she was staring straight at the security camera.

'That's her.'

'*Is* it?' Tanner stared.

Thorne froze the frame and asked Gemelli if they could

get a printout. The manager quickly obliged, stabbing at the keyboard until the printer began whirring into life. 'She came to scope the place out once Sumner had suggested it. Chances are she went straight from here to Gospel Oak to get a good look at where all *those* cameras were, left her car near Sumner's place then came back once, you know ... she'd worked up an appetite.'

Tanner said she wasn't sure. Gemelli just shrugged.

'I'm telling you.' It had been something about the way the woman had held herself, Thorne said, the way she'd moved; at the counter, and later, when she'd stood up and turned away from the dinner table. The shape was the same, too. Short and ... not heavy, but oddly solid.

He asked Tanner to go back to the dinner footage to confirm what he was telling her, to move between the two images. As soon as she'd taken a second look, she told him that he was right.

'It's bugger all to do with how she held herself, mind you. Whatever that means. More about what she's got on her feet.'

Now, Thorne looked again. At lunchtime on Saturday, the blonde woman collecting her takeaway had been wearing a long coat, with – he was now certain – the smart red dress she would wear that evening for dinner underneath. But on both occasions she had been sporting a pair of shiny black DMs.

Gemelli had asked his staff to gather around a table in the centre of the restaurant and the half a dozen men and women looked a little nervous, as though it was an episode of *Ramsay's Kitchen Nightmares* and one of them might be about to get sacked. In Italian, then in English for Thorne and Tanner's benefit, Gemelli told them what was required. Before leaving the office he had printed out a second image – of Sumner at dinner – and once that had been passed around, the young woman who had served them that night shyly raised a hand.

Thorne asked her to tell them anything she could remember.

'They were enjoying themselves.' Though the girl clearly spoke Italian, Thorne heard no hint of an accent. 'I really didn't hear very much ... I mean, it's not nice to eavesdrop, is it?' She looked towards her boss, who smiled and waved a hand, urging her to continue. 'I remember the man telling the woman that his job was a bit boring and she said "mine too" ... something like that.' She nodded, thinking back. 'Oh, I remember they were talking about books ... favourite books or whatever.'

Thorne glanced at Tanner. He remembered standing in that bedroom two nights before, taking it all in. As far as he could recall, the books had been on Andrea Sumner's side of the bed.

'It didn't seem like a first date,' the waitress said. 'You can usually tell, but these two seemed very relaxed.' She thought for a moment and shook her head. 'Well, maybe she was a little more relaxed than he was.'

'How did they settle the bill?' Thorne asked. A signed credit card slip with the woman's name on would have been lovely, of course, though he knew it was an extremely long shot.

The young woman smiled. 'They argued about it ... you know, sort of jokey. It happens a lot with couples. She was offering to pay half, but he insisted.'

61

Thorne saw Tanner rolling her eyes. Considering the app that had brought them together, Sumner's insistence on paying the bill didn't come as much of a surprise. It's what any self-respecting sugar daddy would have done, knowing full well what the young lady wanted, that her protestations had merely been for show.

Just a regular, giggling sugar baby.

He thanked the waitress and asked if she would mind popping into the station later that day to help them put together an e-fit. He was still clutching the grainy printout of 'Jasmine' in cap and sunglasses, but guessed that a description from someone who'd had a good look at her up close would be a damn sight more useful. The waitress looked towards Gemelli who quickly nodded his permission.

OK, so maybe not drugs, but the bloke was definitely fiddling his taxes.

Five minutes later, Tanner pulled away from the restaurant and pointed the car back towards Becke House. 'I wonder what she would have done if Sumner had agreed to go Dutch.'

Thorne was checking messages on his phone. 'She'd have paid in cash,' he said. 'She's not stupid.'

'Well, she reads books.'

'Because of the cameras, all of that.' Thorne reached into his pocket for the printout of the woman in the sunglasses. 'I do wonder what kind of books she likes, though. Nothing too mushy, I'm guessing. Are there any rom-coms where one half of a couple savagely murders the other?'

'Anyway we already knew she wasn't stupid.' Tanner was clearly growing impatient with the driver ahead of her, tutting and smacking the wheel. 'Other than the fact that place does fantastic coffee, I'm not sure we found out anything we didn't already know.

'We're getting there,' Thorne said.

'Are we?'

'Yeah, I reckon so.'

Tanner glanced at him. 'Is this you being *optimistic*? Is there a hidden camera in here somewhere?'

'Just saying, we need to stay positive.'

Now Tanner was shaking her head.

It was not an attitude with which most who knew him would readily associate Tom Thorne and he would be the first to accept that his glass was half empty much of the time. Most of the time. A half-empty glass of hot piss, more often than not. If he *was* ever going to feel . . . upbeat about a case, though, it would usually be at moments like this; when the person he was after began to live and breathe a little in his imagination. When it was no longer a simple matter of gathering together the traces of themself a killer had left behind, but had become about who that killer was.

Thorne held up the printout again and stared at it.

'Now we've got a sniff of her,' he said.

NINE

Time might very well go like the clappers when you were having fun, Thorne thought, but it wasn't as if it dragged its size nines when you weren't. When life was anything but a bowl of cherries. When you woke up and suddenly it was six days since you'd caught a murder, and you were no nearer solving it than you had been when you were minding your own business and the poor bastard who'd been carved up was drawing his last breath.

Well, nearer perhaps, but it was all relative, wasn't it?

I could take a step nearer to a beach in the Maldives, he thought, but I'd still be freezing my tits off in West Hendon.

'Are you ever going to take your jacket off?' Tanner asked.

'Are they ever going to sort the heating out?'

'Looks like you're not stopping. That's what my mother would say.'

Thorne ignored her.

'"Face like a slapped arse". That's something else she would say.' Tanner waited. 'At least take the bloody thing off before we go in to see Russell. He'll think you've only just come in.'

Mooching in their office, Thorne and Tanner were due to bring the DCI up to speed on the case, to talk about the progress the team was making and it was not a meeting either was looking forward to.

'It is what it is,' Tanner said.

Thorne sighed. 'Is that another one of your mother's?'

'The boss knows how it can go sometimes.'

'Does he? OK, I feel much better now.'

'Come on, it's not like we're sitting on our backsides, is it?' Tanner tried hard not to sound as irritated as she was. This was the Thorne she knew best, that she missed if he was not around, then struggled to put up with every day that he was. Miserable as sin, but not nearly as much fun. Stubborn and over-inclined to feel sorry for himself, but with a good heart and the best intentions and ... she tried, she really tried, but sometimes the temptation to slap the shit out of him was overwhelming. 'Everyone's been knocking their pipes out. We've done everything we can and we're building a hell of a case, you know we are.'

'They built the pyramids quicker.'

'Listen to yourself.' Christ, it was tempting. 'It's been a week, not even that. We'll get a result.'

'You just said it.' Thorne shoved his hands deep into the pockets of his leather jacket, like a sulky teenager. 'We've done everything we can. We need ... something else.'

Tanner looked at him.

'No, not that.' They were both thinking it, of course and had been since day one. The break in the case that nobody would ever wish for, that was *un*thinkable.

Another body.

Thorne checked his watch. He knew that Brigstocke was waiting. 'Well, it won't take very long,' he said. 'Small blessings, right?' He looked at Tanner and the smile was one of resignation, but it was a smile at least. 'So, what are we going to tell him?'

Fresh out of ideas, bright or otherwise, Tanner dug into her bag and began to reapply lipstick.

'No worries, Nic, you just put your face on and leave it to me ... "OK, Russell, here's where we are. I know this is supposed to be an update, but we've decided to go in a different direction, you know, think outside the box ... so instead, we're going to tell you a whole bunch of stuff you've been very well aware of for the last week".' He saw Tanner shaking her head. '"Excuse me ... for the best part of a week. More of a downdate I suppose you'd call it.".' He began to pace up and down the small office, rehearsing a speech he would never dream of making, blowing off steam. '"So, basically we're looking for a crazy woman who trots off on a hot date, all dolled up in her smartest Dr Martens with a blade in her bag".'

'And a bottle of roofies.' Tanner was clearly happy enough to join in, to indulge him. To put off the real meeting a little longer.

'Of course, let's not forget *them*.'

The toxicology on the PM had come in on the same day they'd been to visit the Italian restaurant. The traces of Rohypnol discovered in the body matched with analysis carried out on one of the wine glasses found at the crime scene.

'Enough "Mexican Valium" to knock an elephant on its arse,' Hendricks had said. 'Or a darts player at least.'

Thorne was into his stride. "'We've got more forensic evidence than you can shake a stick at, shedloads of digital stuff and a seriously top of the range e-fit from an eye witness. Most importantly ... *most* importantly, we've got a team that's fired up and it goes without saying that myself and DI Tanner remain full of piss and vinegar, so there's really no need to worry because, you know ... it's only a matter of time.'" He turned to Tanner, held out his arms. 'What do you think?'

Tanner dropped the lipstick back into her bag. 'There's only one way to find out.'

'It'll go one of two ways, if you ask me.' Thorne grabbed the case file from his desk and followed her to the door. 'We're either talking handshakes all round, big drinks later on and immediate promotions for the pair of us ...'

Tanner waited.

'Or he'll tell us we're both useless twats and call in a psychic.'

TEN

From: Hari harihari1995@hotmail.com

To: JennyG brghhtm@anonymail.com

Hey Jenny just wanted to check you're still on for later. It's been great getting to know you in emails and stuff but I'm very excited about meeting you IRL! *Tries not to sound overly keen* H x

From: JennyG brghhtm@anonymail.com

To: Hari harihari1995@hotmail.com

Ha! I'm looking forward to it too and I'm very happy you're keen. Hope you're not disappointed! Cameras tell porkies, remember! xoxo

From: Hari harihari1995@hotmail.com

To: JennyG brghhtm@anonymail.com

I'm sure I won't be disappointed but glad you mentioned the photo thing first. Not sure I look very much like the pic I sent either. Also, wanted you to know I'm not exactly minted so is it ok if we go somewhere not too pricey? How do you feel about Nando's? I know it's not posh or anything so I hope you don't mind. H x

From: JennyG brghhtm@anonymail.com

To: Hari harihari1995@hotmail.com

You are very sweet but I'm not the sort of person who's bothered about going anywhere fancy. LOVE the peri peri so no worries! All about the company and where it leads, right? Ring and let me know where. See you later. xoxo

From: Hari harihari1995@hotmail.com

To: JennyG brghhtm@anonymail.com

Can't wait! Hx

ELEVEN

Thorne had wanted to go to *his* local, but Hendricks had pointed out that he came to Thorne's neck of the woods way more often than Thorne came to his, so, you know . . . it was only fair. On the phone at knocking-off time, Thorne had fought his corner for a few minutes, then given up. The place Hendricks was suggesting on Camden Parkway was no more than a fifteen-minute walk from Thorne's flat in Kentish Town – close enough to mean they could easily have downed a couple each in both pubs twice and still been home before closing time – so Thorne had hung up wondering why the hell they'd been having such a pointless argument.

'Because I was in a bad mood,' Hendricks said now. 'On top of which, it's not healthy for you to get your own way too often.'

'Oh, well, as long as there was a good reason,' Thorne said.

Hendricks nodded. 'Trust me, mate, you're much nicer

if you get slapped down now and again.' He jabbed a fork towards the food. 'Plus, these things are seriously amazing.'

They were sitting at a corner table in the Spread Eagle on Camden Parkway. Each had ordered a pint of Guinness and they'd agreed to share two of the home-made bar snacks Hendricks had been raving about on the phone. Hendricks speared his portion of a neatly divided Scotch egg. 'So presumably half a Scotch egg wouldn't count as a "substantial meal".' He took a bite and talked while chewing. 'Remember all that bollocks?'

Thorne nodded and cut into the half sausage roll on his own plate. It was good to just *be* in a pub again. It still felt like a treat.

'I've never been a massive fan of eating in pubs anyway,' Hendricks said. 'Meals, I mean. If you're hungry, there's nuts and crisps, right? That's what's meant to go with beer, not ... chicken nuggets or posh fish finger sandwiches. You ask me, gastropub is just another way of saying shit restaurant.'

'Well, I didn't ask you,' Thorne said. 'But as always, Philip, I'm hanging on every morsel of wit and wisdom.' He took a mouthful of sausage roll and immediately began to nod enthusiastically, humming with pleasure.

'Told you,' Hendricks said.

They polished off the rest of their food quickly and, save for the low chatter from adjoining tables, in silence. For Thorne, this was another reason to give the place a big tick. However good the grub was, it was always ruined by 'atmospheric' background music and it would only have taken a few minutes of Ed Sheeran or God forbid something *ambient* to bring on raging indigestion.

71

'So, why were you in a bad mood?' he asked.

'Just a stupid row with Liam.' Hendricks lifted his glass, shook his head, then took a drink.

'What about?'

'What are rows usually about? Bugger all, right?' Hendricks sighed and swirled the beer around in his glass. 'He'd spent all morning doing the crossword, you know? Really concentrating on it, he was. So, because I thought it was funny ... when he went to the toilet, I grabbed his pen and filled in some of the words he couldn't get.'

Thorne winced. 'What did you write?'

Hendricks nodded slowly, milking it. He was trying to look at least a little shamefaced, but the overwhelming desire to laugh meant that he couldn't pull it off. '*Ballbags*,' he said. 'And *Cockjockey*.'

'You're *such* a child.'

'I'm telling you, mate, he seriously overreacted.'

'You think?'

'*Well* over the top, it was.'

Thorne was trying to catch the attention of the girl behind the bar. 'As it happens, I wasn't in the best of moods myself earlier on.' He caught the girl's eye and signalled for two more pints. 'Got a bit chopsy with Nicola Tanner.'

Hendricks looked at him. 'Oh yeah?'

And there it was. The change in the air, the shift; every bit as strong and sudden as it had been when Hendricks had mentioned Tanner's name after the post-mortem. 'Not a big deal. Getting nowhere with the Sumner case and feeling frustrated and taking it out on her. I was just being an arse, that's all.'

'Maybe I should have a word,' Hendricks said.

'About what?'

Thorne couldn't recall the last time Nicola and Phil had spent any time together, but it was probably arrogant of him to assume he would know if they had. There was, of course, no reason why they shouldn't get together outside work, see one another independently of Thorne, but the idea was no longer one he could ever be comfortable with. He wondered if Phil felt the same way about him seeing Nicola and how she might feel about Phil and him sitting together in the pub right now.

It was a perfectly normal situation, they all were, but even so.

Would she wonder if they were talking about it? Whispering the rights and wrongs of it, despite an unspoken agreement that they never would, worn out by the effort it took *not* to?

'About what, Phil?'

Hendricks was, thankfully, smiling. 'I could tell her my theory about slapping you down once in a while.'

Thorne emptied what was left of the beer into his mouth and held it there for a few seconds before swallowing. 'I wouldn't waste your time, mate. I think she's probably worked that out by now.'

There was a small queue outside Nando's on Clapham High Street. It was only half a dozen people and probably no more than a fifteen-minute wait, but still, Hari felt bad about it. It was cold and had started to spit with rain and Jenny was only wearing a thin jacket.

He watched her shiver and stamp her feet, and even though she smiled at him, which was nice, he knew that the night was going wrong before it had even started. 'Listen, I'm really sorry,' he said. 'We can go somewhere else if you want.'

'Don't be daft, it's not your fault,' she said.

'You sure? I didn't think it'd be so rammed.'

'Saturday night, isn't it?'

'I suppose.' Hari told himself he should have thought about it a bit more, checked the app on his phone to see what the weather would be doing. He'd been too busy tearing around his flat, choosing which shirt to wear, getting his hair right, all that. She hadn't looked horrified or anything when she'd turned up though, and you could always tell when someone was faking, so that was something.

'A few more minutes doesn't really matter, does it?' She smiled at him again. 'We'll just be that bit hungrier.'

Hari peered in through the window. 'There's more people leaving.'

'Yay.' She held up her hand for a high-five and when their palms met she wrapped her fingers around his. It was only for a few seconds, but although she looked a little bit embarrassed Hari thought it was a pretty good sign.

They watched as the couple up ahead were called inside and when Hari shuffled forward the staff member waved him in so they could sit in the waiting area. He handed them menus and said it was only going to be another few minutes until a table was ready.

Hari flapped his menu. 'Don't really need this, to be honest. Bit of a regular.'

'Oh, so you bring loads of girls here then, do you?'

'No.' Hari could feel himself redden. 'I mean no, it's usually just me or sometimes me and my flatmate. And no, there aren't . . . loads of girls.'

'I'm kidding,' she said. 'Relax.' She leaned against him and turned her head until her mouth was close to his ear. Then, she sort of whispered his name, as if she was trying it out for size; like she thought it was sweet or maybe even sexy. 'We're going to have a brilliant night.'

Thorne and Hendricks walked down Parkway towards Camden High Street. There was drizzle in the air, so Thorne turned up his collar, while Hendricks was sporting the black pork-pie hat he'd taken to wearing.

'What are you supposed to be?' Thorne had asked the first time he'd seen it. 'A rude boy?'

'Go fuck yourself,' Hendricks had said.

'The prosecution rests.'

The rain had become just a little heavier by the time they reached the tube station. From here they would be going in different directions, but Hendricks, a very occasional smoker, stepped under the cover of the station entrance and lit a cigarette. Thorne was happy enough to hang around with him while he smoked it, before they went their separate ways. Neither of them had very far to walk.

'Sorry to hear the case isn't going very well,' Hendricks said.

Thorne thought about what Tanner had said. 'It is what it is.'

'Doesn't stop you feeling shit, though.'

'I've been here before,' Thorne said.

'At least you're still walking around, mate. With both your ears. Things couldn't have got much shitter for *that* poor sod.'

'He ended up with you working on him, didn't he?'

'What are you on about?' Hendricks threw his arms wide in mock outrage. 'I'm the best there is. He won the post-mortem lottery.'

'Yeah, right.' Thorne had watched his friend work more times than he could remember and knew the boast was justified, but the insults and the constant wind-ups were one of the things that made them friends in the first place. 'He'd have been better off with Stevie Wonder.'

'I'm thinking I should leave some kind of . . . signature, you know? Same as any great artist. So, if one of my bodies ever gets dug up by someone a hundred years from now, they'll know it was worked on by the Master.'

'The master *something*, definitely.'

'I could get a few business cards laminated, pop one in the chest cavity before it gets sewn up.'

'I'm not even sure you're joking,' Thorne said.

'Or maybe just a plastic toy. Like a Kinder egg type thing.'

'You're a disgrace.'

Four pints to the good, Hendricks had been annoyingly cheerful up to that point, but now the grin became a grimace, as though his cigarette had suddenly begun to taste bitter.

He let what was left drop to the wet pavement and stamped on it.

'Ain't that the truth.'

They had eaten a *lot* of chicken – legs, wings, livers – with chips, peas and coleslaw, and afterwards they'd somehow found room for a couple of the Portuguese custard tarts, which Hari had never tried before. They'd drunk two bottles of lager each and talked more or less the whole time.

Hari stared down at the carnage and slapped a hand to his belly. 'I'm not sure I can walk.'

'Yeah, that was awesome,' she said.

'Sorry it wasn't anywhere a bit more . . . '

'Like I said, it's all about the company. And the company's . . . pretty great.'

She told him a bit about her job in a supermarket, about her brother who she didn't get on with, then asked him what kind of books he liked. She was always reading, she told him. It was like a doorway into a different world. He said he had to read so many stupid textbooks for his course that he didn't have much time to read stuff with stories and she said that was a real shame.

'My flatmate reads tons,' Hari said. 'Science fiction, mostly.' He pulled a face. 'We don't have the same taste in music either. He's great, I mean he's probably my best mate, but he listens to some weird shit.'

'I quite like weird shit,' she said.

'Oh, you'll definitely get on with him, then. He's gone to a gig tonight, actually. Some band with a stupid name.'

'Yeah?'

'Yeah, somewhere up west. He'll probably be going to a club or whatever afterwards, so who knows what time he'll be rolling in.'

They didn't say anything for a while after that, but it wasn't awkward. It was virtually the first time either of them had drawn breath, and besides, Hari was happy enough just to look at her for a bit. To enjoy how well it was all going.

'I think we've been dead lucky,' she said. 'Well *I* have, anyway. I mean you stick a profile up and bang off a few emails, but you never know who you might end up with.'

77

Hari nodded. *Lucky* didn't even come close. 'I meant to ask . . . what's with that weird email address you were using?'

'Oh, yeah.'

'Anonymail?'

She looked down and began fiddling with the cutlery. 'Well, because it's all just a bit . . . embarrassing.' Seeing Hari's expression, she quickly reached a hand across the table. 'Not *this* . . . this is ace. I mean, just going on a site like that in the first place. I suppose I'm worried it makes me look a bit sad and desperate and everything you send stays *out* there, doesn't it? So I was just hiding a bit. That's probably why I put a picture up that doesn't look a lot like me. Just covering my arse in case I end up feeling like an idiot.'

Hari was laughing by the time she'd finished. 'You were worried *you* were going to look desperate? Oh, and no, you don't look much like that picture . . . you look way better.'

She laughed. 'That was *so* smooth.'

'Yeah it was, right?'

'Especially the way you left that little pause.'

'I rehearsed it, if I'm honest.'

She laughed again. 'So, how far away do you live?'

Hari pointed out towards the High Street. 'It's only five minutes away. I know, not the most adventurous outing.'

She turned to lift her jacket from the back of her chair. 'Come on then. I mean, I presume you *can* actually walk.'

Hari stared at her, desperately trying to appear cool. 'Are you saying you want to come back to mine?'

'Well, not if you don't want me to.'

'No . . . yeah. Course I do.'

'You were the one who made a point of telling me your flatmate wouldn't be back until late.'

'Yeah, but that was just conversation, honest. I wasn't . . . hinting.'

She pulled on her jacket, grinned as she picked up a cold chip and popped it into her mouth. 'Look, bearing in mind how we got together, I don't think either of us should waste time pretending we're hard to get.'

TWELVE

'Well, no prizes for guessing there's at least one more coming,' Thorne said. 'Or what *that* poor bastard's going to be missing.' He stared out of the window. The scenery had become a lot greener since they crossed the bridge at Dartford and the houses had been getting bigger and further apart since they'd passed the first sign for Sevenoaks. 'Hear no evil, speak no evil, see no evil. Jesus . . . '

Tanner shook her head. 'Isn't it supposed to be *see* first?'

'What?'

'The three wise monkeys. See then hear then speak.'

Thorne was not surprised that Tanner would know and care about such things. This was someone whose books were colour-coded, who laid out her clothes for the morning before going to bed. 'I don't think "Jasmine" or "Jenny", or whatever the hell she's going to call herself next time is that bothered about the running order.'

'No, probably not,' Tanner said.

They slowed when the sat-nav announced that they had

reached their destination and drew up outside a large, mock-Tudor house set back from the road. Tanner turned on to the drive and parked behind a black four-by-four.

'Nice place,' Thorne said, when he stepped out of the car. 'Home comforts for the lad look seriously comfortable.'

Luke McGovern, the twenty-one-year-old they were here to interview, had discovered the body of his friend Hari Reddy in the flat they shared in Clapham at lunchtime on Sunday, two days previously. He'd been staying with his parents ever since.

'You think a big house helps?' Tanner keyed the remote to lock the car. 'Right now, I think "comfortable" would be anywhere there aren't bloodstains.'

The woman who answered the door studied their warrant cards and told them she was Luke's mother. She showed them into a sitting room and said that she would go and fetch her son, who was in his bedroom. He'd been there nearly all the time, she said, since the police had brought him home on Sunday evening.

Thorne and Tanner sat down on a vast sofa and waited.

'I just meant there are worse places he could be,' Thorne said. 'That's all.' He looked around the room. 'It's better that there's someone taking care of him.'

Tanner nodded. 'Times like this, you run for home. If you've still got one.'

A few minutes later, while his mother stood watching from the doorway, Luke McGovern wandered over and dropped into an armchair. He was barefoot and wearing what Thorne would later learn was called a onesie. It was nearly midday but he gave the impression that he'd just woken up. He looked more like a schoolboy than a second-year student.

'I'll leave you to it.' Luke's mother was staring at her son. 'Let me know if you need anything.' Had he and Tanner been visitors of any other sort, Thorne was sure that the woman would have offered them refreshments by now, but politeness was trumped by concern for her child. She did not want him reliving what had clearly been a hugely traumatic experience any longer than was strictly necessary.

'Thank you.' Tanner waited until the door was closed, then turned to the young man opposite her. He had drawn his knees up and wrapped his arms around them. 'So, Luke . . . I know you've already spoken to several officers in Clapham, but I'm afraid we weren't made aware of this until yesterday morning. We're keen to speak to you because we think what happened to Hari might be connected to a case we're already working on.'

In an effort to keep track of any murders with similar characteristics, flags had been set up on the Police National Computer in the days following the discovery of Richard Sumner's body. *Neck wound. Evidence pointing towards a romantic/sexual encounter. Missing body parts.* Each of these alerts had been activated the day before and details of the Clapham crime scene sent through to Becke House.

They had known straight away.

'I know it's horrible,' Thorne said. 'I swear we wouldn't be asking you unless it was absolutely necessary . . .' He heard a creak outside the door and wondered if the boy's mother was listening in. ' . . . but could you tell us about finding Hari?'

Luke dropped his chin on to his knees and turned to look out towards the garden. 'I got back really late on Saturday night and I'd had quite a lot to drink, so I didn't get up until like, midday.' His voice was flat and accentless and he spoke so quietly that Thorne and Tanner had to lean towards him to make it all out. 'Even then, I didn't know anything was . . . I mean, I went into the kitchen and made some coffee and I was like shouting for him. To get his lazy arse out of bed, you know? I knocked on his door for a bit. Then I went into his room.'

Tanner watched the boy close his eyes. She had studied the crime scene photographs and knew very well what he was seeing, what he would see for a long time to come. She still opened her front door sometimes and saw blood blooming on the hall carpet, the scatter of white spots from the bleach they'd fired into her partner's eyes.

'What about the night before?' she asked. 'When you got back.'

'Yeah, so I could see that he'd got somebody round,' Luke said. 'That he'd brought her back with him. Like they'd got stuck into the wine in the kitchen.' Tanner glanced at Thorne. Luke had been confronted by the same evidence of a romantic liaison as Andrea Sumner, although his reaction on seeing it was very different. 'I was seriously made up for him, you know? It was the first time Hari had got lucky since I've known him.' His arms tightened around his knees, as though he was trying to make himself as small as possible. 'Well, I thought he'd got lucky.'

'Course,' Tanner said.

'So, you think he got catfished?' Luke turned his head suddenly and stared at her. 'That this woman wasn't really a woman at all?'

Tanner hesitated, so Thorne stepped in. 'If by "catfish" you mean that the person Hari thought he was seeing was actually someone else entirely, then yeah, he got catfished.'

83

Thorne had no idea what Luke McGovern was studying or even if he was a particularly good student, but he was obviously not stupid. His expression made it clear he could see that Thorne and Tanner were keeping something back. 'So, it *was* a woman?'

This was an investigation that would not stay out of the press for very long, so Thorne could see little point in being even operationally coy. 'We believe so, yes,' he said.

'Fuck.' Luke shook his head. 'I mean . . . fuck.'

'So, you knew all about it?' Tanner asked. 'What Hari was doing that night?'

Luke was still shaking his head. 'Yeah, we'd both put profiles up on the site. Looked at all the pictures. It was a laugh, you know?'

The nerds had already extracted and analysed the relevant information from Hari Reddy's phone and computer. Thorne and Tanner knew about Hookupz.com. They had studied transcripts of the emails, sent using one of the countless guerilla email sites that were freely available.

They knew all about 'Jenny'.

'Hari was like, really excited. He showed me the messages she sent him, told me where they were meeting up, showed me a picture of her. Oh, wait . . . ' Luke sat up suddenly and dug into his pocket. 'I've got it on my phone . . . '

Thorne watched and waited while the boy tapped and scrolled.

'Here . . . '

He leaned forward to look at the picture Luke had found. 'Yeah, we've seen that one.'

'He'd talked to her on the phone as well,' Luke said.

Thorne nodded. The nerds had checked. Another burner.

'Hari said she sounded nice, you know?' Luke stood up and began to pace back and forth in front of his chair. 'He was properly keen. I mean I know it's called Hookupz and I'm not saying he wouldn't have been up for, like, just a shag or whatever, but he was really hoping it might lead somewhere else.'

Thorne said nothing. Thinking: It *did*. He watched as Luke walked all the way across to the French windows and stared out, leaning his head against the glass; tearing at his scalp like there were things crawling across it.

'What about . . . ?' He turned, and he raised his arms, and the tears began to fall. 'I mean, I saw all the blood around his mouth. What the hell was that about?' He nodded, struggling to get the words out. 'She took his tongue, right? She took his fucking *tongue?*'

Thorne said, 'Luke,' and Tanner stood up when the sobbing started. The door opened a few moments later and Luke's mother walked in. She moved halfway across the room and stopped, her own eyes brimming as the young man began to bawl. This time, Thorne and Tanner had no trouble hearing him.

'What kind of person *does* that?'

'It's a fair question,' Tanner said, her eyes on the mirror as she reversed off the McGoverns' drive.

Thorne was searching for something on his phone. 'Even if we knew the answer, I'm not sure it would help us find her.' He opened an attachment and stared down at the same picture Luke had been so keen to show them. The photograph sent to Hari Reddy.

'She's enjoying herself,' Tanner said. 'I know that much.'

The woman was pale with dark eyes. The blonde hair had now been dyed black and was cut shorter than it had been on her visits to Arturo's a week before. The smile was shy, not quite fully formed.

Now, they had plenty of pictures.

As well as the profile shot posted on the Hookupz website, Thorne had seen stills from the security footage at Nando's, which had been checked immediately after Luke's initial statement. He had seen the grainy pictures from CCTV cameras near the restaurant and from others close to the crime scene; images captured as Hari and his date had arrived at the flat, then again, a few hours later, when the woman had walked away on her own.

It was all very helpful, but still. Thorne could not help wondering why, despite the untraceable phone and emails, the woman they were trying to find did not appear overly bothered about hiding any more.

THIRTEEN

Thorne sat in front of his laptop at the small table in his kitchen. Melita had pulled up a chair next to him and watched as he guided her through the contents of the Hookupz website, scrolling slowly through the hundreds of pictures.

'No shortage of punters, is there?'

'No big surprise,' Melita said. 'They make it very easy.'

'Not sure I could do it,' Thorne said. 'Even if I *was* in the market for . . . ' he looked at the website's forthright mission statement, '"no strings nookie".'

'You sure?' She leaned against his shoulder. 'I'm only watching to make sure you don't "accidentally" match with someone.'

'Yeah, it would be easy to make a mistake. You know, click on the wrong thing.' He held up his hand. 'My big sausage fingers.'

Melita looked at the screen. 'To be honest, I *am* surprised there's as many women as men.'

'Well, it's not *quite* fifty-fifty.'

'Even so. It's far easier for women to simply go out and get sex if they want it.'

'Yeah,' Thorne said. 'I've always thought that was a bit unfair.'

'And in a bar or whatever, at least you get to see the person first.'

Thorne opened some of the tabs he'd saved and together they looked through a few of the other sites available, offering associated services. 'Look at this lot,' Thorne said. Many were even less subtle about what was on the menu than Hookupz. Adult Pursuits, Get-Off, ShagNow. There were plenty tailored towards specific demographics – Milfs, Dilfs and Gilfs – and no shortage of those geared towards those of more particular sexual tastes and persuasions. Thorne's favourite was a site aimed at the older customer who fancied some immediate, no-questions-asked bondage, called Instant Whip.

'Something for everyone,' Melita said.

'There's probably a site on here somewhere for your enema man.' Thorne smiled. 'FastFlush dot com?'

Melita sighed. 'He's not the only person on my books, you know. As it happens I'm seeing a number of very interesting clients at the moment.'

'Such as?'

'You know I'm not comfortable discussing that.'

'You told me about the enema bloke.'

'And now I'm wishing I hadn't,' she said. 'It was only because it was relatively harmless and I knew you'd find it funny, because you have a juvenile sense of humour. Trust me, some of the issues my other clients are dealing with are rather more serious.'

Thorne deleted his open tabs until he was back on the Hookupz site and looking at the profile and picture of the woman who had called herself Jenny.

'So, what do you think?' Thorne asked. 'First time round she's keeping well away from the cameras, now she's all over them. Is she getting careless?'

Melita stared at the picture. They had discussed it over pasta an hour or so earlier, but she was someone who preferred to think about things a while, who shied away from making snap judgements. 'I think you may be right, but not in the way you mean. Not careless in the sense that she's being sloppy and making mistakes ... but perhaps she simply does not care any more.'

Thorne looked at her.

'I'm not saying she doesn't care about getting caught. I see no reason to believe that she wants that. Maybe she's rather more concerned with being noticed. Getting proper credit.'

'We'll take care of that.' Thorne closed the laptop. 'You reckon life without parole will be enough credit for her?'

Melita topped up her wine glass, Thorne grabbed a bottle of lager from the fridge and they walked into the living room.

'Something else I was thinking.' Melita sat down. Thorne turned off the spectacularly dull Southampton v Leicester game he'd been watching and joined her on the settee. 'This whole wise monkeys thing.'

'If we're right about that.'

'Let's presume you are. It's all a bit ... *showy*, don't you think? A bit theatrical. As if she's been studying murders like this which, as you know, are incredibly rare and she's just ... doing an impression of a serial killer.'

'She's not doing an impression,' Thorne said. 'She *is* one.'

'Yes, of course, but only in terms of the statistics. I don't think she's being herself when she's doing it, that's all. I think she's playing a character.'

'Like someone in one of those books she's obviously so keen on.'

'Perhaps,' Melita said.

Thorne sat back and stared at the blank TV screen. 'What about the victims, though? You've got a middle-aged white accountant and an Asian student. She clearly doesn't have a type. I mean they usually do, right? And if she's following some *Serial Killing For Dummies* script, like you said, you'd think there'd be more of a pattern in terms of the victimology.'

'Well, both victims do have one thing in common.' She turned to look at him. 'Yes, one was cheating on his wife and the other was single, but they were both men who were basically after sex.'

'So, what . . . you're suggesting this might be some kind of ultimate feminist revenge thing?'

'I'm not suggesting anything. We're just talking.'

'Maybe a rape victim?'

'Well, it might be worth considering,' Melita said, 'but it works against your three wise monkeys theory. I mean, if that *is* what's behind these murders, and I have certainly come across cases like that, I think there might have been one body part she'd have been somewhat keener to remove than a tongue or some ears.'

Thorne puffed out his cheeks and went back to staring at the dusty TV screen.

'You can put the football back on,' Melita said.

'Trust me, this is more exciting.'

'I don't dislike sport as much as you think I do.' She tucked a strand of dark hair behind her ear, then laughed when she saw the look on his face. 'There's still all *sorts* of things you don't know about me, Tom.'

'Actually there *is* something you might like.' Thorne turned the TV back on and scrolled through the channels, but sadly there wasn't any axe-throwing available. 'Never mind,' he said.

They sat in silence for a while, finished their drinks, then Melita moved closer. 'You OK?'

'I'm fine,' Thorne said.

She reached across and rubbed his arm. 'Sure?'

'Yeah . . . ' Thorne flicked back to Sky, to see if the match had got any more interesting. 'I'm grand.'

They watched for a few minutes, until Melita grew understandably restless. 'So, early night?'

Thorne nodded, like he was thinking about it. 'Yeah, you're right about how much easier it is for women to get sex if they want it. Basically, they just have to ask.'

FOURTEEN

A few minutes' walk from Thornton Heath station, DS Dipak Chall stopped and pointed. 'Do you think that might be it?'

'I reckon there's every chance,' Thorne said.

To be fair, it was hard to miss the place. The gleaming white pavilion certainly caught the eye rather more effectively than the nearby nail bar, the second-hand furniture shop and the 'best hand car-wash in the UK'. What marked it out most particularly though, making its function obvious to anyone without the most serious eyesight problems, were the enormous, cartoonish letters that ran along three sides of the entrance.

LIBRARY

Thorne and Chall showed their warrant cards at the reception desk and waited.

While the obvious links between the murders in Clapham and Gospel Oak had seen the case officially handed over to the team at Becke House, it had been the nerds south of the river who had been given first crack at Hari Reddy's phone and computer. Having quickly established that 'Jenny' had made use of a guerilla email account, they had now traced the ISP back to a public computer at Thornton Heath Library.

'I'm not sure what the point of libraries is,' Chall had said on the train.

Dipak Chall was a young officer brought on board by Nicola Tanner when she'd joined the team and, even if he hadn't quite had the enthusiasm for the job knocked out of him yet, Thorne thought he was a solid enough copper and a nice enough bloke. He'd heard him say smarter things, though.

'What the *point* is?'

'I mean, why would you want to borrow a book when you can buy them for next to nothing in charity shops or whatever?'

'Well, if you don't have a lot of money, I'm guessing the difference between *next* to nothing and *nothing* is pretty important.'

'Yeah, but there's free ones you can download on to your phone or whatever.'

'If you've *got* a phone. If you know how to do that stuff.'

Chall looked at him as though he was suggesting there were people who still couldn't walk upright.

'Anyway, it's not only about books,' Thorne said. 'People use libraries for all sorts of things.' Seeing that Chall was waiting for him to elaborate, Thorne had reached for the folder on the seat next to him, containing the transcripts of the emails sent to Hari Reddy. '*This*, for a kick-off.'

'I'm very sorry, but it's council policy.' Now, the woman at the library's reception desk was sliding a form across the counter. 'Before we can allow access to the security footage, you need to fill in an application which we then forward to the borough's IT department.'

'Oh, come on.' Thorne smiled, but saw immediately that it would not get him anywhere. 'Seriously?'

'I know, it's daft,' the woman said. 'But it'll only take a few minutes.'

Chall had already picked up the pen. 'Why didn't we sort all this before we left?'

'Why didn't *you*?'

While Chall filled in the form, Thorne wandered away from the desk and, looking around, found himself every bit as surprised by the library's interior as he had been by what he'd seen from the street. There were high ceilings and avenues of stripped-oak flooring snaking between splashes of plush carpet. Customers sat on comfortable-looking armchairs lined up against the glass walls or perched on benches with deep, green and purple cushions. The books were shelved on a seemingly haphazard arrangement of ultra-modern units on shiny wheels. Nothing seemed ... fixed and there were no sharp edges. There was light and colour everywhere, and though Thorne would never have described it as noisy, it was certainly not quiet.

The fact that it wasn't what Thorne had been expecting was odd, he thought, considering he could not remember the last time he'd been inside a library. He blinked, and, from nowhere, a long-submerged memory bobbed suddenly to the surface; of being taken to the local library by his mum, being dragged along, probably.

He sat down on one of the benches and let it come.

Highbury, was it? Or Islington . . .

It was fuzzy round the edges, just a sense of the place, really . . . standing looking up at floor-to-ceiling shelves, and of everything being very dark and very quiet. The smell of polish and the echo of footsteps on marble and his hand inside his mum's as she led him round.

He couldn't remember her taking any books out, but she must have done.

It made sense, because his mum had been a reader. He could still picture the names on some of the books he'd seen around the house. Norah Lofts, Jean Plaidy, Catherine Cookson. Romances or sagas, and some racier stuff, too. Harold Robbins and Jacqueline Susann; something about dolls that had a cover with tablets on.

His mum had encouraged him to read, but aside from *Whizzer and Chips* and *Shoot!* it had never been something he was keen on. Even now, other than the newspaper – back pages mostly – his country music magazine once a month and the occasional revelatory post-mortem report, there wasn't anything that had him turning the pages in excitement.

Considering how . . . unbookish he was, Thorne wondered why he'd felt the need to argue with Chall on the train and defend something that, ostensibly, meant so little to him. Why he'd fought his corner, despite feeling out of his depth, like someone pushing the merits of vegetarianism while they were working their way through a KFC bargain bucket.

He saw Chall beckoning him from the reception desk and started walking back across.

Valley of the Dolls. Thorne smiled when the title came back to him. If there was time when he and Chall had finished, he might see if the library had a copy; if there were still tablets on the cover.

Five minutes later, they were seated in the library office, reviewing CCTV footage from four days previously. They watched the formerly blonde 'Jasmine', who was now dark-haired 'Jenny', walk to the reception desk, chat briefly to a member of staff, then move across to an area not covered by cameras, where the public computers were.

'She's got quite a showreel now,' Chall said. 'When there's a jury watching this, we might need to have an interval. Chuck in some popcorn.'

'Let's hope it comes to that,' Thorne said.

They scrolled through the footage until, half an hour later, 'Jenny' came back to the reception desk, had another short conversation and went back to the computer. Fifteen minutes after that, she left the library.

'Christ,' Thorne said. 'Is it just me . . . ?'

Chall shook his head to indicate that he had seen it too. On her way out, the woman they were looking for had glanced up at the security camera above the main library doors. A second or two, no more than that; just long enough to smile.

They sat at a table in the corner of the library's small café with the library supervisor – a woman in her thirties called Melanie – and an older man called Robin: the library assistant who had confirmed that he was the member of staff who had spoken to 'Jenny' the previous Saturday.

Chall laid out half a dozen photographs on the table: printouts from several CCTV cameras, including the library's own, as well as the picture that had been posted on the Hookupz website.

Thorne gave them half a minute to study the images, then pointed to the photo from Hookupz. 'So, can we start by confirming that this is the same woman who was using one of your computers last Saturday afternoon?'

'Certainly seems to be,' Melanie said.

Robin nodded. 'Yeah, that's her.'

Two children were snuggled up with a book on a beanbag against the wall. They began to giggle and a woman at a nearby table gently shushed them and put a finger to her lips. One of the kids stuck his tongue out and the woman, who Thorne presumed was their mother, did the same.

'So, we're guessing she'd have needed some sort of ID,' Chall said. 'To use the library's facilities.'

'Well, theoretically,' Robin said.

Melanie shook her head. 'Not if she was a member.'

This was not a possibility Thorne had even considered. It was far too much to hope that they would be trotting back to the train station with a facsimile of the killer's library card bearing her full name and address. 'I seriously doubt that's the case,' he said. 'And we don't have a name anyway, so there's no way to check.'

'No.' Melanie cradled a plastic cup of herbal tea. 'And even if there was, I don't think you'd be very happy about the number of forms you'd need to fill in to look at our membership records.'

Thorne was rather more concerned with what Robin had said. 'What did you mean, "theoretically"?'

'Well, she only wanted to use the computer, and I know that because I was the one who spoke to her—'

'Can you remember what you spoke about?' Chall asked.

'Yeah, like I said, her wanting to use the computer.'

'Anything else?'

Robin looked flustered suddenly. 'Well, I suppose . . . just general chit-chat for a minute while I was sorting out the code or whatever. I can't remember anything specific. Sorry.'

'It's OK,' Thorne said. 'What were you about to say?'

'Just that . . . yeah, *theoretically*, you need some sort of ID to get the access code, but . . . it's not always like that.' He glanced a little sheepishly at his boss, as though he might have done something that could get him into trouble, but Melanie nodded as though it was no big deal.

'It used to be a lot stricter,' she said. 'Proof of address, photo ID, all that. But these days it's all about encouraging access. We want people to use the facilities and there are plenty of people who don't have fixed addresses or bank accounts. So, if people want to just sit here and use the Wi-Fi that's fine. If they want computer access, and they've got some form of ID, a bank card or something . . . they can just pay a pound and they get a guest code which gives them half an hour.'

'Right.' Thorne was already starting to think they'd got as much, or as little, as they were going to get.

'I did ask to see a bank card,' Robin said. 'She definitely showed me one.'

'Can you remember anything about it?' Chall asked. 'The name of the bank or the name on the card? Did you write anything down?'

Robin shook his head. 'Just the fact that I'd seen it.'

'Why did you talk to her twice?' Thorne asked. 'She came back to the reception desk.'

'Because she'd run out of time,' Robin said. 'She paid another pound to get another thirty minutes on the computer.'

'OK.'

Chall began gathering the photos together and Thorne reached for his leather jacket. The children on the beanbag were laughing again.

'I suppose you'll be wanting to take it,' Melanie said. 'The computer.'

'Well, not us.' Once again, responsibility would be given to the Digital Forensics team based south of the river. 'But yes, officers will be along later on to collect it.' Thorne sensed this might be important. The email exchange with Hari Reddy had taken place over no more than fifteen minutes, but now he knew that 'Jenny' had used the computer for the full half-hour, then gone back to buy extra time. 'They'll need to check out anything else she might have looked at while she was using it,' he said. 'Websites, contacts, whatever.'

'I think they might be wasting their time,' Melanie said. 'Our system uses Deep Freeze.'

Thorne had no idea what she was talking about, but the look on Dipak Chall's face made it clear that *he* did.

'It's software designed to wipe any identifying information from the computer as soon as a user has signed off. Browsing history, payment details, the lot.' Chall shook his head. 'Thinking about it, she didn't even need to use that guerilla email address.'

'We need to protect our users,' Melanie said. 'Sorry.'

Thorne thanked both members of staff for their help and, though he guessed they would be unable to provide any further information that might be of use, he handed over cards and asked them to get in touch if they thought of anything. Melanie walked back to the reception desk and Robin escorted Thorne and Chall towards the exit. Thorne was wondering why he'd bothered coming, why they hadn't just dispatched a couple of local uniforms. Aside from a few more evidential frames of security footage, the journey south had been largely a wasted one. He was about to ask Robin about that book of his mother's when the library assistant said, 'Oh,' and laid a hand on his arm.

'Actually, I *do* remember what I talked to her about. When I was getting the access code for her.'

Thorne stopped, waited.

'Well, not all of it . . . but I definitely said something about her hair.'

'What about her hair?'

'Just how different it was, you know? I mean, I probably didn't say as much, but I thought it suited her better when it was blonde.'

Thorne stared at him.

'She'd been there before.' Thorne pressed the mobile to his ear as he and Chall hurried back towards the station, the younger, fitter DS struggling to keep pace with him. 'A few times, the bloke in the library reckons. That's got to mean there's a chance she's local, right?'

'A chance, yeah,' Brigstocke said. 'It's definitely worth chasing up.'

'We need to make sure every officer in the borough gets a copy of this picture on the hurry-up,' Thorne said. 'Every uniform . . . pinned to the wall of every squad room. First thing on the agenda at every shift briefing.'

'I hear you, Tom, but it's going to be happening anyway.'

Thorne slowed a little. 'Right . . .'

'I've had the DCC and the press office in with me and we've decided to bring the media in.' Brigstocke grunted. 'Well, *they've* decided, but it amounts to the same thing.'

'When?'

'Tomorrow. Papers, TV, the full monty.'

Thorne was actually surprised it had taken this long. It was a major step, and not always one that worked in an inquiry's favour, but right now he didn't think they had any choice. It was time to ask the general public for their help. That would be the official line, at any rate. It was pointless to quibble, because they did need the public to pitch in where they could, but as with all half-truths, it was about what was unsaid.

Because it was also time to warn them.

FIFTEEN

In a small room above a dry-cleaner's in Crystal Palace, Rebecca Driver sat at her computer and ate crisps and thought, *I could do this in my sleep now.* So she let her mind drift and thought about other things, while she told a few more lies just because she could, filled out unnecessary questionnaires and uploaded another set of pictures.

She wondered when it had all become about the monsters.

Probably right after the first time she'd been woken by the door *shushing* across her bedroom carpet. That would make the most sense, though she wasn't sure how old she'd have been back then. How young. From that point on, there were monsters everywhere. She'd glimpsed them, squatting in the dark corners of the house and in branches waving from the end of the garden. They stared at her from passing cars, lay silently in wait for her after school and, of course, they'd been there on every page of every story she wrote.

Sea monsters, ice monsters, space monsters.

They were invariably deadly and it always took someone very special to defeat them. They stalked and they devoured, mercilessly. They were invisible sometimes, and the very worst ones were able to change their shape and become something that seemed totally harmless, but whether they had claws like knives or robot pincers or the pale, cold fingers of a corpse, all her monsters liked to *touch*.

It was only once she'd begun to *read* about monsters, though, that she'd started to seriously appreciate them. The properly scary ones that were jolly doctors or caretakers or car mechanics, who made her realise it was time to grow up, because the monsters that actually wandered the streets and stood behind you in the shop weren't really monsters at all. They were just ... ordinary. They weren't actually scary either, not to her, because the more she found out, the more she came to understand them, the more sympathy she felt. Not for *him*, of course not, never for him ... but always a little for those poor souls who'd been forced on to the fringes. Why wouldn't you share the pain of those who'd lived as outsiders, freaks even, for so long that eventually they'd taken the only course of action possible and done what they'd been stuck on Earth to do? To immerse yourself in lives like that, in *half*-lives, and not feel some sort of compassion ... now that really *would* be monstrous.

One otherwise dull day, a few years before, she had opened the right book and her stupid little world had been turned on its head, when she'd come across that one very special life. A life that was still being lived, uniquely ... *gloriously* and, for her, the opportunity to become even a very small part of that life had been like the last piece of a puzzle sliding into place. Not in any religious way, she thought, none of that crap, but she knew what that lot meant when they talked about being born again. Chosen, whatever. Like when someone smacks that golden buzzer on *Britain's Got Talent* and shiny stuff rains down on you and everything changes.

Rebecca smiled and sucked the salt off her fingers. No, not shiny stuff. Ears and tongues.

It had all been very obvious, in the end. Simples. If you wanted to become a monster, if that's what you were clearly destined to be, why wouldn't you learn from the best?

SIXTEEN

'So ... what are you wearing?' The voice was husky, seductive.

Thorne turned down the volume on the TV, the excitement of top-flight axe throwing undimmed by the absence of sound. 'OK ... I'm currently rocking a pair of tracksuit bottoms with a stain on the crotch that I'm guessing is chilli sauce ... and a ratty Townes Van Zandt T-shirt I should have thrown away years ago. Is that doing it for you?'

'God, yes,' Tanner said. 'That might turn me.'

Thorne sucked in a breath. 'Steady.'

Once Tanner had stopped laughing, they settled into a comfortable silence. Thorne watched a man throw an axe which hit the target. The man was probably pleased, but the vast amount of facial hair made it hard to be sure.

'You ready for tomorrow, then?'

'As I'll ever be,' Thorne said. They both knew that once the photos of their prime suspect were shown on the morning TV shows, printed in the papers and posted on all the news websites, the incident room would become as much a call-centre as anything else. Weeding out the cranks and checking out any lead that sounded remotely kosher would be full on for several days at the very least, though that was, of course, the point of the exercise.

'So, which tie do you reckon Russell's going to wear for the press conference? My money's on the dark blue.'

'Well, I don't think it'll be that red one with the little golfers on it.'

Tanner grunted another laugh, after which they said nothing for a while. Thorne heard Tanner mutter 'Stop it' and, as he didn't think she had company, he could only guess she was admonishing her cat.

'You think she *is* local?' Tanner asked, eventually. 'Down that neck of the woods?'

'I can't see any other reason why she'd go back to Thornton Heath.'

'Maybe we'll find out tomorrow—'

'Three more days, Nic.'

Tanner said nothing.

'Three more days until the last wise monkey. Christ knows what she's got in mind after that, but I mean it makes sense, right? Saturday night is date night and it doesn't look like she's got any intention of slowing down.'

'Well at least we're making it harder for her,' Tanner said.

'Are we?'

'Getting her face out there.'

Thorne stared at the TV, then at the wall above it, then at a large cobweb dancing in the corner, where the wall met the ceiling. 'Right . . . I'm going to bed. Knackering, isn't it, doing bugger all?'

'Just you then, is it? No sexy shrink around, tonight?'

'We don't spend *every* night together.'

'So, a cosy evening of ready meals and internet porn, was it?'

'Well, now you mention it,' Thorne said. 'I did spend a fair amount of time on my laptop before you called.'

'Not sure I could even guess what kind of filth you're into,' Tanner said.

'Oh, you won't, because we're talking *seriously* bizarre. I tried to fight the urge, but what can I tell you? Twenty minutes online, but I managed it in the end.'

'I don't think I want to know—'

'I joined my local library.'

SEVENTEEN

I can't remember her name but I'm sure I was at school with her.
She really looks like this girl I used to go out with.

I don't know who she is, but she's proper evil. You can just
tell . . .

Responses from the public had been pouring in for hours. From those who'd seen the appeal on morning TV programmes, logged on to news websites or simply read the bulletins arriving on their phones. From others who had seen the photograph in their daily newspaper or picked up a dog-eared copy of *Metro* on the bus or the train into work. Call handlers at the Lambeth control centre had their work cut out because, as was always the case, more than a few public-spirited citizens were phoning simply to express an opinion or to pass on bogus information, but once the mischief-makers and those acting maliciously had been discounted there was still enough being sent through to set at least some pulses racing.

To galvanise the less experienced members of the team.

Several names had been passed on – though unfortunately none more than once – and among sightings of their suspect from almost every part of the country a significant number had been reported in south London. Given time, everything would be followed up, but these tips in particular would be prioritised.

'Anywhere south of the river,' Thorne had said. 'Watch out for those, and straight to the top of the list if it's anywhere within spitting distance of that library. Croydon, Bromley, Crystal Palace.'

He had prowled the incident room all morning, sullen and snappy. Sifting through intelligence as and when it came in from Lambeth. Reminding himself that the more excited he allowed himself to become about this or that lead, the worse he would feel when it came to nothing. It was a tactic that had stood him in good stead when dealing with senior officers or the desperate relatives of victims – with anyone pushing hard for a result – but it worked equally well in the somewhat trickier dealings he constantly had with himself.

Under-promise and over-deliver.

He knew from bitter experience that a life lived the other way round was only ever going to make him, and those unfortunate enough to get near him, blunted and miserable.

'Works with sex as well,' Hendricks had told him once; into the Guinness and happily gobbing off. 'I mean, there's no point bigging yourself up, is there? They're only going to be disappointed. But you tell them you're hung like a hamster, you can't go for more than a few minutes and you always blow your wad too early … then, however you perform, it's always a nice surprise. Happy days for everyone, right?'

Thorne watched the notes being scribbled, listened to the phones ring and tried not to think too much about what would make him happy today.

Just before midday, he and Tanner moved from the incident room into their office. Tanner sat at her computer and logged on to Sky News, which was broadcasting the proceedings live from Scotland Yard.

They watched the Chief Superintendent make the introductions then hand over to Russell Brigstocke. The DCI stood up and glanced at his notes.

'You were right,' Thorne said.

Tanner looked at him.

He nodded at the screen. 'The blue tie.'

The usual Met Police backdrop had been replaced by a huge photograph of the woman responsible for bringing them all together: the police officers and the members of the press; the couple in their fifties sharing the platform with Brigstocke and his boss. Andrea Sumner had declined to take part, but the Powers That Be had pronounced themselves happy enough to have Hari Reddy's mother and father. Shell-shocked parents would probably play better than a grieving widow.

Thorne wondered if the usual shoutline should be updated for occasions such as this.

Metropolitan Police. Hoping you'll help us make a safer London.

'We're urgently seeking to trace the whereabouts of the young woman you can see in the photograph behind me,' Brigstocke said.

They had plumped for the photo 'Jenny' had posted on the Hookupz website. It had been suggested they might also show an earlier photo of the suspect when she was 'Jasmine' and had long, blonde hair, but had decided this would only lead to confusion and perhaps twice the number of unhelpful calls to chase up. The information was all in the press pack anyway. The aliases, the dating apps and websites, the changes in appearance.

'We believe that this woman is responsible for the savage murder of Hari Reddy on Saturday evening and that this murder is connected to that of Richard Sumner, one week before that . . .'

'You want to translate?' Thorne asked.

'You know how it works,' Tanner said.

'And furthermore,' Thorne said, 'we believe that they will both be connected to the murder of some as yet unidentified individual two days' hence . . .'

Tanner shushed him.

It was standard procedure to withhold the specifics of the crime, but grislier details aside, the language of the DCI's statement had been carefully chosen. *Responsible . . . connected to.* The experienced journos would know what was being said, of course, and those who took the tabloid shilling would not hold back on sensationalism when they ran the story. That was not Brigstocke's job. On top of a basic appeal for information, Brigstocke was there to ensure the public remained vigilant, but it was in nobody's interest to scare them to death.

The use of the word *savage* had been seriously debated.

It was also why there would be no questions taken afterwards.

So, are we talking about a serial killer on the loose in London? Could you explain why there's been so little progress on this case? How confident are you of catching this woman?

The press had a decent line in mischief and malice, too.

When Brigstocke had finished, he introduced the parents of the second victim. Hari Reddy's father gulped down water from the tumbler in front of him. He stood up and fumbled with his glasses for a second or two, before reading a short statement. He begged those watching to do anything they could, to pass on any information they had, in the hope that no other parents would have to suffer in the way he and his wife were. The man's voice was quiet, but remained steady. At one point, without taking his eyes from the piece of paper in his left hand, he reached out his right to brush the shoulder of the woman who sat next to him with her head bowed, weeping silently.

'Hari was a wonderful boy,' Mr Reddy said. 'We loved him more than anything and he did not deserve this. Burying him will be the second hardest thing we have ever done. The first was identifying his body.'

Thorne and Tanner watched as the 101 contact number scrolled across the bottom of the screen; as the Detective Superintendent stood to wind things up and Brigstocke leaned across to whisper something to Hari Reddy's mother and father.

'What do you reckon he's saying?' Tanner said.

Thorne shook his head. 'I don't know ... thank you or well done or whatever. Nothing he'd be wise *not* to say.' He knew Brigstocke well enough. Whether or not they ended up delivering anything, he never over-promised.

Thorne didn't feel quite as wiped out as he had been the previous night, but it was pretty close. He put away three slices of cheese on toast while Hank Williams sang *Live At The*

Grand Ole Opry, then texted Melita to find out if she was still awake. As soon as he'd received a thumbs-up emoji, he rang.

'Is this a booty call?'

'A *what*?'

Melita explained.

'No, it isn't.' Thorne lay back on the sofa. 'It's . . . whatever the opposite of that is. I just called to say goodnight, really. Anyway, as far as sexual advances are concerned, I think it's your turn to make the first move.'

'What about the other night?'

'Oh . . . yeah.'

'Well, it obviously wasn't that memorable.'

'No, it was. It doesn't matter . . . I just wanted to make a shit joke about the booty being on the other foot.'

Melita laughed, but she sounded tired, too. Or distracted. Thorne asked if she'd seen the press conference.

'Sorry, I've had back to back clients all day. I'll watch it online when I go to bed. Was it useful?'

'Hard to tell yet,' Thorne said. The volume of calls had certainly been high immediately afterwards and had increased towards the end of the day, when people had begun getting home from work. By the time Thorne had knocked off, there had been a significant number of sightings in the borough of Croydon – South Norwood, Crystal Palace and two in Thornton Heath – as well as half a dozen names which were being checked out at that very minute by the team on the overnight shift. 'Should have something to chase up tomorrow.'

'Let me know how it goes,' Melita said.

'As long as you won't just think I'm calling for a bunk-up.'

'Perish the thought.'

Thorne was trying to formulate another joke based around booty being in the eye of the beholder when the tone on his phone told him that another call was waiting. He looked at the handset to see who the caller was and told Melita that he needed to take it.

Dipak Chall was working the late turn.

'Dipak . . . ?'

'There's a call I think you should hear,' Chall said. 'Came in about ten minutes ago.'

'Right . . .' Thorne heard a click and a hiss. He sat up. All calls were routinely recorded and he guessed that Chall had loaded the relevant sound file. He listened to a civilian staff member answer the incoming call and ask how she could help. The voice was tinny and Thorne presumed that Chall was simply holding his phone close to the computer speaker.

Then, a second voice.

'Well, it's just information, really.' High and light, an estuary accent. 'I mean, that's what you want, isn't it?'

'What information do you have, madam?'

'Only that sometimes a date can go a bit wrong. That's all. Sometimes there just isn't that . . . spark. Like, you know from the off there's no future in it, so you just have to make the best of things and do whatever it takes to enjoy yourself. You know what I'm saying?'

'I'm listening . . .'

'I've had a few dates like that recently, where I was the only one enjoying themselves, but only a couple of them seem to be common knowledge. It's like, one's gone . . . under the radar.' She waited. 'You still there?'

The woman in the incident room confirmed that she was.

'So, there's a house in Hadley Wood. All very posh.' She

gave a street name, spelled it out. 'Sorry, I can't remember the number, but it's a big one down near the end. There's a white fence . . . '

There was another click and Chall came back on the line. 'Boss . . . ?'

Thorne already had his jacket on. 'You trace the number?'

'Unregistered pay as you go,' Chall said. 'Not much we can do until people are back at work in the morning.'

'Right, get all the usual bodies over to Hadley Wood. I'll meet everyone there.' He snatched up his car keys. 'And call DI Tanner.'

'You reckon that was *her*?'

Thorne said they would find out soon enough, but as he slammed the door behind him he was asking himself why he was even bothering to hedge his bets. He already knew the third wise monkey had shown up two days early.

EIGHTEEN

She'd had one large vodka before making the call and a couple more since. Lager to chase them with. The pub was noisy, but she was enjoying herself at her table in the corner, tuned out from the chatter and the music; wondering if the police had got there yet and remembering the fun she'd had in that lovely house.

Thinking the place was enormous and how full of old furniture and dusty knick-knacks it was. How nice the old man seemed to be.

'I don't have much female company,' he'd said.

'Well, I hope I'm not a disappointment.'

'Oh, no. I think I'm the one that's likely to disappoint.'

She'd laughed then and put a hand on his knee. 'You'll do.'

Thinking that the bottle of wine he'd produced probably cost more than she earned in a week and that, seeing as the poor old soul was knocking on a bit, it wouldn't be too long before he'd need the toilet and she could pop a little something into his glass.

'I'm feeling rather odd,' he'd said twenty minutes later. Blinking very slowly and sucking in air. 'Awfully tired, suddenly.'

'Well, we'd better go upstairs then, before you conk out completely.'

'I haven't done this before, you know.'

'Course not.'

'No, really. I wouldn't want you to think I pay for this kind of thing all the time.' A few more deep breaths. 'I'm not even sure I can remember what you're supposed to do. It's been such a long time.'

'You'll be fine,' she'd said. 'It's like riding a bike.'

He'd laughed at that, then coughed for a while. 'You might have to bear with me, that's all.'

'Don't worry, I'll talk you through it.'

She'd helped him up from the sofa then, and now, down-ing the last of her vodka, she remembered thinking that he weighed bugger all, that his comb-over hadn't been doing him any favours and that the silly old bugger had overdone it on the aftershave.

He'd said, 'You're very sweet,' as they slowly climbed the stairs and she'd felt like she was his mother or something, that she should be making him hot chocolate and tuck-ing him in.

'I aim to please,' she'd said.

He was as good as asleep by the time she was helping him off with his clothes and it had all been very easy after that.

All the houses were big on Claremont Road, but they'd found the place easily enough. Set back and detached, with a sizeable front garden and an expensive car in the driveway, same as most of its neighbours, though it was almost certainly the only property on the road whose occupant was dead as mutton. In terms of desirability, the location of this latest atrocity might have been a step up from the Sumner house and was certainly a far cry from Hari Reddy's student flat, but the crime scene itself was much the same as the previous two in all the ways that mattered.

The clothes scattered on the bedroom carpet. The wine bottle and glasses in a sitting room two floors below. The strands of hair recovered by the CSI team, the colour of which suggested that the dark-haired woman who was formerly blonde had been a redhead before that.

The latest murder scene, but not the latest murder.

Thorne watched Hendricks work, delicately taking samples and measurements, muttering into a recorder. He had called him on the drive north, but he didn't need a pathologist to tell him that the victim had been dead a while. The smell had made it obvious enough; that punch of ripe cheese and foetid meat as soon as the Tactical Support Unit had put the front door in.

What remained of the victim was grey-green and marbled. The tissues had already begun to soften and Thorne could see the first signs of adipocere, or grave wax, across the distended abdomen and the top of the legs. The organs had burst, and fingernails and teeth had fallen out. There was a pattern of reddish-brown stains around the body left by the blood and a variety of purged fluids.

And there were insects.

In other circumstances, Thorne might have guessed that maggots had consumed the dead man's eyes, but the ragged black holes told him there had been nothing there for them to feed on. He'd known what the killer had taken before they'd got there.

'At least three weeks.' Hendricks closed his bag. 'Heating's been on to help things along. I'm guessing nobody's too gobsmacked by the cause of death.'

Thorne was only surprised by how much more obvious the injury had become during decomposition. The gash in the man's neck had widened as the skin had grown loose and slipped; a grisly second scream.

'Victim's name is Thomas Bristow.' Tanner appeared in the bedroom doorway. 'The woman next door says he'd been living alone since his wife died a few years ago, kept himself to himself. I've got a number for a daughter in Leeds. We're tracing the address.'

Thorne knew that some unlucky local officer would be dispatched to deliver the death message. A far worse job than any of them had tonight.

'So, she had the order right after all,' Tanner said. 'The wise monkey business. See then hear then speak.'

They stared at all that remained of Thomas Bristow; what little there was left for his daughter to identify. He was disappearing and it didn't look like there'd been a lot of him to begin with.

'Well, maybe that's the end of it, then,' Thorne said.

'Yeah, maybe.'

He didn't need to look at Tanner to know she was no more convinced of it than he was.

Watching him bleed out, she'd remembered a random line from a book or a play she'd read at school, or had read to her. Something about *not knowing the old man had so much blood in him.* Three weeks on, in the pub, with a few more drinks inside her, she thought it was odd, because she didn't actually remember much from school at all. Just that feeling of being constantly got at and written off. Underestimated. Knowing, when she walked into a classroom, that the kids who were already in there had been talking about her.

She sniggered into her glass.

So much blood ...

It hadn't just been that old bloke she'd been cutting or the one in Gospel Oak or that soppy student. She'd done it all for the man who'd changed her life, of course, like a thank you, but while she'd been doing it she'd been happily slicing up all those wankers from back then, too. The kids who'd laughed behind her back or ignored her completely. She'd been lopping bits and pieces off everyone who'd told her she was ugly or weird or taken the piss because of what was happening to her at home, even when they didn't know the half of it. Doing it to *them*, popping her souvenirs into a plastic bag, then standing back to watch her touchy-feely stepdad die.

Thrashing around like he could fight it, but not for very long.

That's what it had been like in that flash house in Hadley Wood, same as the others. A story about monsters with a happy ending. A story that she was *in*. She couldn't swear the old man had been dead by the end. It wasn't like she took a pulse or anything, but he'd certainly stopped moving by the time she put the scalpel back in her bag and took the spoon out.

Knelt across him and said 'Be quiet,' just like her stepfather had done.

Rebecca – 'The Bookworm', 'Morticia Addams', 'Unsexy Bexy' – told herself that the tears were stupid, and were only because she'd had too much to drink and got herself into a state, as she stood up and walked, a little unsteadily, towards the Ladies.

'Slippery bastards, eyes,' Hendricks said.

They were sitting in Thorne's car on Claremont Road. Tanner was in the passenger seat and Hendricks, who had collected coffees from the all-night garage round the corner, was sitting in the back. The engine was running and the heater was on.

Tanner turned to look at him. '*What?*'

Hendricks leaned forward. 'They're all soft tissue, aren't they, and they're constantly lubricating to enable rotation. We already know she doesn't bother wearing gloves, so I'm just saying, she'd have had a right job keeping hold of them. Probably chasing them all over that bedroom . . . like trying to pick up a sliver of soap when you've dropped it in the shower.' He saw the look on Tanner's face and sat back. 'It's all right for you. I'm the one that has to live with me.'

Thorne stared out of the window and watched as more officers, CSIs and auxiliary staff came and went from Thomas Bristow's house. Equipment carried in, bags and boxes carried out. Thinking that evidence was all well and good, that they already had a shed-load of it, but that none of it would amount to anything until it was presented. There were police lock-ups stuffed with evidence all over the country. Hard drives and rock-solid data, murder books full of statements and fridges full of samples; all of it gathering dust and degrading while cases cooled and the relatives of the dead struggled to move on. Precious, vital, *damning*, but ultimately worth no more than the shit people carted up to their lofts and forgot about.

Tanner watched the comings and goings too, and it wasn't hard to work out what Thorne was thinking, because he wasn't the only one.

'It all helps, Tom,' she said. 'And we'll have plenty to get stuck into tomorrow.'

Thorne turned to look at her. 'Melita reckons she's putting on a show, you know? All the wise monkey stuff, the trophies. Like she's playing a part.'

'Sounds feasible,' Tanner said.

'She's making a good job of it,' Hendricks said from the back.

'What about the victims, though? There's no connection. These killers she's emulating usually target specific types . . . age and appearance, whatever, and I don't think the fact that they're all men is enough. It just feels . . . ' He stopped.

'What?' Tanner stared at him.

'Their *names*,' Thorne said. He swore and slammed his palm against the steering wheel. He looked at Tanner and waited, like it was obvious. 'The dead men's names. Yeah, course it looks random. Christ, it even *sounds* random. Thomas, Richard . . . '

Hendricks got it, slapped the back of the seat. 'Ah.'

Tanner nodded, just a second behind him. 'Any old Tom, Dick or Hari.'

NINETEEN

Saturday, late afternoon; over thirty-six hours since the body of Thomas Bristow had been discovered. Two nights earlier, outside the house in Hadley Wood, Tanner had talked to Thorne about 'getting stuck in', but the all-important process of following up on leads provided by the public had, by necessity, slowed a little. Now a third murder had been added to the caseload. Officers had been given new jobs to do, with associated evidence needing to be urgently gathered and another crime scene still being processed. There was fresh information coming in all the time via phone and email, but the focus had shifted and now it felt to Thorne like the team was playing catch-up.

Sitting in Brigstocke's office he made his feelings perfectly clear, and the DCI was more than happy to respond, with interest.

'I've been doing this a while, Tom—'

'I'm not exactly new to the game myself—'

'And I'm not sure there's any such thing as "too much evidence".'

'You know that's not what I meant,' Thorne said. 'I'm saying, we've got *enough*. For now, certainly. Enough to put her away a hundred times over, but until we actually catch her, or get a half-decent sniff of catching her, all the evidence in the world is worth jack shit.'

'I hear what you're saying, but we can't just ignore new evidence, can we?'

'No, but we can try not to kid ourselves it's getting us anywhere.'

The new evidence consisted of yet more CCTV footage showing that a woman had visited Thomas Bristow's house and departed approximately ninety minutes later, having left behind forensic traces that were, to nobody's astonishment, quickly matched to those from the previous two crime scenes. The pay as you go phone the suspect had used to call the hotline had been purchased from a shop in Forest Hill the day before and paid for with cash. The computer removed from the victim's home office had revealed a booking made the previous day through a website euphemistically called *Capital Companions*, and a bank transfer shortly afterwards as payment for the agreed service – £350 for a two-hour home visit from Bristow's chosen 'companion'.

'So, she's using escort sites as well as dating apps.' Thorne shrugged. 'I'm not convinced that really gets us anywhere and, to be honest, we probably should have assumed it anyway.'

Brigstocke was staying surprisingly civil. 'You know as well as I do that *any* piece of evidence can be the one that gets you the result. Some stupid thing. You never know where it's coming from.'

'Well, it won't be from wasting more time looking at bloody camera footage,' Thorne said.

'You know that, do you? Because all *I* know is there's been another murder and we've got to investigate it properly. Same as we investigated the others. Do you remember doing that?' Brigstocke stared hard at him, then took off his glasses, rubbed at the bridge of his nose. 'Christ, why do I feel like I'm talking to a teenager doing work experience? Look, I'm really sorry if the way we've been doing things round here like . . . *for ever* doesn't meet with your approval any more—' He raised a hand when he saw Thorne about to interrupt. 'And the only reason I haven't told you to fuck the fuck off out of my office already is that you're clearly very frustrated. Or you haven't been getting enough sleep. Or maybe there's medication I don't know about that you've forgotten to take . . . but the fact remains, it is what it is.' Brigstocke put his glasses back on. 'So, suck it up, all right?'

Thorne said nothing; turned away to look out of the window.

'What, now you're going to sulk?'

'Just . . . why aren't a few more people working on the intel that's coming in and a few less . . . doing the investigating?'

'You do know how stupid that sounds, right?' Brigstocke didn't bother waiting for an answer. 'Try asking Thomas Bristow's daughter that question. I think we owe it to her to investigate her father's murder every bit as thoroughly as we would any other. Every bit as properly.'

'Yeah, I get that, but—'

'Maybe you should take it up with the suits who allocate the resources around here. Better yet, why don't you give the

Home Secretary a bell and spend ten minutes getting on *her* tits for cutting our budgets?'

Thorne's phone rang. He took it from his pocket and saw a number he didn't recognise on the screen. He looked at the DCI.

'You go right ahead, mate.' When Thorne hesitated, Brigstocke pulled across the paperwork he'd been working on before Thorne had interrupted him. 'Might be somebody else you can annoy, give me a break.'

The caller identified himself as a DS Brunt based at a station in Crystal Palace and began to tell Thorne a story. After listening for half a minute, Thorne was waving to get Brigstocke's attention, and fifteen seconds later he was out of his seat. 'Listen, I've got the SIO with me, so I'm putting you on speaker . . .' He laid his phone down on Brigstocke's desk.

'DCI Brigstocke here. I'm listening.'

'Hang on.' Thorne moved quickly to open the door and called Tanner in from the incident room. As soon as she had stepped into the office, Thorne said, 'OK, go ahead.'

'So, it's like I told DI Thorne . . .' Brunt's voice was echoey, but clear enough. 'Just after eleven on Thursday evening, uniform arrested a young woman for drunk and disorderly . . . pissing in the street outside the Sparrowhawk pub on Westow Hill, if you want to be specific. They probably wouldn't even have nicked her, but she took a swing at one of them, busted the lad's nose. So anyway, they brought her in . . .'

Tanner and Brigstocke were both looking at Thorne. Brigstocke shook his head, mouthed, *What the fuck?*, but Thorne held a hand up.

'We took prints and DNA, as per, and she was bailed

yesterday morning, but, here's the thing ... when they got round to running them through the database an hour or so ago, we got a hit on two of your crime scenes. I've checked the reference numbers and we're talking about the Sumner and Reddy murders? Prints *and* DNA. Hundred per cent match.'

Brigstocke said, 'Bloody hell.'

Tanner just stared.

'What's the name?' Thorne leaned down to the phone. 'The woman's name?'

'Rebecca Driver,' Brunt said. 'Twenty-six. Works in a local supermarket, home address on Anerley Road.'

Thorne looked at Tanner. She nodded.

'I can send you all the details. She was very cooperative, once she'd sobered up a bit—'

'So, any idea where she is now?' Brigstocke came quickly around his desk, stood over the phone. 'What's happening?'

'I dispatched a couple of units to Anerley Road five minutes ago,' Brunt said. 'Thought you'd want to move quickly. I'm waiting to hear, but fingers crossed we can pick her up and get her across to you asap.'

Brigstocke asked to be transferred to Brunt's DCI, and while he began to make what would hopefully be the necessary transfer arrangements Thorne and Tanner stepped out into the hallway.

'We've got that name on file,' Thorne said. 'Somebody phoned it in.'

'Yesterday, I *think*.' Tanner still looked shell-shocked. 'I've definitely seen it on one of the lists.'

'But it's not been checked out yet?'

Thorne didn't need anyone to confirm what was already

obvious. The bullet they had ... *might have* ... dodged. A cock-up of seismic proportions that, whatever anyone had to say about 'investigative priorities' and 'allocation of resources', was the kind of thing that could end several careers. A mistake that could, had they not just got very lucky, have cost many more men their lives. As it was, the call of nature after one too many, and a young PC with a broken nose, might just have let them all off the hook.

A little under two hours later, Thorne leaned against the wall of the custody suite at Colindale station and watched as Rebecca Louise Driver was booked in for the murders of Richard Sumner, Hari Reddy and Thomas Bristow. As per standard procedure, D&D and assaulting a police officer would be added to the charge sheet when the time came, though neither offence was likely to make a great deal of difference if and when it came to sentencing.

'You never know,' Hendricks had said, when Thorne had called to give him the news. 'Some judge with a wasp in his wig about public urination, they might slap another six months on.'

Thorne watched as handcuffs were removed and the woman calmly handed over the contents of her pockets, then those of a small plastic handbag. A hairbrush, bits and pieces of make-up, a shiny black purse, tampons. He watched her sign for her possessions once the custody sergeant had logged them and passed the requisite form across.

He heard her say, 'Thank you.'

He saw the look of disinterest as she turned down the offer of legal representation; a stare and then a nod when the custody sergeant asked if she was sure. He saw the expression

128

of mild amusement as she was informed that she would be taken to a 'dry' cell – where her clothes would be removed for forensic testing and where swabs and samples of blood and hair would be taken – before being given something to eat.

'I'm allergic to nuts and shellfish,' she said.

Then, as the arresting officer moved forward and laid a hand on her arm, Thorne saw Rebecca Driver turn to look at him, as though well aware he'd been watching her the entire time. She ran fingers through her short dark hair and, just for a second or two before she was led away, Thorne saw the same smile he'd seen her give to that camera in the library. As though there weren't too many places she'd rather be and she was happy that Thorne was there to welcome her.

Like she was pleased to see him.

TWENTY

DS Dipak Chall and DC Susan White stated their names for the recording. Chall looked at his watch and announced that it was seven thirty-six p.m., glanced at the woman sitting on the other side of the table, then opened the folder in front of him. An hour and a half since officers from Crystal Palace had escorted Rebecca Driver into Colindale station.

A 'first account' interview.

'You have declined the offer of legal representation at this stage,' Chall said. 'Is that correct?'

Driver nodded, stared around the room.

'For the recording, please.'

'Yes, I have declined it.' A half-smile. 'That is absolutely spot on.'

'Thank you,' Chall said. 'So, now I'm going to show you photographs of a number of items that were removed from your home address at the time of your arrest.' From the folder, he removed three large colour photos of the plastic bags found behind the peas and oven chips in the freezer at Driver's flat. He laid them out in a row. The contents of the bags were iced up, compacted, but – certainly as far as the eyes and ears went – it was clear enough what they were. 'Can you explain what these items were doing in your flat?'

Driver didn't bother to look. 'No comment.'

Chall produced a fourth photograph. A partially rusted scalpel that had been discovered wrapped in tissue paper in a shoebox beneath Driver's bed. 'Can you explain why officers found this hidden in your flat?'

'No comment.'

'Can you explain what appear to be dried bloodstains here, on the blade?' Chall pointed. 'And here, on the handle?'

Nobody was in any real doubt that the scalpel, currently being tested for prints and DNA, was the one that had killed Sumner, Reddy and Bristow. As far as moving to charge their suspect went, there was already sufficient evidence for what would surely be as quick a thumbs-up as the Crown Prosecution Service ever gave, but while they were waiting for forensic confirmation of the murder weapon, Brigstocke had been keen to put Driver into an interview room. To get her side of the story.

'The scalpel's going to put the tin lid on it,' the DCI had said. 'But it can't hurt to see what she's got to say for herself.'

'No comment,' she said.

White sat forward and began to make the same speech she'd made many times before. The spiel about the suspect's right to say nothing and the right of a jury to draw an adverse inference from her silence down the line. The DC hadn't got very far when Driver leaned back and folded her arms.

'I'm only messing about,' she said. 'I've got plenty to say.'

In an otherwise empty office two floors above, Thorne and Tanner sat staring at the screen of a computer broadcasting the live video and audio feeds from the interview room. Tanner shook her head. 'I've seen people done for not paying their TV licence who looked more nervous.'

'She's not nervous at all,' Thorne said. 'Look at her.' Driver was wearing a regulation grey sweatshirt and tracksuit bottoms, her Dr Martens replaced by dirty-white training shoes. The collection of thick silver rings and bracelets had been taken away, but she was still sporting the make-up she'd been wearing when she came in. A thick layer of pale foundation that made her look almost doll-like, heavy mascara and eyeliner, and purple lipstick that Thorne saw cracking just a fraction, now, as she smiled. 'She's like a pig in shit.'

'Let's get back to these photographs, then.' Chall pushed the first three a little closer together. 'We'll start with the items found in your freezer.'

'What about them?'

'Well, could you explain why they were in your freezer?'

'You serious?' Driver grimaced. 'They'd've been stinking the place out otherwise.'

'Cocky little bitch,' Tanner said.

'Let her enjoy herself,' Thorne said. 'She'll be on remand this time tomorrow.'

'You want to tell me what they are?' Chall asked.

Driver leaned forward, made a show of carefully studying each photograph. 'This isn't exactly the most difficult quiz ever . . . ' She stabbed a finger at each one in turn. One, two, three. 'Eyes, ears, tongue. What's next?'

'How about telling us who these body parts were taken from?'

She sighed and shook her head. 'Wouldn't this be a bit more fun for you if you were asking me questions you didn't already know the answer to?'

Thorne picked up his phone and sent a text message to Susan White.

Monkeys.

'These are the eyes you harvested from Thomas Bristow.' Chall pointed at a photograph.

White took her phone out when she felt it vibrate. She glanced at the message.

'*Harvested*?' Driver laughed, repeating the word as though she'd never heard it before. 'Well, I actually scooped them out with a soup spoon, but I don't mind if you want to get all fancy about it.'

'We do get the pattern,' White said. 'We understand the whole "see no evil, hear no evil" thing.'

Driver shifted in her chair to look at her. 'Well, thank God for that. I was starting to think I'd been wasting my time.'

'And the business with the names. Tom, Dick and Hari.'

'Yeah, did you like that?' She seemed delighted. 'It makes everything a bit more interesting, I reckon. For you as well as me.'

'Why the three wise monkeys, though?' White looked at Chall and shook her head.

'Was it something you read about in a book?' Chall asked. 'We know how much you like your books. Hundreds of them back at your flat by all accounts. Must be just about every true crime book ever written, that's what one of the lads said.'

Driver had stopped smiling.

'Something you nicked out of one of them, was it?' Chall leaned towards her. 'Your three wise monkeys. Some pathetic copycat thing?'

Driver's head dropped and she sank down in her chair.

'Doesn't look so cocky now,' Tanner said.

Thorne stared at the screen. He watched as Driver slowly put up her hand as though she was about to ask a question, raised four fingers and waggled them at the two detectives, like she was waving at them.

'What the hell's she doing?' Thorne said.

'It's actually four.' Driver lifted her head and smiled at Chall, like she was revelling in a joke they hadn't got yet. 'Four wise monkeys. See no evil, hear no evil, speak no evil and . . . *do* no evil. Maybe you should go and look it up. It's only in some of the stories . . . the statues and whatever, and it's usually ignored, because four is an unlucky number in Japanese. The whole idea comes from Japan, you know that, right?'

Chall and White looked at each other and, two floors above them, Thorne and Tanner did the same.

Driver sat back and slowly raised her fingers again, one at a time, counting off. 'One, two, three . . . four.'

'What's she talking about?' Tanner asked.

'*Sedzaru.*' Driver looked from Chall to White, as though she was searching for some glimmer of understanding she knew would never come. 'That's the name of the fourth wise monkey, if it helps.'

Thorne grabbed his phone and fired off another text message.

Break now.

134

Thorne spent ten minutes talking it through with Brigstocke. It took the DCI another forty-five to get the necessary authorisation from higher up and for the technical arrangements to be made. Then somebody pressed the send button.

Melita called when Thorne was halfway back to Kentish Town.

'Have you watched it?'

'Twice,' Melita said. 'And I don't think you need to be so worried. I think she's winding you all up.'

'It has to be a possibility, though, right?' Thorne had already told her what he and the rest of the team were concerned about. The fourth wise monkey, suggesting a fourth body, as yet undiscovered. 'Or maybe there's someone else involved we don't know about yet and the fourth murder's been assigned to them.'

'Which is exactly the kind of thing she wants you all thinking,' Melita said. 'It's about power, Tom, and right now, playing games is the only power she's got. It's not like you don't know all this.'

'You're probably right, but we're still waiting on the scalpel so we're going to carry on talking to her.'

'Whatever you think, but I'm not sure the games will stop.'

'Can you come in tomorrow morning?'

'I've got patients.'

'I wouldn't ask if it wasn't important.'

'My patients are important.'

'I think it might help if you have a look at her, that's all.' Thorne slipped into boyfriend mode, though he wasn't confident it would be any more persuasive. 'Come on, I know you're interested and maybe you'll get some kind of . . . paper out of it. A chapter in a textbook or whatever.'

'Again, exactly what she wants.'

'Just for an hour,' Thorne said.

TWENTY-ONE

'Where's the other one, today?' Driver asked, once the formalities had been completed. 'The Indian bloke.'

Nicola Tanner did not bother looking up from her notes. 'Detective Sergeant Chall is busy on another investigation this morning.'

Driver nodded, thinking about it. 'So, like a rota kind of thing then, is it? Same as in a supermarket, basically.'

'Not really.' White checked her phone was switched to silent and slipped it into her inside pocket.

'So, I might be getting other detectives as well?'

'Others?' White asked.

'Different ones, once you've finished.'

'It's possible,' Tanner said. 'If we're needed elsewhere.' Now she looked across the desk. 'Yours is not the only case we're dealing with.'

Two floors up, Thorne and Melita sat in front of the computer. Thorne had laid on the coffee and a selection of pastries, as a thank you. Melita had her notebook open and had already begun to write.

'Very nice,' she said. 'Don't let her think she's all-important.'

'Nicola's good at this,' Thorne said.

'She'll need to be.'

'Can we go back to your wise monkeys?' Tanner glanced at DC White, like she might be a little confused. 'However many of them there are supposed to be.' White shrugged as though she wasn't sure either.

'It's four, I told you.' The flash of irritation had been brief, but had not gone unnoticed. 'It's four.'

'Yes, we were wondering what you meant by that.'

Driver had put four fingers up again, the way she had done the previous evening. She waggled them slowly. Then, having clearly worked out where the camera was, she turned and looked up to give it a wave.

'What did you mean, Rebecca?'

Thorne stared at the screen, at the young woman staring back at him. A hammy pout, then the deliberately goofy smile of someone trying to ruin a photograph. The make-up had been removed overnight and, stripped of her mask, pallid and pimply, she might just have been a stroppy teenager showing off.

'She wants your attention,' Melita said.

Thorne turned. 'Mine?'

'Whoever she thinks is watching. Anybody's.'

'What did you mean when you told DS Chall that there were four wise monkeys?'

Driver turned back to the two detectives, considered Tanner's question, and shrugged. 'I didn't mean anything.

I was just telling you the truth. It's important to get the facts right, isn't it? Why does everything have to *mean* something?'

'That's very helpful,' White said.

'Well, I'm *trying* to be helpful,' Driver said.

'And we appreciate it.'

'That's the whole point, isn't it?'

Melita scribbled something in her notebook, underlined it.

'I'm interested in where the idea came from,' Tanner said.

Driver seemed interested, too. She sat forward and drummed her fingers on the table. 'The murders, you mean?'

'Yes, the murders . . . and the manner of them. The things you did to the victims afterwards.'

'Not always afterwards,' Driver said.

'No . . .'

'I got a bit over-excited sometimes.' There was another glance up at the camera, a small shrug. 'I couldn't wait.'

'Jesus,' Thorne said. 'Is she actually proud of that?'

'Probably,' Melita said. They watched as Tanner simply nodded and pressed on. 'That's good.' Melita was scribbling again. 'It's important not to rise to her bait . . .'

'We've already talked about the great many books that were found in your flat,' Tanner said.

'I like books,' Driver said.

'Who doesn't?'

'You'd be amazed. Some people are morons.'

'Only I don't recall seeing too many about Japanese mythology on the list. So . . . ?'

'Something I saw on the telly,' Driver said. 'The internet, maybe. You just pick stuff up, don't you?'

'I suppose so,' Tanner said.

139

White took her turn. 'Last night, you seemed to get a little agitated when DS Chall suggested it might all have been something you'd ... borrowed. Something you were copying.'

Driver appeared to find that funny. There was certainly no sign of the irritation she'd shown the night before or a few minutes earlier. 'There's a difference between borrowing something and being influenced by it. We're all the sum of our influences, aren't we?'

'So, you committed these three murders because something influenced you?'

Driver sat back. There was a half-smile. 'Well, not exactly some*thing*.'

Thorne sat up a little straighter. 'What?'

'More games,' Melita said.

'Some*one*,' Tanner said. 'You're saying you've done these things because someone influenced you.'

'Not influenced,' Driver said. 'Asked me to.' She seemed pleased at the look she saw pass between Tanner and White; at the reaction she was perhaps imagining from those observing proceedings from elsewhere. 'No, *asked* isn't quite right, either. *Suggested* it ... yeah, that's better. Knowing that I was very suggestible, you see what I'm saying? Knowing I'd already done it a hundred times in my head, that I'd been doing it all my life, really.' She smiled and shook her head, like she was confessing to a lifetime of minor shoplifting. 'Someone special who just gave me that little nudge, that's all. Made me feel brave enough to step over the edge.'

Thorne began composing a one-word text message, but Tanner asked the question before he could send it.

'Who?'

Driver slowly shook her head, unable or unwilling to answer. She stared down at the tabletop for half a minute before finally looking up; uneasy suddenly. Paler than ever. 'Sorry,' she said. 'I don't feel too clever ... I think I need a break. I can have a break if I want, can't I?'

TWENTY-TWO

There were six of them, seated around a table in an over-heated conference room on the second floor. Brigstocke watched Melita open her notebook and said, 'I think it would be useful to hear Dr Perera's thoughts before the interview recommences.'

Thorne was sitting next to her. He glanced across at the word she'd underlined fifteen minutes before.

'Your suspect's being too *helpful*,' Melita said. 'She's giving you too much, too quickly, and I think that might be a cause for concern. It's something I would ask you to think about, certainly.'

'You think she's stringing us along?' Brigstocke asked.

'No, not necessarily. I'm not saying that what she's telling you isn't true, or true for *her*, at least. It all just feels a little too easy.' She turned to Thorne. 'Don't you think?'

'She definitely seems a bit over-eager,' Thorne said.

'I've already spoken to Tom about this—' She paused,

flustered for a second or two, and corrected herself. 'To Detective Inspector Thorne ... and the more I think about it, the more I begin to see discrepancies.'

Tanner looked at her. 'In what she's saying?'

'From the word go,' Melita said. 'From when the murders started.'

Brigstocke glanced at Tanner and Thorne. Said, 'Go on.'

'You all believe that this young woman is clever, yes?' Melita looked around the table. Chall and White nodded. 'Right. I mean most of the people who do this sort of thing *are*, even if it's not what you might think of as conventional intelligence. It doesn't mean she's good at chess or crosswords ... but she's got a highly developed sense of guile, at any rate. An animal cunning, if you like. But, if we accept that's the case, why did she start off hiding from the cameras, taking all the steps she could to avoid them, and then very quickly start showing herself to them?'

'Right.' Thorne nodded to Tanner and Brigstocke. 'Suddenly she's in more photos than a Kardashian.'

'She uses a burner phone and untraceable email addresses, she changes her appearance for each murder ... but she makes no effort whatsoever to destroy forensic evidence, despite titles on her bookshelf which would indicate that she knows all about it. It would have been simple enough to take her victims' phones and computers. That would have made your jobs a lot harder, but again, she chooses not to. She was very well prepared for the killings, with her selection of the victims, with the sedatives and so on ... so, why so sloppy afterwards?' She looked at Brigstocke. 'I'm just asking the question.'

'Are you saying she's exactly where she wants to be?' Tanner asked.

143

'I'm putting the possibility out there, that's all. For one victim she's a young girl looking for love. For another she's an escort. She's all things to all men, so perhaps she's being something entirely different for you.'

'It starts to make sense when you put it together,' Thorne said. 'That maybe she wasn't trying quite as hard as we thought not to get caught.'

'Exactly,' Melita said. 'Look at how she *was* caught.'

'So, maybe not the bit of luck we thought it was,' Brigstocke said.

Melita closed her notebook. 'It's just a suggestion.'

'Arrested for having a piss?' Thorne looked at his boss. 'More like *taking* it, I reckon.'

Brigstocke thanked Melita for her input, then turned to Tanner and White. 'Well, at the very least you should be bearing in mind everything Dr Perera has said, when you go back in there—'

'Can I talk to her?' Melita asked suddenly.

Thorne stared at her. This was something they had *not* discussed.

'Well, it wouldn't be something I could authorise just like that,' Brigstocke said. 'It's not ... standard, put it that way.'

'Sounds like a good idea to me,' Chall said.

'What were you thinking?' Brigstocke asked.

'I don't think it would be very sensible to go marching in there with a plan,' Melita said. 'Not one that can't change from moment to moment, anyway. There's certainly reason to believe the woman has narcissistic personality disorder, so the prevailing wisdom would suggest an initial approach that makes her feel special. Exalted. But, until I can be sure of that diagnosis, such an approach might actually be counterproductive. I think I should just sit and ... talk to her and see where that goes.'

'Suck it and see, Russell.' Thorne immediately decided that he could have chosen his words better, as this was not an approach the DCI was known for. 'She's going down anyway, so if she's playing some game we haven't figured out yet, I can't see the harm in it.'

'Fine with me,' Tanner said.

Brigstocke still looked far from comfortable with the idea as he worried at what remained of his quiff. 'OK, but we'll have to inform her of our intentions when she's well enough. Make the offer of legal representation again. She would need to give her consent, obviously.'

'Course,' Thorne said. 'I reckon we're in with a shout, though.'

'She'll bite your bloody hand off,' Melita said.

TWENTY-THREE

Thorne had been stared out by some seriously scary individuals in his time, but even though she appeared no more dangerous than the average sixth-former, sitting face to face with Rebecca Driver was definitely disconcerting. He stared back for as long as he could manage, remembering the look she'd given him the night before in the custody suite; the welcome in it. She hadn't stopped staring at him from the moment he'd come into the interview room. Sitting up straight, a nod here and there, like she was saying hello. A half-smile, and her wide eyes fixed on his as he ran through the pre-match formalities for the tape.

'I'm glad you feel able to carry on, Rebecca,' he said.

'No worries.'

'The doctor said there was no reason why you shouldn't.'

'I told you I didn't need to see a doctor.' Still staring. 'I just wanted a break, that's all.'

Calling the shots, that's what Melita had said. Wanting to

do things at her own pace, to set the schedule and perhaps even the agenda.

'And thank you for agreeing to see Dr Perera.'

'Oh, *I'm* seeing *her*, am I?' Now, Driver turned to the woman sitting on Thorne's left; her gaze equally keen, every bit as hungry. 'I thought she'd come to see me.'

'It's just an expression,' Melita said. 'We're seeing each other.'

'Right. But not like you're seeing *him*.' She smiled and nodded at Thorne. She made a hole with a thumb and forefinger and slowly pushed the finger of her other hand back and forth through it. 'Not like that.'

Thorne felt like he'd been gut-punched. He glanced at Melita and fought the overwhelming urge to get involved. He had agreed to let her run things, to try not to get in the way, but now, more than anything, he wanted to know how the hell Driver could know about their relationship. He sucked in a breath and told himself that of course she didn't, that she was simply being suggestive. Trying it on. She'll do her best to provoke us, to get the upper hand, wasn't that what Melita had said?

He almost convinced himself.

Melita ignored Driver's comment and opened her notebook. 'Like DI Thorne, I'm happy you agreed to this. I hope it will be useful.'

'For you or me?'

'Well, you know I'm working with the police,' Melita said. 'So I'm sure you can work that out.'

'So, what? You're telling me you're not interested in me? Professionally or whatever.'

'I'm very interested.' Melita glanced down at her notes.

'Why don't I save you a bit of time?'

'Sounds good to me,' Melita said.

'Great stuff.' Driver leaned forward and cleared her throat. 'Was I bullied at school? Yeah, a bit. Was I a bully at school? Yeah, that, too. Did I have a happy childhood? No, not especially.' She was firing off the questions, then answering them like someone reading out football results. 'Did Mummy and Daddy buy me a bicycle? Good question . . . yes, they did, but it was a rubbish second-hand one with no gears. Was I fiddled with as a kid? Yep, plenty of fiddling and diddling, thank you very much. Do I hear voices? Yeah, course I do, but doesn't everyone? The voice telling me that working in a supermarket's a bit shit, but what else am I going to do with three GCSEs. The voice that tells me to buy a particular pair of shoes, then another one telling me not to be daft because I can't afford it. *My* voice, that's what I'm saying. Mine.' She sat back and sucked her teeth, pleased with herself. 'So, the big question. Does any of that lot explain why I'm sitting here in this horrible tracksuit? Why that old bloke's eyeballs were bagged up in the freezer behind my onion rings? You tell me.'

Thorne stared at her; her gaze now fixed on the ceiling. Melita had been banging on about Driver's wanting to run the show, but he wasn't convinced the woman was quite as confident as the bullishness suggested. He remembered what Melita had said to him several days before, about the killer playing a part. The smile looked like something she was plastering on and he sensed that there was plenty bubbling up and ready to burst, just beneath the couldn't-give-a-shit surface.

Rage and shame. Guilt.

'Actually, I wanted to ask you about something you were talking about earlier today,' Melita said. 'About influence.'

'Oh.' Driver sounded a little disappointed, but she shrugged and leaned forward. 'Well, I can't even say that I'm paying for our little therapy session, can I? So I suppose it's up to you.'

'Good.' Melita nodded and went back to her notes. 'This came up during the discussion about your books ... about how something you'd read had influenced you? Someone you'd read about. Someone special, I think you said.'

'That's right.'

'So, I'm presuming this isn't anyone you've actually met.'

'Sadly not.'

'But aren't we usually influenced by people we know?'

'You can know someone without actually meeting them.'

'By parents and friends?'

'Maybe, If you're lucky.'

Melita leaned closer, lowered her voice a little. 'I really want to understand what you're trying to say, Rebecca. How can someone be influenced by a stranger?'

'What are you on about?'

'I'm not talking about just liking someone or admiring them. Actually *influenced*, I mean, to do the sorts of things you're accused of doing.'

'By who they are, by what they say.'

'What they *say*?'

'Their ideas.'

'Yes, but if I believe in peace, in not hurting anyone else, it's not because John Lennon told me to.'

Driver laughed. 'What kind of loser wants to believe in *that*?'

Thorne turned at a knock to see Chall's head appearing round the door.

'Sir . . . ? Sorry, but I need a minute.'

Melita closed her notebook and Thorne bit back a swear word as he began the process of suspending the interview.

'Shame.' Driver shook her head. 'I was quite enjoying myself.'

While Driver was escorted back to her cell and Melita hung around by the door to the interview room, Thorne followed Chall to the far end of the corridor. He said, 'This had better be good.'

'Well, I don't know about *good*,' Chall said.

'Come on, Dipak—'

'The lab came back with the results on the scalpel.'

'Murder weapon?'

Chall nodded. 'DNA matches on Sumner, Reddy and Bristow. We've got every victim's blood on there.'

It was the news they had all been expecting, so Thorne couldn't help wondering why Chall hadn't just sent a text message or waited for a natural break in the interview. Why the DS didn't seem quite as thrilled about it as he should have been. 'Why do I think there's a *but* coming?'

Now, Chall was actually looking nervous.

'Well, it's a mixed profile . . . obviously, plenty of prints that we weren't able to identify, but they found another blood profile on the blade. It's a bit more degraded than the others, but we got a match on that one, too.'

'And . . . ?'

'It's Dr Hendricks.'

Thorne stared, aware that he should be saying something,

150

but he could only reach up slowly to the nape of his neck; the spidery fingers that had begun to creep across it. He tried to swallow but couldn't. He felt sick; dizzy.

'Maybe somebody messed up,' Chall said. 'I mean, it doesn't make any sense, because Dr Hendricks hasn't been anywhere near that scalpel. He hasn't even seen it.'

'Right.'

'Sir . . . ?'

Thorne turned and began to walk back towards the interview room. He understood that finding Phil Hendricks's blood on that blade made perfect sense. There could only be one explanation and, terrifying as it was, he knew exactly where that scalpel had come from. The name of its previous owner.

He knew who Rebecca Driver's special someone was.

PART TWO

A GAME

TWENTY-FOUR

Sometimes, he struggled to remember who he was supposed to be.

There was so much juggling to do, so many things to get right and keep track of. Names and accents and the details of whichever brief biography he'd created and drip-fed. Then, perhaps most important, there was his appearance. It wasn't *hugely* complicated, because it wasn't as if there were umpteen versions of himself knocking around at any one time. That would cause more problems than it solved. That was how you tripped yourself up. No, he only ever took the precautions he felt were sensible and necessary, but even then there was always plenty to bear in mind, and apart from the simpler things he needed to think about each time he ventured outside – glasses or coloured contact lenses, the state of the facial fuzz, clothing, all that – he had made any number of more radical changes over the years.

The dental work and the bits and bobs of cosmetic surgery.

Nose and jaw and ... *ears*, for heaven's sake. Thanks to 3D scanning and facial recognition software, the unique geometric features of an individual's ears were now pretty much as good a way of identifying someone as fingerprints. Who knew?

Those bloody hair transplants ...

Stuart Nicklin carried his tea across to the sofa and browsed on his iPad for a few minutes. Running fingers gently across a still-tender scalp, he looked at a few of the sites where he might occasionally get a mention, killing time while he waited for the next afternoon quiz show to start. He preferred the shows that were on early evening, but the slightly cheaper ones they trotted out after lunch or repeated on the more obscure cable channels were entertaining enough. You could spend all day watching quiz shows if you fancied it. He didn't, of course, because he had other things to do.

His own show to organise.

Young Ms Driver had been a fantastic contestant, all things considered, even if she had been a bit star-struck by the host. Not that he didn't know very well that this was why her sort wanted to play his game in the first place. He was always the big draw. Fair play to her, though, she had done as well as he could have hoped. She'd gone all the way, had loved every minute of it and, most significantly, won the big prize. Not that most people would consider life imprisonment – which she would surely be given – as something very desirable, but she'd always known what the rules were, what would be waiting for her at the end of the final round, and she'd been very happy to go for broke. Good girl.

Watching his favourite shows, he never had any time for

the lightweights who bottled it at the final hurdle. The ones who'd 'had a lovely day, thank you very much'. The losers who shook their heads, perfectly content with whatever pitiful amount they'd won getting to the final and refused to take the final gamble.

What was the point of not seeing it through?

What was the point of anything if you weren't going to go all the way?

He put his iPad away and reached for the newspaper, turning straight to the back pages to see how Tottenham Hotspur were getting on. Averagely, as it turned out. He had no interest in football, thought it was pointless and dull like the people who watched it, but he always made a point of checking on Spurs.

Strange, that.

He reached into his pocket for a small tin, opened it and picked out an embossed yellow pill which he quickly swallowed. He'd always thought it was funny that by adding just two letters, MDMA could become MADMAN. Not that he was that, of course, not in a million years, but he'd been described as such plenty of times in the past. Because it made for a better story, because people were lazy and lacked imagination. It didn't make him angry, not any more, and besides, one man with whom he would soon be having an interesting conversation certainly knew better.

He wondered how Rebecca was going to cope in prison. He'd managed well enough; *very* well by the end, learning quickly how to get through the days, then how to thrive thanks to the reputation he'd already earned by the time he got there. She would be there a lot longer than he had been, of course, and he wasn't sure she would handle things quite as gracefully as he had. Whatever reputation she would bring inside with her, she was still a young woman at the end of the day, and, though he had never met her in person, she did not strike him as someone particularly . . . hardy.

The programme started and he nodded along with the jaunty theme tune, thinking about swings and round-abouts. Silver linings. At least Rebecca would have plenty of time to read.

Most important of all, of course, the silly mare would finally have the notoriety she craved. That had always been the jackpot she was playing for, and now she'd have the rest of her life inside to enjoy it. She'd wanted what he had, and he understood that, because a lot of people did. The big difference was that now *he* wasn't behind bars any more and, given the choice, he would prefer the situation to stay that way. Ultimately, the choice would not be his, but that was fine, because that was the new game. The big decision that the new player would have to make at the end of it.

Nicklin sat back and sipped his tea. Considered the various outcomes.

Everything would depend on whether the next, very special contestant was willing to take that final gamble.

TWENTY-FIVE

'So, you've come to my local, again ...' Hendricks stared round the bar of the Spread Eagle and narrowed his eyes, suspicious. 'You've got the first round in *and* you're paying for the snacks.' He sipped the top off his Guinness, thinking about it. 'So either it's something bad, like you've got cancer, or you've found God ... or maybe the idea is to ply me with strong drink until my standards start to drop, because you're finally going on the turn and you want me to break you in gently.' He looked at Thorne. 'Am I close?'

'I'm afraid not,' Thorne said.

'Good, because trust me, I would not be gentle with you.'

Thorne managed a weak smile and let Hendricks laugh. It was fine, because it might be the last time either of them laughed for a while. There were two things his friend was guaranteed never to find funny: the secret the two of them shared with Nicola Tanner, and the man Thorne had asked

Hendricks here to talk about. The man who he now believed had finally resurfaced.

Thorne took a drink himself and got it over with.

'Fuck,' Hendricks said, when Thorne had finished. He said the word quietly, his voice colourless. He said it again, then quickly downed half of what beer he had left and nodded towards the bar. 'You'd best get a couple more in, mate.'

'I'm sorry, Phil—'

'Are you *sure*, though?' Hendricks leaned across the table. 'So, yeah, she uses *that* scalpel . . . the scalpel Nicklin's mates used on me, to kill those three blokes, but how do you know Nicklin had anything to do with it?'

'Because she as good as told us,' Thorne said. 'She never actually named him, but only because she knew damn well we were about to find out for ourselves. Playing games, like Melita said she would. She just kept banging on about the "special someone" who'd inspired her, like he was her fucking spirit guide or something.' Thorne stared down at the food in front of him and wondered why he'd bothered ordering it when he doubted either of them would manage so much as a mouthful. 'He's the one who made it happen, same as he always does. I don't believe they ever met, but he might just as well have put that scalpel in her hand.'

'Why, though?'

'Come on, Phil, you know him as well as I do. It's just his way of letting us know he's around. Using bodies to wave hello.'

Hendricks sat back and closed his eyes, as though he was in pain.

Or perhaps, Thorne thought, he was just remembering it.

160

Six years before, Thorne had escorted Stuart Nicklin to a remote island off the Welsh coast. After ten years in prison, Nicklin had promised to reveal the whereabouts of a body: the young man he had killed and buried on the island many years before. It had, of course, been part of an elaborate plan and had resulted in Thorne being made a fool of and Nicklin escaping from police custody. The key part of the enterprise had involved the kidnap and imprisonment of Phil Hendricks, and in order to make the seriousness of Thorne's predicament perfectly clear, Nicklin had arranged for an A4 sized piece of skin to be neatly cut from Hendricks's back with a scalpel and delivered to Thorne in a Jiffy bag.

Thorne had known what he was looking at straight away.

He had recognised the tattoos.

In the end, faced with a choice between his friend's life and Nicklin's liberty, Thorne had taken the only decision he could; the decision Nicklin had known he would make all along. Though obviously thankful to Thorne for choosing to save his life, Hendricks had been all too aware that Thorne was the reason he had been taken in the first place, so even though tears were shed when they saw one another again, there had been no conventional display of gratitude. There had only been a few dark jokes when Thorne had handed Hendricks back his own skin; tentative banter and mock-macho posturing, until eventually it had just become ... awkward. There was little time for emotion-drenched post-mortems on either side anyway, what with the press fallout to deal with, a career in the balance and the ongoing hunt for an escaped lunatic; with umpteen skin grafts to be endured, and weeks of trauma therapy.

It had taken them both a good while to recover.

They had not seriously talked about it since and Hendricks had never shown Thorne the scars.

'I understand if you want to stay well away from this,' Thorne said. 'If you just want to lie low, or whatever.' Hendricks opened his eyes. 'It would probably be the sensible thing to do, bearing in mind what happened on Bardsey.'

'You're kidding me, right?'

'I don't want to take any chances, Phil, that's all I'm saying—'

'*You* bear in mind what happened on Bardsey. I was never *on* Bardsey. I was busy being tasered and handcuffed to a bed in a freezing fucking basement. That's what *I'll* be bearing in mind, if it's all the same to you.' Hendricks looked down at the table. 'What I've been bearing in mind ever since those arseholes cut me.'

Thorne knew when to shut up and take a drink.

They sat in silence for a minute or more. Hendricks tore a beer mat into a dozen pieces, then said 'Fuck' again.

'Trust me, Phil,' Thorne said. 'I wish this wasn't happening every bit as much as you do. I'd be perfectly happy if I never heard that sick bastard's name again, even if that meant him staying out of prison.'

'Don't talk shit to me,' Hendricks said.

'I mean it.'

'No you don't, and you should really remember who you're trying to kid, mate. Nicklin's been messing with your head for as long as I can remember, so I know full well how badly you want to catch him and bang him up for the rest of his unnatural. How much you want to hurt him.' Now, there was the trace of a smile. 'Every bit as much as I do.'

Thorne also knew when he'd been rumbled. How easily

he'd been seen through. He nodded, then slowly pushed his glass across the table and touched it to his friend's.

'There you go,' Hendricks said. 'No point living in denial.'

'That's a bit rich coming from an Arsenal fan,' Thorne said.

'So, two things.' Hendricks ignored the dig and raised his glass. 'First off, congrats on charging the Driver woman. That's a proper result and, whatever else might kick off, you shouldn't forget that.' They touched glasses once again and Hendricks finished off what remained in his. 'Second of all . . . and we can talk about this when you get back from the bar, is the big question.' Against all expectations, Hendricks picked up half a sausage roll and pushed it into his mouth. 'Where did she get that scalpel from?'

TWENTY-SIX

It was, of course, the first question Thorne had asked Rebecca Driver when the interview had recommenced the previous day, but it quickly became clear he was never going to get an answer. If not struck exactly dumb, the woman had suddenly become a lot less keen to talk – about anything – than she was when she'd first been arrested. She had merely shrugged or grunted, impatient and keen to crack on, throwing in a 'no comment' now and again to keep herself entertained while she waited to be charged with three murders. She had simply sat there, seemingly content with her doomed lot, as if her role in proceedings had come to its perfectly scripted end. Like her job had been done.

Thorne was starting to suspect that it had.

With no possibility of offering Driver a reduction in sentence in return for her cooperation, and no indication that she'd accept such an offer anyway, Thorne had been left with little option but to go back to basics. To continue sifting through the evidence gathered at Driver's home address.

There was plenty of it.

Aside from her own frozen 'souvenirs', the search team had recovered a small trove of items related to the crimes of other serial killers past and present: crime scene pictures and photocopies of autopsy reports; a letter from Peter Sutcliffe to a roofing company; a doodle signed by Ted Bundy; a bag which, according to the label, contained the toenail clippings of John Cooper, a man who had committed a series of murders in Wales in the 1980s and whose crimes had been made into a TV drama a couple of years before. If these were not enough to highlight the extent of Rebecca Driver's macabre interests, there were always the books.

Hundreds of them. A collection of true crime studies, 'shocking' exposés and dog-eared murderer's memoirs that, judging by their sheer number, must have accounted for the majority of Driver's supermarket wages. It was these that a small team of unlucky officers had been given the thankless task of meticulously poring through, paying particular attention to those passages that had been underlined and the notes that had been scrawled in the margins.

Wow, he was so clever!
That's SO brilliant.
LOVE how he's making the police look stupid.

On the second day, the search paid off. A chapter towards the end of a tawdry paperback 'biography' of Fred and Rose West described how certain ghoulish individuals had stolen patio stones and other items from the killers' property on Cromwell Street, the writer commenting with just enough self-righteousness – and clearly unappreciative of the irony – on the growing trade in such grisly souvenirs. This passage had been underlined and, in the margin next to it, a name had been scribbled.

Margaret Herbert.

At the same time, the Digital Forensics Unit had been working on the computer equipment taken from Driver's flat. The laptop had revealed plenty of evidence about her online dating and escort activities, but no more than that. They had a bit more luck with the clumsily hidden USB drive, found to contain an autonomous operating system that would have allowed its user to visit any site on the web without leaving a trace; the sort of site where she could freely purchase Rohypnol as well as the required murder weapon. Predictably, it was impossible to access the system to see the search history, and with Driver – already on remand in HMP Bronzefield – cheerfully refusing to disclose the necessary password, the nerds had quickly run out of road.

Thorne was every bit as frustrated. The only Margaret Herbert on the Police National Computer was a thirty-three-year-old in Cornwall who had once poured paint over her partner's car when she discovered he'd been sleeping with her sister. She had been interviewed and quickly eliminated from the inquiry. Thorne was well aware that, as far as leads went, a name scribbled in a book might be stretching the definition, but in something like desperation he had passed it across to the Digital Forensics Unit in the hope that it might open up other avenues.

Initial feedback suggested that it had done, and now he

was about to find out if those avenues had proved to be dead ends.

Thorne and Tanner showed their warrant cards at reception, and were escorted to a vast, open-plan office on the third floor of a nondescript block in Wembley. Thorne had visited DFU hubs before, in Islington and Charing Cross, but was always amazed at the sheer number of computers on display. At the number of screens, at any rate. He presumed that the computers themselves were the sort of huge, powerful machines that you'd find at NASA or the Pentagon and were probably hidden away beneath desks or in locked rooms. He muttered as much to Tanner as they were led through the office and she looked at him like he was an idiot.

'So, what . . . you thought it would be a couple of teenagers with iPads?'

'Just . . . it's impressive, that's all.'

A man waved from a desk in the corner and beckoned them across.

'Best let me do most of the talking,' Tanner said.

Like most of those working at the DFU, Greg Hobbs was a member of the civilian support staff. He and Thorne had spoken a couple of times on the phone and he certainly hadn't sounded like a nerd. As Thorne and Tanner shook his hand, then sat down on either side of his wheelchair in front of three enormous screens, Thorne decided that he didn't look much like a nerd either. He had an impressive and neatly sculpted beard, slicked-back hair and a row of large silver earrings that was only revealed when he removed an equally oversized set of headphones. He wore skinny jeans and a mouse-brown waistcoat over a shirt and tie. He was probably pushing forty.

167

'Right, so I think I know what we're doing, but I just need to clarify a couple of things.' He talked fast, with the trace of a northern accent. 'We're still thinking murderabilia, yeah?'

'Looks that way,' Tanner said.

'Nasty word, but it does what it says on the tin. OK, cool ... now second, before we get too far into this, are we absolutely sure that Rebecca Driver wrote that name in the book?' He looked at them, drumming his palms on the arms of his wheelchair. 'I mean, if she bought it second-hand, it might already have been there.'

'She wrote it,' Thorne said. 'We matched the handwriting with the signatures from her arrest paperwork. We're not daft.'

'Course you're not, you caught her, didn't you?' He shook his head, reddened a little. 'I'm an idiot. OK, cool, *so* ... Margaret Herbert.' He leaned towards the centre screen and began typing. Pages appeared and disappeared faster than Thorne or Tanner could take them in. 'I reckon she'll be easy enough to trace, in terms of current address and what have you, and I'll show you how in a minute, but there's not much point going after her just yet, is there?'

'Isn't there?' Thorne asked.

Tanner could see what Hobbs was getting at. 'We need to prove she sold that scalpel.'

'I want to know where she got it in the first place,' Thorne said.

Hobbs was still typing. 'Yeah, course, and that's obviously more your job than mine ... once we've established that she's the one who sold it and you can interview her or whatever.'

'Show me,' Thorne said.

168

'OK, cool.'

After a few more seconds of clicks and keystrokes, a familiar-looking page appeared on the screen. Thorne and Tanner leaned forward to look.

'eBay?' Tanner said. 'Looks different.'

'Because it's an archived page,' Hobbs said. 'Twenty years old. They made it illegal to sell this kind of stuff on eBay and the other big retail sites back in 2001, but this wasn't too hard to find.' He moved his mouse to highlight the seller's name. murdermags48. 'There she is.' He scrolled down. 'She was mostly selling paperwork back then ... photocopies of bus passes, utility bills ... look, Ian Brady's old school report. Nothing too gruesome and nothing very pricey. She was flogging this kind of stuff on here for a few years, but once they made it illegal ...'

'She moved somewhere else,' Tanner said.

'Right, and I'll give you three guesses where. I mean, there are still plenty of legitimate sites in the US selling the really nasty stuff ... *Murder Auction, Serial Killers Ink* ... plenty of them. I suppose Driver *could* have got the scalpel from one of those, but Margaret Herbert certainly used to trade from the UK, so let's work on the assumption that she still is. Now, the only sites still operating in this country are probably a bit tame, judging by some of the things you found at Driver's flat. It's all kitschy repro stuff ... Manson's face on a T-shirt or a mug or Ted Bundy on a phone case ... serial killer colouring books, all that. I could buy any of those things on Amazon right now, if I was, you know, *weird* ... but the kind of site we're looking for, that Margaret Herbert's selling from, has gone underground.'

'The dark web,' Tanner said.

169

Hobbs smiled and nodded, like those were the magic words. 'It's tailor made for it.' He tapped his mouse and the old eBay site disappeared. A few clicks and pastes later, they were looking at a very different sort of page. Hobbs began to navigate through sites that were predominantly black with white print, but Thorne knew that was not where the dark web's name had come from. A series of search categories appeared: Financial Services, offering crypto and fake currencies; Commercial Services, including hackers for hire, weapons and ammunition and any fake ID you could think of; page after page of illegal drugs for sale.

'I can get Margaret Herbert's old details from eBay records,' Hobbs said. 'And from there it shouldn't be too difficult to get a current address. Like I said, though, there's not much point right now. What she's doing isn't actually illegal, so there's nothing you can arrest her for.'

'We need to find the site she's selling from now,' Thorne said.

'Obviously,' Tanner said.

'We'll have our link to Nicklin if we can establish that she sold that scalpel.'

'Right, but I'm not sure there's anything we can nick her for even then.'

'I'll think of something,' Thorne said.

They watched as Hobbs loaded more pages, navigating various sites and mini-sites as though he was giving them a tour. Thorne's exposure to the workings of the dark web up to this point had been very limited, but even he knew it wasn't as simple as typing a name into a search engine. He wasn't even sure there *were* conventional search engines, certainly not without a compatible browser, but he knew that there were rarely names to look for and that traders did not tend to advertise or care much about promoting themselves in search results. He knew that hunting Margaret Herbert down online was unlikely to be straightforward.

'You reckon you can find her?'

Hobbs cocked his head, confirming Thorne's suspicions, but then a smile appeared. 'I'll need to be sneaky,' he said. 'But that's fine, because I *am* sneaky. I'm a snake on wheels.' He began typing again and a different page appeared. *Social Networks; Message Boards; Hidden Answers; Intel Exchange.* 'It's just a question of lurking about on the right forums and in the right chat rooms, making a few comments to let people know what kind of stuff you're interested in buying. Websites like the one we're after might only be online for an hour or two a day and they're not easy to find any other way. I'll need a recommendation, someone to vouch for me. If I hang around long enough in all the likely places and make the right noises, I reckon I can get someone to point me in the right direction.'

'So, do it,' Thorne said.

Hobbs put his headphones back on and eased his chair forward, as if Thorne and Tanner had already gone. 'OK, cool . . .'

TWENTY-SEVEN

They picked up a takeaway from the Bengal Lancer and ate at the table in Thorne's kitchen. Melita asked Thorne if his masala prawn was better than the curry she had made. He lied and assured her it wasn't. She told him she knew he was lying, but that she didn't mind. It was three days since Rebecca Driver had been charged, since her connection with Stuart Nicklin had come to light and the first evening Thorne and Melita had spent together in over a week.

Later, in the living room, Thorne told her about the trip he and Tanner had made to the Digital Forensics Unit. Their meeting with Gregory Hobbs.

'Do you think you can be a nerd *and* a hipster?'

'I'm not really sure what either of those look like,' Melita said.

'Well a nerd looks like ... a nerd,' Thorne said. 'And a hipster's one of those twats in Dalston or Shoreditch, with wax moustaches like they're sergeant majors and shirts buttoned up to their necks.'

'So, did he look like that?'

'No, not really.' Thorne took a swig from his bottle of Kingfisher, watched Melita turn a page of the *Standard* and reach for her wine glass. She hadn't yet made any objection to the Margo Price album he'd chosen and there was even a little foot-tapping going on. 'Do *I* look like a copper?'

She turned and stared at him, weighing it up. 'You don't *not* look like a copper.'

'Well, that clears that up,' Thorne said.

They sat in silence for a while. Melita looked as if she was thinking about something. 'So, do you think he can find Margaret Herbert?' She kicked off her shoes and pulled her feet up. 'Mr Hobbs, who's not really a hipster-nerd.'

'I think he knows what he's doing.'

'And what then?'

'Well, if she *is* the one who sold Rebecca Driver that scalpel, we pick her up and find out where she got it from.'

'You're making it sound very easy.'

'Best-case scenario.'

'What if she refuses to tell you?'

'I'll find a way to make sure she does.'

'Really?' Melita did not look convinced. 'You should remember what you might be up against, Tom. If Margaret Herbert has had direct dealings with Nicklin, she might be someone else who's only willing to do or say what he's allowing her to. You know better than anyone how good this man is at getting people to do what he wants, however much they might be the only one who suffers as a result. I saw what he'd done to Rebecca Driver myself, don't forget that. How much . . . in thrall to him she was. If you're right about their relationship, she was willing to butcher three complete

173

strangers and spend the rest of her life in prison, because that's what he wanted. Because he'd made her believe it was what *she* wanted. I just think you should be prepared for something that might not be . . . best-case.'

'Is this professional advice, or . . . ?'

'Both.' Melita looked away for a few seconds. 'Obviously I care about catching this man, but I care a lot more about you.'

'Like a caring voice of doom,' Thorne said.

'That's not fair.' She sounded angry.

'OK.' Thorne took another swig. 'Sorry.' He knew that she was right, of course. She usually was. If not necessarily about how things might go with Margaret Herbert, then right about how close Thorne was to committing the cardinal sin of over-promising.

He pushed himself up from the armchair, walked across and dropped down next to Melita on the sofa.

He leaned into her and said, 'Shove up.'

Melita grunted and scowled as she reluctantly made room, but Thorne caught the glimpse of a smile when she said, 'This music's terrible, by the way.'

Any impartial post-coital analysis would probably have concluded that both participants had performed better and with rather more commitment in the past. That, were they being honest, neither had really had their head in the game.

Melita put her latest murder mystery down and said, 'One of my clients spends hours on the dark web every night.'

Thorne looked at her.

'He's got a thing about privacy, that's all. Thinks people are spying on him.'

'Fair enough.' Thorne knew that for every weirdo, criminal, or 'tourist' surfing the dark web, there were many more whose presence was entirely innocent. Investigative journalists, anti-censorship and free speech campaigners or those simply seeking to keep their activities hidden from totalitarian regimes. There were a lot of pages in Russian and Chinese.

'I thought I might take a look myself,' Melita said. 'It might give me a bit more to talk about in our sessions.'

'I'm not sure that's a good idea,' Thorne said.

She turned to him. 'You seriously think anything on there could shock me?'

'No, that's exactly what I'm talking about. I think you'd just find it all a bit . . . dreary.'

'You didn't make it sound dreary.'

'No, most of it really is. Dreary and bleak. It'd be a rubbish busman's holiday for you. You'd be like someone who's been on the world's scariest rollercoasters stuck on a shit ghost train in Margate.'

Melita laughed. 'I'm quite partial to a shit ghost train.'

'That's our next weekend away sorted,' Thorne said. 'I like a cheap date.'

'Anyway, I think it might be interesting to poke around, that's all.' She picked up her book again. 'At the very least, it sounds like a good place to scout for new clients.'

Thorne hadn't been entirely honest, of course. Yes, a lot of what he'd seen earlier that day had been grim, yet entirely humdrum. He could not deny, though, that there were areas he'd found horribly fascinating. As far as Melita went, he just thought that someone who spent their day dealing with behaviour that was . . . transgressive, to put it mildly, deserved a break from such things when they were off work.

Some time and space to let a little light in.

Half an hour later, turning on to his side, he was still thinking about one thing in particular he'd seen while Hobbs had been showing them around. The Commercial Services section; the hacker for hire. *I will do anything for money. I'm not a pussy. If you want me to destroy a business or a person's life, I'll do it! Ruining opponents or persons you don't like. If you want someone to get known as a child porn user, no problem!* That particular service was offered at a very reasonably priced 500 euros and, as Thorne drifted off in the dark, he began idly composing a list of those he might consider shelling out for.

A Detective Chief Inspector named Trevor Jesmond.

The lecturer his ex-wife had left him for.

José Mourinho . . .

There was one man, obviously, who would always top any such list, though Thorne was hopeful that he'd be able to properly fuck that man's life up very soon without any help, and without it costing him anything.

Financially, at any rate.

TWENTY-EIGHT

It was stupid, Rebecca knew that, but still, she was a little bit disappointed that Stuart hadn't been in touch. Stupid, because it had only been a few days, and she knew he was already busy with other things. Because even if he wanted to, it would be tricky. Yes, there was some internet access, but you couldn't receive encrypted emails, nothing like that, so he couldn't contact her like he normally did anyway.

She wouldn't want him to do anything to put himself at risk.

She had taken a table on her own, in the corner of the canteen. She raised her head occasionally from her book, or the food she wasn't eating, but made sure to quickly lower it again if anyone glanced in her direction. Only a few days, but she'd already learned that you did not want to attract attention. Not early on, anyway.

Maybe when the dust had settled, he might find some other way, she thought. He might even write and get someone to post it from a different place. That would be safe enough. She knew that her mail would be intercepted, but he was far too clever to make it obvious to anyone that it was him. There would be just enough clues for her to know though, and that was all that mattered. To know that he appreciated what she'd done and that he was thinking about her. To know she'd earned his respect.

She jumped slightly when someone sat down opposite her and she looked up to see a woman smiling and pointing at Rebecca's lunch with a plastic fork.

'I'll have that if you're not going to eat it.'

Rebecca nodded and the woman reached quickly across, scraped the contents of Rebecca's plate on to her own and began to eat.

'Oh,' the woman said, a minute or two later. 'Just so you're aware . . . everyone in here knows exactly what you done.' She pointed with the fork again, at Rebecca's face this time. 'And if you're going to try and be a smartarse and say that you're on remand which means you haven't actually done *anything* officially, don't bother. Everyone knows, all right?'

'OK . . .'

The woman cheerfully shovelled in another mouthful. 'It doesn't mean anything, that's all I'm saying. Nobody cares.' She smiled again and shook her head. 'What you done doesn't count for shit, and wherever you end up, it doesn't mean you're safe.'

The woman wasn't any bigger than Rebecca and didn't seem particularly dangerous, but something in her eyes – or rather something that was missing from them – caused Rebecca's to prick with tears.

She blinked hard and stood up.

She had also learned that it was a very bad idea to show weakness.

She quickly left the canteen and walked back on to the wing. She just wanted to get back to her cell and for the door to slam shut again. Once it had, she dropped on to her bunk and let the tears come. She thought about Stuart and about those three men and about what her solicitor had told her the last time she'd seen him.

Mad will work out better for you than bad.

She decided then and there to change her plea after all, to go for the whole diminished responsibility thing. She wouldn't say anything about Stuart, of course, she would never do that, but the solicitor had said that she definitely had grounds. *Compelling* grounds, he'd said.

Rebecca began to feel more positive, knowing she would have a new story to tell, an even more exciting one. So she lay down, and soon she wasn't quite as scared any more, thinking about the best way to tell it.

A secure hospital had not been what she'd planned on, but surely it was preferable to prison. She'd be treated, for what it was worth, and she'd be safe, because it would be the same as it was with animals. She guessed it would, anyway. The way that predators stuck together to protect themselves, and carnivores didn't eat other carnivores.

She *hoped* it was the same.

That monsters didn't hurt monsters.

TWENTY-NINE

On Wednesday morning, two days after their visit to the DFU, Thorne and Tanner both received a text from Gregory Hobbs.

We're in business.

He'd signed off with an emoji of a snake.

An hour later, they were back in Wembley and Hobbs was showing them what he believed to be Margaret Herbert's murderabilia site. 'Wasn't that tricky in the end,' he said. 'Just left a few comments saying what kind of "souvenirs" I was interested in and eventually some weirdo pointed me here.' He highlighted a line at the top of the page. 'She's still using the same name, see?'

murdermags48

Hobbs scrolled down the page. There were pictures and descriptions of hundreds of items for sale. At the pricier end of the inventory were passports and driving licences purported to have been issued to Robert Black, Levi Bellfield and Steve Wright; a stethoscope which had apparently once belonged to Harold Shipman; a dog collar and lead described as having been worn by Dennis Nilsen's 'beloved dog Bleep'.

'Christ on a bike,' Thorne said.

'If he had one,' Tanner said, 'I'm sure it'd be for sale on here somewhere.'

'Now, from what I can see, Margaret Herbert's basically just the go-between. People send her this stuff to put on the site, and, if she sells it, she takes her cut then passes on the profit. Here we go . . . ' Hobbs highlighted and enlarged one item in particular. 'I think that's what you're after.'

Scalpel owned by Stuart Nicklin, used for unknown purpose. SOLD.

The photographs, displaying the scalpel from several angles, clearly showed the murder weapon seized from Rebecca Driver's flat and now safely stored in a pre-trial evidence locker. It had been purchased from murdermags48 for £2,000, corresponding almost exactly with an amount withdrawn from Rebecca Driver's building society account two months earlier.

'She must have been saving up for a treat,' Tanner said.

'Most of these places leave their sold items in the listings,' Hobbs said. 'To show punters the kind of stuff they can get. Free advertising, really. So, that's your proof. That this woman sold it, at least.'

'Good enough,' Thorne said.

'Hopefully,' Tanner said. 'Depends if we can find out where she got it from.'

'OK, cool . . . oh, wait. There's one more item on here you might be interested in.' He scrolled again until he found what he was after.

Empty pill bottle once owned/used by Stuart Nicklin. £750.

'Still for sale,' Hobbs said. He enlarged the image and peered at the photographs. 'There's no label, so God knows what your friend kept in there.'

'Let's ask the woman selling it, shall we?'

'Oh, right.' Hobbs clicked off the screen and opened another. An address in Colchester. 'Not too far away,' he said.

Tanner began thanking Hobbs for his help, but Thorne was already on his feet and reaching for his jacket. 'Text it to me . . .'

Margaret Herbert did not seem particularly surprised to find a pair of detectives on her doorstep, or perhaps she was simply enjoying their poorly disguised shock at being confronted by a plump, white-haired woman who was well over seventy. As she stood back to let Thorne and Tanner inside, her answer to a question they hadn't asked made it clear she had a fairly good idea why they'd come knocking at her door.

'Forty-eight,' she said. 'In case you were wondering. My user name . . . the year I was born.'

She showed them through to a small front room crowded with mismatched furniture. Moving slowly and with a slight limp, she made straight for the armchair that was obviously her favourite. On top of the small table next to it was a pile of magazines, a pair of reading glasses and assorted TV remotes. She sat down and waited.

'Right then,' she said.

While Thorne and Tanner found chairs for themselves, Thorne quickly took the room in. An old glass-fronted cupboard stashed with knick-knacks; net curtains and antimacassars; framed family photographs on the mantelpiece above an iffy-looking gas fire. It looked as much like a stereotypical old lady's room as Herbert looked like a stereotypical old lady, but Thorne knew better than to be taken in by appearances.

He remembered a woman known as the Duchess with whom he'd had dealings a few years earlier. Despite the candyfloss hair and the whiff of lavender, the woman had actually been a skilled drug smuggler with serious gangland connections; way more likely to be carrying a flick knife in her handbag than a packet of pear drops.

'I haven't got all day, mind you.' Herbert grunted as she shifted in her chair. 'I need to get my tea on and I'm not exactly quick on my feet these days.'

'We've been looking at your website,' Tanner said.

'Course you have, but I'm not doing anything illegal.'

'That remains to be seen.'

'Unless of course you're here because you've got something you want me to sell.' The woman smiled and winked. 'I've handled plenty of stuff from coppers over the years.'

Tanner told the woman that they were not there to sell anything, that they had a number of important questions they were hoping she could answer. Margaret Herbert told them that was a shame, and promised to do her best. Thorne had just begun to talk about the one item that was of particular interest to them when there was a noisy skittering in the hall and a scruffy white dog scampered in. Thorne watched as the dog turned circles on the carpet for a few seconds, before settling down at Herbert's feet.

The woman reached down to rub at its ears. 'You're all right, he doesn't bite,' she said. 'Not even coppers.'

'We need to talk about this scalpel,' Thorne said.

'Oh, right, that. Sitting there for ages, that was. I finally got shot of it . . . what, two months ago?'

'That'll be about right,' Tanner said.

'We're here, Margaret, because, after you "got shot of it", that scalpel was used to murder three people.'

Herbert stared at Thorne. 'You're kidding.' She shook her head, looked down at the dog for a few moments. 'Well, that's horrible, obviously, but I don't think it's my fault. There's no way that's down to me. I mean, if you were going to do people for selling things that people went on to use for . . . something like that, you'd have to prosecute John Lewis because they sell carving knives, wouldn't you? Every branch of B&Q. Besides which, I'm only an agent, aren't I? People send me their items to sell because I've got a certain reputation.'

'Congratulations,' Thorne said.

Herbert smiled, showing a good many teeth that were almost certainly false. 'I handle the sale of this stuff on behalf of other people, that's all I'm saying. I take a small commission then pass the money on to them. I'm just the shop window. You can't do me just because the nutter who bought that scalpel went out and used it on someone.'

'Her name was Rebecca Driver,' Tanner said.

'Well, if you say so, love. People don't tend to use names in this game. I mean sometimes they do, but it's always usernames. DeathGatherer, The Reaper, all that rubbish.'

'I take it you believed the scalpel was genuine,' Thorne said. 'That it had been used by the man you claimed it had.'

'Stuart Nicklin, that the one?'

The casual way Herbert said the name made Thorne's gut tighten momentarily. 'That's right. Nicklin.'

'Yeah, as far as I know. You take people on trust though, don't you? I mean, I'm not daft, there's plenty of chancers around, so I know some of it's probably a bit iffy. I can't swear that stupid stethoscope was *actually* Harold Shipman's, and as for the Nilsen dog lead . . . well, I reckon someone just roughed up a new collar and got *Bleep* engraved on the tag. But there's always a risk when you're buying stuff online, isn't there? It's no different if you stump up a few hundred quid for Frank Sinatra's autograph. I mean, how can you ever be sure?'

'So, what about the scalpel?' The DNA results had already made it clear that the scalpel was the one Stuart Nicklin had once used – or that had once been used on his behalf – but Thorne needed to know what the woman thought she had been selling.

'Yeah, I reckon so. It certainly *looked* old. All rusty, you know? The people who supply the stuff for me to sell always sound convincing, but they know I'm not a mug.'

'So, who supplied that scalpel?'

She hesitated. 'I'll have to check my records, but like I said—'

'Where are they?'

'Well, my grandson looks after that side of things. It was

my son who used to do it, years ago when I was on the proper internet, but now Cameron does all that stuff for me. He's always been good with computers and it's a good job he is, because I don't know a hard drive from a soft one.' She nodded to the photographs. 'I've only just learned how to get *them* on to the computer.'

'Where does Cameron live?'

'Oh, it's very handy, because he's only five minutes away. He comes over most days to go over everything . . . keeps the stock up to date, does the book-keeping.' She smiled, looked at Tanner. 'He's a good lad and what I pay him keeps him in weed, so everyone's happy.'

'You need to call him,' Thorne said. 'Wherever he is, you need to get him over here, right now.'

'Really?'

'Really.' Tanner stood and walked across to the table next to Herbert's armchair. She picked up a mobile phone that might well have qualified as vintage and passed it to the woman. 'Oh, and don't tell him why.'

Herbert put her glasses on, then stabbed at the oversized buttons, shaking her head as if she thought it was all a bit silly.

'Cam, it's me . . . can you pop over?' She stared resentfully at Thorne and Tanner as she spoke. 'Oh, nothing urgent, love, but I really need your help with something. Better bring the computer with you . . . '

She put the phone back on the table.

'Thank you,' Tanner said.

The woman shrugged. 'There won't be a name. I've already told you.'

'Well, let's wait and see.'

'Suit yourself.'

'We'd like to ask about another item listed on your site,' Thorne said. 'A pill bottle ...'

'That's another Nicklin one, isn't it?'

Thorne told her that was what her listing claimed.

'Surprised it didn't get snapped up, if I'm honest,' she said. 'The Nicklin stuff usually is. Might need to drop the price a bit.'

'You think that one's genuine?'

'Oh, yeah, a hundred per cent. The bloke who's selling it certainly sounded kosher. Said he'd had personal contact with the bottle's previous owner.'

Thorne sat forward. 'Do you have that person's details?'

'No, I told you. It's never more than a couple of emails and they're always ... cryptic, or whatever the word is. Cameron knows all about that, so you can ask him in a minute. I think it was something to do with the bloke who had the bottle and Nicklin being in France together.'

'Which you never thought was worth reporting to the police?' Tanner asked. 'What with Stuart Nicklin being on the run from the authorities.'

For the first time Herbert began to look uncomfortable. 'Well, I can't swear the bloke was telling me the truth, can I? I mean, I wouldn't want to waste anyone's time.'

'Very thoughtful,' Tanner said.

The doorbell went and, a few minutes later, a scrawny teenager sloped into the room. He tried and failed to look intimidating, then demanded to know who the fuck Thorne and Tanner were.

They told him exactly who the fuck they were and ran through it all again; pressing on despite Herbert's persistent heckling and her insistence that it was all pointless.

Cameron perched on the arm of his grandmother's chair, still doing a piss-poor impression of a hard case. 'Yeah, so this bloke who was flogging the pill bottle definitely said he'd hung around with Nicklin in France, but that's about all there is to it. I can check to make sure, but it's like my nan told you. Everything's anonymous and all the emails are encrypted end to end—'

'*Encrypted*,' Herbert said. 'That's it.'

Cameron nodded. 'Right, so there's no way to trace anything. I'm talking serious security, because that's what the people buying and selling this stuff want.'

'What if you refused to do that?' Tanner asked. 'If you asked for real names and contact details?'

Herbert smiled, like Tanner was a simpleton. 'We'd lose customers very bloody quickly if we did that, love. If word got out our business wasn't secure and ... discreet, we wouldn't be trusted, simple as that. It's a strange old racket, I know, but those are the rules and it's how I pay the rent, so ...'

Cameron stood up. 'Are we done, then?'

Thorne told him to sit down again.

'So, what happens now?' Herbert shuffled forward in her chair. 'I've still got my tea to put on.'

Thorne took a few seconds, pretending to think about it. 'Now, we arrest you.'

'Fuck's sake,' Cameron said.

'OK.' Herbert sighed and sat back again. 'But you know as well as I do that's daft.'

'Is it?'

'You'll only be arresting me so as you can search the place and take my stuff away. It saves pissing about getting a warrant, but you know very well there's nothing you can really arrest me for.'

'Well, you've already admitted to thinking some of the stuff you sell is fake,' Tanner said. 'So we can start with fraud.'

Thorne nodded at Cameron. 'And we can nick *you* for possession of the weed she very kindly told us we're likely to find at your place.'

Cameron looked at his grandmother, horrified. 'What the fuck?'

'Yeah, but you know none of it's going to stick, don't you? It's a lot of fuss for bugger all.' Herbert smiled, waited. 'Look, it sounds like you've got plenty of better things to do, so why don't I save you a lot of pissing about?' She held out her arms. 'Help yourselves . . . take anything you want. Take anything you want from Cameron's place, too.'

Cameron turned again. 'Nan!'

'Shush, love.' She looked back to Thorne and Tanner. 'I mean it. Fill your boots.' Groaning, she heaved herself to her feet. 'Listen, why don't you have a quick think about it? I'm going to the toilet, and that'll take me at least ten minutes.' She nodded at her grandson. 'Cam, you make yourself useful and put the kettle on or something.'

As soon as they'd left the room, Tanner said, 'She's got a point.'

It rankled, because Thorne badly wanted anyone with so much as a tangential connection to Stuart Nicklin to suffer in one way or another, but he couldn't disagree.

'If we can take the stuff anyway, why the hell lumber ourselves with all that paperwork?'

'Fair enough,' Thorne said. 'But I don't just think we should take it. I think we should *use* it.'

Thorne told Tanner his plan, and when Herbert and her grandson came back in, he explained what was going to happen. 'We're hugely grateful for your cooperation and very happy to accept your offer. So, we'll be taking everything. All your stock, all the computers, the lot. Oh, and Cameron needs to come with us, but I promise we won't keep him very long. You ever been to Wembley, Cameron?'

Cameron sucked his teeth and glared.

'It's very lovely,' Tanner said.

Suddenly, Herbert didn't seem quite as relaxed about things as she had been. Her hands fluttered in her lap. 'I'll want it all back when you're done.'

'I can't promise anything,' Thorne said.

'But it's my living.'

'Well, maybe, instead of pissing on the graves of murder victims, you should find something a bit more dignified to do at your age, Margaret. Like being a drug mule or a crack whore.' Thorne got to his feet. 'Actually, if you've got no objection to whipping old blokes for a few quid, there's a website I can point you towards.'

THIRTY

Thorne called in a team of local uniforms who searched
Herbert's house and seized computer equipment from
Cameron's flat, while others cleared out the nearby lock-up
which served as the murdermags48 stockroom. Having spent
the best part of an hour carefully packing up cardboard boxes
with dozens of items – including the less-than-uplifting
poetry and artwork of several serial killers, numerous plastic
bags containing hair, the all-important pill bottle and one
dodgy dog lead – officers driving an unmarked van, with a
disgruntled Cameron Herbert on board, followed Thorne's
car back towards London.

Tanner was driving, so Thorne made the call.

'So, just how sneaky *are* you, Greg?'

'Oh, super-sneaky,' Hobbs said. 'If I need to be. Will I
need to be?'

'Only in a good way,' Thorne said. 'You reckon you can

pull off a decent impression of a teenage toe-rag? I mean, you don't have to dress up or anything.'

'That's a relief,' Hobbs said.

'It's more about convincing people that you're him online. The way he might word his emails or whatever. He's the one who does all the techy stuff for Margaret Herbert's website.'

'Gotcha. Sounds simple enough.'

'Good, because I'm bringing Cameron – he's the teenage toe-rag in question – over to see you right now, so you can have a chat. Get the measure of him.'

'OK, cool.'

'Oh, and we'll need to get my bosses talking to your bosses, to sort out the financial side of things. We're going to be buying something that Cameron's grandma's the agent for. Then Cameron, by which I mean you *pretending* to be Cameron, can make the necessary arrangements with the actual seller.'

'The pill bottle, right?'

'Right.' Hobbs was clearly way ahead of Thorne, who was starting to appreciate just how lucky they were to have him on their team. 'So we'll need to send the funds over, get all that arranged.' He was already guessing that the simple budgetary liaison between departments would prove to be the trickiest part of the whole enterprise.

'It'll be Bitcoin,' Hobbs said.

'OK,' Thorne said.

'All these transactions are made using Bitcoin. Well, *fractions* of Bitcoin for a smallish purchase like this. What's the bottle on for ... seven hundred and fifty quid? You're probably talking about ... 0.034 Bitcoins, somewhere round there, but obviously the rate changes every few seconds—'

'I'm already losing the will to live.'

Hobbs laughed. 'Don't worry, it's not complicated. I can open a Bitcoin account in five minutes.'

'As long as we get it sorted,' Thorne said. 'We should be with you in about an hour.'

Three hours later, just after eight o'clock, Thorne finally walked through his front door in Kentish Town. He'd picked up a lamb shish and chicken wings from the Turkish place round the corner. He felt as though he'd been working for several days straight.

Once he'd eaten, he called Melita and then Phil Hendricks, to let them know how the trip to Colchester had panned out.

'Sounds like it went well,' Melita said.

'Yeah, it could definitely have gone worse.'

'I think it's a good plan, too. Especially now you've managed to get your clever hipster friend to play along.'

'He didn't need to be talked into it,' Thorne said.

'Really?'

'I swear.'

Melita didn't know how keen Hobbs had been to get on board, so Thorne could guess what she might have been thinking and he was grateful she didn't actually say it. That Thorne could be almost as persuasive as the man he was trying to catch.

Hendricks was more concerned with why Margaret Herbert had not been taken into custody. Why, to his mind, she was getting away with it. Thorne tried to explain and voiced his own reservations, but however much sense he knew the decision had made, it didn't cut any ice with the man that scalpel had been used on.

'I just wish you had her in a cell for like . . . a day.'

'I understand, Phil—'

'Just ten fucking minutes, so I could march up to the bitch, turn my back and lift my shirt up.'

Thorne was nodding off in front of some panel show on Dave when Greg Hobbs called.

'Don't you ever go home?'

'I'm enjoying myself,' Hobbs said.

'I'm glad one of us is.'

'I had a *very* useful session with young Cameron, not that *he* seemed to be having a lot of fun.' Hobbs laughed. 'In a slightly different world, he'd be working for us. I got what I needed, though. He's in a car on the way back to Colchester, just so you know . . . and I've made contact with the seller.'

Thorne wasn't nodding off any more. 'Great, so—'

'Don't get too excited . . . I've sent the first email, that's all. As Cameron, I mean. I've told the seller – calls himself "K-Man" – there's an offer on his pill bottle, but it's less than he was asking. I thought it would be a good idea to string him along a bit.'

'OK . . .'

'Look, if I just tell him I've got a buyer, then that's it. He asks for the money, I transfer the Bitcoin and we're done. I already explained, there's absolutely no way of tracing this K-Man's Bitcoin account without getting hold of his computer. We need to communicate with him as much as we can, see if we can find a crack in his security set-up somewhere.'

'You're even sneakier than you told me you were,' Thorne said.

194

'Trust me, I'm surprising myself,' Hobbs said. 'I'll let you know when he gets back to me.'

'Right, thanks,' Thorne said. 'Now, go home.'

He had just got into bed when his phone rang again. He got up and padded across the bedroom to where the handset was charging. He saw who was calling and took it back to bed with him.

'Everything OK, Nic?'

The pause was enough to answer his question. 'Sorry, I know it's late.'

'No worries.'

'Just a bit . . . all over the place.'

Thorne could guess what was on Tanner's mind and it was already obvious she'd been doing as much drinking as thinking. 'Come on, Nic, today was a good day, right?'

'That's usually the problem,' she said. 'It's good days that make you think about bad ones, isn't it? About the really bad one. That and your little speech today about pissing on victims' graves. Well, I'm pissing on Graham French's grave every day. Every day I'm walking around like nothing happened. Every day I try to do my job and uphold the *law*.' She barked out a laugh, ragged and bitter. 'It's a fucking joke, Tom. *We're* a joke.'

'Come on, Nic.'

'Come on *what*?' She was getting angry and he knew where it was heading. This wasn't the first time she'd had a wobble and it usually involved her lashing out at Thorne like it was his fault. It would end up with her crying or shouting and telling him that, were it not for the fact that she'd be destroying his career, and Phil's, she'd have owned up to what she'd done a long time ago. 'Come on *what*, Tom?'

'You won't always feel like this,' Thorne said. 'I know that sounds stupid right this minute, but you won't. It'll get easier.'

'The three of us keeping our dirty little secret, you mean?'

Yes, because that's all we can do. Because at the time we did the only thing we could and yes it was wrong, and yes it was terrible, but the fact is our lives are still worth far more than that animal's ever was.

'I don't know what else to say.'

'Does it *sound* like I'm finding it any easier?'

Now, Thorne was getting annoyed himself, but he knew better than to let it show. He said, 'You need to stop drinking, OK? Or keep on drinking until you don't give a shit. I'm tired, Nic, so I don't really care which, right now.'

There was a long silence before Tanner hung up.

Their dirty little secret.

Thorne closed his eyes, and for a few minutes at least he forgot all about Stuart Nicklin. A knot grew and tightened in his stomach as he sat up then lay down again; as guilty as Tanner was and even angrier with himself than he had been with her. Because the truth was that, thanks to him, it wasn't just their secret any more.

A month or so before, Hendricks had called late one night, every bit as wound up and pissed as Tanner had been. Eaten up by the small but significant lie he'd told on that crucial post-mortem report. Thorne had talked him down, eventually, but afterwards Melita had walked in from the next room and told Thorne that she'd overheard the conversation. Enough of it, certainly.

196

So he'd told her.

She'd been shocked, he could see that, but mercifully quickly she'd told him that she understood and that the last thing she would ever do was judge him; judge any of them. She'd wrapped her arms around him, in the very bed Thorne was lying in now, and told him she was there if he ever wanted to talk about it.

'It helps,' she said. 'I *know*.'

He'd thanked her, but had never taken her up on the offer. The last thing he needed was to watch her nodding, *knowing*, as he tried to explain that he had been saving a friend and that Phil had only been doing the same. That ten minutes before his death, Graham French had been torturing Nicola Tanner, with every intention of killing her afterwards. Thorne didn't need a professional, least of all one he slept with, to tell him what self-justification was, or denial.

Look them up in a dictionary, he thought, and there's a picture of me.

Now, Thorne could only lie there and feel the knot tightening, slippery and non-undoable. He thought about trust, and betraying it. He thought about blood clinging to a scalpel blade or running down the blackened body of a poker, and sleep was a long time coming.

THIRTY-ONE

At the same time, less than five miles away, someone else was considering the issue of trust, though Stuart Nicklin's thought process was, unsurprisingly, very different from Tom Thorne's. The light from the small television was more than enough to illuminate the overpriced shoebox he was renting and besides, he enjoyed the effect. The fades and the sudden flashes, the reds and the blues flickering across the walls. There was always plenty of colour in the quiz shows he now watched obsessively; picking a contestant to root for, getting annoyed at the host's feeble jokes and speaking the answers out loud as though there was somebody listening.

He said 'Venezuela', then sighed, exasperated at the moron who didn't know where the world's highest waterfall was. Thinking that never trusting anyone, while at the same time having an almost supernatural ability to make others trust *you*, had pretty much been his recipe for success.

His signature dish.

It was like having a superpower, he decided.

He couldn't remember ever trusting anyone. Not other kids at school, not his friends and not even his mother. Actually, least of all her ... but he remained convinced that keeping that part of him smothered – if it had ever been there in the first place – was one of the things that had allowed him to stay safe. Not safe from getting caught or going to prison, which had been unfortunate, but safe from the simple, stupid feelings he saw people crippled by every day. Beaten into submission. It was a shield which had kept him happily immune from so many of those things that trust could lead to; *would* lead to when it was inevitably broken.

Disappointment, pain, regret.

On the other hand, getting others to trust *him* had always been something he'd found ridiculously easy. ABC. Candy and babies. It was just a question of seeing what other people wanted, even if often they couldn't see it themselves. Letting them know there was nothing shameful about those dark thoughts they kept hidden and that he understood; bringing those thoughts and ideas scuttling into the light so they could breathe. It was about knowing which buttons to push and what nerves to poke at, that was all. It wasn't *complicated*.

It was ironic, he thought. Funny even, considering what was always trotted out about people like him, what it was they were supposed to lack. Funny because in the end, it was all *about* empathy.

Actually, he wasn't even sure that trust was the right word. It was about having enough *belief* in him and his ... outlook on life to step up and do the things he was suggesting. The Driver girl had been a case in point. She'd believed in him long before he'd ever come across her or responded to the torrent of sycophantic messages she'd left on an assortment of forums. There was a degree of faith, of course, and he had always believed she would do what she needed to. That was something he'd clocked nice and early, because on those rare and wonderful occasions when he came across someone with the capacity for killing, he knew it at once.

Like, oh, *hello* . . .

Like smelling someone who used the same soap as he did.

The Tom, Dick and Harry business had actually been her idea, but any leader worth their salt should encourage initiative. When she'd first suggested it, he'd thought it was over-egging the pudding a bit, but it was all about getting attention, so, in the end he'd decided that it couldn't hurt. When he'd given her the go-ahead, she'd been like a kid on Christmas morning.

Stupidly grateful and mad keen to play with her new toy.

Well, second-hand, strictly speaking, but that was precisely why she'd wanted it.

He thought that leader was perhaps the wrong word too, and even now he wouldn't describe himself in those terms, but there was no denying that he had followers, so he supposed it made a kind of sense. Even if the majority of them were idiots, or just desperate losers like poor Rebecca, he'd been grateful for the help they'd given him over the years. For the entertainment, too, not to mention the fact that those of them who were a bit more . . . obsessive than others had provided a steady source of income.

Ridiculous, the stuff they'd pay good money for, and how much.

But he would never *trust* any of them. He couldn't know

exactly what was in Rebecca Driver's messed up little head or what she might say or do when the likes of Tom Thorne turned the screws. He wasn't a mind reader or a hypnotist. If she'd chosen to break down in that interview room and say, *Stuart made me do it, Stuart was behind the whole thing,* there would have been bugger all he could do about it. It wouldn't have mattered, because as soon as they'd worked out where that scalpel had come from they'd have figured it out, just like they were meant to, but the girl spilling her guts early would have spoiled things slightly; thrown the game off course a little. There would have been no real damage in the scheme of things, though. He would always be unreachable until he decided otherwise, because he'd never trusted Driver or anyone else enough to give them anything that might be used against him. That could lead the police to whichever door he was waiting behind at the time.

He knew that soon, when the moment came, Thorne would be desperate to get through that door. It would not be Nicklin's own door, of course, but that was the whole point. Full of laughable, self-righteous fury, Thorne would be beating at that door alone; kicking and screaming to be let in, and when he did finally come charging through it he would discover that the prizes you struggled most to win always came with a cost.

That you could come out on top and still lose everything.

He tore into a chocolate bar with his teeth and took a bite; his weakness, if he had one. It had proved to be the case in more ways than one, when DNA from a discarded wrapper – like those scattered on the floor next to the sofa – had helped to convict him, first time around, though he could laugh about that now. He bit off another chunk and went back to his quiz show. It was getting exciting. He reeled off the seven wonders of the ancient world, then shook his head when the woman in the final could manage only three.

Truth be told, he talked to himself almost constantly. It was comforting, and, despite the loony-bin connotations, no dafter than talking to a cat or a dog, same as most people did when there was nobody else around. He preferred it when there *was* someone to talk to, of course. He'd missed out on a lot of that over the years he'd been away, and what was not to like when the topic of conversation was one he was so fond of?

Everybody's favourite, if they were being honest.

He'd been talking about himself rather a lot lately.

THIRTY-TWO

Thorne spent a good deal of Saturday clock-watching. When he wasn't doing that, he was putting a barely scraped maths O-level to good use; trying to calculate what kind of pension he'd get if he chucked the job in now and work out if it would be enough to start a small business flogging second-hand albums, or go halves with someone buying a rundown pub, or set himself up as a Z-list gigolo. He knew his phone conversation the night before had a lot to do with his mood, but still.

It passed the time.

Most of the day was taken up with necessary admin, which suited the likes of Nicola Tanner, but had never been Thorne's strong suit. Tits-deep in files and folders, they were alternately frustrated at hearing nothing from Hobbs and then excited when they did, though the excitement wore off quickly enough once the paperwork fairy began politely coughing to reclaim their attention.

There was plenty that demanded it. The cases Tanner and Thorne had been working before catching the Richard Sumner murder had not gone away or been passed on to others. Thorne still had work to do on a gang-related stabbing in Finsbury Park, while Tanner was chasing the forensic results on a domestic in Hornsey.

Understandably, both were finding it hard to focus.

The first call from Hobbs came mid-morning, to let them know that not only had K-Man rejected his lower offer for the pill bottle, but that he'd actually upped the asking price to £900.

'Looks like we've rattled his bars a bit,' Hobbs said.

The call was on speaker in Thorne and Tanner's office. 'Is that a good thing or not?' Tanner asked.

'Got to be good,' Thorne said.

'I agree,' Hobbs said. 'Now he knows he's got someone who's interested, he's seeing how far he can push it. That, or he's annoyed about the lower offer and thinks the buyer's taking the piss. Either way, he's hooked.'

'Tell him you might lose the sale,' Thorne said.

'I already did that. Went back and forth a few times. He said it's take it or leave it.'

'OK, good. So, tell him you've passed that message on and now the buyer's thinking about it.'

'Will do,' Hobbs said.

The 'buyer' was thinking about little else.

The majority of everyone's time was naturally spent on pre-trial preparations for the three murders with which Rebecca Driver had been charged. The court date would be months away and the CPS had as solid a case as they could wish for, but that didn't mean there wasn't a lot more work still to do. In many ways, the team had made a rod for their own backs, because the better a prosecution case was, the harder they had to work to ensure it did not get screwed up by some stupid failure in procedure; by being careless or taking the result for granted. A good many cases fell apart because someone forgot to feed a suspect often enough or have their fitness for interview assessed by the Force Medical Examiner; to get the correct form signed or say what was legally required of them on a recording. Simply put, that could not be allowed to happen with a case as high-profile as this one and with as much media interest.

*I*s needed to be dotted and *T*s crossed, then everything had to be checked again to ensure that the dotting and crossing had been done correctly.

Thorne got his head down and only raised it to look at the clock.

When he saw that it was nearly lunchtime, he called Greg Hobbs.

'OK, *Cameron* . . . tell him your buyer has agreed to the higher price. That they're *so* desperate to own Nicklin's pill bottle, they'll take it for £900.'

'You sure?'

'Let's see what K-Man does now he's got a deal,' Thorne said. 'If he acts any differently. Sometimes people get careless when they can smell the money.'

Thorne walked to the Royal Oak for lunch on his own. He was just about done with a microwaved shepherd's pie that was all but welded to the plate, when Tanner, who had eaten alone in the other room, came through to join him.

'I hope you didn't have what I had,' he said.

'Cheese salad.'

Thorne pushed his plate away. 'Good choice.'

'I didn't want to talk about this in the office.' Tanner swirled her mineral water round in the glass. 'I mean, obviously . . . but I just wanted to say sorry about last night.'

'It's fine, Nic.'

'No, it's not, but . . . you don't need to worry, all right? I really don't want you to think there's anything to be concerned about. I was just feeling sorry for myself, that's all, and the wine kicked everything up a notch. It was stupid. So . . .'

'I told you, it's fine.' Thorne reached for his Diet Coke. 'And I get it, OK?'

Tanner nodded.

'It's never going to sit well, course it isn't, so you shouldn't feel bad about having a glass too many and getting worked up.' Thorne leaned towards her and lowered his voice. 'Listen, it could just as easily have been me freaking out and calling you.'

'I don't think so.'

'Trust me—'

'I do,' Tanner said. 'That's the whole point. Look, I know Phil can get a bit jumpy about what happened, and well, you don't need telling *I* can, but you're the only one who doesn't panic. The one who just gets on with things.' She sipped her water and managed a smile. 'Thank God at least one of us is solid.'

Thorne straightened his knife and fork. 'Yeah, that's me,' he said.

They said nothing else until one of the bar staff had cleared Thorne's plate away. They finished their drinks and Tanner began to reapply her lipstick.

'Russell got a call from the CPS,' she said. 'Apparently Driver's brief's going to push for diminished responsibility.'

'Always on the cards,' Thorne said. 'Her getting "nutted off".'

'So, what do you think?'

Thorne had known a great many killers whose legal teams had played the same card, and in some cases, bearing in mind the degree of violence or the apparent loss of control, it had been hard to quibble. This was different though, because however firmly Thorne believed Rebecca Driver to be responsible for those murders, he knew that someone else had given her that responsibility. Stuart Nicklin had suggested, insinuated, cajoled . . . until she'd decided it was a responsibility she wanted; that she was destined to bear.

As usual, Thorne's train of thought left its tracks across his face.

'How's things going with Hobbs, d'you reckon?'

Thorne shrugged. 'As of now, he's the only hope we've got.' He checked his phone in case there was a message from Hobbs that he'd missed. There wasn't. 'If the bloke who's selling that pill bottle doesn't lead us to Nicklin, I haven't got the first idea how we get to him.'

Tanner thought about it. 'Obviously I don't know Nicklin as well as you do, but from everything you've said . . . isn't there at least a possibility he might come to us?'

Thorne looked at her and shifted in his seat. The sudden stab of discomfort was probably down to no more than the shepherd's pie oozing into his gut and doing its worst. It was not something he wanted to think about for very long.

Tanner reached for her jacket. Said, 'We should probably get back.'

*

It was half an hour before going-home time when Hobbs called again.

'K-Man's very happy,' Hobbs said. 'Says he's letting it go cheap and that our mystery buyer's getting a good deal.'

'Very generous of him,' Thorne said. 'So, he wants his money, right?'

'Oh yes. He's mad keen to have the Bitcoin transferred to his account as soon as possible.'

Thorne thought about it. 'So keep on stringing him along, Greg. Tell him there's no problem, but you're having trouble getting hold of your buyer.'

'OK . . . cool.'

Seeing as the 'mystery buyer' was actually the Metropolitan Police, Thorne knew he should probably have sought further authorisation before agreeing to a higher asking price. He told himself that he'd been far too busy with paperwork. 'We need to drag this out.'

'I'm not sure I can drag it out too much longer,' Hobbs said. 'I don't get the impression he's all that patient.'

Thorne did not know that what he was asking Hobbs to do would achieve anything, but he was out of ideas. 'Just do your best, mate,' he said. 'You're doing a top job, by the way.'

A few minutes later, he was pulling on his jacket and heading down towards the car park. Chall passed him on the stairs and asked what the hurry was. Thorne considered a lie – a sick relative or an urgent lead – but in the end he couldn't be arsed.

He said, 'I need to get to the library before it closes.'

THIRTY-THREE

It was not the book with which Thorne would have chosen to pop his library card's cherry. That said, there wasn't a long list of contenders. Or indeed any list. It was even more disheartening to see that dozens of people before him had chosen to borrow *Killing On Command: The Life And Crimes Of Stuart Nicklin* since it had first been published three years before.

Once he'd eaten and lined up the couple of beers he felt sure he would need, Thorne sat down and put on his reading glasses.

The library had been the only option in the end, because Thorne certainly wasn't going to put money in the author's pocket by buying the bloody thing. He'd been all too aware of what critics had apparently called a 'hard-hitting portrait of evil' when it had first come out, but he'd had no interest whatsoever in reading it then. He wasn't awfully keen now, but there was always the possibility he might come across something that would help, so at this stage of the game he didn't mind holding his nose. The book had, of course, been one of many in Rebecca Driver's collection, but that copy – with its handwritten musings and schoolgirlish words of admiration – was now a crucial piece of evidence and, as such, unavailable for thumbing through again without the use of nitrile gloves.

Opening the slightly battered volume from Kentish Town library, Thorne felt as though he should be wearing them anyway.

'Jesus ...'

The author – Stephen J. Campbell – had dedicated his book 'to all the victims of Stuart Nicklin and to those they left behind'. Thorne wondered if 'those they left behind' had seen any of the profits.

Thorne knew he could safely skip the first few chapters. He had no desire to find out anything he didn't already know about Stuart Nicklin's childhood; whether he had been made to wear girls' clothes or locked in a cupboard under the stairs. Thorne could not have cared less about the killer's family tree. So, as he presumed most people did when reading a book in which they themselves would feature, he went straight to the index and searched for his own name.

It wasn't difficult to find.

The descriptions of the murders for which Nicklin had first gained notoriety, and which had seen him sentenced to life imprisonment, were horribly familiar. Unnecessarily graphic perhaps when described on the page, but more or less accurate. Some killings Nicklin had carried out himself, while others had been the work of a hapless, ill-fated individual named Martin Palmer, a young man Nicklin had been able to terrify into doing his will since they'd first met at school who had been shot dead just before Nicklin was arrested.

Suicide by cop; that was what Thorne had always believed.

There were plenty of quotes from Thorne himself, though he could barely remember some of the things he was alleged to have said back then. The text of the speech he'd given on the steps of the Old Bailey after Nicklin had been convicted was printed in full, as well as extracts from interviews given while Thorne was still hunting for the killers. He would be the first to admit that several of those early confrontations with the media had been somewhat ... testy, but he almost spat out his beer when he saw himself described by the author as 'truculent and over-sensitive'.

'Twat ...'

He turned the pages hard and fast enough to tear a couple. He wondered if he'd be fined. He decided he could claim it on expenses, so he accidentally tore a couple more.

There was no mention of the murders committed several years later by a man named Marcus Brooks, the photographs of the victims that had been sent to Thorne's phone, or the crucial part Stuart Nicklin had played in their deaths by orchestrating events from behind bars. It wasn't a surprise. Nicklin's role in that case had never become public knowledge and the justice later meted out to him – which Thorne may or may not have had something to do with – had been dished out privately in the prison canteen, in the form of a lasagne laced with broken glass.

Thorne smiled, remembering.

The details of what had transpired on Bardsey Island were

sketchy to say the least, but Thorne had expected as much. He had certainly never spoken to Stephen Campbell. He was fairly sure Nicklin never had, and virtually everyone else who'd been on that island at the time was dead.

There was no mention of what had happened to Phil Hendricks.

Nobody except Thorne, Nicklin, and the men Nicklin had paid or otherwise persuaded to do the job, knew what had been done with that scalpel.

Nicklin had got away. That was the gist of two entire chapters and, thanks to what Mr Campbell could only describe as the 'foolishness and over-confidence' of Detective Inspector Tom Thorne, a dangerous killer had not only been allowed to escape custody, but still remained at large; an ever-present danger to the public.

There was a picture of Thorne; a snap taken by a local reporter just after he'd stepped off that helicopter back to the mainland. His face was bloodied and swollen, the result of the beating he'd taken from Nicklin at the end, that he'd begged for. Looking at it now, Thorne could remember how much worse he'd felt on the inside.

Scalded, empty.

He tossed the book to one side, deciding that the label on his beer bottle would provide a more fulfilling read, which it did.

Well into a second bottle, Thorne wondered if, when all this was done with, when Nicklin was safely back in custody, he should seek out Stephen J. Campbell and pay the man a visit. He would perhaps ask him to autograph a copy – could you do that with library books? – and then politely suggest that now might be a good time to publish a fully up-to-date edition. Then, just to show the author how truculent and over-sensitive he could be, he would shove the man's shitty book up his arse—

Thorne's phone rang.

Hobbs.

'You were spot on.'

'What?' Thorne sat up.

'What you said about him smelling the money and getting sloppy.' Hobbs was gabbling, fired up. 'I'm ninety-nine point nine per cent sure who K-Man is.'

'How?'

'So, I've already explained that these emails are fully encrypted at both ends. Basically, he's untraceable, right?'

'Right.'

'Now, with every email he's sent so far I've made a point of checking the header. All the gobbledegook you don't ordinarily see, yeah? The routing, the source and most importantly the IP address of the computer. Up to now it's been a dead end because he's been using a VPN, right? You know what a VPN is?'

'Visible panty something?'

'It's a virtual private network.'

'I'm kidding,' Thorne said.

'Oh, OK. Well, it basically encrypts all your data, but the main thing is it disguises your IP address . . . your computer's location. With the last email he sent, though, the IP address was actually *resolvable*. Do you see what I'm saying?'

Thorne *wanted* to say *hurry the fuck up*, but the man had earned his moment. 'Yeah, I think so.'

'He forgot to switch on his VPN.' Hobbs waited for Thorne to grasp the significance of what he'd been told.

'Or maybe the connection to it dropped out at the crucial moment, because that can happen . . . but, either way, his last IP address resolves to a regular service provider – Virgin, if you're interested – and from there it was like shelling peas, basically. I mean, this is what we do round here all day long, right? One call to Virgin – well, a couple of calls in the end – and I had the name of the bill payer.'

'Which is?'

'Oh . . . Kevin Bartley. K-Man's name is Kevin Bartley, and it gets even better because I've already run the name through the PNC. I know that's a bit above my pay-grade . . .'

'I forgive you,' Thorne said.

'He's in the system.' Hobbs paused again, as though he was waiting for a round of applause. 'Kevin Bartley is *in the system*. Various offences, most of them drug-related, going back years. I mean, we could check that pill bottle, see if his prints are on it . . . you know, if we really want to make sure it's him.'

'Yeah, we *could* . . .' The bottle was already being examined forensically, but Thorne knew that would take time.

Clearly, Hobbs knew it too. 'So I did a bit more digging, and . . . this is the good bit.'

'It's already good.'

'Yeah, I know, but Kevin Bartley's got a record in France, too. Did six months in a prison in Marseille two years ago for supplying heroin. So it checks out, right? The story about him and Nicklin knowing each other when they were both in France.'

'Fuck me, Greg.' Thorne was on his feet, trying to decide who he should call first. Brigstocke was the obvious choice, but more than anything he wanted to tell Phil. 'What do you do for an encore?'

'Would a current address be any good?'

THIRTY-FOUR

By just after three o'clock on Monday morning, they'd been sitting in the unmarked command car for twenty minutes. There was frost forming on the windows and Thorne was starting to lose the feeling in his legs. He leaned forward and prodded the shoulder of the officer in the driver's seat. 'Any chance of turning the heating up a bit?'

'High as it'll go, mate.' The officer looked round and smiled, slapped his palms against his jacket. 'I've got thermals on under here.'

'Me too,' Tanner said.

Thorne looked at her. 'Why didn't you remind me?'

'I think there were more important things to worry about.'

Squeezed in between them on the back seat, the Tactical Firearms Commander, a heavy-set superintendent with a Peaky Blinders accent, stared down at the screen of his laptop; at the separate feeds from the helmet-mounted cameras of the six-man Firearms Operations Unit which had taken up various positions outside the target address.

He keyed his Airwave radio. 'All units from TFC. State Amber, repeat State Amber ... stand by.'

'Besides which,' Tanner said, 'I'm not your mother.'

Thorne could not argue, about that or the number of things that had needed organising the day before. The address Hobbs had provided for Kevin Bartley was in Coventry, which had meant urgent liaison with West Midlands Police and all the authorisation necessary for a full-on firearms operation. Thorne had wondered initially if they were going a little over the top. He'd been all for jumping straight in a car with three other members of the team and charging up the M1, until Brigstocke had pointed out that whatever their target's criminal history might be, any association with a suspect as dangerous as Stuart Nicklin meant that the strictest degree of protection for officers and members of the public alike would be needed when attempting an arrest. It meant taking no chances and *that* meant firearms.

'How do we know Kevin Bartley isn't still knocking about with Nicklin?' Brigstocke had asked.

'Unlikely,' Thorne had said.

'How do we know Nicklin won't *be* there?'

'He won't.' Thorne had been ready to push, until he'd seen the look on his boss's face, remembered that quote about foolishness and over-confidence and stopped making a fuss.

As well as getting things set up with the team from the West Midlands, there was a good deal of back-and-forth with police and prison authorities in Marseille. Predictably, it being a Sunday, this had been somewhat less *vite* than it might have been. Appeals for a little more speed had been met with the emailed equivalent of a Gallic shrug, and it hadn't been until the end of the day that all the records, and crucially a recent photograph of Kevin Bartley, had eventually been sent.

'That's Brexit for you,' Tanner had said

'Roger, State Amber received.' The voice of the FOU team leader was loud and tinny through the superintendent's radio. 'Standing by on red.'

'What are we waiting for?' Thorne asked.

The superintendent ignored him, kept his eyes fixed on the screen, at the images lit by the torches mounted on six SIG Sauer carbines: patchy grass and blackened brick, a metal door next to a row of large plastic bins at the rear of the two-storey block; the foot of a concrete stairwell.

'Repeat, standing by on red . . . '

Thorne and Tanner had finally left London just after ten-thirty the night before and were sitting down with the Firearms Operation Unit in Coventry by one a.m. Thorne had quickly told them everything he knew about Kevin Bartley and explained exactly why they needed to talk to him. He was informed that officers from West Midlands Police had already conducted a drive-past of the target address as well as a helicopter sweep, and reported no signs of activity in the second-floor flat.

'If your man's in there, he's probably asleep, which is exactly what we want,' the superintendent had said. 'All being well, we can get in there and have him in handcuffs before he's woken up properly.'

A floor plan of the property was produced and projected on to a screen as each member of the FOU was given their individual instructions. The superintendent had briefed his team carefully, talking them through every detail of the operation several times, and had only stopped when he caught the look on Thorne's face.

'Sorry if we're boring you.'

'No, I was just . . . sorry.'

'How many deaths did you say he was responsible for? Your Mr Nicklin? I mean just the recent ones.'

'Three,' Thorne had said. 'Indirectly.'

'All right then.'

The superintendent wore the same blank expression now as he continued to stare down at the laptop.

Thorne slid numb fingers beneath his thighs.

Now he needed a piss.

'State Red.' The superintendent sat up straight. 'Go when you're ready.'

Thorne knew what would happen next; that it would not be the chaos of shouting and screaming they were so fond of on cop shows. He watched the moving images as two armed officers moved slowly and silently up two flights of stairs. The torches illuminated a scarred front door and a few seconds later, a short stretch of dark hallway as the door was smashed open with a metal battering ram.

'Armed police. Come to the door slowly with your hands on your head.'

Thorne and Tanner stared at the screen.

There was movement from a third camera and another torch lit up the shape of a firearms support dog which was let off its leash and immediately bounded through the door into the flat. The dog had been trained to bark at any sign of life, but there was no sound from inside and after a minute or so the dog reappeared.

In the car, the superintendent shook his head. He glanced at Tanner and Thorne, then leaned towards his radio. 'OK, all officers. Go ... '

Now the shouting began, the thud of boots on the stairs, the rasp of breathing behind helmets.

'Armed police .... '

The images on the superintendent's screen lurched and tilted, shifting violently as the officers poured into the flat and scattered, yelling.

'Room to the left.'

'Room to the right.'

'Clear ... '

'Kitchen clear ... '

Struggling to take in the six camera feeds at once, Thorne watched bulky shapes in black body armour flashing across the screen, pressed against walls or reflected in mirrors. He stared, holding his breath, as thin beams of light danced over grey Anaglypta and doors crashed open. He saw a gloved hand pulling at a wardrobe door and a bottle kicked across curling lino, and everywhere he saw the barrels of semi-automatic guns pointing at nothing and briefly lighting up the gloom.

'Flat clear.'

'Shit,' Thorne said.

Then: 'One in the back bedroom. We need a medic.'

'*Shit*,' Tanner said.

The superintendent let out a long sigh and said, 'That's not good,' and by the time he was closing his laptop Thorne already had the door open and was stepping out into the cold.

On the way up the stairs, he passed several members of the FOU on their way down, the fizz of the adrenalin still clear on their faces. As Thorne and Tanner approached what was left of the front door, someone inside turned all the lights on and an officer who'd been waiting just inside nodded, then pointed them towards the back of the flat.

Thorne heard a message come through on someone's radio.

The medic was on the way.

The place was small and pretty basic. A kitchen immediately off to the right and a cluttered living room to the left; needles on a low table, a laptop computer. It was not anywhere Thorne would have chosen to live, but even taking into account the stench of cigarettes and sweat, he and Tanner had both been called to plenty of worse places. They glanced into the larger of the two bedrooms, saw a bed that had not been slept in, and kept walking until they reached the smaller room at the back, where two of the armed officers were waiting for them; where the man in the chair was.

The victim was sitting in a straight-backed chair, naked from the waist up. His arms had been tied behind him and each foot bound hard to a leg of the chair with what looked like washing line. His head hung to one side, like he was thinking about something, and the long red hair and scraggly beard were both matted with blood.

There was no reason for the medic to hurry.

The damage to one side of his face – almost certainly the result of the blunt force trauma that had killed him – meant that, even after pulling out the photograph from his pocket, Thorne could not be certain he was looking at Kevin Bartley. The tattoos on his arms were clear enough, though: the same as those listed on the man's PNC file.

An acid-house smiley face; another with crosses for eyes; *COMING ON STRONG*.

A child of the eighties.

The two officers who had remained in the room were staring at the body. One shook his head. 'What the fuck's *that* supposed to mean?'

'Not a clue, mate.' His colleague turned away, nodding at Tanner as he headed out of the room. 'Not our problem.'

Thorne had only met these men a few hours before, so there was no reason why they should have known his first name. No reason at all why they would have understood the message carved deep into the dead man's chest.

Tanner stepped across to stand close to Thorne. She asked if he was OK and leaned gently against him, and they both stared at the rivulets of blood that had snaked down Kevin Bartley's mottled torso, leaking from every letter scored into his flesh and now dried into rusty-brown trails. Thorne understood only too well.

He knew exactly who the message was for and who was sending it.

BUYER BEWARE, TOM.

While a full debrief of the firearms operation was taking place, a local homicide unit was securing the crime scene in Coventry. A murder inquiry had been set up and discussions were already taking place between the heads of major crime teams from the Met and West Midlands Police as to how two investigations which were obviously linked could be brought together and worked.

The Top Brass, doing what they did best.

At WMP headquarters, Thorne and Tanner sat together

at the back of an otherwise empty office, high above the city. It was their first chance to talk privately. They drank coffee and ate bacon sandwiches, while the sky pinked and the sun heaved itself up from behind a ragged line of tower blocks.

'It was Nicklin all along,' Thorne said.

'Looks that way.'

'He was the one who supplied that pill bottle for Margaret Herbert's website. Waiting for a buyer to come along, posing as K-Man and then deliberately making that "mistake" in his last email to set Kevin Bartley up.'

'Then killing him.'

'The same way he put that scalpel up there and then told Rebecca Driver exactly where she could buy it. How perfect it would be.' Thorne sat and chewed for a few moments. 'I think it might be how he's been funding himself all this time. Putting a few of his mementoes up for sale whenever he's running short of cash.'

'Why wouldn't he?' Tanner shook her head. 'If I could get fifty quid for a few locks of hair, I'd have the scissors out every five minutes.'

They sat in silence for a while.

A cleaner poked her head round the door, saw that the office was being used and quickly withdrew again.

'What you're saying makes sense.' Tanner picked at the rim of her Styrofoam cup. 'We've got one major problem though.'

Thorne waited.

'That message . . .'

'I'm fine,' Thorne said. 'Well, not fine, because it's scary as fuck, but when it comes to Stuart Nicklin, I'm *always* scared.'

'That's not what I'm talking about.'

'If I wasn't scared I'd be stupid—'

'He knew we were coming, Tom.' Tanner put down her coffee and turned to look at him. 'He put Kevin Bartley in the frame and killed him, knowing that you'd be the one to find his body. He laid it out for you.' She began to talk faster, a grim urgency in her voice. 'Everything Greg Hobbs did was ... ultra-secure at our end, right? Using Cameron Herbert's computer, all the right passwords ... it was completely anonymous. Yes, Nicklin put that pill bottle up there with just enough evidence tying it to Kevin Bartley, but in the end his buyer could have been ... anybody.' She took a deep breath as she saw it on Thorne's face: the realisation that there was one more thing to be seriously scared about.

'So, how did he know it was us?'

PART THREE

A CHOICE

THIRTY-FIVE

There was a Christmas tree in the corner of the restaurant, silver with red decorations, and Thorne found himself staring at it. He thought how nice it looked; simple and perfect. It was not as if he didn't know Christmas was just over a fortnight away because, as always, it was impossible to avoid. He had heard all the usual songs on the radio or in shops and passed plenty of suitably decked-out houses, but they had just been ... noise and lights, and with so much else to occupy his mind this was the first time it had fully registered.

There would probably be a few decorations up at work by now, a bit of tatty tinsel round the doorways and a card or two on desks, but he had not really noticed.

Unlike the tattooed curmudgeon sitting opposite him – Phil Hendricks, who, with immaculate timing, was actually grinning, having seen that their food was on its way – Thorne actually quite liked Christmas. This year was shaping up to be another one of those when work meant he would not really get time to do all the things he wanted, but given the chance he would usually try to celebrate, same as everybody else. To think about unwanted socks for a few days, instead of unwanted bodies. He would sing along tunelessly with Slade and Wizzard and the Pogues and he never needed an excuse to stick on Christmas albums by Johnny Cash or Willie Nelson. He would buy the necessary gifts for the few people who mattered and plenty of unnecessary ones for himself. He would find time to visit his Auntie Eileen and his father's only surviving friend Victor and, when the big day came, if he was spending it alone – though there had been occasions when he'd turned up at Ebenezer Hendricks's place, bearing gifts of beer and turkey sandwiches – he would sit, happily sozzled, in front of *Elf* or *The Great Escape* and eat half his body weight in nuts and Quality Street.

It all came down to that, in the end. He wouldn't bother with decorations unless he was with someone, because there didn't seem any point. With everything that had been going on, he and Melita hadn't had a chance to discuss how they'd be spending Christmas yet, but he didn't think it would take him long to stick up a tree like that one in the corner.

'Get *in*,' Hendricks said, rubbing his hands together.

The waiter laid the pizzas down. Spicy meat feasts for Thorne and Hendricks, something with rocket and goat's cheese for Greg Hobbs and Tanner's usual abomination.

Hendricks shook his head in disgust. 'You should be banged up for that.'

'Pineapple on a pizza isn't actually illegal,' Tanner said. 'I know you and Tom would like it to be.'

228

'It's a crime against nature.' Hendricks reached for the chilli oil.

'A crime against humanity,' Thorne said.

He and Tanner had not returned from Coventry until lunchtime and had immediately been summoned to a meeting, during which Russell Brigstocke had outlined the way the two forces would handle the investigation going forward. A PowerPoint presentation had already been prepared. The last few hours of the day had been taken up with the kind of operational briefings that Thorne always thought of as 'bullshit bingo', and in the forty minutes since arriving at the restaurant in town he and Tanner had already told Hobbs and Hendricks everything that had happened in the early hours of that morning.

'Let's try not to talk shop,' Tanner said now.

'Fine with me,' Thorne said.

'Just for fifteen minutes, just while we eat. Let's talk about something else. *Anything* else.'

Hendricks seemed keen to get the ball rolling. He nodded towards Hobbs, or more specifically to his wheelchair. 'So, how d'you end up in that thing, then?'

'Fuck's sake, Phil.' Tanner stared at him.

Hobbs was laughing. 'It's cool. Most people haven't got the bottle, but I know they're desperate to ask.'

'So?' Hendricks shoved the best part of an entire slice into his mouth.

'Driving back from a party when I was at uni,' Hobbs said. 'My own fault really, because I knew the bloke who was driving was pissed. He died . . . so.'

'That's terrible,' Tanner said.

'I'm kidding.' Hobbs chewed, enjoying himself. 'Jammy

sod walked away with just a broken leg. Well, he didn't *walk*, obviously.'

Hendricks waved another slice of pizza in Hobbs's direction. 'I *like* this lad ... he can stay. So, you got a girlfriend, Greg?'

Hobbs nodded, his mouth full.

'Right. Is *she* ... ?'

Thorne groaned and began shaking his head. Tanner muttered something about not being able to take Hendricks anywhere.

'I'm only asking,' Hendricks said.

'My girlfriend's legs are fully functional.' Hobbs grinned. '*Fully.*'

'Nice,' Hendricks said.

'So, what about you?' Hobbs looked at Hendricks. 'You got a girlfriend?'

Thorne snorted and Tanner laughed so hard that there was genuine concern she might choke on a piece of pineapple.

Hobbs looked at Hendricks as though seeing him for the first time and reddened a little. 'Oh, I see. Sorry.'

'How *dare* you.' The two bottles of Peroni he'd necked in quick succession were making Hendricks slightly flirtatious.

'You can hardly blame him.' Thorne pointed his fork at Hendricks. 'You are a bit ... closety.'

They talked about other things after that. Football, once it transpired that Hobbs was a Crystal Palace supporter and the Spurs and Arsenal fans at the table had united for once in their derision. Films, which prompted a heated discussion about whether *Die Hard* qualified as a Christmas movie. Cats, when, much to Hendricks's disgust, Tanner and Hobbs began showing each other photos of their precious pets. It was only once the dirty plates had been cleared and more drinks ordered that Hobbs jerked the conversation back to the rather less controversial topic of corpses.

'Have they got a time of death for Kevin Bartley yet?'

'Some time on Saturday by the look of him,' Tanner said.

'Specifically, I mean.'

Thorne said that if they had, he was yet to be told about it.

'Definitely a poorer class of pathologist in the Midlands,' Hendricks said.

'I think I can help.' Hobbs reddened again slightly when the other three looked at him. 'Well, there are only two ways Nicklin could have sent that last email showing Bartley's IP address. Either he somehow managed to get his Wi-Fi code ... say he nips round to see his old friend and asks for the code because he needs to check Twitter or something ... then he could have sent it sitting in his car outside before going back into the flat and killing him. *Or*, he goes round there, kills him straight away, then sends the email from Bartley's computer.'

'That sounds more likely,' Tanner said.

'Agreed,' Hobbs said. 'The man you're after certainly doesn't sound like the sort to waste time unnecessarily. Now, I received that final email at seven forty-three p.m. on Saturday, so ... allowing maybe half an hour for Nicklin to tie Bartley up and kill him and whatever else—'

'Carve his little note,' Hendricks said.

Thorne stared into his wine glass.

'Right, the note.' Hobbs sat back as though he'd just explained something blindingly obvious. 'Anyway, I think we can therefore assume time of death would have been somewhere between seven and seven-fifteen that evening. Like I say, give or take.'

Tanner nodded and nudged Hendricks. 'I think Greg's after your job.'

'Considering he was the one who led you to Bartley,' Hendricks said, 'I think he's after yours, too.'

'Nicklin led us to Bartley.' Thorne looked up at them. '*Nicklin*. Led us by the fucking nose.'

'We couldn't have known that,' Tanner said.

'*I* should have known. He's been one step ahead of us the whole time . . . no, make that several steps ahead, because he always is . . . and I should have sussed it. When I saw what he'd cut into Bartley's chest, I wasn't even surprised, you know? Just angry at myself for being such an idiot.' He picked up his glass and drained it. 'Christ, you'd think I'd have worked the fucker out by now.'

Hobbs may have been oblivious to the change in mood, or perhaps he was simply unwilling to indulge it for very long, but either way he was the one who finally broke the awkward silence.

'Nicola's right,' he said. 'There's simply no way anyone could have known Nicklin was the one sending those emails. Or what he was planning to do once he'd sent them. It does beg one question, though.'

'We know.' Thorne said it rather more aggressively than he had intended. The same concern Tanner had raised back in Coventry. The question they had been wrestling with all the way back to London.

How had Nicklin known who he was sending those emails *to*?

'We're going to see our two prime contenders tomorrow,' Tanner said.

'Margaret Herbert and her grandson?' Hobbs nodded. 'I guessed they'd be the obvious suspects.'

'You are *so* wasted as a nerd, mate,' Hendricks said. 'You should seriously think about becoming a detective. Come on, it's obvious they need all the help they can get, right?'

'Well . . .'

'I mean, coppers are still not the most switched-on lot when it comes to diversity and all that. Not overly sensitive, some of them. Just saying, you'll probably have to put up with a few idiots calling you Ironside, or whatever.'

Tanner reached across to pat Hendricks on the arm. 'OK, Phil, that'll do.'

'What?'

'I think you've demonstrated your woke credentials very nicely already.'

Hobbs started to laugh.

'Listen, mate.' Hendricks looked offended, but was clearly enjoying the attention. 'I was . . . *woke* when most of these Generation Z snowflakes were still in a fucking coma.'

Now, three of the four people at the table were laughing, but Thorne simply turned and signalled to the waiter that they were ready for the bill.

As soon as Hobbs had driven away, waving, Thorne, Hendricks and Tanner walked through Soho towards Leicester Square tube station. It was dry, but the wind had teeth and there was ice on the pavement. Once they were underground – marginally warmer and with less chance of going arse-over-tit – Tanner said a brisk goodnight and veered off to catch the Piccadilly line back to Hammersmith.

'Just thee and me, mate,' Hendricks said.

They managed to bag seats on a crowded Northern line train, and somewhere between Tottenham Court Road and

Goodge Street Thorne leaned close so as to be heard above the noise.

'We got the forensics back on that pill bottle, by the way.'

'The genuine article?'

'Looks like it,' Thorne said. 'Bartley's prints and Nicklin's.'

'Oh well, at least they weren't trying to rip anybody off.'

'What's a bit more surprising is what had been in it.'

Hendricks looked at him. 'Well, I'm guessing it wasn't Nurofen Plus.'

'They found traces of MDMA.'

'Bugger me.' Hendricks let his head fall back against the window. 'So Stuart's developed a taste for disco biscuits, has he?'

'There's every chance.'

'Scary thought.'

Thorne said nothing, remembering what he'd said to Tanner; the pair of them eating bacon sandwiches and watching the sunrise as though everything was normal. The only thoughts he entertained about Stuart Nicklin that *weren't* scary involved handcuffs, or a dock, or a prison van.

Or a gravestone.

Ten minutes later Hendricks stood up as the train approached Camden Town. Thorne raised a hand, told him he'd call if there was any news. The train slowed, but instead of moving towards the doors to beat the rush, Hendricks lingered, hanging on to the metal safety pole while others pushed past him.

'Are you OK, mate?'

Thorne looked up.

'You seem a bit . . . off.'

'I just need to catch up on some sleep.' Thorne winced and closed his eyes as the wheels screamed, grinding suddenly against uneven rails, but in truth it was not much worse than the cacophony growing daily inside his head.

THIRTY-SIX

It had been quite the Saturday night up in the Midlands and now, forty-eight hours later with a pill kicking in very nicely, every memory of it was heightened – charged and bright as neon – so that Nicklin could remember exactly how he'd felt minute by minute. The noises and the colours as they'd changed. The stupid laughing for a while, then the computer stuff and the cutting; all of it, like he was back there watching it happen, from that first delicious moment when K-Man had opened the door and peered around it at him like he was a stranger.

Fuck do you want?

He says, *Come on, Kevin, it hasn't been that long,* and he holds up the bottle he's brought with him and grins and says, *France, mate, France,* and then Kevin remembers, and he's in.

The stink of sweat and mould and fags . . .

Yeah, France. Good times . . .

. . . and the vinegary smell of cooked heroin that tells

him Kevin hasn't changed a whole lot, and he's smiling and thinking how he's picked the perfect time, and how very much easier it's all going to be because the idiot's *high*.

The bottle's opened straight away and, sitting around in the rancid little kitchen, the pair of them are rattling on like they'd only seen each other the day before or something.

We were good mates, yeah?

Course we were, Kevin. Those few weeks we were knocking around together in France, you were always a mate, always gave me a bottle of pills when I needed one.

Is that what you're here for?

I'm fine for pills, don't you worry about that. Listen, there's something I need to show you. You'll piss yourself, I swear . . .

Through to the living room then, carrying the bottle, and it couldn't be better because the computer's already open. It's sitting there on a table because Kevin's probably been looking at porn or playing some stupid game.

He's logged on, though, that's the main thing, and now . . . two nights later, lying on the bed in his flat, Nicklin remembered that lovely moment when he'd checked himself. When he'd really relaxed into it, knowing he could have killed Kevin there and then, but had decided to wait just that bit longer, because he'd wanted to have a little fun first.

He sits down and makes himself comfortable.

A blast from the past, Kev . . .

A few clicks on his host's grimy laptop and *voila*. He calls Kevin over, patting the sofa cushion and seeing the dust fly up, watching the daft junkie drift across like he's in a dream, then pointing so he can see it on the screen.

Recognise that?

It's a bottle, right? For pills . . .

237

One of yours. One of the ones you gave me when we were in France.

Kevin leans in then, squints as he reads, not getting it. *Who's K-Man?*

That's you, because it's your bottle. Well, it's me pretending to be you.

Nicklin laughs, then Kevin laughs, without actually understanding why.

I still don't know what I'm looking at . . .

Read what it says about the bottle. Who it belonged to.

You, yeah? One of the ones I gave you, that's what you said.

Read it.

So Kevin reads the full description of the bottle on the website and then he shakes his head, confused. Kevin doesn't really take the name in the first time, only sees that it's not the one he's expecting.

That's not your name.

I was using a different name when I was in France. I've used lots of names over the years. That's my real name . . .

Kevin looks again and now he really *sees* the name and of course he recognises it. This is when his face changes, and Nicklin enjoys that spasm of piss-yourself terror, but not for long enough to give Kevin time to get away or anything. To *try* to get away. Nicklin's already bringing the wine bottle up, then smashing it into the side of Kevin's head, and after that, everything's just the way he imagined it would be.

He sends the email, because the computer's right there.

The one he knows will lead them here.

He drags Kevin into the back bedroom and ties him to the chair because he wants him sitting up nice and straight; he wants him to be seen.

He pulls off Kevin's shirt and takes out the knife.

He has to hit Kevin with the bottle again, because Kevin wakes up before Nicklin's finished working with the blade. Hits him many more times than he needs to, actually. He's annoyed, because Kevin jerks and thrashes about when he comes round and it means that the *M* in that final word isn't going to be as perfect as he would have wanted.

Now, lying on the bed in the dark, Nicklin's heart was racing. The pills did that anyway, but this was the rush of the memory as much as anything, and the expression he imagined on Thorne's face when he walked into that room and saw the message.

His less-than-perfect *Tom*.

THIRTY-SEVEN

Thorne did not want the Herberts to be comfortable.
He did not want them to feel *safe*. No favourite armchair
for Margaret to sink into, no doggie to fuss over and no
opportunity for Cameron – Herbert by name, herbert by
nature – to snuggle up close to his nan.

Even if the old woman *had* grassed him up last time.

A quick phone call first thing that morning had secured
facilities at Colchester police station and two unmarked cars
had subsequently been dispatched, arriving unannounced to
collect their guests. By the time Thorne and Tanner pulled
into the car park just before lunch, Margaret and Cameron
Herbert had been sitting alone in separate interview rooms
for the best part of an hour.

Thorne decided that another half an hour wouldn't
hurt, so he and Tanner made themselves tea. They flicked
through a couple of dog-eared papers in reception. They

swapped gossip with the custody sergeant and ate the sandwiches they'd picked up on the way.

'You take the old woman,' Thorne said when they'd finished. 'I'll have a crack at her stoner technical adviser.'

'Am I under arrest, then?'

Tanner had barely closed the door of the interview room behind her. She smiled at Margaret Herbert and walked across to the table. She took off her jacket, sat down and informed the woman opposite her that although it wasn't evidential, the interview was being recorded. 'Now, what did you ask when I came in?'

'You heard me.'

'Well, I think you'd know if you were, Margaret. You sounded pretty clued up about that kind of thing last time we met. If you're still unsure though, I'm guessing that someone would have said, "I'm arresting you for ... " I don't know ... whatever they thought you needed arresting *for*.' Tanner smiled again. 'Has that happened?'

Herbert looked ready to spit.

'I mean we *can* arrest you, obviously, and we still might. I suppose it depends on how this conversation goes.'

The old woman stared back at her, clearly in no mood for pleasantries or piss-takes. 'So, I'm free to go whenever I like, then.'

'Absolutely,' Tanner said.

'Well, maybe I will.'

'It'll have to be the bus, I'm afraid.'

'I'll call a taxi.' Herbert was suddenly a little fuller of herself. 'Or Cameron can order us an Uber on his phone.'

'Whatever, but bear in mind we'll be asking ourselves

why you aren't very keen to cooperate with a murder investigation.'

'I've already cooperated.' The woman sounded horrified. 'I let you take all my stuff, if you remember.'

'I can see why you're confused,' Tanner said. 'That was a different murder investigation. The three men who'd been killed using that scalpel you sold . . . if you remember. Unfortunately, since we last spoke there's been another murder, and I'm sorry to say it's another one directly connected to an item on your website.'

Herbert seemed to shrink into her chair as she let out a long breath.

'I mean, that's got to hurt your reviews, hasn't it? Well, maybe not, considering the sort of people you're catering to. Either way, you can see why we wanted another chat, right?'

'It's that pill bottle you were so interested in, isn't it?'

'That's correct.' Despite her appearance and the obvious mobility issues, Tanner had never thought for one moment that Margaret Herbert was the harmless old lady she might have been mistaken for. The woman was obviously in possession of every last marble. Still, it didn't hurt to be reminded of just how sharp she actually was.

Unless, of course, she had known all along where the sale of that pill bottle would lead; had let Kevin Bartley's killer know exactly who he was exchanging emails with and who would be on their way to discover the body. The message carved into it.

'What happened?' Herbert asked. 'Who was murdered?'

Tanner inched her chair forward. Whether Herbert knew or not, there was no reason to go into details. 'Have you ever had any direct communication with Stuart Nicklin?'

'*What?*'

'He's the man we believe to be responsible for the most recent murder and to have been instrumental in the previous three. He's also responsible for countless other murders and conspiracies to murder going back almost twenty years.' Tanner saw that Herbert was shaking her head, but pressed on. 'He's an extremely dangerous individual and his whereabouts are currently unknown.'

'I know who he is, for God's sake. You know full well I do. I sell his stuff, don't I?'

'*His* stuff?'

'Things he's ... connected to. I sell all sorts of things connected to all manner of nutters and psychos like him. Plenty *worse* than him, I promise you.'

'I doubt that,' Tanner said.

'Oh, there's a lot of sick bastards in this world.' Herbert nodded sadly; words of wisdom from an old soul.

Ignoring the temptation to remind the woman that the sicker the bastard the bigger her profits were, Tanner simply waited a few seconds. 'So, I'll ask you again,' she said. 'Have you ever had any direct communication with Stuart Nicklin?'

'Of course I bloody haven't. Why the hell would I?'

'Well, you've already admitted to knowing that the man selling that pill bottle was an associate of his.'

'That's hardly the same thing.'

'And, bearing in mind that Nicklin is a wanted criminal, I asked you why you hadn't informed the police of that fact.'

'Yeah, and I told you why, didn't I? Because I thought it was probably rubbish and he was just talking up his stupid pill bottle to get a bit more money for it. Happens all the time.'

Tanner sat back, ready for one last push. 'So, you've never talked to Stuart Nicklin on the phone?'

'Never.'

'Never exchanged written correspondence with him?'

'No.'

'Text messages or emails?'

'*No*. For heaven's sake . . . '

'I need to tell you, Margaret, that this is your last chance to be straight with me. If we find out later on in the investigation that you've been lying to us about this, we won't be able to help you.' She waited until she'd found the woman's watery blue eyes. 'Trust me, we won't *want* to help you.'

'Are you done?' When Tanner didn't reply immediately, Herbert reached into her handbag and took out her mobile phone. She showed it to Tanner, as if she might not know what it was. 'Because either I'm calling that taxi or I'm calling my solicitor. You choose.'

'I want to start by saying how much we appreciate the help you've given us so far.'

Cameron shrugged. 'I didn't have much choice, did I?'

'Greg Hobbs was seriously impressed by your computer skills.'

'Who?'

Thorne watched Cameron lope from one end of the room to another, then lean back against the wall as though he was bored stupid. 'It would be easier for both of us if you sat down,' Thorne said.

'Would it?'

'I think so.'

'I don't have to though, do I?'

'I'd rather you did.'

'When am I getting all my stuff back?'

'Sit *down.*' Thorne's reservoir of politeness was never particularly well stocked and it had finally run dry. He enjoyed the look of shock on the boy's face; watched him swallow, then quickly manufacture a couldn't-give-a-shit sneer as he ambled across to the empty chair like he was doing Thorne a favour.

Cameron sat, stretched his legs out and brushed at the bum-fluff on his chin. 'Happy?' He leaned back and folded his arms. 'So, when am I getting it back? My computer and that.'

'It's not going to be any time soon,' Thorne said. 'I'm guessing it'll need an update, put it that way.'

'Fuck's sake.'

'Out of my hands, Cam. Your computer's likely to be an important piece of evidence in a murder trial. In a couple, as it happens.'

Cameron shook his head; lost or trying very hard to appear that way.

Thorne told him much the same thing as Tanner was telling his grandmother in a room across the corridor. Once again, watching the lad's face change as the implication of what he was being told dawned on him, gave Thorne a moment or two of pleasure, which, of late, had been few and far between.

'Surely I'm entitled to compensation or something?' Cameron said.

'For what?'

'My computer. It's not my fault you need it, right?'

'We don't know that yet.'

Cameron narrowed his eyes. 'I'm not with you, mate.'

'Well, yes, you might be able to claim the cost of replacing all your electronics,' Thorne said, 'but not until we can establish that you had no involvement in the murder they played a considerable part in.'

'*What* involvement?'

'That's what I'm trying to find out.'

'How can I be . . . *involved*?'

'You knew what the plan was.'

Cameron took a few seconds, rubbed his face. 'Yeah, kind of . . . I mean, no, not really.'

'You knew that we would be posing as you online, sending those emails, talking to the man selling that pill bottle. You knew, because you'd met the man who'd be doing the pretending. You'd gone through all your passwords with him, all the technical stuff.'

'All right, I knew what you were up to. So what?'

'Because somebody else knew, and we're keen to find out how. You understand what I'm saying, Cameron?'

'Yeah, but I don't see what it's got to do with me.'

'Really?'

'I still don't know what I'm doing here, if I'm honest.'

'You're here to help, I hope.'

'Not sure I can.'

'You do remember who that bottle used to belong to?'

Cameron nodded, sighed. 'Nicklin, right? Yeah, he's one of my nan's top brands.'

The casual way the boy said it caused something to twist in Thorne's gut and he could feel the tension taking hold everywhere else. 'Yeah . . . that's him. A top brand. Now, the thing is, someone told him what our plan for that pill bottle was. I don't suppose you'd know anything about that?'

The penny dropped. 'Now hang on, mate—'

'The plan you've just acknowledged that you knew all about—'

'No way.' He sat back, shaking his head. 'No way ... you're not putting this on me. Why the hell would I want to tell him? I mean, never mind *how*, because I wouldn't have the first idea ... why would I?'

'Because you're afraid of him.' Thorne was staring, searching for a reaction. 'Or maybe because he told you that tipping him the wink when the likes of me came knocking would be worth your while financially. He's someone who can be very persuasive.'

'I wouldn't know.'

'Did he persuade *you*, Cameron?'

'Are you deaf or what?'

'I'm saying, it would be understandable.'

'Doesn't matter, because it didn't happen, I swear.'

'If it *was* you, I need you to tell me,' Thorne said.

'I'm *telling* you. Christ ...'

It was Thorne's turn to sigh, to shake his head. 'Well, we've got a problem then, because I'm not convinced that you're telling me the truth. Because you need to know that, until I am, I will not leave you or your grandmother alone. I will turn your pathetic little lives upside down and I won't lose a moment's sleep. I'll probably kick off by making sure the council knows that on top of the income support you're claiming from them, you've got a cushy little job going on the side with Grandma. Then I'll tell them that not only are you failing to declare earnings, but you're spending it all on drugs. Are you listening to me, Cameron? I will do whatever it takes. I'll have every copper in the area banging on your door three times a day and nicking you if they find so much as a packet of king-size Rizlas.'

'Shit.' The boy smiled. 'You're really getting desperate, aren't you—?'

Thorne's chair fell back as he jumped up, roaring, and with equal speed the boy was away from the table and scuttling back towards the wall.

'You've got no *fucking* idea.'

THIRTY-EIGHT

While Margaret Herbert was still arguing with the desk sergeant about claiming back the cost of her Uber, Thorne and Tanner were already heading south on the A12.

'I can't see it.' Thorne pulled into the outside lane and accelerated past a white van. 'Trust me, I wish I could, but the only thing those two care about is money.'

Tanner nodded. 'I don't think Margaret's quite as useless with technology as she pretends to be, but I don't buy her sending secret messages to Nicklin either. Cameron barely seems to know what day it is. So ... ?'

'So, Christ knows,' Thorne said. 'I don't know who the hell else it could be, but Nicklin found out what we were doing somehow. Unless ... I mean, he knew Driver would lead us to that scalpel, right? That was always the idea, and he could probably have figured out that from there we'd eventually get to murdermags48 and find that pill bottle.' He tapped at the steering wheel, staring hard at the white lines as they were sucked beneath the wheels; reaching for some explanation of what had happened over the previous few days that might be a little less alarming. 'So, when there's suddenly a buyer for that bottle, it might be a reasonable assumption that it's us.' He glanced at Tanner. 'So that's when he decides to set Bartley up.' He glanced again. 'Do you think?'

'He *knew*,' Tanner said. 'He wasn't guessing or assuming anything.'

Thorne leaned on the horn until the driver ahead indicated and moved over. 'No, course he wasn't. I'm just . . .'

Tanner watched Thorne's hand tighten around the wheel. 'Look, it could be that Margaret or Cameron or both of them are playing us every bit as much as Nicklin is. Maybe it *was* one of them, in which case there's every chance they'll make contact with Nicklin again.'

'I don't see why.'

'Neither do I, but we should consider the possibility, at least,' Tanner said. 'To be on the safe side.'

'OK.'

'We should get basic surveillance organised.'

'You think Nicklin might pop round to Margaret's place for a chat? Meet up with Cameron in the pub?'

Tanner ignored him. 'We've got the kid's computer, so any activity using his accounts or passwords, Hobbs would know about it. Obviously, that doesn't stop one of them just picking up the phone, so I think we should check all the landline records and get a warrant sorted for a phone intercept on both their mobile numbers.'

'It wasn't them,' Thorne said.

'It can't hurt though, can it?' Tanner took the grunt

she got in return as the correct response and immediately reached for her phone to set things in motion.

Thorne drove, half-listening to the call. He thought it was almost certainly a waste of time, but was willing to accept that it was probably the right thing to do. He had overlooked the obvious so often that it was starting to seem like a pattern.

A few miles further on, he said, 'I lost it a bit back there, in the interview room. With Cameron.'

Tanner turned to look at him. 'Right . . . '

'I mean, nothing . . . *bad*.'

'OK.'

'Just the red mist, you know.' Thorne saw the look on Nicola Tanner's face, watched her turn away, and wished he'd found some other way to say it. Or hadn't said it at all. They both knew how familiar she was with the red mist; exactly how bad it could get. 'Felt like it's been coming a while, if I'm honest. Ever since . . . well, when we found out who we were dealing with.'

'Understandable, Tom.'

'Trust me, I'm as angry with myself as I should be, because . . . well, we're not in an episode of *The Sweeney*, are we?' He laughed, but there wasn't much to it and it died quickly enough.

They both stared ahead for another minute or so; passed a sign that told them they were only half an hour away from London.

'Do you think you should talk to someone?' Tanner asked.

Thorne turned to stare at her for as long as was safe. 'I'm talking to you, aren't I?'

THIRTY-NINE

As always, when they were spending the night at Melita's place, they sat and had dinner at the island in her kitchen. She'd bought a baguette – which Thorne's father had always called a 'French stick' – and laid out a selection of cheeses, though Thorne was happy enough with Cheddar. There was a small TV in the corner and as they ate they watched a documentary about an executive business programme which, in the end, had turned out to be a sex cult, and Thorne wondered when islands had become a thing.

How had he missed that memo?

He couldn't remember seeing any when he was a kid. There'd been a kitchen table in his house growing up and a kitchen table in the house he'd lived in when he and Jan were married. Thinking about it, it might well have been the same kitchen table he now had in his flat. So, when did people decide to throw out their perfectly good kitchen tables and have islands installed? He guessed it was probably around the same time sheets and blankets were replaced by duvets – which his father had always called 'continental quilts' – and people started having showers instead of baths.

Melita watched him slather butter on his bread before cutting off a healthy slice of Cheddar. 'That's very un-French,' she said.

'What?'

'Butter *and* cheese. The French think that's appalling.'

'Exactly why I'm doing it,' Thorne said.

On the documentary, people had begun to ask serious questions after some of the programme's female members were branded with the leader's initials. Melita grunted her disgust.

'I should know better by now,' she said. 'But it still amazes me.'

Thorne looked at her and she nodded towards the screen.

'The things people are prepared to go through or do to other people when they believe in someone enough.'

Thorne reached for more bread. He wasn't amazed at all.

'So what's next?' Melita asked.

'You haven't got any Branston pickle, have you?'

She laughed. 'With the case?'

This was the first time Thorne had seen her since the clusterfuck in Coventry. He'd called her on the way back to London to let her know how it had gone and she'd sounded especially concerned about the message left for him on Kevin Bartley's body. She'd asked him how he felt about it and, with Tanner sitting next to him in the car, he'd brushed it off; made some stupid joke about how a postcard would have saved everyone a lot of trouble.

'Maybe he just didn't want to pay for a stamp.'

While Melita had been opening wine and laying out the bread and cheese, he'd told her about the fruitless trip to Colchester to talk to Margaret and Cameron Herbert. He'd told her they were still none the wiser about how Nicklin had known what they were up to. He hadn't mentioned losing his temper in the interview room.

How good it had felt.

How he'd lied to Tanner about being angry with himself.

'Back to Rebecca Driver, I suppose,' he said. 'She's still the only genuine connection to Nicklin we've got.'

'Really? She didn't seem very willing to answer questions last time.'

'She might be a bit more inclined to talk, now she's had a week in prison.'

'Just remember, it's probably exactly what she wants. You going to see her. The power to withhold information, even if she hasn't actually got any, is the only power she has left.'

'I know,' Thorne said. 'If you've got any better ideas . . . ?'

'Sorry.'

A few minutes later, loading the dishwasher, Melita said, 'Is everything all right?'

Thorne immediately wondered if Tanner had said something; called or sent an email. After all, why would he need to *talk to* anybody when his girlfriend was a professional?

'Everything's fine,' he said.

She smiled and nodded. She closed the dishwasher and moved back to the island. 'You've just been a bit quiet, that's all. I thought maybe you were pissed off with me for some reason.'

'Oh. I thought *you* were pissed off with *me*.'

'Why?'

'I don't know. Like ... you were being distant or something.'

'Well, I'm sorry.'

Thorne shook his head. 'Forget it, I'm just being stupid. Seriously, this is the best I've felt in days.'

'Good.' She leaned to kiss him, then reached for her wine. 'It's hard to tell with you sometimes.'

The documentary finished and she began looking for something else to watch.

'I was thinking about Christmas,' Thorne said.

'OK.'

'What you wanted to do.'

She nodded.

'I mean, you've probably got some family stuff.' Melita's parents had moved back to Sri Lanka a few years before, but there was a sister Thorne hadn't met yet; nephews and nieces. He guessed there would be commitments.

'Only on Boxing Day, but if you're planning to whisk me off to Barbados I'm not going to argue.'

'Unlikely, if I'm honest,' Thorne said.

'Well, Crouch End works just as well. Or Kentish Town. I don't mind.'

'Whatever's easiest ... but I'm happy to cook Christmas lunch.'

'I'll cook,' she said.

Thorne nodded, relieved. 'Fine. I'll sort out a tree.'

'You're on,' she said. 'Just not one of those horrible silver ones.'

FORTY

If Rebecca Driver was as happy to see Thorne as Melita had suggested might be the case, she wasn't letting her face know about it. Thorne guessed it was the fact that they were surrounded by dozens of her fellow prisoners and their visitors, even if nobody else in there seemed remotely interested in him or the woman he was here to see. The choice of the public visits area had been a deliberate one, based on what Melita had said to him the previous evening. It was not an official interview and he was here alone, so a private visits room was not necessary anyway. More important, though, he did not want Rebecca Driver to feel special.

She sat staring down at her shoes or up at the ceiling; glancing across once or twice towards a woman on the other side of the room. Thorne wondered if it was a prisoner Driver had become friendly with, or perhaps one with whom she'd fallen out. It didn't much matter, because he was in no mood to waste any time.

'I want to talk about Stuart Nicklin,' he said.

Now she looked at him. In their last conversation, before Driver had been charged and taken away, Thorne had tried and failed to ascertain where she had obtained the scalpel, knowing full well who it had once belonged to. In her first interview with Tanner and Chall, Driver had been happy enough to talk about the person who had influenced her so much, and before the session with Melita had been cut short she'd seemed more than willing to discuss that special someone all over again.

This was the first time the *someone* had been mentioned by name.

'Well, course you do,' she said. 'You've got a thing for him.'

'What makes you say that?'

'I read all about it.'

Thorne nodded. 'The Campbell book.'

'You read it?'

'I've got better things to do,' Thorne said.

'You're a liar.'

She sat back and folded her arms. It had only been a week, so the change was subtle, but Thorne could see it. Rather, he could see the effort she was making to disguise it; the sullen expression and the slumped shoulders. The regulation attitude to go along with the regulation grey sweatshirt and blue bib. He'd seen it at the station a week before, or thought he had. A glimpse of the lost and lonely girl who had become a vicious killer.

Only a week, but now she'd had a taste of it.

The noise and the stink and the bludgeon of time that would beat out the rest of her life.

Thorne sensed the fear and he hoped it might give him a chance.

'I'm not here to talk about my relationship with Nicklin,' he said.

'That's a shame.'

'I'm much more interested in yours.'

She blinked and shrugged. She said, 'You wouldn't understand.'

'You think you're the first? You think you're the only one he's ever chosen? You obviously didn't read that book very carefully.' She looked away again and Thorne could see the muscles working in her jaw. 'I'm guessing it was all emails, the communication with him. I know you'd have preferred handwritten letters doused in his after-shave, but we can't have everything we want.'

She looked back at him and smiled. 'I got what I wanted.'

Thorne looked around. 'Really? Was this what you signed up for, Rebecca?'

The smile stayed in place, but her eyes slid away from his. 'I got what I wanted.'

'I'm happy for you. So, what difference would it make if I saw all those emails? I know they're just sitting there on that flash-drive we found, so where's the harm in letting us take a look? All I need is the password, then I'll have the full story. *Your* story. Isn't that what you want? I know how proud of it you are.'

'Yes, I am, but that doesn't mean I want to share it with you. It's between me and Stuart.'

'So there are things Stuart wouldn't want me to see?'

'You'll see what he wants you to see, when he decides it's the right time.'

'What does that mean?'

She shook her head, gnawing at fingernails that Thorne

could see were already bitten to the quick. 'Isn't this where you offer me something?'

'What do you want?'

'Nothing you can give me. I mean you can hardly promise me a reduced sentence, can you?'

'No, I can't.'

'Not when I did *three*.' She held up three fingers, just in case Thorne had forgotten.

Richard Sumner, Hari Reddy, Thomas Bristow.

Thorne wanted to reach across and snap every finger. He wanted to see her face distorted by pain and ask just how *special* and *different* she felt now. Instead, he nodded, acknowledging her achievement. 'I know you're doing everything you can to serve your sentence in a hospital, but even with those there are good places and bad places. A secure unit's still a prison, just with a few more doctors around and a couple of beanbags. We can make sure you wind up in one of the better ones.'

'You could do that?'

'If you help us, I'll do my best.' He wouldn't, of course, but right then Thorne was willing to promise anything.

It didn't matter.

She pressed a hand across her mouth, as though she was trying to stop herself laughing. 'You really are a shit liar, but fair play for giving it a go. Don't feel too bad, though, because even if I thought you could work some miracle and get me acquitted, I still wouldn't give you what you wanted.' She leaned towards Thorne, eyes wide and bright. 'I would never give up the smallest piece of him.'

'I'm sure he would be very moved by your loyalty,' Thorne said.

'He deserves it.'

'People less sensitive than me might say it just goes to show how stupid you really are . . . what with him still out there and you spending the rest of your life inside.'

She stared, as though Thorne was the stupid one. 'Him *being* out there . . . that's the main thing.'

Thorne remembered what Melita had said about the power of information; of holding on to it. He leaned close and said, 'I'm not convinced you know anything that would be of any use to me at all, but just supposing that you do . . . you keep it to yourself. See how much good it does you six months from now, when people are pissing in your tea every day, or someone you've looked at the wrong way gets clumsy with a kettle of boiling water.' Thorne reached for the jacket he'd folded over the chair behind him.

'Stuart *has* got plans for you.' She enjoyed seeing Thorne freeze, then turn slowly back to her. 'Just in case you were feeling a bit neglected.'

'You talking about Kevin Bartley?'

'Who?'

'K-Man. The message.' Thorne waited for a reaction, but he could see that she did not recognise the name.

'*Fun* plans. Now, don't waste your time asking what they are, because that would spoil the surprise. Like I said, when the time comes.'

Thorne stood up and pulled the jacket on.

She sat and watched him. 'Why are you even here?' She waved to one of the guards to make it clear she was ready to go back to the wing. 'Why would you even think I might want to help you?'

It was a good question. 'Fuck knows.' Watching the guard

walking towards them, Thorne felt as though he was the one about to be led away to a cell, and for a few moments it seemed perfectly reasonable. Like it would be no less than he deserved. 'Because I'm an idiot. Because I thought maybe there was still some bit of you in there, some sliver of something that hadn't been . . . poisoned. Stupid, obviously, because nothing he's touched can ever be good again.'

The guard arrived and stood behind the chair, waiting for her prisoner to move, but Driver wanted the last word.

She looked up at Thorne. 'Does that include you?'

FORTY-ONE

Thorne had left for HMP Bronzefield just after ten o'clock, but even though Ashford was only an hour's drive away, Tanner guessed he wouldn't be back until the afternoon. She didn't know how long his conversation with Rebecca Driver would last, but she knew very well that security procedures meant nobody got in and out of a prison very quickly, not even police officers. She was just trying to decide what to do about lunch when Phil Hendricks called and asked if she fancied the Oak.

Tanner was at the pub before him. She ordered Diet Coke and a bowl of soup and sat at a table in the corner. She remembered the last time she had eaten here, the day after she'd called Thorne in a state, and now here she was waiting for the only other person who would understand exactly why she'd been so upset.

Not that she had any intention of talking about *that*.

It wasn't *exactly* like they were in a saloon with the music stopping when Hendricks eventually pushed through the doors, but the man knew how to make an entrance and, in a bar almost full of besuited coppers or business types, his appearance was certainly noticed. Tanner waved to let him know where she was, then watched him walk to the bar to order.

When he sat down, he raised his glass in a toast to the two women staring from the next table, then stuck his tongue behind his bottom lip to move the spike around.

'You're such a child,' Tanner said.

'Trust me, there's far worse things I could show them.'

'Please don't put those pictures in my head.'

'You know you love it.' Hendricks leaned across and whispered. 'Lying there every night, thinking about the studs in my ball-bag and flicking your peanut into the wee small hours—'

He stopped and sat back, grinning when the barman came across with his meal; laying down the plate then setting out oversized salt and pepper grinders and cutlery wrapped in a paper serviette.

The barman smiled and said, 'Enjoy.'

Hendricks stared at the atrocity in front of him. 'Is he kidding?' He turned the plate around, as though what was on it might look more appetising from a different angle. 'This looks like it might have actual shepherd in it.'

'Oh.' Tanner was laughing. 'I should have warned you.'

'This is why you should only ever eat snacks in pubs.' He shook his head. 'What the hell.' He dug in, wincing at the first mouthful, but pressing on.

'I'm honoured,' Tanner said. 'You coming all the way up here for lunch.'

Hendricks swallowed, grimacing. 'I'm starting to wish I hadn't bothered.'

'Don't you usually go to that greasy spoon opposite the hospital?'

'Just fancied a change ... and I'd forgotten how warm the welcome was in here.' He turned to smile again at the women at the next table, but they'd lost interest. 'So, what's happening?'

While they ate, Tanner gave him what little news there was. Stuart Nicklin's fingerprints had been found on the computer taken from Kevin Bartley's flat in Coventry. This confirmed Greg Hobbs's theory about when K-Man had been killed, while the brain matter caked on to the empty wine bottle in the living room had given them a pretty good idea how.

'The pathologist up there reckons Bartley was still alive when Nicklin started cutting.'

'Yeah, he's fond of that,' Hendricks said.

'So, that's where we are.'

'Which is ... ?'

Tanner held up her hands. 'We know exactly who we're looking for, but we haven't got the first bloody idea where to start.' She used a last chunk of bread to mop up what was left of her soup. 'He hasn't been Stuart Nicklin for a long time, that's our biggest problem. There's no point looking for phone records or car registrations or council tax or in any of the places we'd normally go to, because we don't know who the hell we're actually trying to find. Basically, we don't know who he *is*.' She brushed crumbs from her lap and sat back. 'We don't even know what he looks like any more.'

'You think he'll have changed his appearance?'

'Well, unless he's an idiot and we know he's not that. Tom

told me that the first time he went to see him in prison, Nicklin was almost unrecognisable.'

'Yeah, well, prison can do that.'

'Right, but when he showed up on Bardsey Island a few years after that, he looked different again. He'd made the effort to change himself even when there wasn't much point. I'm just saying, with access to money and plastic surgery or whatever . . .'

'Yeah, I get it.' The mood was darkening a little, inevitably and when Hendricks sat forward suddenly, it was obvious that he was keen to do something about it. 'So, who would *you* look like, if you had the choice?'

'Well, I haven't got the money, for a start.'

'If you did, though.'

Tanner thought about it. 'Elle Macpherson, maybe?'

'Christ, I didn't mean *that* much money.'

Tanner laughed and gave him the finger. Said, 'What about you, then?'

Hendricks raised his hands up to frame his face. 'You can't improve on perfection, mate.'

They both laughed, needing it; smiling at each other while the barman cleared their dirty crockery away and shaking their heads in unison when he asked if they would like to see the dessert menu.

'So, what now then?'

'Well, most suspects do the job for you in the end,' Tanner said. 'They slip up. Nicklin's not most suspects, though. I don't know . . . maybe he'll take one too many of his ecstasy tablets and we'll find him dancing in the middle of the road somewhere, off his tits.'

'Maybe Tom can get something out of Rebecca Driver.'

265

Tanner nodded. 'Right.'

So Hendricks knew about Thorne's trip to Bronzefield. Thorne had obviously mentioned it to him, but more important, it meant that Hendricks had known, when he'd called her, that Thorne would not be there when they were having lunch. She watched him lean towards her and began to breathe just a little faster, the panic starting to build; knowing now that Hendricks had come to talk about the very thing she so desperately wanted to avoid.

'I wanted to ask you something.'

'Listen, Phil—'

'Do you think Tom's OK?'

Tanner tried not to let her relief show. 'How do you mean?'

'He seemed a bit ... off, the other night. He told me he was fine, but you know what he's like.'

Tanner certainly did, though she didn't know him nearly as well as Phil Hendricks, so she wasn't going to take the pathologist's concern lightly. 'He blew up a bit yesterday, as it happens.'

'Blew up?'

'He just lost his temper, but we can all do that, so ...' She looked away and they both waited a few seconds, until the charge of what should have been a harmless comment had dissipated.

'I think it's starting to get to him, that's all.'

Tanner nodded. 'He was definitely shaken up by that message. Well, he's been a bit edgy ever since he found out who we're dealing with, but why wouldn't you be? I'm not exactly chilled about it, myself.' She watched Hendricks as he fiddled with one of the many rings in his ear. 'What about you?'

'What about me?'

'How are *you* doing? I mean, apart from Tom, if anyone has a right to be freaked out that Nicklin's knocking around again, it's you.'

'Don't worry about me.' Hendricks shrugged and sniffed, carried on worrying at the metal in his ear. 'I'm right as ninepence, mate.'

'Are you sure?'

'Just ... keep an eye on him, will you? You see a lot more of him than anyone else. For which you deserve a medal, obviously.'

Tanner said, 'No worries, Phil.'

Once they'd paid the bill and stepped away from the table, Hendricks put an arm through Tanner's. 'Trust me, Nic, you are way hotter than Elle Macpherson.'

'You're full of shit.'

'I'm telling you.' He leered theatrically. 'If I was straight ...'

'Yeah, and if I was.'

'If we were *both* spectacularly pissed.'

Tanner could see that Hendricks was still drawing the attention of several customers as the two of them walked towards the exit. She opened the doors and they stepped out into the afternoon chill. They shivered and swore.

'Tell me you haven't got studs in your ball-bag,' she said.

'That's for me to know and you to find out.'

Tanner dug a scarf from her bag. 'There isn't enough booze in the world.'

FORTY-TWO

'What the fuck does *plans* mean, anyway?' Thorne asked.

'It doesn't mean anything,' Tanner said. 'This is what she wants . . . you worrying about it.'

'Who's worrying?'

'Nicola's right,' Brigstocke said. 'By the sound of it, she knows bugger all about bugger all. She's just winding you up.'

Mid-afternoon and the three of them were sitting in Russell Brigstocke's office. It hadn't taken very long for Thorne to run through the highlights of his trip to HMP Bronzefield. The visit with Rebecca Driver that had kicked off with an over-enthusiastic pat-down after going through the security scanner, then gone downhill from there.

'That's what I told her,' Thorne said. 'That I didn't think she actually knew anything useful, but to be honest I couldn't swear to it. I was just trying to get a read, you know?'

'It's just games,' Tanner said. 'It's what they do . . . the likes of Driver and that arsehole she bows down to.'

'Bang on,' Brigstocke said.

'Ask Melita what she thinks.'

Thorne was thrown momentarily, annoyed for no reason he could put his finger on, until he realised that Tanner was talking about a professional opinion.

'Yeah, that's what she thinks,' he said.

'Well, that lad Hobbs at the DFU is still on the case,' Brigstocke said. 'If there *is* a way to get into Driver's memory stick without a password, he'll find it.'

'I wouldn't bet against him,' Tanner said. 'There's nerds and there's . . . *super* nerds, right?' She smiled and looked at Thorne, but his expression didn't change. It hadn't changed a great deal since he'd got back from Ashford. It was not an expression she recalled seeing too many times before, but the truth was, he looked . . . cowed.

'Even if he does, I doubt very much there'd be anything in those emails that would help us find Nicklin.'

'Worth persevering, though,' Brigstocke said.

'Yeah, if you like.'

If Brigstocke's sigh wasn't loud enough, the look on his face made his irritation clear enough, and the removal of the glasses was rarely a good sign. 'Sorry, Tom . . . there I was thinking this was a strategy meeting. A catch-up between senior members of the team. I hadn't realised we were basically here to cheer you up. I mean, you can sit in the corner with some crayons, if you want, and me and Nicola can get on with . . . you know, working.'

Thorne mumbled an apology, threw in a 'Sir'.

'Look, I know this is personal for you. Our suspect, being who he is, has made it personal. I accept that, but if I start to think it's interfering with your ability to do your job—'

'It isn't.'

Brigstocke glanced at Tanner. 'Or with anybody else's.'

'We're good.' Tanner looked at Thorne. 'Right?'

Thorne just stared, confused and panicky suddenly at the turn things were taking. He wasn't sure what he'd done wrong.

Tanner rolled her eyes at Brigstocke. 'I think maybe Spurs lost again last night.'

'Can we just crack on?' Thorne said.

'Absolutely.' Brigstocke put his glasses back on. 'So, the West Midlands lot are still looking at cameras near to Bartley's flat, running every registration plate, hoping we can identify a vehicle. They're also checking all the local taxi firms, in case Nicklin went up to Coventry by train and got a cab from the station.'

'What about witnesses?' Tanner asked.

Brigstocke nodded and looked at his notes. 'The house-to-house turned up a couple from the block Bartley lived in. One who reckons they saw a man arrive at a time that fits and another one who might have seen him leave. They're putting together an e-fit.'

'That'll be huge,' Tanner said.

Thorne certainly looked as though he was paying close attention, but he had already begun zoning out, knowing he was not going to hear anything to get very excited about. He made the occasional supportive comment and nodded in all the right places, but it was like hearing snippets of a tune he vaguely recognised through a wash of hiss and feedback. He could focus on little else but the plans Rebecca Driver had mentioned; had been thinking about them all the way back to London.

Fun plans.

Yes, of course she'd been playing games and no, Thorne did not believe for one minute that she knew exactly what those plans were.

But he was in no doubt whatsoever that Nicklin had them.

Outside Brigstocke's office, Thorne stopped and said, 'What the hell was all that about?'

'All what?'

'"Maybe Spurs lost again last night" . . . like you've got to make stupid excuses for me, like I need . . . explaining away.'

'Now, hang on—'

'Like the way I'm feeling about all this is a joke.'

'Nobody thinks it's a joke, Tom.'

'And all that "we're great" bollocks, which was probably meant to sound reassuring and all for one and one for all or whatever, but which sounded to me very much like "don't worry, I'll keep an eye on him".'

Tanner looked at him. 'Have you finished?'

'It is allowed, you know,' Thorne said. 'To look at where we are with this . . . to count the bodies, then count up all those white-hot leads we've got and decide that, all things considered, we're up against it. That's putting a positive spin on it, by the way.'

'I'm not disagreeing with you,' Tanner said. 'It's pretty much what I said to Phil.'

'When did you talk to Phil?'

'We had lunch,' Tanner said. 'In the Oak.'

'OK.' Thorne tried his best to look as if it was. It would take something fairly serious to distract him – even briefly – from the Nicklin-shaped shitstorm he knew was on its way, but Tanner and Hendricks having a cosy lunchtime chin-wag about a very different kind of disaster would do the job nicely. 'How's he doing?'

'Same as ever,' Tanner said. 'Talking filth and scaring the horses.'

Thorne said nothing.

She glanced up and down the corridor, shook her head. 'We didn't . . .'

Thorne nodded then walked away towards the incident room. Tanner followed a few seconds later, but made no attempt to narrow the distance between them.

By the time Tanner caught up with him fifteen minutes later, Thorne was at the drinks station, trying to decide if the disgusting coffee might give him something else to think about for a while.

Tanner stepped close. She said, 'Don't do it.' Then, 'Fancy a drink at close of play?'

'Not sure I'd be the best company.'

'Oh, stop feeling so sorry for yourself, you silly twat.' She leaned against him, but nothing seemed to give. 'Come on, I reckon you could do with a few beers and I know I could.'

Thorne knew that, later on, he would need those beers, but he wasn't so sure that he wanted anyone else around while he drank them. 'Seriously, Nic . . . I think I'll probably give it a miss.'

'Suit yourself.'

'Oh, and Spurs didn't *have* a game last night.' Thorne wasn't smiling when he said it, but it didn't much matter because Tanner had her back to him, already walking away.

FORTY-THREE

There were nicer pubs than the Railway; *far* nicer ones if he could be bothered to go into the centre of Ashford, but it was handy. It was ten minutes' walk from work and from there – once he'd had his pint, his two pints at the most – it was only another five to the bus stop.

You looked at it like that, the pub was on the way home.

Gordon Ames didn't call in at the Railway every day, nothing like, in fact, but some days were tougher than others. It was the nature of the job, he accepted that, and the day he'd just had was definitely one of those that called for a certain amount of ... decompression. He smiled, pushing through the scarred wooden doors into the bar, because it was something Jill always ribbed him about. On those very rare occasions when he stopped off for more than one or two and eventually rolled in squiffy, she'd always be waiting up with that look on her face; shaking her head while she pulled something together from the fridge and asking him if he was feeling nice and *decompressed*.

As decompressed as a newt.

His wife didn't mind, though; she told him often enough. She knew how hard the job could be.

Tonight it would be just the one though, because Jill was making that chicken and pasta thing he loved, on top of which he'd promised his eldest boy that they could play a bit of *FIFA 22* together. Actually, a session on the PlayStation helped take the edge off every bit as much as the beer, and he joked with some of the other officers that he was turning into something of an addict.

'Pint of the usual, Gordon?'

That was another thing that made it worth dropping in for a quick one. He felt like he was in an episode of *Cheers*, and even if the banter wasn't quite up to that level it *was* nice that the barman knew his name and what his tipple was. Some of the things he got called at work, some of the shit that got thrown at him – literally, on several occasions – it was a relief to feel human again.

He carried his pint of Black Swan across to an empty table. He tore open a bag of crisps, which was OK because Jill wouldn't have the pasta ready for at least an hour yet. He took out his phone and sent a text message to his son.

Hope you're ready to be owned x

He got a reply before he'd finished his crisps.

bring it on loser

'Do you mind . . . ?'

Ames glanced up to see a man pulling out the chair

opposite him. He shook his head, grunted, 'Help yourself,' then looked away again as the man sat down.

He did mind, obviously. It was like when you bagged a table and four empty seats on a train, then some bugger came and sat down when there were plenty of other seats available. Ames lifted his glass and looked around; it was early, so there were loads of other tables this bloke could have chosen. It didn't matter that much, he decided. As soon as he'd finished his drink, he'd be away.

'Tough day at work?'

Ames looked up again. 'Sorry?'

The man shook his head, like it didn't matter, like he was only messing about. He raised his glass and said 'Cheers', so Ames did the same because it was only polite, then went back to his phone.

'Rather you than me.'

Ames looked up again.

'I mean, I should imagine *every* day's tough.'

Same as on a train, it was even worse when the unwelcome companion was a talker, and Ames wondered how rude it would look if he just got up and moved to another table. He quickly decided it would be easier to just neck his beer and head out. It was a shame, because he'd wanted to savour it and relax a little, but the last thing he needed was a row.

He took a healthy gulp.

'I'm just saying, it can't be a picnic, stuck in there, every day.'

Ames watched the man nod in what he could only assume was the direction of the prison. 'What?'

'I certainly don't envy you, Gordon.'

'Sorry . . . do I know you?' Ames asked.

There was a half-smile before the stranger bobbed his head like a bird to take a drink. 'You do now.'

Ames looked at him. The man was wearing a dark puffa jacket and a baseball cap and there was something weird going on with his face. The nose and the chin were . . . all wrong, and his skin was far too smooth. Shiny, almost. Ames reckoned the bloke was forty or thereabouts, but it was hard to be sure and he was starting to wish he'd just got up when he'd first thought about it and marched straight out of the pub.

'Listen, I don't know what your problem is, but I think—'

'Hard to come away unscathed, I would have thought. Working in a place like that. You're on a knife-edge all the time, aren't you? All that pent-up aggression, and women are worse than men . . . trust me, I know what I'm talking about. I mean, it can't be good for you, can it? Being hated.' The man shuffled his chair forward a little, hunched his shoulders and leaned across the table. 'Because nobody likes a screw, do they?' He shook his head, sadly. 'Who in their right mind loves a kanga?'

Ames knew now that he should leave, that whatever was going on, it could not possibly end well. He looked towards the bar, hoping to catch the barman's eye and somehow let him know that there was a problem.

'I can see why you'd need a little something at the end of the day, I mean, who the hell wouldn't? Something to make you feel a little better, to make you feel normal. So you're not carrying all that hatred home to Jill and the boys.'

'*What* did you say?'

Ames moved to stand up, but the man quickly reached across and took hold of his wrist; squeezed it just hard enough.

'Calm down, Gordon, for pity's sake.' There was a chuckle in the man's voice and his tone remained perfectly calm. Perfectly reasonable. He hadn't actually spoken in much more than a murmur since he'd sat down. He waited until Ames had settled before removing his hand and giving Ames's a little pat. 'Right then. Now you stay there and finish your cheese and onion, while I go and get us another drink.'

Gordon Ames could only stare as the man got to his feet.

'Black Swan, was it . . . ?'

Sometimes even Hank Williams couldn't do the trick.

Yes, there had been a lifetime of physical pain and an addiction to painkillers that had lasted almost as long. There had been a toxic marriage which it had taken him far too long to escape and several thousand bottles in which he'd tried to lose himself. He had worked like a demon and died at twenty-nine looking like a man twice his age, but Thorne doubted that Williams ever had to deal with someone sending him messages carved into human flesh.

Hank did sadness like nobody else, but he didn't write about fear.

Thorne briefly tried to distract himself by imagining just how the Hillbilly Shakespeare might have turned the machinations of a madman into a jaunty jukebox hit. A yodelling serial killer. He gave up when the only word he could come up with to rhyme with Nicklin was picklin' and even the spasm of pleasure that gave him immediately soured and became unbearable.

He got up from the sofa and turned the music off.

He walked through to the kitchen and made himself a sandwich, but left half because the bread tasted stale.

He went back and laid down on the sofa again.

Sometime later, Melita called, but he couldn't bring himself to answer it, or listen to the message that she left.

Stop feeling so sorry for yourself, you silly twat.

Tanner was right of course, on both counts, but knowing didn't make him feel any less sorry, did it? It didn't shine a light that might show him the way out. So, instead he lay there and tried and failed to lose himself in somewhat fewer bottles than Hank might have reached for. He gave in to it until he became sorrier still and felt like even more of a twat, consoling himself with the thought that, unlike Hank's, his own pain would surely not last a lifetime.

He thought about calling Tanner to apologise, but didn't.

He thought about calling Phil, just to listen to him talk for a while.

He thought about *plans*.

He might even have slept at some point, it was hard to be sure. There might have been dreams, but the darkness that swirled, solidified and wrapped itself like a stinking hand around his face could just as easily have been something he'd justifiably imagined while he was wide awake. Either way, when Thorne looked at his watch, it was several hours later than it had been the last time he'd checked, and he was still staring at the spot where the wall met the ceiling.

Watching that fucking cobweb dance.

FORTY-FOUR

By the time Thorne got to his office, it was apparent that Nicola Tanner had been there before him. He sauntered into the incident room and found her and Dipak Chall working at HOLMES, inputting intel on the domestic murder case they were still both working.

He held out the box of crayons that had been left on his desk. 'Funny,' he said, deadpan.

'I thought so,' she said.

'Russell's idea?'

'Mine.'

Thorne couldn't maintain the non-committal expression for very long. He smiled and nodded, rattling the box. 'Yeah, funny.'

Chall looked up. 'What is?'

'You had to be there,' Thorne said, though he was rather glad that, Brigstocke and Tanner aside, no one else had been.

He was embarrassed about the way he'd behaved, felt that Tanner at least was owed an apology.

'How was your evening?' Tanner asked.

'I've had better. What about you?'

She waited until Chall was staring at his computer screen, then looked at Thorne and nodded back towards the office they shared. Thorne talked to Chall about sod all for a couple of minutes, said 'I'll leave you to it', then headed back the way he'd come and waited for Tanner to join him.

'What's the big mystery, then?' he asked, when she'd closed the door behind her.

She sat down at her desk, straightened some papers. 'I had a date.'

'Bloody hell,' Thorne said.

'See, that's why I wasn't sure I should tell you, because I knew you'd make a song and dance about it.'

'I'm not,' he said. 'I'm just . . . I think that's great.'

Tanner looked dubious; about Thorne or about the date, it was hard to tell which.

'So, where did you meet her?'

Tanner found more papers to straighten, a pen to pop back into the mug where it lived with a dozen others. 'It was a dating app.'

'OK . . .'

'It's called *Scissr*, if you really want to know.' She shook her head, watching Thorne struggling to suppress a smirk. 'Screw you.'

'Sorry, it's just the name.'

'I'm registered on a few of them, actually,' Tanner said. 'I started looking around when we were checking out all those apps Rebecca Driver had used. Just logged on and started swiping, you know? Felt a bit weird, if I'm honest . . . using a series of horrible murders as a springboard for putting myself back out there. Is that bad?'

Thorne shrugged. 'I worked with a DC once who shagged a murder victim's wife the day after the bloke's funeral. I mean, I don't think the couple had been all that close, but still.' He clapped his hands. 'Anyway, never mind . . . let's have some details. Blonde? Brunette? Younger than you or older? OK, forget all that . . . was she hot?'

'She was, as it happens. Well, I thought she was.'

Thorne saw the hesitancy. 'But . . . ?'

'I knew more or less straight away it wasn't going to work out.'

'Don't tell me, she doesn't like cats. Or she doesn't wash up as she goes along. Oh, I know, she doesn't reorganise her handbag once a week.'

'She's a copper,' Tanner said.

'Ah . . .'

'Uniform, over in Hackney.' She shook her head. 'I reckon that's just asking for trouble. Too much Job all round. Well, you know that better than anyone.'

Thorne was in no position to argue with Tanner's hypothesis. She had been on the spot to witness his relationship with DI Helen Weeks going down in flames. She had provided a shoulder to cry on, or more accurately been someone sympathetic to rant at.

Thorne wasn't sure he'd ever thanked her properly.

'Sadly, I do know,' he said. He watched Tanner logging on to her computer, as though the conversation was done with. 'Hang on . . . so there might not have been any wedding bells ringing, but you said yourself she was hot. So, I mean, did you not just fancy . . .'

'No,' Tanner said. 'I did not *just fancy*, and even if I did, I didn't get the impression that's what she was after.' She shrugged. 'Dinner was nice, though.' She began to type.

Thorne watched her for half a minute. 'Listen, I wanted to say sorry for being such an arsehole yesterday. More of an arsehole than usual, I should say. I was out of order.'

Tanner didn't look up. 'It's fine,' she said. 'Gave me something to talk about on my date. Now, haven't you got any work to do?'

Thorne was smiling as he typed his own log-in.

'Oh, and washing up as you go along is just common sense.'

They worked solidly through the morning: on Tanner's domestic and on Thorne's gang-related stabbing; on statements from witnesses to a serious assault that, according to the hospital where the victim now lay in a coma, could well become a murder; and on a fatal hit and run that had come in overnight. They managed the best part of three hours without any mention of Stuart Nicklin or the cases that bore his fingerprints, and had almost finished lunch in the canteen when Thorne's mobile rang.

When the news began to come through about a major incident at HMP Bronzefield.

While the majority of those who worked in the building were already drifting towards car park, bus stop or tube station, Russell Brigstocke was passing information sheets across a large table in the meeting room. Thorne took his and began to read. Details had been coming in – piecemeal and occasionally conflicting – throughout the afternoon, from the prison authorities and from the local homicide unit on site,

282

but this was the first chance he and the rest of the team had been given to find out what had happened.

What those at the scene thought had happened, anyway.

'So, Rebecca Driver was found dead in her cell at HMP Bronzefield just after midday.' Brigstocke looked down at the hastily compiled sheet, the list of bullet points. 'It appears to have been a stabbing with a home-made weapon, and as the victim was seen on the wing around an hour before that they're putting the time of death at somewhere between eleven o'clock and midday. The team from Kent police that are handling this have taken a thirty-nine-year-old woman into custody and are currently questioning staff and prisoners, but at this time there's no obvious motive for the killing.' The DCI laid the sheet of paper down and sat back. 'Jesus, what a nightmare.'

Whatever their personal thoughts about what had been done to Rebecca Driver, nobody around the table was in any doubt that the DCI was talking about logistics; the organisational complexities involved in what would now be three different forces working together on cases that were obviously linked.

'Maybe she just pissed the wrong person off,' Chall said.

'No chance,' Thorne said. The connection between the three cases – the man who connected them – was blindingly obvious and he didn't think his colleagues in Kent police would need to spend too long looking for their motive. 'She was killed because I went to visit her.'

'We don't know that, Tom,' Brigstocke said.

'Course we do.'

'It's possible, I'm not saying it isn't . . . or Dipak might be

283

right.' Thorne was shaking his head, but Brigstocke ignored it. 'Either way we need to let the Kent team get on with it. We pass on any relevant intelligence, obviously, we pass on our thoughts, but we don't tell them how to do their job. If we do, it'll be muggins here that has to deal with the fallout.'

'I get that, Russell.' Tanner well understood the delicate position her boss was in. 'But I'm with Tom on this. It's got to be Nicklin, surely?'

Brigstocke nodded. 'Yeah, I know, but I'm not convinced Tom's visit necessarily had anything to do with it. Nicklin might have been planning to kill Driver all along.'

'I don't see it,' Thorne said. 'If he was . . . and I don't see why he would be . . . far easier to do it *before* she's in prison, I would have thought.'

Tanner grunted her agreement. 'So, maybe Driver really did know more than she was telling. Maybe Nicklin had her killed because of something he thought she'd told Tom. Or something she might tell him if he visited her again.'

'He knew I was going.' Thorne looked at Tanner, then at Brigstocke. 'I mean yeah, he could have found out I'd been there because he's got some contact in the prison, but that's unlikely . . . it's not like he's got eyes *everywhere*, is it? It's possible he found out I'd been there because Driver told him, but I don't see how, and, more to the point, it was *yesterday* for Christ's sake.' He waited a second or two, as though it should be obvious to everybody. 'There's no way he could have arranged all this that quickly . . . found someone willing to stick a knife in her, bribed them or threatened them, whatever.' Thorne's hands tightened around the edge of the table. 'He knew I was going to Bronzefield in advance.'

'Like he knew about Coventry,' Tanner said.

Thorne thought he could hear the ticking in his blood; the thrum of it gaining a little speed. Since discounting the Herberts, he remained clueless as to where Nicklin was getting his information from.

'OK, well, that's something we need to bear in mind,' Brigstocke said. 'In the meantime . . . Tom, you need to get yourself down to Ashford first thing in the morning and talk to the Kent team.'

'Don't worry, I'll play nice,' Thorne said.

'Well, when the time comes, I would hope so . . . but they actually want to interview you as a witness.'

'Come again?'

'Like I said, they're just doing their job. Aside from guards and her fellow prisoners, you were the last person to talk to Rebecca Driver before she was killed.'

FORTY-FIVE

Nicklin wasn't arrogant enough to believe he was incapable of making mistakes. People who thought like that usually made a hatful. He was always careful, obviously, but who was to say he hadn't taken his eye off the ball when he'd been communicating with Rebecca Driver; his mind going walkies maybe, when one of those lovely yellow pills was working its magic, and letting something slip?

He didn't think so, but he couldn't be sure. That had been the issue.

That's why he'd felt the need to make certain arrangements at the prison.

The only disappointment was that he hadn't been able to get it together a little faster. He'd done his best, but he wasn't a miracle worker and he'd been obliged to wait until that prison officer had been thirsty enough to visit the pub on his way home. The ideal scenario would have been for his little helper to have got busy with her shiv on the day Thorne got there.

Terribly sorry, Detective Inspector, but I think you've had a wasted journey. Thorne's face . . .

He thought a lot about Thorne's face.

He always felt good and relaxed after a session; at ease with himself and with the world. He turned his head and stared out at it from the top deck. It was dark already and he checked out every lighted window as the bus went past, hoping for a glimpse of something that might fire his imagination when he got home. Those moments were always very special: arms and legs moving behind glass or shapes glimpsed through thin curtains; a torso moving across the frame and even, once or twice, a blank face staring straight back at him. Later he would flesh out these snapshots of what he supposed were ordinary lives and imagine the things he could do which might transform them into something very much out of the ordinary.

Nothing yet, but he kept on looking.

That niggle about possible carelessness hadn't been the only reason for deciding Driver had to go. If he was being honest, he'd been irked at all that diminished responsibility rubbish. That was not what had been agreed. On top of which, he sensed that she might be the sort to get above herself a bit and he wasn't going to have that. He'd given her a golden opportunity to be part of his game, to work alongside him for a little while, but he couldn't tolerate anyone with aspirations to become the main attraction. He couldn't bear the thought of her swanning about like a queen bee in her secure hospital, dropping his name to see people's reactions and loving how dangerous they all thought she was. Cheeky little bitch.

If she was dangerous, it was only because he'd made her that way.

So, yes, he would admit that in deciding to have Rebecca Driver killed, there'd been a degree of . . . petulance involved. How could he deny that when he'd been accused of it before?

He smiled, remembering the teacher who'd written it on his school report.

Stuart's behaviour often appears deliberately petulant.

He'd paid for that when his mother had seen it, but of course the teacher had paid for it too, in the end. Nicklin had found out where the man lived and watched his house for a while. He'd watched him leave home every evening at the same time to walk his dog, until one day, when the teacher and his pooch were in the park, Nicklin had broken into the back garden and sprinkled a little rat poison around. There wasn't much dog-walking needed after that.

When the bus passed Kensal Green tube station, Nicklin got up, rang the bell and began walking down the stairs.

There would come a time when he would think fondly of Rebecca Driver, he knew that. He remembered all of them that way, eventually; the same way, he supposed, that people thought about old sweethearts. Martin Palmer and Marcus Brooks and poor old Jeffery Batchelor, who'd played such an important part in his adventure on Bardsey Island.

It would sound odd to most people, he was aware of that, but there were even times he thought fondly of Tom Thorne. Not *that* odd, he decided, considering the amount of pleasure the man had given him over the years; that he would be giving him again, soon enough.

Nicklin thanked the driver then stepped off the bus. He tugged his baseball cap down a little and began to walk.

He did seriously doubt that the feeling was mutual.

*

Melita called when Thorne was driving home.

'I rang you last night,' she said.

Thorne did not want to try to explain why he hadn't picked up. 'I must have been in the shower or something.'

'I left a message.'

Thorne had still not listened to it. He'd meant to, then forgotten, then been far too distracted by the day's events to remember. He wondered why he was feeling quite so bad about it. There had been several occasions recently when *he'd* been unable to get hold of *her*, when she hadn't responded to the messages he'd left, and he hadn't made a big deal about it. He'd just presumed she'd needed time to herself, to unwind after a stressful session. It was understandable. 'Sorry . . . '

'It's fine.' She laughed. 'I don't want you to think I'm needy.'

'A lot on, you know?' He told her about Rebecca Driver. His visit to the prison and what had happened the following day.

'So, do you feel guilty?'

'Why would I feel guilty?'

'You just said that she was killed because you'd been to see her.'

Thorne accelerated to beat the lights on Archway Road, but he didn't quite make it and was forced to brake hard. He swore quietly. 'Yeah. I mean . . . I think she was, but that doesn't mean I'm feeling guilty about it.'

'Because you're not to blame?'

'Of course I'm not to blame.' Thorne had been thinking about it all day. He still believed that Nicklin had known about his visit in advance, but he could not help regretting

289

the fact that he'd chosen not to make use of a private visits area. Driver would be dead anyway, he knew that, but it still nagged at him a little.

'Do you feel sorry for her?'

'Is this some kind of unofficial therapy session?'

Melita laughed again. 'I'm just saying it would be perfectly natural, despite everything she'd done.'

'That's exactly why I don't feel sorry for her.' He remembered trying to scare her; the speech he'd made about staying safe. 'Look, I'm not saying she deserved to be carved up in her cell . . . then again, I don't think the three men she murdered deserved what she did to them.'

'She still has friends and family, though, Tom. There are people who loved her. They'll be grieving every bit as much as her victims' loved ones.'

'I know that,' Thorne said. He understood that the parents of those who had done terrible things, while they might lie awake at night questioning what *they* had done wrong, did not love their children any less. He struggled to find any real sympathy himself. No, he was not happy that Rebecca Driver had been killed, but how he felt about it had far more to do with the fact that his only direct line to Stuart Nicklin had now been cut. 'Can we talk about something else?'

'Are you pissed off with me?'

Thorne *was* pissed off with the woman driving the Audi in front of him who had spent the last two minutes slowing for turnings, indicating, then changing her mind. He wanted to get home. 'Sorry . . . just got the nadgers, that's all.'

'The *what*?'

'Something my mum used to say.' Thorne smiled, remembering. A family word for that feeling of generalised tetchiness you couldn't really explain. Or didn't particularly want to. 'I'm just knackered.'

'I was hoping you might want to come over.'

'Can we do it tomorrow?' Thorne asked. 'I've got to drive down to Kent first thing in the morning. Could do without it, if I'm honest.'

'OK, I'll cook.'

'Sounds great.' The Audi finally turned off the main road and Thorne put his foot down. 'I could do with slobbing out for a night . . . something to take my mind off all this for a few hours.'

'Oh, I can do that,' she said.

FORTY-SIX

To begin with, Thorne thought that he and Clive Coleman were going to get on.

His opposite number from the Homicide Unit at Kent Police had been waiting for him in reception at Ashford station. He'd all but bounded across to shake Thorne's hand and thanked him for coming. *Very much appreciated ... I know it's a pain in the arse* etc etc. He was tall – at least six foot four – and the shape of him suggested someone who didn't drink a great deal and rarely got up close and personal with a full English or an entire packet of Hobnobs. Despite what Thorne would normally class as irredeemable character flaws, the man seemed genuinely welcoming, so Thorne was willing to give him the benefit of the doubt. The cheap suit and shoes were another good sign. In Thorne's experience, a copper who spent a month's wages on tailoring was usually one to avoid.

'Good journey down?' Coleman asked, as they walked

towards the interview room. An estuary accent: class-less, edgeless.

'Piece of cake,' Thorne said. 'Forty minutes door to door.'

'I gather you're a Spurs fan.'

Thorne said that he was, wondering just where Coleman had gathered it from. Was it in a file somewhere? Alongside his arrest reports and service history and the disciplinary records that probably had a drawer all to themselves?

'I'm Man United,' Coleman said.

'Can't be helped.'

'Well, we're not exactly spoiled for choice when it comes to local teams.'

'Glory hunter, then.'

Coleman laughed. 'Yeah, I suppose.'

'What about when it comes to the job?'

'Oh Christ, no. I'm all about keeping my head down.'

'Best way,' Thorne said.

Coleman stopped outside a door. 'We're in here.'

'So, how's it all going?' Thorne asked, nice and casual.

If there was hesitation, it was only momentary. 'We've got a prison guard ... Gordon Ames. He was approached in a pub on Wednesday night and encouraged to look the other way while Driver was attacked. Threats against his family.'

Thorne nodded. At the very least this would put paid to the ludicrous idea that Driver's murder had been random; a coincidence. 'What about the woman who shanked her?'

'Karen Sinclair,' Coleman said. 'A lifer, which would make her an ideal choice.'

'Nicklin obviously got to her too.'

'Well, someone did, but we're not sure exactly how or

when just yet. Sinclair's not denying that she murdered Driver, but she isn't saying a fat lot besides.'

Thorne remembered the woman Driver had been glancing at when he'd visited and wondered if that might have been the woman who had stabbed her to death the next day. Brigstocke's words of warning from the day before were ringing in his ears, but he couldn't help himself. 'I presume you've checked to see what visitors Sinclair had on Wednesday.'

Coleman took a little longer this time. Long enough for the flash of annoyance to flare, then settle into a fixed, impatient smile. 'Obviously,' he said. 'But Karen Sinclair didn't have any visitors on the day you were at the prison.'

'Oh, right.'

'She did have a visitor the day before that, though.'

'And . . . ?'

'Her mother.' Coleman reached for the door handle and pushed. 'Shall we?'

Once inside, the Kent DI was all business. He strode across to a desk and sat down. Waiting for Thorne to do the same, he took out his notebook and said, 'It's always a bit awkward interviewing a colleague, even when it's non-evidential.' He had the good grace to look at least a little uncomfortable. 'Obviously you know how this works. The blah blah blah I have to say about rights and recording before we kick off.'

'Fill your boots,' Thorne said.

As soon as Thorne was seated and the blah blah blah was out of the way, Coleman said, 'So, you attended HMP Bronzefield to visit the victim the day before yesterday, is that correct?'

Thorne told him that it was.

'Would you mind telling me what you talked about?'

'We talked about a man called Stuart Nicklin.'

'Right. The man you believe murdered . . .' He reached for glasses and glanced down at his notes. ' . . . Kevin Bartley.'

'I don't *believe* he murdered Kevin Bartley. I *know* he did.'

Coleman's grunt sounded like a shrug, as though the distinction was unimportant.

'He's murdered a lot of people.'

'Oh, don't worry, I know who he is.'

'Well, that's a start,' Thorne said.

'Can you be a bit more specific? About what you and the victim discussed.'

'I was trying to persuade her to give me the password to a flash drive we found at her flat. I think there may be records of her communication with Stuart Nicklin on it. She said no.'

'Did she say anything else?' Coleman waited. 'Apart from no.'

'Not really.'

'You were there for almost forty minutes.'

Thorne shifted in his seat. 'We talked about her relationship with him. Her misplaced loyalty. She mentioned a book about Nicklin we'd found on her shelves.'

Coleman nodded. 'The one you're in.'

'Right.' Thorne was feeling tense and fidgety; starting to get a little short of breath. 'We talked about what it was going to be like for her in prison. I tried to put the wind up her a bit, to give her a sense of what she might be in for. The dangers.'

Coleman wrote something down.

Thorne settled himself, or tried to. 'Look, I really don't see what this has got to do with anything or how any of it helps. Rebecca Driver was killed because I went to see her ... because Nicklin found out I was going to see her. Simple as that. You've got the woman who did it and you've identified the prison officer who colluded, so what do you need from me?'

'Well, if, as you say, your visit was the reason this offence was committed—'

'It was.'

'—I'd suggest that the details of your conversation have *everything* to do with our investigation.'

'I asked for her help,' Thorne said. 'She refused. What else is there, for fuck's sake?'

Coleman looked up at the swear word, as though he'd never heard it spoken before. He removed his glasses, but the gesture did not carry the same threat as when Russell Brigstocke did it. The man just looked faintly amused. He leaned back and said, 'I was warned this might be tricky.'

A few seconds crawled by and suddenly the room felt very warm.

'Warned by who?'

'Doesn't matter, does it?'

'Oh, I think it does,' Thorne said.

'I'm just saying, it's ... well known that you're a bit closer to this case than you might be to some others. That's all. That you might be taking it a bit personally.'

'Too bloody right I am.'

'There you are, then.'

Thorne was leaning across the table now, but he made every effort to keep his voice calm. Every effort. 'We're talking about a very dangerous man who I put away when you were still in uniform.'

Coleman smiled.

'Who I've had dealings with several times since.'

'I read the book,' Coleman said, still smiling.

Thorne stopped bothering to sound calm. 'Someone who's murdered colleagues of mine and seriously assaulted others. Who's made threats against me many times in the past ... serious threats ... and the other day Rebecca Driver intimated that he was making those threats again.'

'*Intimated*?'

And then, though he couldn't quite remember how he'd got there, Thorne was on his feet and, despite the fact that Coleman's face had become a little blurry, he could see the man's eyes widen and that stupid fat mouth falling open, right before his own spittle started flying into it.

It didn't go very well after that.

FORTY-SEVEN

This time, they did the sensible thing and went to bed before dinner.

'It's a question of timing,' Melita said.

'It's a question of priorities,' Thorne said.

Melita had already put a chicken in the oven, so by the time they'd finished in the bedroom there was only a salad to prepare. Thorne was keen to help, but it wasn't the biggest kitchen – certainly not with that bloody island taking up so much space – so while she sat there chopping tomatoes and spring onions, she asked Thorne to sort the drinks out and put some music on.

Thorne poured wine and opened beer, then approached the Alexa in the corner as if it were a potentially dangerous animal. He'd recently done the unthinkable and bought one himself, though in what he thought of as his defence he mostly used it for news updates, settling arguments with Phil Hendricks about football trivia or setting alarms.

Alexa, wake me at eight AM with 'Folsom Prison Blues'.

'What do you fancy?'

Melita didn't look up from the chopping board. 'Something singer-songwritery?'

This was a challenge and Thorne knew he had to tread carefully. His idea of what constituted a great singer-songwriter and Melita's were entirely different, so a compromise of some sort was called for. He settled on Tim Hardin, then watched for a reaction when the guitar kicked in on 'If I Were A Carpenter'. Melita didn't turn and pull a face, so he guessed he'd done pretty well.

'I'm sorry for giving you a hard time the other night,' she said.

'Don't be daft.' He moved behind her and kissed the back of her neck.

'All that waffle about guilt and shame.' She reached around to stroke the back of his head. 'You were right. It *was* a bit like I was giving you a session for nothing, and I didn't exactly pick the best time, what with having the ... what did you call them?'

'The nadgers,' Thorne said. He certainly didn't have them now; he was good and relaxed. On top of which, chicken and salad was only a light dinner, so there was always at least the possibility of sex again later on.

Or maybe he was just talking a good game.

'I need to get better at leaving the work behind,' she said.

'Well, you couldn't be worse at that than I am.'

'Nobody could be worse than you are.' She fetched the ingredients for the dressing, nodding along to the music. 'It's just not that easy to switch off, is it? Especially when I've got a ... problematic client.'

'Which I'm guessing you have.' Thorne knew that the men and women Melita saw were rarely easy, so for her to be remotely troubled by a client meant that *problematic* was almost certainly putting it mildly. 'You want to talk about it?'

'Oh God, no.' Her expression hardened for a moment, but she quickly shook off whatever was troubling her, conjured a half-smile. 'That's exactly what I'm trying not to do. Even if I did . . .'

'I know, the confidentiality business.'

She sliced up the remaining tomato and stared down at it. 'I *want* to work with these people. You do get that, right? I need to.'

'Yeah, I get it.'

She stood very still, the knife in her hand. 'Most people with mental health issues never commit an act of violence, and even the ones that have done seriously bad things . . . their brains aren't really any different from yours or mine. That's what's so fascinating, how delicate the balance is.' She thought for a few seconds, slowly shook her head. 'It's a thin line.'

Thorne sipped his beer and watched her.

'I'm not saying it's easy or that it's a lot of fun. I mean, even if people haven't done anything bad . . . some of the things going on in their heads are tough to deal with.' She scraped everything on her chopping board into a bowl. 'You know?'

Thorne said nothing. Instead, proving that what Melita had said about him just a minute earlier was right, he downed the rest of his can and thought: *Haven't done anything bad . . . yet.*

He laid out the knives and forks and tablemats while Tim Hardin sang 'Reason To Believe'.

They'd only been eating for five minutes when Brigstocke called.

Any call from his DCI at this time was unlikely to be unofficial and Thorne found himself wondering if Greg Hobbs had worked another miracle. The tone of Brigstocke's voice when he said Thorne's name quickly killed that optimism stone dead.

'What's up?'

'As I remember,' Brigstocke said, 'when you came bowling back into the office this afternoon, and I asked you how everything had gone in Ashford, you said, and I quote, "All good".'

'Yeah.'

'Define *all good*.'

'DI Coleman asked me some questions and I answered them.'

'Really? Nothing else you maybe should have mentioned?'

Thorne could see where this was heading; had seen it from the moment Brigstocke had said his name like it was a hazard. 'It was nothing, Russell. It was a spot of handbags—'

'You called him a "useless cunt".'

'Well, he is.'

'Your fists were clenched.'

'I don't think they were.'

'I saw the fucking *tape*, Tom. Jesus . . . '

Thorne looked across and saw that Melita was watching him. He didn't doubt for one second that she could sense there might be a problem. She mouthed a *What?* and Thorne shook his head before turning away.

'Anyway, the long and the short of it is, he's made a complaint.'

'Oh, for God's sake.'

'And it's not like it's the first time, is it? You losing your rag.'

Thorne said nothing, because he knew what was next.

'I'm surprised that little shite-hawk Cameron Herbert didn't make a complaint as well, because he had every right to.'

'Who told you about that?' Thorne had a pretty good idea, but he wanted Brigstocke to confirm it.

'I run this team.' Brigstocke sounded exasperated. 'How would I not know about it?' Thorne could almost hear the glasses coming off. 'So anyway, I need to make a call on this.'

'Come on, Russell, don't do that.'

'No, *you* fucking come on. *You've* put me in this position and it's not like you haven't got plenty of other cases to be working, is it?'

Half a minute later, as soon as Brigstocke had hung up, Thorne dialled Nicola Tanner's number. It went straight to voicemail, but he didn't bother leaving a message.

FORTY-EIGHT

At the morning team briefing, Russell Brigstocke got the 'call' he'd been forced to make out of the way good and early. He explained that, effective immediately, there was to be a degree of . . . reallocation when it came to caseloads. It paid off sometimes, he said, to shift personnel around and it was always useful to get a fresh pair of eyes on things. He went on to announce that DI Thorne would be providing that fresh pair of eyes when it came to the fatal hit and run that DI Tanner was currently working, as well as the domestic murder investigation that he would now be running alongside DS Chall.

'It's a minor bit of rejigging, that's all.' An arm was raised, but he waved the question away. 'I've got no concerns because you're all good officers, so it doesn't much matter which cases you're on.'

Thorne sat listening, at the back of the room, head down, ignoring the sly glances he knew were being thrown in his direction. Thinking: *All good, but some not considered quite as good at this precise moment. Not quite as reliable and most definitely not at the top of their game.*

Not needed . . .

As to the investigation with which DI Thorne would no longer be so closely involved, Brigstocke went on to say that strictly speaking there wasn't one; not in the conventional sense. The murder of Kevin Bartley in Coventry was being run by West Midlands, the murder at HMP Bronzefield was being investigated by officers in Kent and, for obvious reasons, preparations for the trial of Rebecca Driver were no longer necessary. All this was not to say that the hunt for Stuart Nicklin was no longer a major priority, because it absolutely was. Every team in the Met had been made aware of its importance, with red flags ready to be activated should Nicklin's DNA and prints show up at any crime scene and a careful monitoring of intelligence right across the city.

'We're not easing up on this,' Brigstocke said. 'Make no mistake, it's of vital importance that we apprehend this man, but until such time as that opportunity presents itself . . . we've got plenty of other cases to be getting on with. So bugger off and get on with them.'

As the officers trooped dutifully away, Thorne ignored the looks he was getting from Nicola Tanner, the invitation to talk; moving quite deliberately so as to put as many people as possible between the pair of them. He'd done much the same thing on the way in. He'd dropped several calls from her first thing that morning and taken careful steps to avoid her for the half-hour between getting to the office and the start of the briefing.

He wasn't interested.

At his desk, he began working through the evidence on the hit and run, a young man named Alistair Savage who had died instantly after being struck by what was probably a Vauxhall Insignia in Dalston. Though there was nothing to indicate that the hit had been deliberate, the run certainly had, so that meant a manslaughter suspect who needed to be caught. A witness had provided a partial registration, so unless and until ANPR came up trumps, Thorne was looking at a long spell of computer-bashing and several hours on the phone with the DVLA.

It would take his mind off things, if nothing else.

Halfway through the morning, Dipak Chall ambled over. He stood next to Thorne's chair and kept his voice low.

'Do you mind me asking . . . is everything OK between you and Nic?'

'Yes.'

'That's good, because—'

'Yes, I do mind.'

Chall nodded and sniffed. He thrust his hands into his pockets and waited a while. 'She stuck up for you,' he said. 'Just so you know.'

Thorne carried on staring at his screen, stabbing at the keys.

'When she found out what the boss was thinking of doing. She said it was a mistake and tried to get him to change his mind. She told him that you were just . . . '

'Just *what*?' Thorne pushed his chair back and looked up.

'Just under a bit of pressure or something. Look, I thought you should know, that's all.' Chall waited a while longer, then, when Thorne showed no inclination to discuss things any further, he wandered away again.

Thorne was unconvinced.

He went back to the hit and run files, or tried to.

Whatever Tanner had told Chall she'd said, Thorne had a pretty good idea how it had all played out, late the day before. She would have been the person Brigstocke had called in to discuss the situation; same rank as Thorne, supposedly close, the obvious choice. Once she'd been told about what had happened at Ashford, she'd have had to at least mention what had happened with Cameron Herbert, even if Brigstocke had already known. She'd have made sure he knew on which side of the line she stood when it came to serious disciplinary matters such as this.

Sir, you should probably be aware that . . .

Of course she'd have mentioned it, because that was what Tanner was like. Job-pissed. A degree of reluctance at the end perhaps, before she was forced to agree, then resignation, a show of sadness even, once the decision had been made.

He picked up the phone to call the DVLA, then put it down again.

Could he actually blame her? Tanner had only been doing her job after all and doing it a damn sight better than he was. She was a good copper and he'd behaved like a bad one. There wasn't much more to it than that. If he was really being honest with himself, he would probably have done exactly the same thing in her shoes: shunted the officer concerned sideways and not given it a second thought.

He understood why Tanner had done it.

He would never forgive her.

Just before lunchtime, Thorne came out of the Gents to find Tanner waiting for him. He briefly broke stride, then carried on.

'Tom . . . ?'

Thorne kept on walking. It felt childish, it *was* childish, but he couldn't stop himself.

She moved quickly past him then stopped and turned to stand in his way. 'This is ridiculous.' There was blood rising to her cheeks and she sounded nervous, breathless. 'I just need a minute, that's all—'

'I haven't got a minute.' He stepped close enough to leave her little choice but to step out of his way. 'I've got work to do.'

Tanner shouted after him as he walked away, asked if they could talk later, but Thorne did not turn round.

He'd been lying about the work, trying to make a point. There was nothing that wouldn't wait. But he did need to be somewhere, for reasons that were far more important.

He was having lunch with an old friend.

FORTY-NINE

'Do people ever cry?' The man sitting in the chair opposite Melita Perera nodded down to the low table between them; the box of tissues within easy reach. 'Really lose it, I mean. Not just a few sniffles.'

'Sometimes,' Perera said.

'Do *you* ever cry?'

Perera said nothing.

'I mean some of the things you hear must be upsetting.'

'I think it's significant that, at least once during every session, I need to remind you that we're not here to talk about me.'

'I apologise.'

'You're forgiven. Again.'

The man smiled. 'You can't blame me for trying, though. I promise it's not because I don't want to talk about myself . . . I mean, that's why I'm here, isn't it? I'm interested, that's all.'

He stared at her. 'Go on, just answer that one question and I promise it'll just be me, me, me from now on.'

Perera sighed and shook her head. 'Well, I'm not a robot,' she said. 'But I don't think I'd be doing my job properly if I sat here weeping. It's not exactly . . . professional.'

The man nodded and said, 'Thank you.' He sat back and turned to stare for a few moments out of the large French windows in Perera's sitting room, towards the garden at the back of the house. 'I read somewhere that it's supposed to be some kind of breakthrough. If you cry, I mean . . . during therapy. I haven't cried once yet, so I was wondering if this is actually getting me anywhere, that's all.'

'I thought you were going to cry last time,' Perera said. 'There was a moment, when we were talking about your mother.'

'You thought wrong.'

Perera waited.

'Well, if I was, they would have been tears of laughter. You suggesting that I missed her.'

'I wasn't suggesting anything. It was just a question.'

'I don't really want to talk about her any more.'

'That's fine. What would you rather talk about?'

'Have I got to do all the work?'

'You were married once, weren't you?'

'A long time ago.'

'Would you like to tell me a bit about that?'

'Not particularly.'

'You're not making this very easy,' Perera said.

The man shrugged. 'It wouldn't be of any use to either of us if it was easy,' he said. 'Come on, be honest . . . would you rather sit here with some loser blubbing like a baby and moaning about their childhood? Telling you their stupid dreams? Surely someone like you gets a bit more out of customers who are a bit . . . trickier?'

'Clients,' Perera said. 'Not customers.'

'It's just an expression.'

'I suppose I'm still asking myself why you're here, that's all. What you want to get out of this.'

'It's a fascinating voyage of self-discovery, isn't it?'

'I know you're being sarcastic, but I'd really like to know. You came to me, and I'm happy that you did, but I really think we'd get a lot more out of these sessions if I understood why. I don't believe that you're unhappy.'

'You're right,' he said. 'I'm not.'

'So is it self-indulgence?'

'Oh, quite probably. I do like to spoil myself . . . well, I think you already knew that, and to be honest I've been deprived of decent conversation for a long time.'

'It's good to hear that this is at least . . . enjoyable for you.'

'Oh, it is. Look, I've never seen the point of denying yourself anything you want if you have the means to go out and get it. I've never understood the value of that and I think people who believe they're somehow more saintly or better human beings just because they choose to forgo certain . . . pleasures are a pointless waste of space. Life is there to be lived, wouldn't you say? Otherwise you're just counting down a clock.'

'Talking of which,' Perera nodded towards the clock on the wall, 'I've got another client in five minutes.'

'That's another good sign,' the man said. 'How quickly the time always seems to go. Actually, I think I'd like to start coming more than once a week, if that's OK with you. If you can fit me in, obviously.'

'We can do that,' Perera said.

The man seemed delighted, though he didn't have much more to say as their final few minutes ticked by. He simply sat, perfectly relaxed until he saw Perera glancing at the clock again. Then he leaned forward and nodded down towards the box of tissues on the table.

'I bet I could tell you things that would make you cry.'

FIFTY

'You're not seriously telling me this is the first time you've been bumped off a case? I always thought that was like a badge of honour with you, back in the day.'

Thorne did not have a snappy comeback and would not have bothered even if he did. If there was one person with whom he could not pretend his disciplinary record was any better than it was, it was his former DC – now a DS – Dave Holland.

'It's not like it ever stopped you, though, did it . . . doing whatever it was you'd have done anyway unofficially? I don't think for one minute it's going to stop you now, either. Certainly not considering . . . who it is you're after.'

'You can say his name, Dave. He's not fucking Voldemort.'

Thorne had called Holland the day before and filled him in. They'd arranged to meet in a café in Islington. It was a notch up from the place Phil Hendricks was so fond of – sourdough sandwiches and no tomato-shaped ketchup dispensers – but it wasn't poncey.

'I think you should stop feeling sorry for yourself,' Holland said. 'Don't beat yourself up about being booted off the investigation and get on with catching him. That's all I'm saying.'

'That's why we're here, Dave.'

'Oh.' Holland tried to look sad. 'I thought it was just because you'd missed me.'

Back in the day . . .

It was hard for Thorne to equate the man on the other side of the table with the floppy-haired newbie loping towards him on the first morning they'd worked together, almost two decades before. There was no longer enough hair to *be* floppy and what there was had begun to grey, but there weren't too many lines just yet and Holland certainly still looked fit enough. He looked every bit as up for it as he had been the last time they'd worked together, though by the time he'd got back from Bardsey Island he'd been every bit as battered and burned-out as Thorne had been.

Only one man had come away from Bardsey undamaged.

When they'd eaten, Thorne said, 'I know we've never really talked about this, but I always wondered if you left because of what happened on Bardsey. Put in for a transfer. I mean, I wouldn't have blamed you.'

Holland shook his head. 'Don't get me wrong, it didn't exactly help. It wasn't . . . great, was it?'

'No. It wasn't great.'

'I was already thinking of getting out of London, though. Sophie and I had decided to get divorced . . . you knew that, right?'

Thorne nodded. The woman who had eventually fallen out of love with Dave Holland had hated Thorne right from the beginning, so he hadn't been overly upset when Holland had mentioned that they were going through a rough patch. He would have felt very differently had he known it would eventually lead to Holland leaving the Met.

'So we were going to have to sell the house, I heard there were better opportunities for promotion in Bedfordshire and I could just afford a place in Milton Keynes. So . . . '

'All seems to have worked out,' Thorne said.

'Yeah, I reckon so. Decent enough bunch to work with and, best of all, it's not too much of a schlep to get back and see Chloe. Seeing her tonight, actually.'

Holland's daughter. 'She must be what . . . seven?'

'Nine,' Holland said, grinning.

'Bloody hell.'

'Yeah, she comes to stay one weekend a month, which is great. Sophie's shacked up with a new bloke, but it's all pretty civilised. Oh, and I'm engaged.'

'What? Tell me she's not a copper.' Thorne was remembering his recent conversation with Tanner. Back when he and Tanner were having conversations.

'Civilian support staff,' Holland said.

'That's all right then.'

'Pippa.' Holland smiled. 'She's a bit more . . . easy-going than Sophie, so I think you'll *probably* be getting a wedding invitation.'

'Count me in.'

'So, what about you, then?'

'Well, Helen and I split up.'

'Yeah, I heard. Nothing since?'

Thorne told Holland about getting together with Melita Perera, went on to explain that she was someone whose

314

input on certain cases could be invaluable. She had certainly provided useful input when it came to this one, but now, with the support of his team dragged from underneath him, Thorne felt the need to talk to someone who knew Stuart Nicklin almost as well as he did.

Holland had seen colleagues die on Bardsey Island, had fought in vain to save at least one of their lives, but he had also been there years before that, when Nicklin had first been arrested. When a fellow officer, who had also happened to be Holland's lover, had been gunned down in a playground.

Dave Holland knew all too well what Nicklin was capable of.

'Do you fancy a coffee or something?' Thorne asked.

'No, I'm good.'

They sat and stared at each other for a few seconds, while people at adjacent tables laughed or chatted or tucked into fancy cakes, the past and their shared memories of it emerging from the shadows and squatting between them suddenly like an uninvited guest. A great deal of pain and a good deal of blood, much of it spilled by the same man.

'So, what do you think?'

'I think you'll catch him,' Holland said. 'Because you have to, and you're good at this, whether you're getting your wrists slapped or not, and ... when you do, if he should happen to tumble out of a window or fall in front of a train or accidentally get kicked to death, I'll be the first person to buy you a drink. I'll be the one at the head of a very long queue.'

Thorne nodded, grateful for the sentiment at least. 'Problem is, it feels like Nicklin's the one ... setting the agenda, you know? The ground rules or whatever.'

'Because he *is*. It's what he always does.'

Thorne nodded again and let out a long slow breath, thinking about the streaks of blood on Kevin Bartley's chest.

'We need to do something to change that.'

Thorne liked the sound of that *we*, though he knew that Holland didn't mean it literally. 'It doesn't help that he seems to know exactly what I'm going to do before I've done it.'

'Yeah.' Holland thought about it. 'You said.'

'All *I* know is that *he's* going to do *something*.'

'Those "plans" Driver mentioned . . . ?'

'I feel like I'm getting fucking buried here, Dave. Like all this shit's coming down on me and I don't know where it's coming from. I don't know if I'm strong enough to stop it, not physically and not . . . ' Thorne rubbed at an old stain on the table then leaned closer. 'Between you and me, what happened with that prick in Ashford? It could have been a lot worse.'

Holland's expression made it clear that he understood, that he at least was not being judgemental. Finally, he said, 'He'll come after the people close to you. Like he did with Phil last time. If he wanted to kill you, he could have done it on Bardsey or he could have had it arranged before that, when he was still in prison, so I really don't think that's what he's planning. What he wants more than anything is to make you suffer.'

'Well, he's already done that.'

'No, he hasn't. I don't mean worrying about suffering, or suffering because you've been kicked off the case.' Holland shook his head. 'That's not even going to be close.'

Thorne managed a rueful smile. 'Well, this is cheering me right up.'

'You asked.'

He knew that Holland was right, of course. Assuming that Nicklin was aware of it – and based on what had happened so far, it was a reasonable assumption – he would be delighted that Thorne was no longer in charge. He would enjoy knowing he had already got inside his head enough to cause such ... erratic behaviour, but it would be a bonus, no more than that. It would put a spring in Nicklin's step to know that Thorne was losing his way, that he was stressed out and struggling to sleep, but it was never going to be a substitute for causing genuine pain.

'That's all I've got,' Holland said. 'I'll keep thinking about it, obviously, but for now I'd say your best bet is to keep a close eye on the people you care about.'

Out on the street afterwards, Thorne thanked Holland for coming, told him how good it had been to catch up.

'Let's do it over a few beers next time,' Holland said. 'When we've got something better to talk about.'

Thorne promised him they would.

They chatted for another five minutes. Holland told Thorne what he was getting Chloe for Christmas, then talked a little more about Pippa and the plans for their wedding. He asked after a couple of old colleagues and seemed keen to know how his favourite pathologist was doing. Thorne told him that, a few more piercings and tattoos aside, Hendricks was much the same, and he shared a couple of stories, but all the time he was thinking about the advice Holland had given him.

As they separated, Thorne said, 'Look after yourself, mate.'

The people you care about.

It wasn't a very long list, but he realised that Dave Holland was on it.

Holland raised a thumb and they walked in opposite directions towards their cars.

FIFTY-ONE

Thorne's doorbell rang just after eight o'clock. He wasn't expecting anybody and would normally have ignored it, but he wasn't feeling altogether normal, so instead he marched into the hall and all but threw the door open, bang up for a row with whatever crusty tea-towel seller or Jehovah's Witness or neighbourhood watch nut-bag had been stupid enough to come calling. When he saw Nicola Tanner on the step, he was tempted to close the door just as enthusiastically, but it felt like he'd made enough childish gestures for one day. Besides, before he had a chance to do anything, she held up a plastic bag and Thorne heard the unmistakable clank of bottles and cans.

So, with the door still wide open, he simply turned and walked back into the flat.

Tanner followed him into the kitchen. She emptied the bag, set down a bottle of wine and four cans of lager on the table. 'They're all for you,' she said. 'I'm driving.'

'You can take the wine home with you.'

She put the bottle back in the bag. 'I drove past that Indian place you're always banging on about, but I didn't know if you'd eaten.'

'I could always have had it for breakfast,' Thorne said.

'I didn't tell Russell about what happened with Cameron Herbert.' She looked at him. 'I know you think I did, but I didn't. He already knew, all right?'

Thorne thought about it. 'Did you at least fight my corner a bit?'

'Course I did, but there wasn't a lot of point,' Tanner said. 'He'd already made up his mind. Just so you know, Russell wasn't thrilled about it himself, but it wasn't like you left him a lot of choice.'

'I wish I'd decked the little gobshite . . . Cameron Herbert I mean, not Russell.' Thorne opened one of the cans and took a drink. 'And that arsehole in Ashford.'

'Then you'd have been suspended.'

'Suits me. I wouldn't be wasting my time on some stupid hit and run.'

'Catching the driver of that car is every bit as important as catching Stuart Nicklin.'

'Even you don't really believe that,' Thorne said.

'OK, but that lad's parents deserve justice for their son every bit as much as Hari Reddy's do. Every bit as much as Richard Sumner's wife or Thomas Bristow's daughter. Kevin Bartley's family—'

'You've made your point.' Thorne picked up another of the cans and held it towards her. 'You can have one, surely.'

Tanner hesitated, then reached out to take it. 'I've got something to show you.'

While Thorne carried the remaining cans across to the fridge, Tanner sat down and opened her laptop. By the time Thorne had joined her at the table, she had found what she was after. Thorne could see what he was looking at straight away: a pub interior in black and white, a man sitting alone in the corner of a pub.

'This is CCTV footage from the Railway in Ashford,' Tanner said. 'The night before Driver was killed. That's Gordon Ames, the prison officer from Bronzefield.' She pressed *play* and half a minute later a second man joined Ames at the table. 'And that's the man who threatened his family.'

'I know exactly who that is,' Thorne said.

Tanner turned and looked at him. 'Really? I sort of presumed he'd paid someone to do his dirty work for him.'

'Maybe he just fancied a drink.' Thorne leaned a little closer to the screen. The image was far from pin-sharp, but he knew he was watching Stuart Nicklin. 'He was a lot bigger the last time I saw him. Must have been on a fitness kick.' They watched, but the image remained much the same until Nicklin got up again to walk over to the bar. 'Jesus, what's he done to his face?'

'Surgery? It's what I was talking to Phil about—'

'Is that ... *hair*?' Thorne pointed to what certainly looked like tufts of hair, just visible at the back and sides of a baseball cap. 'He was bald as an egg when we were on Bardsey, with scars and fucking ... craters on his head. Fat and bald. He still looked better than that, though.'

'At least we know what he looks like now,' Tanner said. 'We can get this blown up and get his picture out there.'

They watched the rest of the footage; a twenty-minute

conversation before Ames stood up and left. Nicklin stayed on another few minutes to finish his drink, and when he finally left he kept his head down. 'That's a surprise,' Thorne said. 'Felt sure he'd look up to the camera, same as Driver did. Give us a wink.'

'Maybe he's come over all shy and retiring.'

'Sadly, that's the last thing he is.'

Tanner closed her laptop. 'So . . . '

'What happens now?' Thorne asked.

'Like I said, we get the picture out—'

'No, with everything . . . going forward. How do I fit in?'

'You don't,' Tanner said. 'Not officially, anyway. Look, any developments, I'll make sure you're the first to know about them, OK? To be honest, I think Russell knows that's what's going to happen. Just . . . don't be too obvious about it.'

'You know me.'

'Yeah, that's why I'm telling you.'

They sat in silence for a while. Thorne watched Tanner perched a little awkwardly on the edge of a kitchen chair, avoiding his eye and taking small sips from her beer can. She hadn't even taken her coat off. 'It's Saturday night, for God's sake,' he said. 'Shouldn't you be out on a hot date or something?'

'What, after the last disaster?'

'It didn't sound like a disaster.'

'Well . . . ' Now she looked at him, just long enough for Thorne to catch a half-smile. ' . . . as it happens, I *have* matched with someone else.'

'There you go, getting back on the horse.'

'Not how I'd have put it.'

'So when's the date?'

'We haven't arranged anything yet,' she said. 'We're still getting to know each other.' She shrugged and the smile broadened. 'Hopefully next week sometime.'

'Text me with updates every fifteen minutes,' Thorne said.

'I'll make it my top priority.'

'And send pictures.'

Tanner grunted and got to her feet. She picked up her plastic bag. 'I'd best be getting off.'

'OK.' She'd barely touched her beer, but Thorne hadn't really expected her to. If he'd wanted to talk about it, or thought for one minute that she did, he might even have said how stupid it was; to be nervous about driving after a few mouthfuls of piss-weak beer.

Ridiculous, if you thought about it, considering what she'd once done.

'I'm glad I came over, Tom.'

'Right.'

Tanner looked at him. 'This is when you say that you're glad, too.'

'Yeah, I suppose.' Thorne nodded. 'I *was* running low on lager.'

FIFTY-TWO

Thorne had never really *got* walking. Walking for no other reason than the walk itself, at any rate. He had no real problem walking to the car or to the fridge and he could just about tolerate a walk outdoors if there was food or a drink at the end of it. That aside, he could think of countless more enjoyable ways to spend a day off. It was his shitty luck, he thought, that all the major relationships in his life had been with women who loved nothing better than tramping about in woods or on heaths, and Melita was no exception. After driving over to Crouch End to join her for breakfast at a Mediterranean café near her flat, his heart had sunk a little at her suggestion that they cross over into Priory Park to walk it off.

He had tried, and clearly failed, to look enthusiastic.

'It'll do you good,' she said.

'It's cold.'

'It's *crisp*.'

'That's just another word for cold,' he said.

'Come on you miserable sod. It's . . . Christmassy.'

Thorne knew he was fighting a losing battle, so made an effort to sound keen. 'Ready when you are,' he said.

It did feel somewhat Christmassy, due in large part to the sprawling pop-up market selling Christmas trees just inside the Middle Lane entrance to the park. There was even talk of buying one there and then and carrying it back to Melita's flat. In the end, they settled for a wreath and Melita bought a few 'organic' decorations, though Thorne thought she'd paid way over the odds for what were basically pine cones glued together and bits of dried fruit on a piece of string.

She squeezed his arm and told him he was a grinch.

He insisted that he wasn't, but that he couldn't bear to be ripped off.

They talked about the arrangements – work permitting – and settled on Thorne coming over to Crouch End on Christmas Eve and staying there for two nights, before Melita went to her sister's on Boxing Day. They agreed that nobody really liked turkey – because if they did they'd be eating it all year round – but decided to do one anyway. Melita said she'd use the leftovers to make a curry. She suggested inviting Phil Hendricks and Liam over and Thorne told her he'd ask.

They walked past the playground and the Philosopher's Garden and then, agreeing that they couldn't wait for the hot chocolate, across to the café where they sat huddled at one of the outdoor tables.

'I'm glad you patched things up with Nicola,' Melita said.

It was the first time they'd seen each other since Brigstocke's call. Thorne had told her what had happened;

his falling-out with Tanner and her visit the night before. He'd glossed over the . . . sulking, because he knew Melita would not approve. She would have thought his behaviour had been juvenile and would have told him so.

'I think it's actually worked out pretty well,' he said. 'Nicola's going to keep me in the loop, but not being part of that team gives me a bit of freedom.'

'To do what?'

Thorne hadn't got the first idea. He hadn't thought it through. 'To pursue leads the way I want to.'

'You mean go after Nicklin without any support?'

'How am I supposed to do that?'

'You tell me. You were sounding like some sort of vigilante, though, and that's a very bad idea.'

'Yes it is,' Thorne said. 'And it's never going to happen, because apart from the fact that I wouldn't know where to start, I'm not stupid.'

They drank their hot chocolate and Melita let her head fall back to enjoy the winter sunshine. Thorne looked around, not quite as able as she was to relax. There were a lot of people enjoying the day; relishing the space and the fresh air rather more than he was. Dog-walkers, couples, joggers. The paddling pool in front of them was covered over, but away to his right there were still a few lunatics playing tennis, albeit in tracksuits, gloves and woolly hats. He watched a man standing alone beneath a tree; a long dark coat and a baseball cap. He only stopped watching when a young woman arrived with hot drinks and the pair of them moved away.

'I don't think you're stupid,' Melita said.

'That's good to know.'

'It's my job to worry, though.'

'Talking of which . . .'

'What?'

Thorne told her about his meeting with Dave Holland, about the suggestion that Nicklin might well choose to attack him indirectly. 'I think it's a real possibility,' he said. 'That he'll come at me through somebody else.'

'Why are you so convinced he'll come at you at all?'

'It's the only reason he's doing any of this. It's what he's been working up to. Even if Driver hadn't said anything . . . it's what I've been expecting him to do.'

'Maybe the fact that you are expecting it is enough for him,' Melita said. 'That might be all he wants. To push your buttons a bit.'

'No chance.'

'So, what are you suggesting?'

'I'm suggesting we don't ignore the risk that the people I'm closest to might be in danger, and I think you might qualify. Just about.' She didn't appear to find it funny. In fact, she wasn't reacting as Thorne had expected at all. He wasn't trying to alarm her, but he wanted her to take his concerns more seriously

'You want me to stop working?'

'No . . . but it wouldn't hurt to be aware of that risk when you are.' Thorne nodded across the park in the direction of her flat. 'Someone rings your bell, you just buzz them in.'

'Only my clients.'

'You don't always know, though.'

'Yes I do. Plus, *you* know very well that I vet all my clients before I agree to work with them. There's any number of phone conversations before I see them face to face, and there's usually a referral from a GP before that ever happens. Are we really going to have this conversation again?'

The argument they'd had several months earlier. It was territory Thorne had sworn to steer well clear of ever since, but that was before Nicklin moved the goalposts.

'What about when you're on the street or when you're on your own at night? I'm just talking about being that extra bit cautious, that's all. For a start, I know you don't always put your alarm on—'

'I can look after myself, Tom.'

'So can I,' Thorne said. 'I'm a damn sight better at it than you are, but that doesn't mean I'm not shitting myself.' He reached for her hand, but she didn't give it straight away. 'Just . . . keep it in mind.' He squeezed. 'Why should you be the only one that's allowed to worry?'

She nodded, finally, conceding the point, but Thorne could see that she was irritated. He was irritated too, because nothing he'd suggested had been unreasonable. Quite the opposite, in fact. He was being caring and uncharacteristically rational and she was picking the worst possible moment to be stubborn and ignore good advice; to let him know just how strong and independent she was.

'You seen those idiots playing tennis?'

She didn't bother to look. 'Up to them, isn't it?'

Thorne was sure she'd see the good sense in what he was saying eventually. *She* wasn't stupid, either. All the same, he guessed that the atmosphere would probably stay *crisp* for a little while longer.

FIFTY-THREE

Given the choice, he'd take warm weather every time, and over the past few years he'd gravitated towards places where he was more likely to get it, but a day as cold as this one was certainly handy when you didn't want to be recognised. He had every reason to be wearing a thick coat and hat. The sunshine was doing him a favour too, because sunglasses would not look out of place.

Nicklin knew Thorne had seen the footage from that pub, so there was no point taking chances. He wouldn't get too close. He wasn't ready to hand himself over on a plate just yet.

He watched them browsing at the Christmas market, like lovebirds in some nauseating film. It was fun, watching them spend their money so pointlessly, and not just because all those chi-chi Christmas bits and bobs were overpriced. If it *was* a film, he thought, it would probably need to be shown after the watershed, bearing in mind how it was going to end.

It would all be a bit much for Granny and the kids.

He was perhaps fifty feet behind them as they passed the playground and headed for the café, so he stopped under a tree and watched them take a table outside. They were almost an attractive couple. It was odd, he thought, how Thorne had always seemed to do pretty well for himself when it came to the opposite sex. Odd, because he didn't think Thorne could be anyone's idea of a catch. There had been a time, many years before, when Nicklin had made a little extra cash having sex with men, and there had even been a copper or two, but looking at Tom Thorne ... he could never imagine needing money that much.

Not that sex of any sort was something that concerned him very much any more. He could certainly not get the kind of sex he wanted in any conventional relationship, so when he did feel the need, he was happy to splash out and pay good money for it; to treat himself perhaps once or twice a year. He was thinking that he might do so again, once his business with Thorne had played out, when he became aware of the woman watching him.

She had a baby splayed in a harness against her chest, and she was talking quietly to a second woman with a pushchair. She looked at the playground, then at him, then back to the playground again. She looked nervous.

She walked over. 'Have you got a child in there?'

'Sorry?'

She looked even more nervous now she was close to him. 'In the playground.'

In other circumstances, Nicklin's reaction might have been somewhat different. He did decide that he would carry the picture of her pinched little face home with him and imagine doing a variety of things she would certainly not approve of. As it was, he simply smiled and said, 'Oh, I see what you mean . . . yes.' He pointed towards a young boy on one of the swings. 'That's my nephew.'

The woman nodded, relieved and burbled an apology.

'It's fine, honestly.' Glancing across at the café, while the woman continued to say she was sorry and that she hoped he understood, Nicklin saw that Thorne and his girlfriend were leaving. 'I'd probably have done the same.'

'Ridiculous, isn't it?' The woman's baby had begun to grizzle and she bounced it against her chest. 'Shocking, really, that you even have to ask the question, but . . . this day and age, you know? You can't be too careful.'

'No, you can't,' Nicklin said. 'It's a sick world.'

FIFTY-FOUR

Monday morning, and the mood in the incident room was as positive as it had been in a while. At least, that's how Thorne would remember it in the long and terrible weeks that were to come. A day when the fear receded a little and the sense of helplessness ceased to be ever-present; when it felt as if a positive outcome might just be more than a pipedream.

The last day before it all turned to shit.

Thorne stood looking at the picture of Stuart Nicklin that had been extracted from the pub's CCTV footage. The image had been enhanced, blown up, and was now pasted front and centre on the case wall, arrows connecting it to photographs of Kevin Bartley and Rebecca Driver. The picture had, of course, already been sent to West Midlands police and copies distributed to every station in the Met area. Nicklin's name would be the first one mentioned at every shift briefing and the last come knocking-off time, that photo passed around until his face was imprinted on the mind of every detective, PCSO and beat officer in the city.

'It's not a face you're likely to forget, is it?' Dipak Chall had moved to stand next to Thorne.

'Let's hope not,' Thorne said.

'You're not fooling anybody, by the way.' Chall waited until Thorne looked at him, then winked. 'I know Nic showed it you last night.'

Midway through the morning, a call came through with a potential ID on the driver of the car that had killed Alistair Savage. The witness, who certainly sounded plausible, worked in Wood Green, so Thorne and Chall were given the job of driving down to interview him.

'What's he like?' Chall asked, in the car.

Thorne didn't need to ask who Chall was talking about. 'You know what he's done, right? I mean, everything's there on the PNC, in the relevant murder books, so you must have a pretty fair idea.'

'You've spent time with him, though.'

'Oh, yes.'

'So ... if someone didn't know what he'd done, would he come across as a normal bloke? I mean, I know he's *not*, but does he seem ... ordinary?'

For a moment, Thorne considered telling Chall to stop asking stupid questions and to read the Stephen Campbell masterpiece if he was so interested. He might have done if he didn't know that, like any copper, Chall would be rather more drawn to the author's descriptions of a certain detective than he would to those of the book's actual subject.

Truculent, over-sensitive, foolish.

'I don't think anyone's born bad,' Thorne said. 'No more than I believe you can be born good.'

'You talking about good and evil, right?'

'Yeah . . . if you like.'

'You saying you don't believe in it.'

'Not really,' Thorne said.

'Well, I do,' Chall said. 'And I reckon if you asked around you'd find that most of us think the same way. I'm not religious or anything like that, but I mean, how can you not? Some of the evil fuckers we have to deal with.'

'It's just an expression, though, isn't it? It's just something people say. I don't think I've ever come across a genuinely *evil* fucker.' Thorne slowed, then stopped for lights. He turned to stare at people sitting in cars, drifting in and out of shops or blithely walking the pavements; men and women lucky enough to live lives that would never be blighted by the likes of Stuart Nicklin. 'He's probably the closest to it, though.'

When they pulled up outside the address they'd been given in Wood Green, Chall got out of the car. He walked a few paces, then stopped and turned back. He tapped at the passenger window, confused by the fact that Thorne was showing no inclination to join him.

Thorne pressed the button and the window slid down. 'You OK to talk to this bloke on your own?'

'Yeah, I suppose.' Chall leaned in, intrigued. 'What's going on?'

'Just a bit of business I need to deal with.'

'Can I ask what kind of business?'

'You can ask,' Thorne said. 'But I'll only be making something up.'

'Go on then.'

'I've had a hot lead on where Shergar might be.'

Thorne pressed the button to close the window, then opened it again when Chall shouted, 'How am I supposed to get back?'

Thorne told him to get an Uber, or catch a bus, or flag down a passing motorist and say 'Urgent police business' the way they only ever did on television. Then he closed the window, turned the car round and headed for Crouch End.

He parked in a resident's bay and took out his warrant card, ready to flash it if a warden came along. He needed to be somewhere that gave him a decent view of Melita's front door. The comings and goings.

Just after eleven o'clock, he saw the door open and watched a young woman step out. Melita's ten o'clock appointment. Thorne knew that the people who lived in the first- and top-floor flats worked all day, so he could be fairly certain that anybody going in or coming out of the house was one of Melita's clients. He also knew that, on her busiest days, Melita would allow herself fifteen minutes between appointments – time to grab a coffee, to write up or read notes – so he guessed that her next client would be along fairly soon. Sure enough, within ten minutes, a middle-aged man was turning on to the drive.

Thorne watched the man walk up to the front door; took a good long look at him as he rang the bell and waited to be buzzed in.

Nothing about the man's appearance or demeanour concerned him but, at the same time, Thorne realised how ridiculous this entire enterprise actually was. He asked himself what he was expecting to see. Aside from Nicklin himself

sauntering up to Melita's front door, would anyone seem ...
dangerous? And what the hell was Thorne proposing to do
if he thought they were? Her eleven-fifteen certainly looked
harmless enough, so Thorne just sat there wondering if this
might be the fabled enema man ...

With an hour to kill until the next client, he walked up on
to the main road and bought a couple of newspapers.

They were still squeezing every ounce of outrage possible
from the Rebecca Driver story. The murders themselves had
already generated dozens of headlines: *Monster's Classroom
Stories*; *First Date Killer's Murder Book Hoard*; *Driver's Grisly
Souvenirs*. Now, her death on remand had provided yet another
angle. While certain higher-end papers bemoaned the levels
of security in an underfunded prison system, some tabloids
had worked themselves into a lather about justice being denied
to the families of the victims – *We Wanted Her To Rot* – and
others were content simply to claim that she'd got no less than
she deserved.

It was a small mercy that none of them, as yet, had made
the connection to Stuart Nicklin.

At twelve-fifteen, the man who almost certainly didn't have
a sexual fetish about enemas emerged, and just before half past
a new client arrived. This one walked right past Thorne's car
and though Thorne kept his head down – riveted by a sports
page he'd already read – he felt sure that the man had glanced
in at him before crossing the road to the house.

Thorne looked up from his paper and watched him.
Fortyish; short but powerfully built, a red puffa jacket and
trainers. The man rang the doorbell, then turned to look back
towards Thorne's car while he waited.

Towards the car or directly at it? Thorne couldn't be sure.

He was thinking about getting out of his car and marching across to find out when the man was buzzed inside.

Normally, Thorne would have felt frustrated. He would probably have stomped over anyway and hammered on the door, but now he was only grateful at being denied the chance to make an idiot of himself.

Again . . .

He walked to the main road a second time and bought himself a sandwich and a can of Diet Coke; sat and ate, listening to people argue about conspiracy theories on a phone-in show. He thought about the conversation he'd had earlier with Dipak Chall and was more convinced than ever that he was right. Aside from anything else, he felt sure that Stuart Nicklin would love to be thought of as evil, and Thorne wasn't about to do him any favours. It also got him thinking that unless the witness in Wood Green had an awful lot to say, Chall would probably be back at the office by now. Brigstocke would want to know where Thorne had been, so he needed to come up with something. He decided that honesty was the best policy and that Brigstocke would probably be OK with it. It wasn't like Thorne was working the case, not really. If anything, what he was doing was closer to *pastoral care*, and the brass always loved that.

It was sunny again and the heating was turned up and he might even have nodded off for a few minutes, but when he sat up again and looked across at the house the man in the red puffa jacket was coming out. The man lingered, fidgety, on the doorstep. He stared across at Thorne's car, then rang the bell to go back in. A couple of minutes later, the door opened again, but this time it was Melita herself who came out; striding up the path and straight across the road towards him.

337

Hands down, the most dangerous-looking person Thorne had seen since he got there.

FIFTY-FIVE

'So, this nosy little arsehole goes straight back in and says, "I think someone's watching your house" and the next thing I know she's out there on the street, laying into me like *she's* the one in need of some therapy, you know?'

Phil Hendricks was struggling to keep a straight face.

'What?'

'I'm sure it was all very traumatic, mate, but I can't get past how obviously piss-poor you are at surveillance. Did you miss that day at training college?'

'It wasn't . . . *surveillance*,' Thorne said. 'Not as such. I was just keeping an eye on her, that's all.'

'Now it just sounds creepy,' Hendricks said.

'I honestly don't know why she was so pissed off. It's not like I'm *imagining* Nicklin's out there, is it? She knows what he's capable of as much as anyone else. *More* than anyone else.'

'Maybe that's the problem,' Hendricks said.

Thorne waited, keen to hear anything that might explain Melita's confrontational attitude. Her reluctance to accept any possibility that she might be in danger.

'She spends so much time dealing with nut-jobs like him, that she's stopped being scared of them. Like these weirdos who keep wild animals as pets, lions and tigers and whatever. You know ... "Oh, Simba would never hurt me, I've had him since he was a cub".'

'Right, and they invariably get eaten,' Thorne said.

It was half-time in the Everton versus West Ham game and the previous forty-five minutes had been less than exciting. Hendricks had turned up with fish and chips and beer which had improved Thorne's mood enormously.

Just after the game kicked off again, Thorne said, 'We never really talked about what happened to you. When I got back from the island.'

Hendricks kept his eyes on the game. 'Yeah, we did.'

'Only stupid jokes,' Thorne said. 'Same as usual. I never really asked you how you felt.'

Now Hendricks turned to him. 'How d'you think I felt?'

'I don't mean ... the pain.' Thorne was struggling, dancing around it. 'I know you blamed me for what they did, and I suppose I just wanted to say that's fair enough.'

Hendricks turned back to the TV, said nothing for a minute, though it was clear he was thinking about it. 'I didn't blame you.'

'That's what it seemed like,' Thorne said.

'Well, I can't help that, can I? I can't help it if you were over-sensitive because you felt guilty.'

Thorne just nodded. Over-sensitive was not something he was often accused of being.

'I blamed those two fuckers who cut me,' Hendricks said. 'I blamed Nicklin for putting them up to it, but he wasn't there and you were. So ...'

'I get it.'

'Sorry if you felt like that, mate. If it helps, I knew I was the reason you let him go, so you weren't the only one feeling guilty. When you think about it, I'm the reason he's still around to put the shits up everyone.'

'No, that's not—' There was a sudden burst of noise when, from nowhere, Everton sneaked a goal, and the excited babble in the studio, followed by a tense VAR judgement, changed the mood; put them back on more comfortable ground.

Stupid jokes, same as usual.

An hour later, when Thorne was cleaning up the debris, he asked the question he'd been wanting to ask for the remainder of what had turned out to be a one-all draw. 'So, how come you're the only one Nicklin *doesn't* put the shits up? I mean, you don't seem nearly as bothered as you should be.'

Hendricks shrugged. 'We're made of sterner stuff in the north, mate. Simple as that.'

His friend had turned away to pick up his jacket as he'd answered, so Thorne couldn't see his face. He wasn't convinced Hendricks was any less scared about what might happen than he was, and guessed he had simply decided that giving into it wasn't going to help anybody. Thorne knew he was right, of course. Worrying about what Stuart Nicklin might do would make no difference in the end. Worrying would not save anyone, but no matter how often Thorne told himself that – while he lay awake coated in sweat or went looking for a fight or struggled to formulate a rational thought – he could not stop.

It was like telling himself not to breathe.

When Hendricks reached for his pork-pie hat, Thorne said, 'Why don't we open another couple of cans and make a night of it? You can kip on the sofa.' He picked up the TV remote. 'I can try and find some axe-throwing . . .'

'I'd best get back,' Hendricks said.

'You sure?'

'Yeah. Liam's heading off for some conference tomorrow and I want to see him before he goes.' He looked at Thorne. 'Well . . . I could always just ring him, I suppose . . . if you really want the company. I know your little heart breaks a bit every time I leave, but what can I say? I'm fun to have around.'

Thorne smiled and said, 'Go on, piss off home,' but five minutes later, when Hendricks had left and he had closed the front door, he wished he hadn't.

Nicola Tanner was trying not to get too excited, but she really liked the sound of Fiona Bridges.

Thirty-six and originally from Edinburgh, a nurse who worked at a private hospital in Bushey. She liked 'good food and bad TV' and didn't make predictable jokes when Tanner told her she was a copper. She was also undeniably fit, which Tanner decided could not be a bad thing. She definitely liked the *look* of Fiona Bridges, too. She had short dark hair and a slightly nervous smile which was seriously sexy.

It didn't hurt that she looked nothing whatsoever like Susan.

We still good for tomorrow?

Tanner texted back straight away. Absolutely.

I won't be upset if you change your mind.

Same.

It had just been messages up to this point; texts and emails once they'd come out of the app. Coy to begin with, both of them a bit wary, but definitely ... flirty. Well, obviously flirty, because they'd met on a dating app, but it was playful as opposed to crude, which Tanner approved of. Now they were talking about the date they'd finally arranged for the following evening. A pub, then maybe a meal somewhere afterwards, but only if they both fancied it. No pressure. Another big tick.

No pressure, but Tanner was already thinking about what to wear and what to say – probably best to say nothing about the dead ex – and praying that she wouldn't get held up at work. Trying not to get excited, but of course it was a big deal, because Tanner had finally decided the time was right to move on, to get out there. To start looking, at the very least.

See you tomorrow then.

Can't wait, Tanner texted.

Me neither x

It was a good sign, Tanner decided, that she had not felt the need to ask Susan what she thought; even better that Susan had not volunteered an opinion. Maybe she'd have something to say the next day, when Tanner was botching her make-up or struggling to pick out an outfit. There might be the odd sarky comment or piece of unwelcome advice, but Tanner knew it would be coming from a place of love, same as always, because Susan would want her to be happy.

She looked back over the text messages she'd exchanged with Fiona.

She smiled through the tears.

She felt sure that Susan would be wishing her well.

FIFTY-SIX

Thorne had not expected to spend so much of the following morning being slapped on the back, but nothing that happened on Tuesday December the seventeenth would turn out the way he had been expecting.

A good result was a good result, though, however it was achieved, and the regulation interview with the witness in Wood Green the previous day had unexpectedly come up trumps. As it transpired, the so-called witness was actually a friend of the man responsible for the fatal hit and run in Dalston and, after his friend had reached out to him panic-stricken to confess what he'd done, the witness – not long out of prison himself and wary of trouble with the law – had decided that their friendship was not worth violating his parole for and contacted the police.

Dipak Chall had used his initiative. He'd told the witness in Wood Green to call his 'friend' and let him know that somehow the police had identified him as the driver of the

345

suspect vehicle and had come round asking awkward questions. 'No, I don't have a clue how they found out,' the man had said, while Chall had listened in, nodding approvingly. 'But they know it was you and the longer they have to spend looking, the worse it's going to be.'

The driver had turned himself in, and been charged, the same night.

Thorne and Chall spent the morning accepting the congratulations for a job well done and being promised a great many drinks. Thorne decided that he actually owed Chall those and several more, for not letting on that he had conducted the interview alone, while Thorne had actually been several miles away, busy making a twat of himself outside his girlfriend's flat.

Chall did not look happy about it, but he played along.

Aside from Russell Brigstocke, the only other person who knew the truth was Nicola Tanner and Thorne was fairly sure that she wouldn't be telling anyone. They shared rather more dangerous secrets. She'd rolled her eyes and muttered, 'Just take it, mate,' when she passed him in the incident room first thing, then later, when they were alone in their office, she seemed far more interested in any reason why she might not be able to leave at the normal time.

'Be good to get away,' she said. And, 'Roll on knock-off.' And, 'Sod's law says we catch a big one at the last minute.'

Thorne was every bit as keen as Tanner to head home when his shift ended, as desperate to leave work as anyone who didn't have a screw loose, and he had to press her a little before she finally told him why it was more important than usual.

'Ah,' he said.

Tanner shrugged like it was no big deal, but she couldn't

hide the grin, and now the cat had struggled from a bag that was less than securely tied, she was a lot happier than she had been a few days earlier to talk about her hot date.

'She's called Fiona and I'm trying not to get my hopes up, and even if it doesn't work out . . . it's just one date, so what's the big deal? I mean obviously I'm hoping that it *does* work out, because honestly, Tom, she seems really nice, which is why I'm nipping off at lunchtime to try and do something with my hair . . .'

There was more after that, but the words began to echo, then seemed to slide across one another and float away. Thorne could see Tanner's mouth moving – speaking, smiling – but he couldn't understand a word of it. He began to shiver and he couldn't control the tremor in his legs. He was freezing suddenly and breathless. It was as if he was seeing all the familiar objects in the room from strange angles, so that they didn't look quite the same; like he'd never been in the room before, even though he knew exactly where he was. His fingers were tingling and when he tried and failed to stand up, he was certain he was going to be sick . . .

It was Tanner who got to her feet.

'Tom . . . ?'

She said his name again, at least it sounded like his name and then she was hurrying across to him, telling him to breathe, and he tried to tell her that he was fine, that it was just . . . fuck, he didn't know *what* it was . . . but he couldn't get the words out. His stomach was churning and he felt sick again, so he closed his eyes, panting. He took hold of Tanner's arm, so that she couldn't leave to fetch anyone, to tell anyone, and he did not let go until he was certain that she would stay with him.

Her hand moved across his and when she squeezed it, he nodded.

Then he laid his cheek against the desk and waited for it to stop.

'Last time, you told me how much you were enjoying this,' Perera said.

'Because I am.'

'That's very nice to hear, but I'm keen to know if you think it's helping you at all.'

The man sitting opposite her smiled. 'Oh, yes.'

'In what way?'

'Understanding myself, I suppose.'

Perera waited. She spent a lot of her job saying nothing.

'Look, I can't be the first person to sit here and worry if he really *is* mad, just because so many people have said he is.'

'That's not really a word I like—'

He grunted a laugh. 'I know, it's a stupid word, really, isn't it? Makes you think of people who're convinced they're Napoleon or something. I certainly don't believe I'm someone I'm not. I suppose what I'm trying to say is that these sessions have helped me understand who I am, and that *different* is not the same as . . . is there a better word for it?'

'Well . . . suffering from mental health issues.'

'Yes, but surely we all suffer from those to one degree or another. It's a sliding scale, isn't it? From mildly anxious to . . . raving lunatic. I'm fairly sure you're on that scale somewhere.'

'Back to me again.'

The man held up a hand. 'Sorry. Can't help myself.'

'So, how do you feel afterwards? When we've finished a session.'

'Fired up,' the man said. 'Raring to go.'

'Well, that's good, but I do still have one major concern.'

'Which is?'

'The drugs.'

The man seemed taken aback. 'You've known about them from the beginning.'

'Yes, you've been honest with me about them, and that's always positive, but I wonder how much of the way you feel is to do with real understanding, and how much might be because of the tablets.'

'I really couldn't say.'

'Have you taken one today?' Perera asked.

'More than one,' the man said.

'I'm sorry to hear that, because I think we'd make a lot more progress without them. I think there's still a lot more work to do.'

The man shrugged. 'Sadly, I don't think we'll have the time.'

'That's a shame,' Perera said.

'The way it is.' The man took out a chocolate bar from his jacket pocket, waved it at Perera and began to remove the wrapper. 'Do you mind?'

'Well, I don't usually . . .'

'Oh, I see.' He reached down to stroke the seat beneath him. 'Worried about your lovely oatmeal cushions?' He bit into the chocolate and began to chew. 'Don't worry, I eat these things so quickly I never get any on my fingers.'

349

FIFTY-SEVEN

There had been a time, not very long ago, when a hug between himself and Helen Weeks would have been awkward. Instinctive, of course, and not out of the ordinary considering their shared history, but a little uncomfortable nonetheless, in light of the fact that it *was* history. Now, though, when Helen opened the door and Thorne moved towards her, the embrace felt perfectly natural, effortless, and he clung to his ex-partner rather longer than he might have done otherwise, because he needed to.

He stepped back to collect the gift-wrapped box he'd set down on the doorstep before ringing the bell.

'Come on,' Helen said. 'Alfie's already excited ... '

It had been a while since Thorne had been back to the flat in Tulse Hill, where he'd as good as lived for a couple of years. It didn't seem very different. A little less messy, perhaps, which Thorne put down to there being fewer action figures and bits of Lego scattered around. Alfie was only seven, but Thorne guessed he spent a lot more time up in his room these days; that he didn't play with toys quite so much.

Computer games, Thorne reckoned. He hoped so, anyway.

While Helen was making coffee, Alfie appeared in the living room doorway. He looked a little nervous and something jumped in Thorne's stomach. Alfie's father had died before the boy was born and Thorne had been the nearest thing to it for a long time. Though he hadn't told Melita about every occasion, he had seen Helen fairly regularly since the break-up and talked to her on the phone every couple of weeks, but this was the first time Thorne had seen her son in almost six months.

'Hello, mate . . .'

Alfie nodded, his hands in the pockets of Avengers pyjamas. He looked down at his slippers. 'How long are you staying?'

'I don't know,' Thorne said. 'For a bit.'

The boy nodded again and looked at him.

'A cuddle would be nice.' Thorne waited. 'Or, I don't know . . . maybe you're too grown up for cuddles now.'

Alfie nodded solemnly, teasing him.

'Oh, well,' Thorne said. He let out a long theatrical sigh, then opened his arms when the boy ran to him. It was another hug Thorne needed badly and he only let go when Helen appeared with the coffees and Alfie began to wriggle.

'Nice to see Uncle Tom, right?' Helen said.

'Yeah.'

'Uncle Phil says hello, too,' Thorne said.

Alfie grinned again. 'Spiky Uncle Phil.'

'Yeah, spiky.' Thorne turned to look at the small Christmas tree in the corner by the TV; a real one like he'd promised Melita. He nodded towards the gift he'd slid beneath it. 'Father Christmas left something for you early.'

Alfie rolled his eyes, put his hands on his hips. *'Mummy's* Father Christmas.'

Helen looked at Thorne and shrugged. 'Yes, well now Uncle Tom's Father Christmas too, so what do you say?'

'Can I open it now?'

'No, you cannot.'

Once the prospect of an unexpected present had disappeared, Alfie seemed keen to get back to his room; he was restless and monosyllabic until Helen put him out of his misery. She told him to brush his teeth and that Tom would be up to say goodnight before he left.

'The lure of that bloody computer,' Helen said, when he'd gone. 'I mean . . . seven years old.'

Thorne nodded. 'I got him some games and a pair of those headphones with a microphone on.'

'You're hardly helping.' Helen shook her head, then smiled. 'Thanks, he'll love that.'

'Oh, and there might be a new Spurs shirt in there, as well. In case he's grown out of his old one.'

They talked for a while about how Alfie was doing at school, about some issue Helen was having with the nosy woman next door, about nothing much. It wasn't until Thorne had finished his coffee that he got round to telling her the real reason he'd wanted to come over.

'Yeah, well obviously,' Helen said. 'I knew what it was about as soon as you called.'

Of course she did, Thorne thought. Helen worked as a DI on a child protection unit, and, once the word had gone out, Nicklin's name would have been mentioned as much at her station as it would anywhere else. His picture on the wall.

'What took you so long?' she asked.

It was a fair question. Helen had been the one waiting for him when he'd come back from Bardsey Island, the one who'd had to live with the man Thorne became for a while afterwards. She had seen first-hand what Nicklin could do and Thorne knew that he should have told her sooner; that they should have been having this conversation two weeks ago, the minute Nicklin's name had first come up.

He thought: *I'm a fucking moron.* He said, 'I didn't want to worry you.'

'So, why worry me now?'

'He's made threats,' Thorne said.

'What sort of threats?'

'Nothing specific, but it might well involve people I'm close to, so . . . you might want to think about getting something organised.'

Helen nodded, like she was thinking about it. 'What, you mean like getting a patrol car to drive by the house twice an hour every night?'

'Yeah, exactly like that.'

'Which is why it's already happening.' Her face was partially hidden by the coffee cup she was cradling, but Thorne knew she was smiling. 'Good job some of us are on the ball.'

Thorne knew that he should not have been surprised, because whenever he'd been stupid enough to underestimate Helen in the past, he'd invariably fallen on his arse. All the same, he could not help wondering why Melita's reaction had been so different. Perhaps it was simply down to the fact that Melita was not a copper and that she didn't have a child to protect.

'So, Nicklin aside,' Helen asked, 'how's work?'

For a few moments, Thorne badly wanted to tell her.

Well, Christ only knows when I last had a decent night's sleep and most of the time I can barely string a sentence together, but if you overlook that, and the full-on panic attack I had this morning, everything's peachy . . .

The attack had lasted less than fifteen minutes, but had left Thorne seriously shaken. Tanner had told him there was no reason to . . . panic. She'd laughed and told him that she'd had a few of them too, soon after Susan had been killed. She said she'd learned not to be afraid of them, that he should look online for the best ways to cope if it happened again, but that, in all probability, it was a one-off.

Yeah, and I did come quite close to beating the shit out of a witness. Oh, and a fellow officer.

He said, 'All good. You?'

Helen talked for a few minutes about her own job, but dealing with those who abused or killed children was never something she was keen to discuss outside the workplace and Thorne wasn't surprised when she changed the subject.

'Everything still going well with Melita?'

Thorne took a few seconds. Helen waited.

'Yeah, I think so.' He hoped so, but sometimes it was hard to tell. It had always been very black and white with Helen. If Thorne had pissed her off, he'd known about it very bloody quickly, and he guessed Helen would probably say the same about him. Melita was somewhat trickier to fathom sometimes. That noise in her head he knew was there, but which she seemed keen to prevent anyone else from hearing. 'What about you? Are you seeing anyone?'

Helen shook her head and nodded upstairs. 'Too busy with his lordship.'

Thorne said, 'Yeah, I bet,' but was wondering what to make of the fact that he was so happy about it.

Twenty minutes later on the doorstep, after Thorne had nipped upstairs to say goodbye to Alfie, he said, 'I've missed him.'

'Well, don't leave it so long next time, then,' Helen said.

'I won't.'

'Maybe don't wait until there's a serial killer running around. Just a thought, Tom . . .'

The hug was perhaps a little more formal this time, a little less desperate, but all the same, Thorne walked back to his car feeling as good as he had done in days. As happy as he could possibly feel, all things considered.

FIFTY-EIGHT

They had chosen a pub just off Trafalgar Square, found a table in the upstairs bar, where it was a little quieter.

'Aye, this is better,' Fiona said, as she shucked off her denim jacket. 'I hate it when you have to shout to make yourself heard.'

'Me, too.' Tanner was already wondering if she was over-dressed.

'I mean, I don't want to get ahead of myself here, but sweet nothings aren't quite the same if you have to yell them.'

The fact that this woman was even tastier in the flesh than she looked in her profile picture meant that Tanner was content to let Fiona Bridges get as far ahead of herself as she fancied. The sexy accent didn't hurt, either.

Tanner told herself to calm down.

Both of them had travelled into town on the tube, so having quickly downed a beer each they decided there was no harm in splitting a bottle of red. Tanner was happy to let Fiona choose.

'I don't want you to think I'm a pisshead,' Fiona said, pouring for both of them. 'I just get a bit nervous.'

'I'm not feeling hugely laid back myself,' Tanner said.

'Well, what's the worst that can happen?' Fiona raised her glass, leaned across and touched it to Tanner's.

'So, have you done this before?' Tanner asked. 'What you said about getting nervous . . .'

'A few times.' Fiona smiled. 'What about yourself?'

'Just once.'

'And?'

'A disaster.' Tanner laughed. 'Well, that's probably putting it a bit strongly. She was perfectly nice, but she was a copper, so . . .'

'That not a good idea, then?'

'Oh, God, no.'

'What about a copper and a nurse?'

'Just . . . as an example, you mean?'

'Aye, just as an example.'

'Sounds pretty good to me,' Tanner said.

'Well, that's all right, then.'

Fiona told Tanner about moving down from Edinburgh a year and a half earlier, the relationship that had broken up just before that, which had been the reason she'd wanted to get away. She talked about her job and how much she loved it. Telling one funny story after another, she ran through what sounded like a fairly hectic dating history since the move south, then asked Tanner about hers.

'I was with one person for a long time.' Tanner stopped, not sure where to go next.

'What happened?'

Tanner had guessed this might come up, but knew there

was no way that talking about what had actually happened could possibly do her any good. It might well put the mockers on a date that seemed to be going pretty well; or, at the very least, make Fiona feel like she was competing with a dead woman. Tanner had felt a sharp stab of guilt when she decided to say nothing, and she tried to imagine how things might go had Susan been the one out on a date, dealing with the fact that Tanner had been murdered several years before.

She could almost hear Susan laughing.

Are you kidding? If you'd been dead this long I'd have probably forgotten your name by now.

'I'd rather not talk about it,' Tanner said now. If things worked out, she would tell Fiona about it later, obviously. 'It was all a bit shit . . . so I'd rather just forget about it and carry on having a good time.'

Fiona smiled over her wine glass. 'You having a good time, then?'

'A great time, so far.' Tanner smiled back. 'I mean, *I* don't want to get ahead of myself either . . . '

'Your hair looks fab, by the way.' Fiona reached across until she could very nearly touch it, then drew her hand back. 'It's a lot different from how it was in your photo.'

'Thanks.' Tanner felt hugely relieved, after an afternoon at a salon in Hendon having every trace of grey taken out, then going a bit mad and having blonde highlights put into what had started as a shaggy mess and was now a sleek bob. The girl in the salon had told her she looked great, that it took years off her, but Tanner still worried that she'd gone a little far. Up until the moment Fiona had complimented her, Tanner imagined she was carrying a big sign saying *Mutton*

Dressed As Lamb. 'Yours is gorgeous, too. It was actually the first thing I noticed.'

Fiona blinked at her, slowly. 'So, not my puppy-dog eyes, then?'

'All right, the second thing.' Tanner grinned and let her eyes drift obviously down to Fiona's chest. 'OK, so maybe it was the third thing.' The laughter masked the shock Tanner felt at how . . . forward she was being, but the chat came easily and the wine was certainly going down *very* easily, and even if she was rather more pissed than she'd been in a while she felt no desire to fight against it.

Half an hour later, Fiona was pulling her denim jacket back on.

'You want to get some food, then?'

'Well, yeah, we *could*,' Tanner said.

'What are you suggesting, Detective Inspector?'

'Just . . . there's food at my place.' Tanner felt herself reddening. 'Unless you'd prefer to go out somewhere.'

'No, food at your place sounds perfect . . . and cheaper, right?'

'Definitely,' Tanner said. 'It's a money-saving exercise when you think about it.'

'Oh, I *am* thinking about it,' Fiona said. 'I'm thinking that what would be even better is if we work up an appetite first.'

They were laughing again as they began walking towards the tube.

FIFTY-NINE

Driving home, Thorne was doing his best to remember the circumstances that had led to he and Helen splitting up. It was hard to get the chronology straight. He recalled some of the arguments all too well, even if the reasons for them eluded him. It was his fault, almost certainly; caring too much about the wrong things at the wrong time, or unwilling to make the final commitment. More likely than not, Helen had simply got fed up with him. All he could remember clearly was that she had suggested a trial separation, and that a few months down the line, neither of them had seemed particularly inclined to wind the trial up. If Helen ever thought she'd made a mistake, Thorne had seen no sign of it, but he certainly did. If he was honest with himself, he had been temporarily excited back then at the prospect of being single again; by the promise of freedom, whatever he'd thought that meant. By the time the gloss had worn off, it was too late and he was stuck with it.

Lumbered with himself, until Melita had come along.

Everything still going well with Melita?

Yeah, I think so.

Up until recently, things had been good ... better than good ... and if they didn't feel quite as perfect right now – if there was a tension between them that neither seemed ready to acknowledge – Thorne knew it was down to him. He had not been himself since Stuart Nicklin had made his presence felt and there had been changes in his behaviour beyond losing his temper or his confidence; more subtle than insomnia or panic attacks. Melita had picked up on it straight away; of course she had. She'd even offered to help, and, being an idiot, Thorne had ignored her. Now it felt as though she was doing the sensible thing and ... withdrawing. Offering a little less of herself, at any rate.

Thorne promised himself that when this was all over he would ask Melita how she felt about moving things on a little. He would find out where he stood. If she was up for it, he could rent out his flat again and move in with her, put the money towards Melita's mortgage payments. They could even do it the other way round ... or, if she preferred, they could keep things exactly as they were.

Either way, though it remained a mystery to him, he would do whatever he could to remind her why she wanted to be with him in the first place.

The alert sounded on his phone as he was approaching traffic lights. He waited until he was stationary before taking his phone out, thinking how proud Nicola Tanner would have been.

A text message from a withheld number.

He was probably sitting there no more than a minute and it felt as if he was hearing the noise from deep underwater, but when Thorne finally became aware that drivers behind him were leaning on their horns, he moved quickly away from the lights then pulled straight into a bus lane and stopped.

He flicked on his hazards, stared at Nicklin's message.

He had no doubt whatsoever that it *was* Nicklin and no concerns as to where Nicklin might have got his number, because stuff like that was child's play. The breaths were coming a little faster and his heart jumped in his chest because of what else Stuart Nicklin knew.

Nicklin had been ahead of the game all along, Thorne was well aware of that, but only in terms of the investigation. The dark web business, the operation in Coventry. Thorne had only bought those presents for Alfie a few days earlier, wrapped them the previous night after Hendricks had left, so how the hell could Nicklin possibly have known about them?

This wasn't a leak from within the team or an email being hacked.

Thorne started when the phone rang on the seat next to him and he snatched at it, certain that it was Nicklin; ready for him. He was as disappointed as he was relieved when he saw that it wasn't. It felt like it was time.

'Hi, Dave . . . '

A few seconds passed before Holland asked him if he was all right. 'You sound a bit . . . stressed.'

Thorne told him why.

'That's sort of the reason I'm calling,' Holland said. 'I was thinking about what you told me ... Nicklin knowing what your plans were.'

'Knowing fucking *everything*.'

'Right, so ... he's always kept an eye on you, hasn't he? Or paid other people to. Wasn't he going through your bins at one time?'

'Yeah.' Thorne remembered Nicklin gleefully telling him that he was ordering far too many takeaways.

'So, I'm guessing that the stuff he knew about was probably stuff you'd talked about on the phone. Conversations with Tanner or Brigstocke or whoever when you were at home.'

'You reckon he's bugged my phone?'

'No. Listen, this is just a thought—'

'Dave, he knew about me giving presents to Alfie. A bugged phone doesn't explain that.'

'I was actually thinking cameras,' Holland said.

SIXTY

It wasn't as if they'd fallen straight into bed.

Tanner had opened another bottle of wine first and put some music on and they'd talked for maybe half an hour. Films they both loved – *Goodfellas, Bridesmaids, Mean Girls* – TV personalities they hated – Piers Morgan, Jeremy Clarkson – and nothing whatsoever was making Tanner think this was a mistake. Quite the opposite, in fact, especially as it looked as though Fiona was feeling the same way. She was every bit as excited about what was going to happen as Tanner was – she said so – but she also seemed completely at ease. There were more funny/bitchy stories about her friends and co-workers, and if she was remotely curious about the woman whose photographs were all over Tanner's front room, she didn't say anything.

Tanner wondered if, had she known she'd be bringing someone back, she would have taken Susan's photographs down.

She didn't think about it for very long.

She tried not to think about Susan once she and Fiona were in bed, but it was impossible. To begin with, at least. This was the first time she had been skin-to-skin with anyone at all since Susan's death and she couldn't help but compare the different bodies. Fiona was slighter than Susan had been and there were sharp angles in places where Tanner had grown used to softness. Fiona tasted different and made different noises, smiled a lot more while they were doing it, and by the time they eventually rolled away from one another, grinning and sticky, it was only Fiona that Tanner was thinking about.

'That was a really good idea,' Fiona said. She rubbed her foot against Tanner's. They were both still breathing heavily.

'And sensible, too,' Tanner said. 'Saving money, remember?'

'Absolutely.' Fiona turned on to her side, leaned on her elbow. 'I'm not hungry yet, though.'

'Me neither.'

'Not tired?'

Tanner smiled. 'Well, I might need a couple of minutes.'

'Don't worry about that.' Fiona threw her leg across Tanner's and straddled her. 'I'll be doing all the work this time.'

'Sounds good,' Tanner said.

Fiona sat up and stared at her, then leaned down fast to take hold of Tanner's arms. 'Oh, it will be.' The smile was there again, but now Tanner thought it was a little weird and ... wolfish. Without releasing her grip on Tanner's arms, Fiona began scanning the room; looking for something to use. 'Because I'm going to tie you up.'

SIXTY-ONE

Thorne did not even bother to take his jacket off.

He started with a straightforward visual sweep of his living room; the corners, the light fittings, the edges of the television and satellite box. He knew that these days a camera could be made to look like almost anything, or simply be small enough to hide in plain sight. He began to prowl around the room a little more quickly, growing angrier and more impatient, and all the time he was racking his brain for some way that Nicklin or someone working for him could have got in to his flat to install a camera in the first place.

He hadn't had any break-ins.

There hadn't been any unscheduled visits from British Gas or BT.

Aside from people he knew, there hadn't been any visitors at all.

The more he thought about it, though, the more Holland's suggestion made sense. He remembered the phone conversations with Hobbs about the pill bottle scam, and there had been several about Kevin Bartley and the operation in Coventry. Most of these cameras had built-in microphones . . .

After fifteen minutes of vaguely methodical searching and finding nothing, Thorne became a little less concerned about making a mess. He stamped around the room, shouting at the walls. He swept books off shelves and ransacked cupboards. He tipped out drawers and tossed what he'd once thought of as ornaments but now seemed like pointless bits of old crap on to the floor. He scattered his carefully ordered albums and CDs, threw aside collections of magazines, and felt nothing, because by now he'd decided that if Nicklin had hidden a camera somewhere he was going to find it, even if that meant tearing the entire flat apart.

By the time he'd finished in the kitchen, he needed to pick his way through the debris.

Forty minutes later, Thorne sat slumped at the foot of his bed, sweating and wasted, surrounded by the carnage of what had proved, in the end, to be a fruitless search. The air was thick with dust and rage. All around him his possessions lay cracked or splintered, and it took him a moment to realise that what he'd thought was some kind of tinnitus or maybe a wheeze in his chest was actually something electrical he'd broken which was now feebly beeping at him from the next room.

Now it looked as though there *had* been a break-in, or a minor explosion.

He let his head fall back, then left, and just as he was wondering when and where the hell he was going to start putting the flat back together again, he saw it.

The camera was on the floor.

He crawled across the carpet, sweeping clothes out of the way, to get a closer look. He'd been stupid, he realised; he'd been searching higher up. This was the perfect place, a gap between the chest of drawers and the wardrobe. Just an inch or two of nothing, but big enough ... with a lead running to a socket behind the chest of drawers that Thorne had forgotten was there.

How many times had he looked and not seen it?

Thorne had to get down on his belly to reach in and pull the thing out. It was black, around the same size as a golf ball, with a lens no bigger than his fingernail. Hidden where it was, Thorne doubted that the field of vision would have been ideal, but it would have done the job. He *knew* it had. He turned it and saw a microphone that he guessed would have picked up any conversation in the bedroom and probably the living room too.

Grunting, he pushed himself up on to his knees and stared down at the lens, seeing only the distorted reflection of his face, puffy and pale. Thorne sensed what was coming, yet strangely the tension began to ease and the roaring in his ears faded, until finally he was calm. It felt as if all the fear and the panic and the anger of the last few weeks – of the last crazed forty minutes – had shrunk and been squeezed into this inevitable moment of stillness and silence.

Thorne stared, and held his breath, and wondered if Stuart Nicklin was staring back.

The question was answered almost immediately when his phone rang.

'Well, *someone's* made a mess,' Nicklin said.

Thorne swallowed, breathed, swallowed again. He had thought many times about what he would say to Nicklin this time around when the opportunity presented itself, but here it was, and he had nothing. There was just the dead, black lens of the camera and the phone, hot against his ear.

'And you look like shit, by the way.'

'You don't look too good yourself,' Thorne said, finally. 'I've seen the pictures.'

Nicklin laughed. 'Jealousy's a terrible thing, Tom.'

'Fuck this.' Thorne reached behind the camera and yanked out the lead.

'Now, what did you do that for?' Nicklin sounded disappointed. 'I was enjoying looking at you, even if you were a bit ... blurry. Then again, I reckon you've been getting blurrier all the time lately.'

Thorne got to his feet, took a few steps backwards then dropped on to the edge of his trashed bed. 'What do you want?'

'Well ... a lot of people think that what I want is to have my head examined, and I'm sure you'd agree with them.'

'It's a bit late for that,' Thorne said.

'Oh, it's never too late.' Nicklin laughed again, a ragged hiss in it. 'On the plus side, the person doing the examining is *very* easy on the eye.' He waited. 'Hello ... ?'

Thorne was getting slowly to his feet and fighting for breath. He had just about managed to suck up enough spit to get the words out when he heard Melita scream.

Heard her say, 'Please ... '

Then Nicklin again. 'Are you still there, Tom?'

'Listen to me—'

'Please don't start listing all the horrible things you'll do to me if I hurt her. All that stupid avenging angel stuff. You're better than that.'

Thorne was already moving, tossing stuff aside and trying to find the jacket which contained his car keys and was now buried somewhere among the carnage.

'Good,' Nicklin said. 'Now, *I* won't insult *you* by telling you not to be silly about this. What the consequences would be if you didn't come alone or if any of your colleagues came charging in later on, all of that. If it was anyone else I would, obviously. I'd spell out exactly what would happen to this lovely young woman if they didn't follow simple instructions, but I think you and me are past all that. I mean, you *know*, don't you . . . ?'

Thorne found his jacket, dug out the car keys and ran to the front door.

The phone was still pressed to his ear.

'Well, you're not saying much, but I'm guessing you're in a bit of a hurry, which is fair enough.' Nicklin's long sigh became a soft hum. 'So, see you soon then, and . . . drive safely. Your girlfriend will be gutted if you don't get here in one piece.'

SIXTY-TWO

Nicklin called back ten minutes later, when Thorne was halfway there.

'Just out of interest, Tom, how many of the seven wonders of the world can you name?'

'What?'

'Come on, surely you can name a couple.'

Thorne swore, at himself and at Nicklin; screamed it as he ran two sets of lights at the Archway roundabout, ignored the cacophony of horns from drivers as he cut them up and accelerated up the hill.

'Too hard?'

'What are you on about?'

'OK then, in which country is the world's highest waterfall?'

'Look, I'm coming, all right . . . what else do you want?'

'Nothing much. We're just getting bored waiting, that's

all. Plus I forgot to say, make sure you bring some handcuffs with you.'

The buzz as he pushed through the front door seemed abnormally loud and Thorne winced when it crashed shut behind him. He stood in the parquet-floored hallway and listened. Just his own breathing and the distant hum of traffic from the main road. A boiler grumbling somewhere. He saw no reason why the occupants of the two upstairs flats should not be at home and, based on the time he'd spent here, he knew that noise in the building carried easily. More than anything, it was vital that whatever was about to happen, happened quietly.

If one of the people upstairs should hear anything untoward and decide to call the police, there would be no time for Thorne to explain that he had nothing to do with it. One yelp of a siren or the glimpse of a blue light and all bets would be off as far as Nicklin was concerned. He was a man who kept his promises and Thorne had no doubt about what that would mean for Melita.

As Nicklin had said, Thorne *knew*.

He was unsurprised to find that the door to Melita's flat had been left a few inches ajar. He sucked in a lungful of air that tasted of floor polish and eased it open. He took a few tentative steps and froze. Melita's small hallway was thickly carpeted, but he obviously had not been as quiet as he thought.

'We're in here.'

Nicklin's tone was casual and welcoming; as if Thorne had arrived fashionably late to a dinner party.

He carried on past the pristine kitchen, then left at the

main bedroom, until he stood outside the door to the smaller one, which Melita had converted several years before into her consulting room. He waited, feeling the tremors build in his arms and legs, but this time Thorne understood only too well why he was shaking. With no way of knowing what was waiting for him on the other side of the door, he wondered if he'd made a terrible mistake. He could simply have told Tanner what was happening and specially trained officers would have been in position outside the house before he'd got there. A firearms unit, surveillance officers, a hostage negotiator. Wasn't there at least a chance that Nicklin could have been taken without endangering Melita?

'You don't have to knock, Tom. No standing on ceremony.'

The quiet confidence in Nicklin's voice was enough to convince Thorne he was right to be afraid, but also that he was doing this the only way possible. If Nicklin faced a return to prison, it would only be to resume a life sentence, and as one of the few offenders in the system for whom life *meant* life, another murder added to his tally would be neither here nor there. Nicklin had never needed a reason to kill anyone, but killing Melita simply to make Thorne suffer would be as good as any.

Thorne pushed the door open.

It was a small room, designed to promote calm and openness; rugs across stripped boards, framed photographic landscapes on the walls, muted colours. There was a desk in one corner and bookcases either side of the window, but the room was dominated by a pair of comfortable chairs facing each other across a low glass table.

Melita sat in the chair furthest from the door and Nicklin stood, leaning against the back of it, the kitchen knife in his hand no more than a few inches from her neck. Thorne stepped into the room.

'So, here we are then,' Nicklin said.

The CCTV footage from the pub had not done justice to the awful peculiarity of Stuart Nicklin's new face. His nose was far too narrow, or perhaps it only seemed that way because his lips were now so absurdly plump, as bizarre as the deep cleft in his chin and a hairline that was crusted and bloody. Thorne looked from Nicklin's ravaged face to Melita's perfect one; to the knife next to it, bouncing gently against the top of the chair.

'Are you all right?'

Melita nodded, but her eyes were fixed on the rug beneath her feet.

'She's fine,' Nicklin said. 'Aren't you fine?'

Melita nodded again, muttered something.

'You'll need to speak up,' Nicklin said.

Now Melita raised her head; shook it as she looked at Thorne. 'I'm so sorry, Tom. He promised he wouldn't hurt you.'

'And I won't.' Nicklin looked at Thorne. 'Not in the way she means, anyway.'

Thorne could see that Nicklin's pupils were dilated; that he was clenching his jaw after speaking. 'Are you high, Stuart?'

'I'm high on life.' Nicklin grinned. 'But the pills certainly help.'

'Look, there's no police coming,' Thorne said. 'I did what you wanted, so why don't you just let her go?'

'Let her go?'

'Then it'll just be you and me and I'm not going to do anything stupid while you've got that knife, am I?'

Nicklin leaned down, his mouth close to Melita's ear. 'He's a bit slow on the uptake these days, isn't he?'

'I'm so sorry,' Melita said again. 'I didn't know it was him, not to begin with, I swear. Then when I did, it was too late—'

'How can I let her go when I'm not actually . . . holding her?' Nicklin drew the knife away from Melita's neck and stepped from behind the chair. 'See? She's free to leave any time she wants, always has been. I don't think she will, mind you. She's . . . invested now.'

'I don't understand,' Thorne said.

Melita stared at him, wide-eyed, as though she was every bit as high as Nicklin. 'It'll be all right, Tom. I promise. I *promise . . .*'

'We just needed to play a little trick to get you over here, that's all. A bit of screaming and what have you.' The look of horror and confusion on Thorne's face brought a smile to Nicklin's. 'It's a lot to take in, I can see that, so why don't you sit down? We've got tons to talk about.'

Thorne walked unsteadily towards the chair and dropped into it just before his knees gave way beneath him. He did not take his eyes from Melita's as she meekly stood to let Nicklin take her seat, then settled herself on the arm.

'Why?' Thorne struggled to get the words out. 'Why would you . . . ?'

'Don't get too distracted by this business.' Nicklin nodded towards Melita. 'You're shocked, course you are, but it's all fairly bog-standard, really. I think it started off as professional curiosity once she eventually found out who I was, and you can hardly blame her for that, can you? After that . . . I'm not really sure. Maybe she thought she could . . . change me, or get to the bottom of me, or something. Maybe she thought

375

she could work a miracle cure and I'd just turn myself in. Whatever the hell she was thinking, we've become . . . close.'

The surprise was giving way to something far darker as Thorne continued to stare at the woman he had trusted and been so keen to protect; whose professional advice had proved invaluable more than once in helping him catch the likes of Stuart Nicklin. A woman with whom he had shared so much more than a bed.

He was starting to grasp the scale of her betrayal.

He asked the question anyway.

'How did you get into my flat to set that camera up?'

'Someone had a key,' Nicklin said. 'Because you gave it to her.'

'The dark web stuff, the operation at Kevin Bartley's place . . .'

Another glance towards Melita, a wink. 'I had a source.' Nicklin nodded, understanding. 'Oh, so you thought I found all that out through the camera? No, that was just a bit of extra mustard.' He grinned. 'I liked seeing you naked.'

Just a few minutes earlier, Thorne was feeling hollowed out and unsteady, but now he could feel his strength returning; rage and adrenaline beginning to boil, to bring the fight back.

He took out his phone and nodded towards Melita, dismissive. 'So, if there's no threat to her, what's to stop me calling for backup right now?'

Nicklin held up the kitchen knife. 'Well, I've still got this.'

Thorne stood up. He was not bothered about the knife.

Nicklin appeared equally unconcerned. 'You need to put your phone away and calm down, Tom, seriously. When we've finished you might well want to call for that backup, but you need to understand what that's going to cost. You need to know that you have options. Trust me on this.' He pointed to the chair. 'You need to sit down and listen.'

Thorne did as he was told, but he was wired and ready to go, desperate to finish this. His own safety had become unimportant. He was confident that when the time was right he could be across the room and on Nicklin in a second; that the blade of a flailing kitchen knife would not be enough to stop him.

'So, you're basically looking at two options,' Nicklin said. 'One is that I simply get up and walk out of here, and if I can't promise that you won't ever see me again, I can assure you it won't be any time soon. The second option is that you just ... arrest me. I wouldn't be winning any prizes by guessing that you'd much prefer that one.'

Thorne said nothing, because he knew there was more.

'Now, obviously you're sitting there thinking that there's a third option and that it's one you'd prefer even more. I do understand, because you've been seriously provoked, but before you get too excited about me being taken out of here in a body bag, there's a couple of things you need to bear in mind.' He patted Melita's arm. 'A witness, for a kick-off, which is not ideal. Secondly, there was quite a good offer on if you bought two of those cameras, and a bargain's a bargain, which is why there's another one sitting behind me on the book-shelf.' Nicklin waited while Thorne looked. 'Just next to the speaker ... see it? All the footage is automatically uploaded to the cloud and easily accessible to several friends of mine who would publish it here there and everywhere if you decided to get all ... murdery. Not that it would be the first time ... which brings me back to that very attractive second option.'

Melita was looking at the floor again and Thorne sensed that the hurt Nicklin had mentioned was not far away.

'I swear that if you decide you'd rather not let me go and choose to arrest me, I will not offer any resistance. I'll be meek as a lamb. What I *will* do, however, at some point, is unburden myself . . . pass on a horrifying story I was told about a man called Graham French. A man who had been detained, who was handcuffed to a radiator as I remember, and was then bludgeoned to death with a poker by your friend Nicola Tanner. The pair of you covered it up with some cock and bull tale about Tanner using reasonable force to protect you, then up stepped Dr Hendricks with a very convenient post-mortem report claiming that the poor man only died because of an abnormally thin skull. Phew! What a stroke of luck.'

Thorne watched Nicklin snake an arm around Melita's shoulders.

'Only three people ever knew what had really happened to Graham French, until you chose to confide in your lovely girlfriend. Now, because she chose to confide in *me . . . I* know, and if you decide to arrest me, to see justice done for poor old Kevin Bartley, then I'll make sure Graham French gets justice too. It's only fair, I reckon.' Nicklin sat back, took a deep breath. 'So, in a nutshell, you can let me go, which isn't a great look for the detective that let me escape once already . . . or you can arrest me, at a price. Prison for DI Tanner, I would have thought . . . for you too, maybe. Certainly the end of Dr Phil's illustrious career, and I think that's going to hurt a lot more than having a stupid tattoo sliced off.'

He leaned forward again, all business. 'It's your call, Tom.'

Thorne opened his mouth, but it was only a reflex. Right

then, he was struggling to remember his name or where he was. Numb suddenly, as though he was shutting down. He could barely string an idea together that was not immediately obliterated by the scream inside his head. The wail and the blackness.

He could not think, or move, or speak.

'It's a toughie, I get that,' Nicklin said. 'Now, I always think big decisions are a bit easier when there's a time limit, don't you? It's a damn sight more fun, I know that much.'

He stared at Thorne for a few seconds, then suddenly reached out and took Melita's hand. She looked at him and he smiled at her. He got to his feet, bringing her with him, then yanked her arm until it was straight and drew the knife hard across her wrist.

All at once: Melita screaming and dropping to her knees; the blood spurting, spilling, then spurting again in time with the pulse; Thorne jumping to his feet and Nicklin reaching to press the blade back against Melita's neck.

'Don't.'

Thorne froze, held up his hands.

'Good.' Keeping his eyes on Thorne, Nicklin nodded down at his handiwork. 'Now *that's* what I call a ticking clock.' He wrapped his hand around the wound then released it again. Pressed and released. Melita screamed again as the blood streamed and jetted across the rugs and the glass tabletop. 'Sorry about all the mess.' Nicklin glanced at Melita then rolled his eyes at Thorne. 'She wasn't happy about a bit of chocolate on her cushions, so you can understand why she's getting upset.'

Thorne watched as Melita moaned and tried to pull away, then reached up and began patting at Nicklin's hand.

'For Christ's sake,' Thorne said.

Patting, not clawing.

'It's make your mind up time,' Nicklin said.

'Please, she needs—'

Nicklin released the pressure again and the blood began to surge; a puddle at his feet. Thorne couldn't tell if Melita was losing consciousness or had simply given up. Nicklin looked at him, waiting for a decision.

'Arrest, OK? I'll fucking arrest you.'

'Good choice.'

'Now just—'

'Let's hear it then,' Nicklin said.

'What?'

'Say it . . .'

They were words Thorne had fantasised about saying ever since Bardsey, that in any other context would have come automatically, like breathing in and breathing out, but now he heard those words falling out of his mouth like someone receiving a terminal diagnosis.

'Stuart Anthony Nicklin, I'm arresting you for the murder of Kevin Bartley. You do not have to say anything . . .'

It was as if everything had frozen for those ten or so seconds, and as soon as he'd finished speaking time immediately caught up with itself, and there was still . . . *this*. Three people in a room, the sobbing, the knife. There was still all that blood.

'Right, it's done,' Thorne said. 'Now she needs medical attention.'

'Did you remember the handcuffs?'

'For God's sake—'

'We should do things properly.'

Thorne scrabbled for the handcuffs in his pocket, then stared at Nicklin's hands. One was holding the knife while the other was wrapped around Melita's wrist; the gash, still pumping blood. He took a step forward, hesitated.

'Yeah, it's tricky,' Nicklin said. 'I can see that. OK, what if we do this . . . ?' He hauled Melita to her feet, dragged her across to the wall and pushed her down again, then lowered himself to the floor next to her. She was whimpering now, still struggling ineffectually to free herself, still leaking blood. 'Cuff me to the radiator.' Nicklin smiled and tapped the knife against the radiator pipe. 'Just like Graham French.'

Thorne moved quickly across, got down on to his haunches and braced himself against the floorboards. As soon as Thorne had fastened the first cuff around the radiator pipe, Nicklin released his grip on Melita's wrist. Thorne watched as she staggered upright and ran from the room.

Nicklin held out his own wrist, slick with Melita's blood. 'Come on then.'

Thorne fastened the second cuff to Nicklin's wrist and stared at that shiny, fucked-up face as Nicklin rattled the cuff against the pipe. More than anything, Thorne wanted to hurt him; to start hitting him and not stop until he was physically incapable of hitting him any more. Nicklin still had the knife in his free hand though and there was that camera to think about . . . but Melita, whatever she was guilty of, was still bleeding out.

Thorne clambered to his feet and reached into his pocket for the radio he'd muted before entering the flat.

'Oh *no*.' Nicklin jabbed the knife in Thorne's direction, like a child play-acting. 'You got me. You got me . . .'

Thorne ran from the room, pressing the radio's *EMER* button. Behind him he could hear Nicklin shouting and laughing.

'Or is it the other way round, Tom?'

He'd radioed control on his way here to pass on the suspect address. Now, the red button gave him fifteen seconds' uninterrupted broadcast to every active unit in the city. He followed the trail of blood into the kitchen, but there was no sign of Melita.

He rattled off his name and warrant card number. 'Requesting an arrest team and emergency medical assistance *now* . . .'

He threw open the bedroom door. Nothing.

He turned back into the hall, skidding in a slick of blood, calling for her.

A few seconds later, Thorne was hammering at the locked bathroom door. He shouted Melita's name, but got no response. He began to kick at the door and he was still kicking two minutes later when he heard the siren.

PART FOUR

THREE VISITS

SIXTY-THREE

Liam was still away at his conference, so when Thorne had suggested a get-together, without wanting to explain over the phone why it was necessary, Hendricks had been quick to volunteer his place.

'I'm always game for a pre-Christmas piss-up.'

Now, hearing laughter and music from inside as he stood, waiting to be let in, it sounded as though Tanner and Hendricks had started without him. Hendricks opened the door, pulled him into a hug, then darted away into the kitchen. Thorne walked into the living room and Tanner smiled up at him from the sofa. There was already a bottle of wine open on the table.

'What was all the laughing about?'

Hendricks came in with the beer he'd been to fetch. He handed it to Thorne, then went back to sit down. 'Nic was just revealing a few more juicy details about the worst first date in history. Freaky Fiona.'

'Oh, yeah?' Thorne moved across and perched on the edge of the sofa, next to Tanner. He didn't take his jacket off. 'How's that working out?'

'Well, first of all she's not freaky,' Tanner said. 'She's just into a bit of light S&M, that's all, but she completely understands that I'm not. She's sexually . . . flexible.'

'Oh, that's always handy,' Hendricks said. 'Bends over backwards for you, does she?'

Tanner smiled. 'It's all good. We're going to see each other again and that's all you need to know.'

'Tease,' Hendricks said.

Thorne looked around, putting off the painful conversation he was there to have. He guessed that Liam had a lot to do with it, but he was struck, as always, by just how tidy and organised Hendricks's flat was. Not in Tanner's league, obviously, but still a surprise, considering the often chaotic lifestyle of its owner. Thorne thought that *minimalist* was probably the right word. A few pieces of ultra-modern leather and chrome furniture, a cowhide rug; a small black Christmas tree in one corner – Liam, again – next to the vast TV and games console. There *were* one or two purely decorative items, though. An elaborate metal chandelier, a stuffed magpie and, for reasons Thorne had never been able to fathom, a full-sized head of the monster from *Alien* glaring down at them from the wall. It was still . . . neat, though, certainly by comparison with Thorne's place which, despite his best efforts, continued to look as though it had been hit by an extremely localised tornado.

'So, how's it going, then?' Hendricks asked.

It had been almost exactly forty-eight hours since the

events at Melita Perera's flat in Crouch End. Two days since police and paramedics had forced entry, then helped Thorne break the bathroom door down. Stuart Nicklin had been quickly charged with Kevin Bartley's murder, but nobody seemed quite sure to what degree he was responsible for Perera's death. He had opened one artery and she had opened the other one herself. Locked in the bathroom with the knife she'd snatched from the kitchen.

'I'm not really sure,' Thorne said.

It was the simple truth.

'Anyway, mate . . . ' Hendricks looked a little uncomfortable. 'Sorry to hear about Melita.'

'Right.'

'Seriously weird, the way it all turned out.'

Tanner nodded and leaned to lay a hand on Thorne's arm. 'Have you got any idea . . . ?' She didn't need to finish.

Why.

Thorne blinked slowly. His chest felt tight, a wheeze in it. He let his head fall back and gazed up at the chandelier, though he remained well aware that Tanner and Hendricks were staring at him, waiting for an answer he was incapable of giving.

There had hardly been a moment since that night at Melita's flat when Thorne hadn't asked himself why she had done what she did. He'd wondered if perhaps Nicklin had threatened her family, those nieces and nephews to whom she was so devoted. It was definitely a possibility, it might well have been enough to force her hand, but it still felt like a straw Thorne was clutching at. Beyond the little he understood about Nicklin's terrifying powers of persuasion, he would never know what had been in Melita's mind.

If he had *ever* known.

He remembered something she'd said to him just a month or so earlier. At his place when he'd wanted to watch the football.

'There's still all sorts of things you don't know about me, Tom.'

He'd seen enough to know that those Nicklin had targeted, or who had chosen to come to him, were usually in need of something. The likes of Rebecca Driver, desperate and doomed. Those from whom something had been taken; the *lifeless*, whose frantic search for purpose had made them ripe for manipulation.

What had Melita been missing? What could she have been looking for?

The realisation that he simply hadn't known her well enough to have the first idea had been sobering. What her demons had been, if in fact she'd had any. They had eaten and slept together, they had talked about work, but the more Thorne thought about it, theirs had been less of a relationship and more of an ... arrangement.

He didn't know the names of those nieces and nephews, not because he'd forgotten, but because Melita had never told him. He had never met any of her friends. He had never so much as spoken to her sister or either of her parents, had never been there when she had spoken to them.

Family had not been part of the arrangement.

Thorne had briefly thought he could remedy that – that he might even find some answers – if he talked to Melita's family at the funeral, to those who were closest to her. Now though, he wasn't even sure he should be there at all.

He would feel like a stranger.

'Tom ... ?'

Hendricks's voice sounded like it was coming from a long way away and Thorne remembered it, teasing and thick with drink; the laugh as his friend had asked the same question Thorne had not stopped asking ever since he'd found himself washing off Melita's blood.

What the fuck does she see in you?

The answer didn't matter then, of course, when it was just a wind-up, but now Thorne could not stop wondering if she had found herself drawn to the same thing in Stuart Nicklin. The thing, whatever the hell it was, that had turned a professional fascination into something else. He was convinced it hadn't been anything physical, and in all the ways that mattered Thorne knew that he and Nicklin had nothing whatsoever in common.

In most of the ways.

So . . .

'Tom . . . ?'

Perhaps Melita had simply been attracted to damage.

Thorne turned to look at Hendricks. At Tanner, smiling at him.

'You any idea how long?' she asked. 'The two of them.'

Something else Thorne had been torturing himself with; exactly when Nicklin and Melita had met and how long *their* little 'arrangement' had been going on for. How long she had known exactly who she had been treating. A few weeks? Longer? Now, only one person knew for sure and it was Thorne's profound hope that he would never have to see or speak to him again.

'It really doesn't matter, does it?' Thorne said.

'Drink up, mate.' Hendricks pointed with his bottle to Thorne's untouched one.

Thorne reached for the beer. 'Any chance of turning this noise down?'

Hendricks looked horrified. 'This *noise* is "Merry Shitmas" by the fine Swedish black metal combo Gehennah.'

'It's making my ears bleed,' Thorne said.

Hendricks got up, muttering, and did as Thorne had asked. As soon as he was seated again, he raised his drink. 'We can still celebrate though, can't we?'

Tanner stared at him. 'Phil . . .'

'Look . . . I'm sorry she's dead and all that, but come on.' Hendricks nodded towards Thorne. 'She fucking *betrayed* him.' He swigged and shook his head. 'Actually, I'm not that sorry . . . but Nicklin . . . yeah.' He raised the bottle. 'Fucker's finally banged up, so I for one am going to drink to that.'

Tanner took a sip of wine, but her eyes were on Thorne.

Thorne nodded, like it was all OK, then finally lifted his bottle and had a drink. A good long one, but only because he needed it; because he was about to spoil everyone's Christmas.

He was about to spoil everything.

He put the bottle down and told them. The price they would all be paying for Stuart Nicklin's arrest. The secret Nicklin would be revealing and how he had found out.

It was Hendricks who broke the long silence that followed, with a burst of hollow laughter. 'Now I'm really not sorry she's dead.'

Thorne looked at him, feeling a flash of anger that was unjustified, that he could not begin to explain. Despite everything Melita Perera had done, Thorne was grieving; as messed up, as broken as the scene that would be waiting for him back at home. He said, 'It was my own fault for telling her.'

'You didn't have much choice,' Tanner said. 'Once she'd overheard.'

'If it's anyone's fault, then, it's mine,' Hendricks said. 'Ringing you up and belly-aching about it.'

'We've all done that,' Tanner said.

They fell silent again, looked at the floor, the walls. Tanner grunted and smiled when the sound of carol singers, tuneless but enthusiastic, drifted up from Camden Road.

'So when?' she asked.

'When what?'

'When's Nicklin going to spill his guts?'

'He didn't say.'

'He'll enjoy it,' Hendricks said. 'Us not knowing when the hammer's going to fall, waiting for it. It's always a power thing with him.'

'He'll do it at the trial, I reckon,' Thorne said. 'The full glare of the media, so maximum coverage. He'll enjoy the theatre of it.'

'If he does it at all,' Hendricks said. 'Maybe just having the three of us shitting ourselves is enough.'

'No chance,' Thorne said. 'He'll do what he promised.'

'Fuck.'

'So that's it then.' Tanner shrugged and sat back. 'It's actually a relief in some ways.' She looked from Thorne to Hendricks, back to Thorne. 'Maybe we shouldn't give him the pleasure, just own up to it before he can say anything.'

'Maybe,' Thorne said.

'So what if he does tell?' Hendricks sounded upbeat suddenly. 'The only other person who can back him up is dead and it's not like Nicklin's word's exactly reliable, is it? Chances are it won't even get taken seriously.'

'If it gets as far as a second post-mortem it will,' Tanner said. 'Once they find out French's skull was a lot thicker than you said it was, the whole house of cards comes down.'

'I'm so sorry.' Thorne looked at Tanner. 'The other week you were saying how lucky it was that one of us was solid. That I was the reliable one, remember? And I'd already fucked it up.'

'You've got nothing to be sorry for,' Tanner said. 'I was the one who . . . killed him. However this plays out, I'll make sure everyone knows that. I'll do everything possible to carry the can for this.'

Hendricks stared at her. 'What, so me and Tom just get our wrists slapped?'

'I promise I'll try.'

'Don't be so fucking daft, Nic.'

They fell silent again. Somewhere on the street below them, the carol singers were still going at it, but nobody in that room was feeling joyful or triumphant.

'Fuck it,' Hendricks said, finally. 'I'll find some other way to earn a crust. I was getting cheesed off with stinking of formaldehyde, anyway.'

Thorne looked across at him. 'Such as?'

'A high-end rent boy, maybe.' Hendricks nodded, enjoying the idea. 'A paid companion for the more . . . *discerning* homosexual gentleman.'

'That's your business plan then, is it?'

Hendricks spread his arms wide. 'Plenty of blokes would pay top dollar for this, mate.'

'I reckon you'd have to pay *them*,' Thorne said.

They both turned to look at Tanner; watched her laughing and crying at the same time.

SIXTY-FOUR

Margaret Herbert knew that HMP Belmarsh was a high-profile place, that it had housed plenty of big name villains, but the security procedures for getting inside were much the same as they had been the last time she'd been to visit someone in prison. Scanners and searches, all that. So she'd known what to expect.

That had been a few weeks back, when she'd been to Bronzefield, pretending to be Karen Sinclair's mother. She still couldn't quite believe that nobody had questioned it. It had been simple enough to get a fake ID with the right name on it, and she'd definitely looked the part. Karen Sinclair hadn't let on, obviously. Not when the silly cow thought Herbert was there to talk about money; specifically, how much of it Sinclair would get for sorting Rebecca Driver out.

As it was, Margaret hadn't mentioned money at all, but she'd definitely had the same sort of conversation she'd have had if she had been the woman's mother. Asked all the same questions. How are the kids, Karen? How are they getting on at school? She'd made it very clear that certain people knew exactly who those kids were, where they lived and what school they went to, so money hadn't even come into it. It had been properly nerve-racking to begin with, but Margaret had enjoyed herself in the end, got right into the part.

The man she'd come to Belmarsh to see had been delighted, told her she should have been an actress. She wouldn't have gone quite that far, but she knew she'd done a good job.

Today, though, she was being herself, and she was excited.

She looked around as prisoners started filing in and the visiting area began to fill up. She knew there'd be some serious criminals in here, terrorists and killers and what have you. The sort of people whose names might make her a few quid somewhere down the line, if she got hold of the right items.

Shame she couldn't hand out a few business cards.

She knew Stuart had come in when she saw other people turn to look, when she heard the whispers. However famous some of the sorts they'd had in here over the years might have been – Ronnie Biggs, Ian Huntley, whoever – they were second division compared to this bloke. He wouldn't be here long, of course, just remanded until his trial, but while he was he'd be top of the bill. Margaret enjoyed people watching as he walked across and sat down opposite her. People looking at her and wondering who she was ...

Nicklin put down a bottle of water and smiled.

'Nice to see you, Mags.'

'You too, love.' She hadn't clapped eyes on him for a good

while, not since he'd come back to London. He was certainly different. 'You're looking good.'

Nicklin smiled again and shook his head. 'Been a long time.'

'So, how are you?' Margaret asked. 'Sorry, stupid question.' She looked around. 'I mean, considering.'

'No, it's all right, actually. I'm not . . . unhappy with the way it all turned out. Better for me than for some others, put it that way.'

'That's the main thing. I mean, as long as you're not bored in here. A clever man like you, stuck inside.'

'Actually, I was thinking I might write a book.'

'Oh, that's a good idea.'

'Well, there's one or two things I need to get off my chest anyway, so why not set the record straight?'

'As long as I get a signed copy,' Margaret said.

'So, yeah, I think I'll be all right.' Nicklin looked at her. 'I'm not saying there aren't one or two things I'll miss, mind you.' He lowered his voice. 'A few treats.'

Margaret nodded and leaned forward. 'That's why I've got a little something for you. Pep you up a bit.'

'You're a star,' Nicklin said.

'Least I could do.' She dug the tissue from her pocket, palming the bright yellow pill that was wrapped inside it before she blew her nose. She reached across to take Nicklin's hand.

'No touching.'

Nicklin saw the guard approaching and pulled his hand away. He coughed, popping in the pill, then washed it down with a swig from his water bottle. Easy peasy.

'Cameron sorted that for you, did he?'

'No, actually it was a present from a bloke outside ... gave it to me specially, said to make sure you got it. You've got quite a few fans out there. Some very strange-looking articles.'

Nicklin shrugged, but she could tell he was pleased.

'Not sure what they're hanging around for. I mean it's nice, but it's not like they can pop in and get your autograph, is it?'

'Not like you, eh?'

Margaret felt herself blushing. 'No.'

'Talking of which, I'll try and send a few more bits and pieces your way as soon as I can.'

'That would be lovely.'

'Just because I'm in here, or wherever I end up after the trial, doesn't mean business has to go on hold, does it?'

'You've always been my favourite,' Margaret said.

'Because I make you the most money?'

'Not just that.'

'You're a good actress, Mags, and a great businesswoman.' Nicklin grinned. 'But you're a terrible liar.'

Herbert shook her head and looked around again. People were still looking. She couldn't remember the last time she felt quite this special.

She turned back when Nicklin began to cough.

'Cough it up, love. It might be a gold watch.' Her mother always used to say that, she said it to Cameron. The coughing only got worse, though, and then it was like Nicklin couldn't breathe properly. She reached across and nudged the water bottle towards him. 'Here you go, get that—'

She leaned away again when he sat bolt upright in his chair and began to convulse, like he was wired up to something.

'Jesus . . . you all right, love?'

Margaret stood up when Nicklin tumbled sideways off his chair and now everyone was looking as guards began to run across. By the time any of them had got there, Nicklin was fitting; red-faced, kicking his legs wildly, with his hands clamped to either side of his head.

She craned her head to watch as she was marched quickly away, as more guards came in shouting and began to empty the visits area.

'Is he going to be OK?'

'You need to move towards the exit,' the guard said.

There were two guards down on the floor with him now, yelling and panicky. It was the last thing Margaret saw before she and everyone else was ushered out of the room. She asked again if Stuart was going to be OK, but didn't get an answer.

She hoped more than anything that he would be.

She couldn't bear to think what it would cost her if he wasn't.

SIXTY-FIVE

Phil Hendricks didn't smoke very often any more, but he was enjoying this cigarette immensely. He mooched around the car park, watching the gate, and it was only when he saw them all coming out together that he strolled back towards his car. He recognised some of the visitors he'd seen half an hour earlier, now deep in conversation with one another.

Clearly something had happened.

He smiled as a couple of them walked past him, complaining; muttering about the prison being locked down.

Hendricks tossed what was left of his cigarette away.

As he started his car, he saw the old woman he'd been talking to before the visitors had been let in, the one into whose hands he'd pressed a special something for the man she was there to visit. A present from a fellow admirer. They'd had a very enjoyable chat as it happened, though he'd had to struggle not to react when she'd told him how she made a living.

He'd been so tempted to say something.

'The dark web, you say? Very good place if you're looking for last-minute Christmas presents. You know, unusual ones . . . '

Stumping up the money had been easy enough, but he'd needed to be creative too, of course. MDMA tended to be rather more . . . colourful than a bog-standard potassium cyanide tablet. So he'd snapped on some nitrile gloves, got busy in his kitchen for a few hours and experimented with food dye until he'd got it right. The first few times the pill had crumbled, but he'd cracked it in the end and then it was just a question of using a post-mortem needle from work to etch on a nice smiley face. All a bit fiddly, and he doubted that Nicklin would even have a chance to examine his free 'disco biscuit' very closely, but if a job was worth doing . . .

As soon as he'd turned out of the car park, he called Thorne.

'Hey, mate . . . just wondered if you fancied a pint later on.'

'Maybe.' It sounded as though Thorne was driving, too. 'Not sure just yet, but I'll know one way or the other in an hour or two. Can I let you know?'

'Yeah, not a problem. Be nice, though.'

'So, what, are we drowning our sorrows?'

'I think we've done enough of that,' Hendricks said.

Thorne ended the call and pushed the car south across Lambeth bridge. He turned the volume back up on the George Jones CD he'd been listening to when Hendricks had rung. A drink sounded great, but Thorne couldn't commit, not yet, because the alternative, if there proved to be one, would be even better.

He wasn't going to make the same mistake as last time,

so he had called Helen as soon as Nicklin had been taken into custody, to let her know she could cancel those nightly drive-pasts. To let her know that she and Alfie were safe. Helen had said how sorry she was about what had happened to Melita. Thorne had yet to tell her the whole story and assured her that he would, but said that he was sorry, too.

They'd left it there.

With only a week until the big day, they'd talked about their Christmas plans. Helen was going to stay with her dad in Sydenham, she'd said, give the old man a chance to spoil his grandson. Thorne had told her everything was a bit 'up in the air' as far as his own Christmas was concerned, though he already knew he'd be spending a good deal of time over the holidays trying to get his flat straight. Disposing of the wreckage and replacing the things he'd broken. He hadn't told Helen that the time would also be spent wondering when the Directorate of Professional Standards would come calling.

If the P45 would come before the arrest.

Helen had suggested that he drop round once it was all over. Thorne had caught his breath, then realised she was talking about Christmas as opposed to his career.

'That time between Christmas and New Year is always so dead,' she'd said. 'Come round here one night and we'll have a proper catch-up.'

Thorne had told her that sounded great.

Nothing had been fixed until she'd called yesterday, told him that Alfie was having a sleepover at a friend's house and asked if Thorne still fancied a trip down to Tulse Hill. He'd said that he did, though he'd tried not to sound too keen. He was probably being stupid, anyway . . .

Half an hour later, Thorne parked the car outside Helen's house and lifted the plastic bag from the passenger seat. She'd said that they could get food delivered, so he'd only brought wine. A couple of bottles.

He rang the doorbell, then quickly leaned forward to check his reflection in the front door's small window.

His hair needed cutting.

He'd missed some stubble on his neck.

Helen opened the door and smiled at him. She stepped forward and pulled him into a hug that felt anything but awkward. She said it was nice to see him and, for no reason whatsoever and for all sorts of reasons, Thorne burst into tears.

ACKNOWLEDGEMENTS

Some books are more fun to write than others and, while I'm fully aware that it can sometimes be the ones you enjoy least that turn out best, I will happily admit that I enjoyed writing this one immensely. Of course, I hope you enjoyed *reading* it every bit as much and, if you did, I would humbly suggest that there are a great many people whose help made *The Murder Book* much better than it might otherwise have been and to whom you should be almost as grateful as I am. That said, if you *do* feel compelled to send cakes or ... cash or even just an email to express your gratitude, then they should come directly to me, obviously ...

Thank you, as always, to my wonderful agent Sarah Lutyens for the furnishings and to Wendy Lee (the Queen of spin/spun/span). To everyone at Little, Brown/Sphere, most particularly: David Shelley, Charlie King, Catherine Burke, Robert Manser, Callum Kenney, Tamsin Kitson, Thalia Proctor, Tom Webster, Sean Garrehy, Hannah Methuen,

Gemma Shelley and Sarah Shrubb. Thank you to Nancy Webber for continuing to spare my blushes, particularly when it comes to the correct spelling of *Gehennah*. On the same subject, an ear-splitting and growly *thaaaanks* is owed to Jack Brookmyre for his encyclopaedic knowledge of all things metal.

I'm grateful (daily) to my brilliant editor Ed Wood and to Laura Sherlock for being the best in the business. I got very lucky.

Thank you to Team Tom (North America Branch), by which of course I mean the fine folks at Grove Atlantic: Morgan Entrekin, Sara Vitale, Justine Batchelor and Deb Seager. I'm not sure if there's a US equivalent of the *nadgers*, but if not, consider it my gift to you. You're welcome.

On matters of police procedure, this is not the first time (and it almost certainly won't be the last) I'm thankful for the advice and creativity of Graham Bartlett. His name-sake Graham Lewendon was equally helpful when it came to the murkier waters of the dark web. His 'tour' was truly eye-opening though I have to say that 500 euros for *certain* Commercial Services seems very reasonable, and I have a list *way* longer than Tom Thorne's. Talking of dark . . . I'm grateful for the work of two friends and colleagues in the plotting of Stuart Nicklin's 'business model'. *Murderabilia* by Craig Robertson and *Still Bleeding* by Steve Mosby were enormously useful, but are, more importantly, fantastic novels which I cannot recommend highly enough.

For their help with the workings and membership reg-ulations of libraries, I have to thank Jo Neville, Caroline (aka @librarylady), Mobeena Khan, Melanie Noland and Robin Miller. I can only apologise for what Tom does to that library book. I'm fully aware that, second only to fictional harm done to fictional animals, fictional damage inflicted on fictional books is probably the most dangerous thing I could do to incur the wrath of a certain type of reader.

I honestly don't know what else I could do to upset them more, other than fictionally murder fictional people.

Oh, wait . . .